GRAND CENTRAL
PUBLISHING

LARGE
PRINT

THE LAST AMERICAN
VAMPIRE

SETH GRAHAME-SMITH

GRAND CENTRAL
PUBLISHING

LARGE PRINT

Grand Central Publishing
Hachette Book Group
1290 Avenue of the Americas
New York, NY 10104

www.HachetteBookGroup.com

Printed in the United States of America

RRD-C

First Edition: January 2015
10 9 8 7 6 5 4 3 2 1

Grand Central Publishing is a division of Hachette Book Group, Inc. The Grand Central Publishing name and logo is a trademark of Hachette Book Group, Inc.

The Hachette Speakers Bureau provides a wide range of authors for speaking events. To find out more, go to www.hachettespeakersbureau.com or call (866) 376-6591.

The publisher is not responsible for websites (or their content) that are not owned by the publisher.

Library of Congress Cataloging-in-Publication Data

Grahame-Smith, Seth.
    The last american vampire / Seth Grahame-Smith. — First edition.
        pages ; cm
    ISBN 978-1-4555-0212-7 (hardcover) — ISBN 978-1-4555-3007-6 (large print : hardcover) — ISBN 978-1-61113-828-3 (audio book) — ISBN 978-1-61113-829-0 (audio download) 1. Vampires—Fiction. 2. United States—History—19th century—Fiction. 3. United States—History—20th century—Fiction. I. Title.
    PS3607.R348L37 2015
    813'.6—dc23
                                                            2014020895

This one goes out to the USS Abraham Lincoln *(CVN-72) and all who sail on her.*

Tell you now children—you're all gonna die.
No hand stamp reentry, no refund, no lie.

*—Found written on a bathroom stall in
Disneyland, June 6th, 1988*

FACTS

1. Between 1860 and 1865, a Confederacy of Vampires attempted to conquer the United States, enlisting an army of men to fight on their behalf.

2. They were defeated by Abraham Lincoln, a gifted vampire hunter, and a small brotherhood of immortals who were sworn to protect mankind. They called themselves "the Union."

3. In the aftermath of the Civil War, these defeated vampires were scattered throughout Europe, Asia, and elsewhere—their numbers smaller than ever before. Just when the vampires were faced with extinction, rumors of a new vampire leader, and a new plot to enslave mankind, began to surface.

THE LAST AMERICAN
VAMPIRE

INTRODUCTION

What a strange thing, to be a vampire. To break free of death's gravity! To think that Henry has observed this earth with the same eyes, the same mind, uninterrupted, for two hundred and fifty years! To think that he has witnessed the fall of empires and the birth of nations! What stories he could tell! What volumes he could fill!

—Abraham Lincoln, in a journal entry,
December 15th, 1832

I was dying, and I wasn't afraid.

After all, I'd asked for this. I'd asked him to bring me as close to death as a man could get. Close enough to see the stitching that holds existence and inexistence together, without actually tearing it. And here I was, perched on a high wire above Hades, nine toes in the grave and the tenth on its way, and all was well and right. I'd heard it said that a certain peace washes over us when we stray close enough to death. That our bodies release chemicals to calm us, to ease us into the inevitable nothing that drapes us all in its black cloak sooner or later. Perhaps that's all it was— a biological calmness. Or perhaps I just trusted that Henry knew what he was doing.

A thought rang through the dark, bright and pleasing, like a church bell on a cold, starry night. *If I do die tonight,* I thought, *at least I'll die in October.* That most American of months, when the first wisps of chimney smoke kiss the crisp apple air, and the promise of a World Series looms large in the imaginations of the good and ever-hopeful people of New England. When children have finished mourning the long summer and grown re-accustomed to the buzzing fluorescents of their classrooms. When Christmas is beginning to take shape on the horizon, just beyond the cousins and food comas of Thanksgiving. Closer still are the masks and glow sticks and cotton spiderwebs of Halloween, the one night when we embrace the darkness from which all of America is descended. October is the gateway to the wonderful, mystical finale of the American year. A place where life ends and the celebration of life briefly begins.

I began to taste blood in the back of my throat. Fear suddenly crept in, cold and unwelcome, tracking mud on the carpet of my cozy little death. I looked into Henry's eyes just before my own began to roll back in my head. Those black vampire eyes that I'd seen only once before, years earlier. He'd shown them to me, those eyes, along with the hideous glass shards of his fangs and the calcified razors that were his claws. He'd shown me because he'd needed me to believe the impossible. His face had been wild then. Animal-like. But tonight it was careful and curious. The tips of his fangs were barely visible beneath his upper lip. His right hand was on my throat, squeezing off my jugular, cutting off the blood to my brain. My brain, in turn, was carrying out its final instructions, ticking boxes on the pre-death checklist that humans have evolved over eons. And all because I'd asked him to.

Perhaps I'd misjudged Henry. Perhaps this ancient, powerful vampire—whom I'd come to think of as a friend—meant to kill me after all. I felt like a zoo-keeper who wanders into a tiger's cage, unafraid, only to be mauled to death. *Why?* he thinks, as he's torn apart by those massive claws and teeth. *How can this be, when I raised you, fed you, loved you since you were a helpless cub?* Only in the final, terrifying seconds does he understand that the love he gave was never returned. That he'd grown too close. Too familiar. *I forgot that it was a tiger,* he thinks as he slips away. *It was always a tiger.*

The edges of my vision went fuzzy…darkness creeping closer to the center of my sight, like those ever-tightening black circles at the end of silent mov-ies and cartoons. I tunneled away into the dark, but there was no light at the end. No feeling of floating

above my body. There was only the inner. The quiet.
I thought of all of the Halloweens and Thanksgivings
and Christmases I would miss. I thought of my boys,
when they were so small and helpless I could hardly
stand it.

And then there were no more thoughts.

It had begun with a jingle, years earlier. A chime that
had been affixed to the front door of the five-and-
dime since the universe was in its infancy and time
just a concept in God's imagination. Its ring was as
old and as quaint as the store itself—a store that had
been a fixture in the little upstate town of Rhinebeck,
New York, since 1946, selling damn near anything to
damn near anybody: school supplies, knitting yarn,
toilet brushes, toys, rain boots, electrical sockets, and
whatever else customers were willing to plunk down
their pocket change for. Packed onto shelves against
wood-paneled walls, or in bins lined with contact
paper.

I'd worked there on and off since I was fifteen,
earning extra money for college, brimming with big
dreams and big ideas, dreams of published novels and
Manhattan book signings, of tenured professorships
and corduroy blazers with elbow patches. College had
come and gone, novels begun and abandoned, vows
exchanged, children born, struggles endured, and
there I was, behind that same counter, fifteen years

and twenty-five pounds later, and not an inch closer to Manhattan than I'd ever been. There I was, thirty years old, greeting customers by name, watching the Yankees on a small color TV under the counter, selling pink pencil erasers and sink stoppers for a penny's worth of profit, from eight-thirty in the morning until five-thirty at night, six days a week. Every week. Wash, rinse, repeat. There I was, clinging to the idea that there was still a place for an old five-and-dime in a Walmart world—still a chance that all those scraps of paper with their half-begun stories would congeal into a dream realized.

By 2006, I'd heard that door jingle a million times. But one summer day, it seemed to ring with a slightly darker sound as a new customer stepped in from the sunshine of East Market Street and onto the checkered linoleum of our floor. I looked up from the sports section of the *New York Post* and saw a young man of twenty-seven or so, with dark, fashionably messy hair. Expensive clothes designed to look tattered and cheap. Dark sunglasses, which he neglected to take off. I'd seen plenty of his kind before—the weekend visitors who drive up from the city to revel in the quaint and backward ways of us simple folk. The young urbanites who brave the Taconic Parkway to ironically spend their discretionary income. But this was no visitor, it turned out. He was a local boy. Not born and bred, but transplanted.

"Hello," I said, the way one does in a small town.

"Hello," said Henry, and went about his browsing. And that was that. I went back to my newspaper, not knowing that I had just been nudged an inch closer to Manhattan.

Henry came in from time to time, bought things, and left. This went on for a number of months, before we slowly evolved beyond the required pleasantries and started talking. Music, mostly. Henry was always eager to talk about music, and I was always happy to oblige. Other than writing, it was the closest thing to a passion that I had, as evidenced by the ever-evolving iPod mix that filled the store's speakers from open to close, its tracks culled from the deepest recesses of "you haven't heard of this band yet" blogs. We talked about what we were listening to, gave each other recommendations, and so on. Henry's taste ran the gamut: the Beatles, Boards of Canada, Stockhausen, Count Basie, Sebadoh, Chick Corea, the Doors, Captain Beefheart, Stravinsky, Sunny Day Real Estate, Elvis, Alice Coltrane, My Bloody Valentine, Patsy Cline… he was a one-man "staff recommends" shelf at a failing record store. I liked him instantly.

Months passed, seasons changed, and life went as it usually did—which is to say, nothing of much note happened, until one evening, in the winter of 2008, the bell jingled, and Henry hurried into the store carrying a package wrapped in brown paper. A package containing a bundle of ancient letters, a list of names and contact information, and ten ancient-looking leather-bound journals, each one filled with tightly packed handwriting.

They were the personal journals of Abraham Lincoln, chronicling his lifelong battle against the vampires that had shaped his destiny and long haunted the American night.

Right. Of course they were. I didn't believe a word of it, just as I don't believe in flying saucers or Santa Claus or happy endings. There were no such things as vampires, let alone ax-wielding vampire hunters who went on to become president of the United States. Henry, anticipating this, had seen fit to convince me that night in a shocking way that left me badly shaken. Once you've seen those glassy fangs, those pulsing blue veins, and the satiation of that bottomless hunger for blood, there's little room left for doubt.

So began nearly two years of research and writing, poring over the journals and letters, chasing down the names on the list he'd given me, and conducting interviews with reluctant subjects. I wrote day and night, much of it in notebooks at the store counter, stopping only when a customer needed help. I'd been given the gift of a story that had already been written. A story that just needed to be carefully stitched together, like the boundary between existence and inexistence. The scribbled notebooks became a typed manuscript, the manuscript became a book, and the book was given to the world to be judged. My dream had been realized in dramatic fashion. Or so I thought.

Writing a book, it turned out, wasn't all that big a deal in the Twitter age. Certainly not as big a deal as which pop star got arrested or which reality TV personality got her prebaby body back. For one brief, shining moment, I was the ringmaster, and then, just as quickly as it had arrived, the circus packed up its tents and steamed on to the next town, and there I was, back behind the counter. A few inches closer to Manhattan, but still miles away. Living a life that suddenly felt two sizes too small.

The idea came in the winter of 2011.

It was a Monday morning, slow and snowy, the sidewalks empty, only the occasional car passing on the unplowed street, hazards flashing. The store was as dead as the world outside. I flipped through the pages of the *Post*, ignoring the chants of Egyptian uprisings coming from the mono speaker of my small television. One of the national morning shows was on, and news gave way to chat, gave way to weather, which was all I was really interested in. The weatherman forecasted—more snow, snow forever, endless winter—then read out the names and showed the pictures of those lucky viewers who'd reached their hundredth birthday. The chosen few who'd seen a century pass before their eyes, gone from horses and buggies to Mars landers in the blink of a lifetime. One of today's celebrants was a man who'd reached the ripe old age of 108.

"My word," said the weatherman. "Isn't that wonderful? Imagine the things he's seen."

Imagine the things he's seen...

I looked up from my paper. Something stirred in me—a vague memory of a passage from one of Abe's journals. I couldn't recall the words, not exactly, but I had the spirit of it. He'd written it as a young man, not long after training with Henry, wondering what it was like being a vampire, wondering what someone like Henry must have seen in his centuries. I went back through the transcripts of Abe's journals on my computer (the originals were safely back in Henry's possession) and found the passage I was looking for: "What a strange thing to be a vampire. To break free of death's gravity!"

Abe's journals had covered only a fifty-year span of Henry's life. But what about the other four hundred years? What of a twenty-first-century man, born before Galileo or Shakespeare? *Imagine the things he's seen.* A man who, with the exception of a brief and turbulent period of being alive, had never had a cold—or a gray hair?

That morning, I did something I hadn't done in twenty years of working at the store: I closed early and braved the snowy roads to Henry's house.

"Not interested," he said.

His answer was immediate and unequivocal. For one, the last thing Henry wanted was more publicity. His fellow vampires had been upset enough when he'd shared the secret of Lincoln's journals. Two, he saw no point in looking back. "Nothing kills a vampire as quickly as the past," he said. To that end, he'd never kept a journal of his own. Never hung on to every letter the way Abe had. You have to keep moving, moving—make a point of staying engaged in the present. Otherwise you ended up like an old car, cautiously creeping along a snowy road with your hazards on. Still talking Beethoven when everyone else has moved on to Batman.

I persisted. He resisted. This went on for months. I would e-mail, and Henry would take days to reply. And when he did, he wasn't encouraging.

```
Yes, I'm traveling. There's nothing to
discuss. I don't see what good will
come of me airing out my dirty laundry
or further aggravating those of my
kind who are already livid that I made
certain details of our past public in
the first place.

HS
```

From: ██████████████@gmail.com>
Date: March 2, 2012 at 2:01:03 EST
To: ████████████@aol.com>

Subject: Book

Henry,

Are you traveling? I haven't heard back
from you regarding my last e-mail.
I understand your concerns about
privacy, etc., but I think there's a
way to get around those issues. Can we
discuss when you return?

                              SGS

Finally, in the spring of 2012, more than a year after I'd first broached the subject, Henry agreed to sit and hear me out. We sat in the study of the giant metaphor that was his mansion—old and Gothic on the outside but completely redone on the inside, all concrete, iron, and glass. Open spaces and clean, tech-friendly surfaces, as if the very décor was there to strengthen his hold on the present. *Nothing kills a vampire as quickly as the past.* There we were, I with my take-out cup of Dunkin' Donuts coffee steaming beside me, he with his hands folded in the lap of his expensive jeans. An incredibly old, experienced mind behind his clear brown eyes.

"So," he said. "What did you have in mind—a

rambling multicentury autobiography? A mopey trea-
tise on the drawbacks of immortality?"

"I want to know what happened in Springfield," I
said. "After Abe's funeral."

I knew that being specific was the only shot I had.
If I'd started with "Tell me everything," or "Oh, whatever you feel like," he would have disengaged. When
you're dealing with a man who has five centuries rat-
tling around in his skull, you have to cast specialized
bait or you'll catch nothing. In the course of writing
about the journals, I'd learned that Ford's Theater
hadn't been the end of Abraham Lincoln. What I didn't
know was how he had escaped death...and what had
become of him after he did. It seemed as good a place
to start as any.

"How?" I asked. "How did it happen? How did
you do it?"

Henry considered me with those old eyes. I could
see his wheels turning, see him debating his next move.
For a second, I wondered if I'd stepped over some
invisible line, wondered if he was going to leap out of
his chair and crack me open, spilling my innards onto
the floor of his museum-quality home.

To my great relief, he started talking.

He talked until the days stretched into weeks and
the summer became Indian summer, then autumn.
And when the leaves of the Hudson Valley had
reached the peak of their crisp, fiery bloom, we weren't
even close to the middle of the story. But we were

hooked, and the experience had infused Henry with an energy that he hadn't felt since the fighting times. He was intoxicated by the distilled memories that had been fermenting for hundreds of years. He was, in the words of Norman Maclean, "haunted by waters."

I asked him questions. Sometimes I stopped him for clarification or elaboration. Mostly I just listened, taking notes and recording every word on my phone—both of us aware of, and amused by, the fact that we were living out a fictional scenario imagined by Anne Rice almost forty years earlier.

I spent the better part of a year conducting these infrequent but intense interviews. When Henry felt he'd rambled as much as he could, I began the task of transcribing months' worth of fragmented recollections (excerpts of these transcripts appear on virtually every page of this book, as indented text), writing the connective tissue between them, and arranging it all into a palatable shape that would fit fashionably between two covers. I wrote about iron and electricity; rippers, Russian mystics, and Indian chiefs; I wrote about world wars and robber barons; about Roosevelts and Kennedys. Blood and murder and lost loves.

Henry gave me the freedom to change and "shine up" his description of certain things (he can be a very matter-of-fact speaker, even when describing the gory or fantastic). But I was strictly forbidden from changing a single word that might alter the truth of what was being told.

And what I was told, it turns out, is something of a caper. A manhunt spanning four centuries. A hunt for the greatest enemy America has ever faced, a shadowy puppeteer who seemed to confound Henry at every turn. Because of that, perhaps, there are some parts of Henry's remarkable life that are simply not relevant to the larger tale and haven't been documented in these pages. Another time, perhaps.

Between running the store and raising two resentful growing boys from a distance, it took me nearly a year to put together the manuscript in its rough form. When I was done, Henry set about making his own alterations—pulling back where he thought I'd gotten too colorful, pushing me when he sensed I was trying to be flattering or respectful. He insisted on naked judgment, warts and all.

One thing Henry found especially lacking were my descriptions of death. "They read like a eunuch writing about an orgy" is how he put it.

I asked him to describe it for me as best he could. I wanted to know what dying felt like in exquisite detail, so that I could convey that experience with my words.

"It's impossible to explain," he said. "You have to experience it."

And so I asked him to kill me. And he obliged.

I shuffled down East Market Street, crisp leaves underfoot, the taste of blood clinging to my teeth like copper fillings. I had no memory of how I'd gotten there. One moment I was dead, the next I was in the center of town, the sun rising in a cold and cloudless sky, my feet guiding themselves down a well-worn path. In that rote, distant manner, they brought me back to the store, to the counter, to my notebook. In my fog, as the first customers began to trickle in, I wrote down everything I could remember, determined to capture the words before the high of being alive wore off.

Just as the towering myth of Abraham Lincoln—honest backwoods lawyer, spinner of yarns, righter of wrongs—tells only part of the truth, so, too, is the myth of America woefully incomplete. The country that Ronald Reagan once called "a shining city upon a hill" has, in fact, been tangled up in darkness since before she was born. Millions of souls have graced the American stage over the centuries, played parts both great and small, and made their final exits. But of all the souls who witnessed America's birth and growth, who fought in her finest hours, and who had a hand in her hidden history, only one soul remains to tell the whole truth.

What follows is the story of Henry Sturges.

What follows is the story of an American life.

Seth Grahame-Smith
Rhinebeck, NY
October 2014

ONE

★ ★ ★

May 8th, 1865

For God's sake, let us sit upon the ground
and tell sad stories of the death of kings.

—*William Shakespeare*, Richard II, *act 3, scene 2*

A braham Lincoln wasn't happy to be alive.
 He'd been roused against his will, pulled from his well-deserved eternal rest with explosive force. One moment, he'd been floating gently through a borderless sea of warm, black nothingness. No more aware or burdened than a man is in the centuries before he's born. And then some lesser god had yanked the plug out of the Great Drain of the Universe, and the consciousness that had once been Abraham Lincoln had been sucked down into it. He was born again. But not into the world outside.

The world of the inner welcomed him first. His brain remoistening with blood, one drop, one vessel at a time. *One cell, two cell, red cell, blue cell.* Synapses beginning to fire slowly, randomly, like the hammers of a typewriter striking a blank sheet of paper but spelling nonsense. Thoughts—*what a strange concept, "thoughts"*—being pieced together, the images and feelings primitive cave paintings on the inside of his skull. Then a filmstrip of disjointed frames flashing before him—*what a strange concept, "him"*—his mind gathering steam now, the fog of death lifting. Here, a dandelion in his six-year-old hand, his feet running across lush green grass. Here, the dirt hearth of a Kentucky cabin. Here, a candlelit book and the smell of bread cooling in the next room. A fleeting feeling of disconnected joy, then grief, then rage, coming and going at random as his brain emerged from its tomb. Each reanimated cell a speck of dirt being brushed off a long-buried fossil. The voices came next. Far-off words in some as yet foreign language. The cries of a child, echoing down a hallway. The moans of lovemaking.

Then, suddenly and unrelentingly, the nightmares. Horrific visions: the faces of his beloved children crying out as they burned away to ash. That ash swirling in a disembodied shaft of light as winged demons flew overhead, their skin so black that only their eyes and teeth showed. His son—*the name...why can't I remember his name?*—reaching out for him, crying out as the impossible hands of the devil himself dragged him away to burn forever. The boy's face streaked with tears, Abe helpless to save him. And then the nightmares broke like a fever, and Abe could breathe again. It was as if God had tired of watching him gasp and flop and had dropped him back in the cool waters of the now.

On the third day, Abe rose again. He heard a different voice beyond the darkness of his closed eyelids. Unlike the screams that had accompanied his nightmares, this voice came to Abe by way of his ears. It was a familiar voice, speaking words that were also familiar, though Abe wasn't sure why. Nor was he certain what language the man was speaking, as those parts of the fossil had yet to be uncovered.

"Nothing in his life became him like the leaving it," said the voice. "He died as one that had been studied in his death, to throw away the dearest thing he owed, as 'twere a careless trifle..."[1]

Abe's eyes opened, though there was no life behind them. He looked around the room—*that's what it's called...a room*—as spare as a room could be. White walls. A fireplace at the foot of his large bed. A single, framed painting of a rosy-cheeked young boy hanging on the opposite wall. Yet as spare as the room was, there was also something vaguely familiar about it. A feeling of being home.

Abe noticed a shape to his right. A dark shape, hovering over him. A man, sitting in a chair beside his bed. There was something familiar about *him*, too. That face. That ghostly face framed by dark, shoulder-length hair.

---

1. William Shakespeare, *Macbeth*, act 1, scene 4.

The tiniest sliver of sunlight squeezed between the drawn curtains and fell on the wall above his head. Abe feared the light. He hated it. It blinded him. It burned him. He wanted it to go away, and it did. As if hearing his thoughts, the curtains were drawn shut, and the burning and blindness were gone.

Now, in the black pitch, Abe saw as never before. Every detail of the room revealed itself, as sharp as day, though drained of nearly all color. Every creak of the house was magnified by his ears. A mouse scurrying behind the walls became a horse galloping over cobblestones. The bristles of a broom sweeping a neighborhood sidewalk sounded like sheets of paper being torn an inch from his ear. And voices. Voices crashing ashore a hundred at a time, the result sounding quite like the jumbled din of an audience milling about in a theater lobby during intermis—

A theater. I was in a theater.

There were other voices—strange voices that didn't pass his ears but were somehow heard just as clearly. Abe looked back to the man in the chair. With the sliver of sunlight gone, he was able to make out the features on the man's face. It was the same face that had greeted him in his twelfth year—the first time he had been spared from the comforting embrace of death. He knew because it was *exactly* the same face. The face belonged to a man. The man who had steadied him when his body convulsed. Dried his skin when it ran with sweat. Who, now that Abe thought about it, had been right there, every time his fevered eyes had chanced to flitter open for a moment over the last days and nights. There was something so familiar about it all. Lying here in bed, with this man—this familiar man—by his side. Waking from a dream without end. They'd been here before, the two of them. *What is your name?*

And suddenly, like a ship enshrouded in fog catching the first faint sweep of the lighthouse beam, it came to him.

"Henry," said Abe. "What have you done?"

Lincoln's coffin is draped in black during a funeral procession in Columbus, Ohio—one of many stops made by the late president's train on its journey to Springfield, Illinois. Henry would steal Abe's body from the same coffin a few nights later.

Abe's mortal body had died in the early morning hours of April 15th, but it was nearly a week before the late president's funeral train departed Washington, D.C., on its way to Springfield, Illinois. The trip had taken thirteen days. Millions had turned out to mourn their fallen leader along the way, some waiting hours to shuffle past his coffin as he lay in state in New York, Philadelphia, and Chicago, some lining the railroad tracks before dawn, hoping to get a glimpse of history as it sped by, to give a last salute to the savior of their Union as he journeyed home. By the time he was laid to rest on May 4th, Abe's body had been an empty vessel for three weeks.

On that warm, sunny afternoon, Henry had stood among the thousands in Oak Ridge Cemetery, waiting through the speeches and the prayers in the shade of his black parasol. And long after the mournful masses had marched back to Springfield on foot and by carriage, Henry remained. He stood alone as hot day became warm night, keeping watch over the padlocked iron door of a receiving vault—the temporary home of Abe's coffin, which he shared with the casket of his son Willie, whose body had been brought on the train from Washington so that it could be interred beside his father. Henry stood there, mourning his fallen compatriot, wading through the memories of their tumultuous forty-year friendship. He'd read some of the scraps of paper that had been left by passing mourners at the foot of the iron gates that surrounded the vault, along with flowers and keepsakes. One of the notes had stirred him like no other. A single scribbled line, taken from Shakespeare's *Julius Caesar*:

I am a foe to tyrants, and my country's friend.

Henry had stared at those ten little words for the better part of an hour, his resolve deepening. Moments coming back to him as if rendered by the dreamy brushstrokes of Manet or Degas...Standing over Abe as a boy, pulling him from the clutches of death after his first ill-fated hunt. Standing in the woods outside New Salem, Illinois, trying to convince a young man who'd just lost his first love that the future held great things for him. *Most men have no purpose but to exist, Abraham; to pass quietly through history as minor characters upon a stage they cannot even see. To be the playthings of tyrants.* In the White House, the last time Henry had seen his friend, when the two of them had been at each other's throats.

I couldn't let it end that way. I imagined all the good that was left to be done. I imagined having the chance to finish what we'd begun. Even then, in death, I believed that it was his purpose to fight tyranny. And there was plenty of it left to fight, by God. To come so far—to bear the weight of a war on his shoulders, to pull a nation back together with his bare hands, only to be cut down at the hour of its splendid reunion. A hero who so often defied death in battle, only to have it ambush him in repose. This was a tragic ending worthy of Shakespeare. Yet unlike Shakespeare, I couldn't find the moral in his death. Only senselessness. Waste. Looking back, I wonder what part my own guilt played in my decision. The fact that we'd parted on terrible terms. Perhaps all I wanted was a chance to make things right.

Whatever his reasons, Henry had broken into the tomb just before sunrise, and with no small effort, he'd spirited the body to a waiting carriage and then to a house on the corner of Eighth and Jackson Streets. Like many buildings and private homes in Springfield, it had been draped with black bunting as the city mourned its favorite son. But this house was different. A plaque beside the front door still read *A. Lincoln*.

I wanted it to be somewhere familiar, to ease the inevitable shock that comes with being pulled from eternal rest. It also had the added benefit of being sealed off for a period of official mourning—its shutters closed and heavy black drapes drawn inside. Darkness, privacy, and a sturdy bed were important when becoming a vampire.

Henry looked down at his old friend, his face caked with heavy makeup, which had begun to dry and crack. His lips had been set in a smile, one that, Henry noted, "Abe never would've made on his own." Three weeks was by far the longest death that Henry—or any vampire, to his knowledge—had yet attempted to reverse. But there was reason to hope. Like anyone who read the papers, Henry knew that Abe had been arterially embalmed in Washington—his blood drained through his jugular, and his arteries filled with a mix of chemicals through a small incision in his thigh. This kept the walls of his arteries and veins moist and staved off the rot of death. Ironically, it was a practice that had only recently come into widespread use in the Civil War, and at Abe's request—so that the bodies of fallen Union soldiers wouldn't rot before their families had a chance to look upon them back home.

> I left the body and ventured into town, where the streets were still crowded with travelers who'd come for the funeral—some of them having spent the night packed together on the floors of over-booked boardinghouses; others on the straw in stables. I made my way to Thomas Owen's drugstore in Statehouse Square, where I sought the item I needed. But Mr. Owen didn't carry it, and so I was forced to seek out a mortuary, where I

convinced the undertaker to sell me a hollow needle and plunger.

Henry returned to the house, taking care not to be seen as he entered through a back door, and began what amounted to a re-embalming of the late president—opening Abe's jugular and draining the embalming fluid into a pan, then drawing blood from his own veins and injecting it, one plunger-full at a time, into Abe's.

Twice during this process, my own supply of blood became dangerously low, and I was forced to venture out and feed. Knowing that Abe would be unable to bear the thought of his resurrection coming at the expense of another's man's life, I fed on the blood of a horse in a nearby corral instead.

When Abe's body would hold no more, Henry began to massage his heart, circulating the blood.

Hours passed. Nothing. *It had been too long,* I thought. My friend had ventured too far down the river Styx to turn back. I began to mourn him again. To contemplate a world without him in it. And then I saw his fingers—those long, weather-beaten fingers, which the embalmers had rendered perfectly straight—begin to slacken. Then twitch. Slowly, the rigor began to ease its grip on

Abe's gray, cold body. Breath, barely a whisper at first, moved in and out of his lungs. And then the sickness came, as it always did. The last, violent throes of living flesh giving way to dead. I sat by his side day and night, cleaning the black vomit from his face and the sheets when it came. Wiping his sweat-soaked brow. Holding him down by the shoulders when his shaking grew too intense, fearing that he might break his own neck. In the quieter moments, I read to him from a copy of *Shakespeare's Complete Works* that I'd found in the downstairs parlor. For two days, I watched him. And then the fever broke. His eyelids fluttered, then opened. I watched him take in the room, unsure if he recognized it or not.

"Henry," said Abe. "What have you done?"

Henry smiled down on him, relieved that his old friend's mind had survived intact—at least intact enough to recognize a face and speak its name.

"Welcome back, Abraham."

"What have you done?"

I took a hand mirror from the bedside table and handed it to him. The changes that I'd witnessed over three days now revealed themselves in a reflected instant. Age had retreated from his face. Gone were the deep lines that a life of heartache and worry had carved over the years, like glaciers across a plain. Gone was the hunch his tall frame had taken on in its later days, and the gray of his beard. His body was lean and strong again. His shoulders square, his skin smooth, and his eyes bright and sharp. Decades of hardship and wear, erased in a relative instant. Yet I knew, even then, that the real hardships lay ahead. The grief of his first kill. The loneliness of his first century of darkness. But I would ease his burden. I would be his companion in grief. His mentor in killing. His light in the dark.

Abe stared at himself for a time. From his expression, it was clear to Henry that he was crying, though his eyes remained dry.

"One of the cosmic ironies of immortality," said Henry. "We cannot cry, no matter how deep our sorrow. Though I suppose the same can be said of living men. Those who cause the most tears often shed the fewest."

"*We...*"

Abe threw the mirror against the wall, shattering it. Henry remained seated, unflinching. The book in his lap.

"It is normal to grieve one's own death," he said.

Abe threw off his covers and rose to his bare feet—still wearing the shirt and trousers he'd been buried in.

He went for the drapes, flung them open, and was instantly repelled by the explosion of harsh sunlight. He cried out in pain and retreated to the corner of the room—shielding his eyes with his forearm. Where the sun had briefly fallen on his skin, there were now red, blistered burns. And even in the relative darkness of his corner, the light reflected off the walls continued to irritate his skin. I rose and closed the drapes. With the return of darkness, he lowered his arm, and the redness retreated at once—the blisters disappearing before his eyes. In moments, he was whole again.

"You'll grow tolerant of the light in time," said Henry.

Abe collapsed in the corner, his back to the wall, head in his hands. It had been a little over three years since they'd been in each other's company, and they hadn't parted friends.

"Henry...what have you done?"

I returned to my chair and took considerable time before answering. When I did, it was with a calm, clear voice. There was no need to agitate him any more than he already was. It was a shock, to be sure. The changes to one's body. To the way one perceives the world. The untrained mind, filled with disconnected whispers that can't yet be shut out. And the hunger. The threat of a great hunger, merely a suggestion at first. A dark cloud rolling

over a distant hilltop. Speaking from experience,
it's no easy thing to wake from one's own death,
especially when one wakes in poor company.

"You were murdered," said Henry. "Assassinated, in
Ford's Theater."

Abe sat in silence for a time.

"By whom?"

"A vampire named Booth."

"Mary?"

Mary . . . poor Mary, standing over another body.

"Unharmed. Though quite stricken with grief, as
you would imagine. The whole nation is in mourning,
Abraham. Even the South."

The South . . . the war . . .

"Where is she?"

"In Washington, with your sons."

My sons . . . Eddie . . . Willie . . .

"Willie," said Abe. "The last time I saw you . . . we
fought about Willie."

"Yes."

"They took him . . . they killed my boy."

"Yes."

Here was the book of Abe's life, its pages filled with
a jumble of random letters. Only minutes ago, it had
been a tale told by an idiot, signifying nothing. But
with every passing second, the letters arranged themselves into words, the words into memories: the mother
he'd buried. The sister, the two sons, and the lover he

mourned. The vampires. The hunts. The nation. The end. The memories began to overwhelm him. Sorrows coming not as single spies, but in battalions—for all of it, every goddamned word of it, was darkness. Loss.

Abe sat in the corner, staring at nothing in particular. Piecing it together.

"I heard a noise," he said after a long silence. "I felt a pain...a hot pain, radiating out from the back of my skull."

"You were shot."

"There was a struggle. Screaming. I heard Mary... heard her shouting. I tried to tell her not to worry, but my mouth wouldn't heed the command to speak, nor my eyelids the command to open. I felt myself floating through the darkness, being carried through some god-awful ruckus. And then it was quiet again. The pain was still there, somewhere in the dark. But it was distant. I felt the cold prodding of instruments on my skin. Heard voices. Hushed voices. People coming and going; crying...but even these noises began to drift farther away, as if I was floating down a lazy river, and all the world was on the banks behind me. Drifting away, until there was only the beating of my own heart as it slowed, like a watch in need of winding. And after a time..."

Abe struggled to find the right words. There weren't any.

"After a time?" asked Henry.

"After a time, there *was* no time."

Abe looked up and met Henry's eyes.

"Henry," he said, "what have you done?"

He'd asked and asked, but now the question struck me with its full weight.

"I've broken a sacred vow," said Henry. "I've borrowed you back. Returned you to a nation that still needs your wisdom and your strength."

Abe shook his head.

"You've undone everything. Whatever good I accomplished, whatever grief I suffered—all that I lost. It means nothing now."

"Abraham—"

"You've made me the very evil I devoted my life to fighting."

"I've made you immortal, so that you and I might continue what we began."

"This isn't what I wanted..."

"You have your youth! Your strength! Think of the good you can do. You'll be able to see your family again. You'll be able to watch Robert and Tad gro—"

"And what kind of father would I be? What kind of husband? A murderer, confined to darkness? You would have me bestow upon those boys and that woman an impossible burden! Just as you have bestowed one upon me!"

"Yes, it's a burden. But I can help you master the bearing of it."

"To what end? Henry, what becomes of me now? You would have me undo all that I devoted myself to. You would have me be the very thing that took my mother! My boy! How can I look upon myself when I am all that I despise? A life! A good death!"

"Think of what you can do with limitless time. Think of the wonders you'll see. The lives you'll—"

"Spare me, Henry. For forty years you've done nothing but blather about the miseries of eternity. Now you sell it as snake oil."

"I can teach you how to make it tolerable. If you'll just listen to me—"

"Listen to you? And then what? Do you expect me to follow you into darkness?"

"That's the only place for you now, Abraham."

Abe rose to his full height, his back strong and straight. His limbs lean and muscular. The last time Abe and Henry had laid eyes on each other, they'd been locked in a fight. A fight between an aging mortal and a vampire. Now they were equals.

For the first time, I saw the hallmarks of his curse. His fangs, which had yet to draw blood— virgin and pristine. His eyes, suddenly as black and lifeless as a shark's. When I'd last faced him, he'd been a living man. Powerful, yes. Trained, yes. But a living man nonetheless, and therefore at a disadvantage. Now we were equals—if not in experience, then at least in strength. Furthermore,

I was weak, having given so much of my blood to bring him back, and having replenished my own with that of animals and all their attendant filth. I was sure he was going to lunge at me, attack.

Henry looked up at him.

"The hunger will come, Abraham. And when it does, you'll be as powerless to stop it as I am."

"By then," said Abe, "I'll be in hell."

Abe stared at Henry a moment longer, then turned and ran across the room.

I realized what he meant to do and screamed his name. He leveled his broad shoulders and met the drapes head-on, shattering the window behind them and crashing through into the harsh light. And I saw, in that unmistakable way only vampires see. Saw his new skin redden and blister the instant the sun fell upon it. I heard him cry out with the agony of it, even as he fell through the air, all of it happening in an instant—too fast for the living to perceive. But to me, helpless and all seeing, he seemed to hang there, in the air, forever. I meant to get up. To jump down after him and shield him from the light. To save him. But it was already too late. All I could do was listen. Listen to my friend burning alive...

Abraham Lincoln was gone.

TWO

★ ★ ★

Five Heads
1888

I know how men in exile feed on dreams
of hope.

—*Aeschylus*

America was at Henry's back.

A thousand miles astern of the RMS *Umbria*—
the steel-hulled steamship that bore him back to the
place of his birth, along with fifteen hundred other
passengers and crew. He stood against the railing
of her promenade deck, a full moon above reflected
in the flat calm of the ageless sea. Marveling at the
speed and steadiness with which it passed. The entire
crossing, from New York to Liverpool, was scheduled to take seven days. *Seven days.* Henry's first,
centuries earlier, had taken months. Packed aboard
a cramped and rat-infested hell, pitching and rolling, grown men puking over the side, sickened by

the motion of the sea and the stench of the rotting rations.

He'd been a mortal then, in 1586. Twenty-three years old. A veritable infant. An Englishman of average height and slender build, with black hair to the middle of his back, and his love by his side, the two of them off to make a life together in the wild. To build a colony and raise a family in the name of the king.

Here he was, on the same sea. An American. Alone. His long hair now sensibly cropped. The swells of that first crossing distant and calm. The virgin shores of that first landing now covered with concrete and glittering with glass. The sweltering, putrid hull of that old pitching hell replaced by a stateroom, appointed with such luxuries as to make royalty blush at its excess. So still, it may as well have been on land.

Henry stared at the sea. Halfway between the continents. Halfway between the Old World and the New. He could hear music from the first-class dining room. Strings softly playing Schubert and Brahms. The clinking of silver on china. The murmurs of the women gossiping over tea, their sleeveless silk evening gowns in shades of coral and sea-foam green, accented with diamond choker necklaces and white kid-leather gloves. The men gossiping over brandy, stuffed into their tailcoats and crisp white bow ties. Henry had no care to join them. Nor did he have any need. Though he'd become adept at giving the appearance of eating—pushing food around his plate, dabbing his lips with a napkin at regular intervals—he found the practice deeply annoying and tried to avoid it at all costs. Better to pass the time alone. Sleeping by day, reading by night. Dressing only to wander the deck in darkness, taking in the unseasonable warmth of the salt air.

Fortunately, the rich had endless reserves of tolerance for strange behavior, at least among their own kind. While a recluse of lesser means might have drawn suspicion, this fellow first-class stranger was merely an "eccentric" who preferred to take his meals in his quarters. An artist, no doubt. A man who needed privacy to summon his muses. Or perhaps he was a wealthy young lord who didn't care to mingle with the merely rich. And, just as fortunate for the well-heeled passengers, I could endure the seven-day passage without feeding. There would be no clumsy ladies slipping on the wet sundeck and breaking their necks on this voyage. No poor, drunken gentlemen getting too close to the railing and falling overboard in the dead of night.

For years I had hungered to see England again. Not the familiar need for a change of pace or scenery that comes every two or three decades, but something else. Something—and forgive me for saying this—something deeper. I missed

England like a man misses his first love, with an intensity tempered by melancholy. And I might never have acted on that longing to see my homeland if an urgent errand had not been thrust upon me in New York. I had no way of knowing at the time, but that errand would consume the next century of my life.

Henry had wandered America in the years after Abe's fatal leap, watching with a sort of detached fascination as the young country rose from the ashes, brushed itself off, and began to move west by way of iron and ink. The purchase of Alaska in 1867; the golden spike of the first transcontinental railroad two years later. America had looked inward. It had gone to war with itself to decide what kind of nation it was going to be. And with that decision firmly and finally made, it pulled itself together and soldiered on, emerging from its near-death experience with a new vitality. A new spirit of progress.

Henry had marked his three hundredth year during America's Civil War. Three hundred years of motion. Of taking new names, making new homes, adapting to the world as it changed around him. In 1888, with the war long over and the greatest man he'd ever known twenty-three years in the grave, he moved again. This time he swam against the westward tide of progress, leaving the Midwest and settling in New York City.

> I'd heard it said that "when a man is tired of moving, he moves to New York, and the movement comes to him." I supposed it was partially this. The need to relax in the anonymity of large numbers. To let the movement of the world come to me for a change. And I suppose I also liked the thought of being closer to the headquarters of the Union.[1] But looking back, more than anything, I think I wanted to be farther away from America. It had been a long relationship, fraught with discovery and upheaval and loss. To me, it was a nation of ghosts, you understand. In every corner of the country, whether it be Richmond or St. Louis or New Orleans, there were a hundred faded memories. The faces of a hundred friends lost to time.

Henry's home in St. Louis was put up for sale and a new one procured in New York. Arrangements were made via letter and cable. Furnishings were bought. A staff hired, sight unseen, based on recommendations

---

1. A mostly below-ground complex, beneath what is currently the American Surety Building, at 100 Broadway, directly across the street from Trinity Church.

from other well-to-do New Yorkers, human and vampire alike. Clothing, keepsakes, books, and artwork were packed up and shipped from St. Louis in advance.

Henry heard the horse first. Then he saw his dinner.

A few hours earlier, upon arriving at his apartment on Park Avenue, Henry had realized that his hands were shaking with hunger. It occurred to him that he hadn't eaten since St. Louis. Fortunately, his new city was practically made of scoundrels and bottom-feeders, their character wanting and their veins bulging.

The Gilded Age was in full swing, and the world was racing to New York's shores by the millions, driven from their homelands by poverty or war or simple ambition. The bricks of new buildings could hardly be laid fast enough, and the bricks of the old were bursting at the mortar as immigrant families crammed three, sometimes four generations into two-room apartments.

Walking the crowded sidewalks at night, or hurrying over cobblestone streets, dodging carriages and trolley cars, one could hear German, Italian, Mandarin; the brogues of Scots and Irishmen joining with the steady hiss of the gas lamps. Streets both paved and unpaved, filled with exotic, overwhelmed faces. The loftiest gentlemen and ladies and the lowest wretches, sharing the same sidewalks. As a brother of the Union, I was sworn to respect the living. To feed only upon the "sick and the wicked." God knows there were plenty of them. They arrived daily by steamship and train. By horse and by foot. Millions of them, lost in this New World. Struggling with a new language. Most of them were decent, but in a city of such size, with such a varied population, there were bound to be scoundrels. Whoremongers and rapists. Men who worked children to death in sweltering factories. Dying drunks sleeping under the stars in Central Park. Extortionists who threatened to break the arms or burn the businesses of those who refused to pay protection money. Men like these existed in every corner of America, but nowhere were they so deliciously packed as in New York. And remember, lightbulbs were still a novelty. Forensic science and surveillance cameras were a lifetime away. It was a wonderful place to be a vampire.

It was a city on the verge of being sleepless, soon to be called the Capital of the World, brimming with electric light, but already brimming with its own brand of electricity. It was a city of contradictions. Noisy and crowded in places, deathly dark and silent in others. Its buildings could be Gothic and grand, yet connected by unpaved streets teeming with horse-drawn

A horse lies dead on the streets of New York after being found with two large puncture wounds in its neck. Animals were often meals of last resort for vampires.

coaches, the stench of manure and uncollected garbage thick and unbearable in the summer months. Construction was just beginning on what was, at the time, a massive apartment building on the corner of Seventy-Second and Central Park West.

> It was a beautiful building, all dormers and spandrels. Gothic. Elegant. But it was also considered an act of lunacy on the part of its backer, Edward Clark.[2] It wasn't the building that was the

---

2. Clark was one of the founders of the Singer Sewing Machine Company, which is still in business today. He died before the building was completed.

problem—it was where he'd chosen to *build* it. You have to understand, the area bordering Central Park was completely undeveloped at the time. There were no neighboring buildings of any note. And here was a towering monument standing in the middle of it all. Apartments only the wealthy could afford, farther uptown than any rich people had need to go. When it was finished, four or five years later, they gave it a name befitting the virtual wilderness that surrounded it: the Dakota.

Henry hadn't been walking long when he heard the familiar groan of a horse in pain. A cart had stopped in the middle of the street farther down the block, so loaded down with scrap iron that its wheels visibly bowed. It was being pulled—in theory, at least—by a lone white shire horse and driven by a stocky, bearded man in a bowler hat. A cigar hanging from one side of his mouth. Even a healthy horse would've had trouble pulling so much weight on its own. This one was clearly exhausted. Malnourished. But that didn't stop the driver from yelling, cussing, and whipping the poor beast to no end. The horse cried out, but it didn't budge, so the driver jumped down from his seat and yanked on its reins, trying to get the beast to move. It didn't. So the driver took a pull off his cigar, until the ashes at its tip glowed red, and thrust it into the animal's left flank beside a grouping of similarly shaped round scars—searing its flesh and eliciting a horrible cry. The driver climbed into his seat and gave the reins a snap. The horse began to move.

> It's interesting. If you're willing to listen, every so often, life—or God or the Universe or whatever you prefer to call it—lets us know that it's paying attention. Here was a man, if you could call him that, whose cruelty would've gone unnoticed and unpunished, if not for the fact that a vampire had wandered onto that very block, at that very hour, on that very night, to witness it. And not just any vampire. A vampire who'd once owned a similar white shire horse as a boy. A horse he'd been quite fond of, named "Alistair."

Henry followed the cart, taking care to keep his distance. North on Broadway. West on Canal Street. North again on Sullivan, the excitement building in him with every block. The anticipation of the kill. The warmth of the giving blood. The night sky was clouded over, the stars obscured, and the moon just a soft suggestion. It was a dark night, and the darkness would do.

> Finding a victim is, in a way, like finding a mate. We venture into the night, hoping to find the right one. That one in a thousand that makes our eyes light up and our breath quicken, for whatever subconscious or chemical reason. Some nights

we get lucky; other nights we settle. Some nights we simply go home hungry. But it isn't a cold, calculated thing. That's the biggest misconception, really. That we simply grab the first warm-blooded human we stumble across and sink our fangs into its neck. No. There has to be some kind of connection between vampire and victim. Something more than the transaction itself. An emotional component, whether it's as simple as physical attraction, repulsion, or rage. And just as when looking for a mate, we have types. Some vampires kill only men. Others women. Some won't touch blondes, or the elderly, or the obese.

The cruel have always been my type, no matter their gender. When I witness cruelty—that is, the powerful abusing the less powerful or the meek— it triggers an involuntary response. A chain of emotions that I never had a name for, until the 1950s, when I began calling it "the Ignition Sequence," after reading about the Mercury space program. First I become flush with righteous anger, which, if you must be angry, is the very best kind. That righteous anger quickly sharpens into determination. Determination, of course, being nothing more than anger with brakes and a steering wheel. Finally, joy. A strange but unmistakable joy, based in the knowledge that here, in this place, on this night, some small measure of justice will be done in the world, and I'll be the one doing it. That feeling—that joy—is something I've never tired of.

It's one of the few true blessings to the curse of being a vampire. For in those ephemeral moments, we cease to be monsters and get to be superheroes. You might ask, is death a just punishment for abusing a horse? Here's how I see it. This man knows it's wrong to hurt this animal, and yet he does it anyway. He allows himself to revert into a base creature, telling himself that a horse is just a dumb animal, after all, well below him on the food chain. So I take my cue from him, and do the same.

The horse struggled up Sullivan Street, passing the dark windows of modest shops and apartment buildings, the driver whipping and cussing all the while, until at last they came to a small, ramshackle house set back from the street and drove through an opening in a wooden fence, its white paint faded and badly chipped, its old boards hanging at odd angles, like a bad set of teeth. The yard was an overgrown nest of weeds, littered with the orphaned treasures of New York—broken wagon wheels; piles of scrap metal; window frames, some of their panes cracked and missing, most clouded over with grime.

The driver unhitched the exhausted animal, the circle of black ash and raw skin plainly visible against its white coat, and led it to a barn beside the house. It was a small barn, little more than a shed, the doorway just tall enough for the horse's head to clear, the stall inside too narrow for it to turn around. The driver pulled off the horse's bridle, closed the stall, and tossed in a flake of hay, which the ravished horse began to eat at once. The driver took off his hat, wiped a dirty coat sleeve across his brow, and took a pull off his cigar.

"Eat up, you lazy old son of a bitch. Not that you earned it."

He reached to give the horse a pat on the snout, but it recoiled and groaned—afraid of being burned again. The driver liked this.

"Good," he said. "You go right on bein' skittish. Maybe next time you'll think twice about stop—"

The barn doors swung shut behind him. The driver spun around, startled. His cigar hung low from the corner of his mouth, a thin wisp of smoke spiraling heavenward like a spirit. He squinted, trying to make out shapes in the dark.

"Who's there?"

No answer.

The wind, he thought. The driver took a pull off his cigar, its orange glow illuminating his face in the blackness of the barn. His eyes began to adjust, and he turned back to the horse—its white form the easiest thing to make out. He looked at it, as if to ask, *Did you have something to do with this?* The horse merely went on eating its hay. *The wind; that's all it was.* The driver put his hat back on and walked toward the barn doors, chuckling at himself for being so jumpy. He reached the doors and gave them a push...but they didn't open.

They'd been latched from the outside.

"What in the..."

He pushed again to be sure. He could hear the rattle of the rusted latch on the other side. It had been closed, no question about it. The driver's heart began to pound. *It wasn't the wind.*

Footsteps on the creaky floorboards behind him. Not the horse's. *There's someone else in here.* The driver spun again, back toward the stall, instinctively holding his hands out in front of his body. Feeling around in the dark.

"Goddammit! Who's there?"

Two more footsteps. Closer this time. The driver took a pull off his cigar and threw it in their direction. The orange dot sailed a few yards through the dark...

Then stopped.

There'd been no impact. No embers cascading outward like a firework shell as it hit the intruder. It had simply stopped in midflight, snatched out of the air. The driver watched the orange dot hover in the darkness—*impossible, it's impossible*—slowly rise to eye level, and grow brighter as someone drew breath through it. And as its glow grew more intense, a face began to emerge behind it. A face unlike any the driver had ever seen. Dead, black eyes. Animal mouth. Veins pulsing beneath its porcelain skin. A demon, breathing smoke through its nostrils.

"Hello," it said.

The driver pissed himself.

He turned and threw his shoulder into the barn doors, and the old latch gave. The doors flung open, and out he ran, stumbling into the night. If he could just make it to the fence, into the street...

He heard the crack of the whip and felt a white flash in the middle of his back. Down he went, face-first into the dirt. He recovered, getting his arms underneath him and pushing himself up. Another crack of the whip. Suddenly he was choking—a black snake coiled around his throat, squeezing the life out of him. The driver clutched at the whip, trying to pry it loose as the demon—*what in God's name was that thing, oh God help me please*—pulled on the other end, dragging him through the dirt and back toward the darkness of the barn.

With the cigar still hanging from his mouth, Henry took the driver by the hair and lifted him off his feet with one arm. The driver howled in pain and grabbed Henry's wrist, kicking his legs wildly, trying to free himself. With his spare hand, Henry grabbed the driver's throat and pressed a clawed thumb through his Adam's apple, opening a small hole and taking away all hope of a cry for help.

> There are endless ways to kill a man. You can be quick. Merciful. Take them in their sleep, unaware. Knock them unconscious before you drink them dry. Or you can take your time. Indulge your creativity. Shake hands with the less savory parts of your personality. Personally, I prefer the latter, especially when the victim is a scoundrel, as mine so often are. I find it's more satisfying to fill their final moments with terror. To let them know the Grim Reaper has come to punch their ticket; to let them feel the tickle of his bony fingers on the back of their neck and give them a little taste of whatever medicine they'd dispensed in their days.
>
> "But, Henry," you say. "Two wrongs don't make a right. Aren't you merely stooping to their level?" In a way, yes. I suppose I am. But that's the wonderful thing about being a vampire. Our hope of heaven is revoked the moment we're made. Every subsequent sin is a teardrop in the ocean.

Henry took another pull off the cigar, holding the driver aloft by the hair, and placed his lips over the bloody hole he'd punched in the man's throat. He blew the smoke into the hole, and out it came, through the driver's mouth and nostrils.

What can I say? Sometimes you get caught up in the moment.

Henry pulled away, the first drops of New York blood running from his chin, and let the rest of the smoke roll slowly from own his pursed lips. With the embers still glowing hot, he pressed the cigar into the driver's forehead. The driver tried to scream—his flesh sizzling, his body thrashing like a fish on a hook—but all that came out was a pained, gurgling wheeze.

Enough. Henry pulled the driver close and bit into his neck, through the sternocleidomastoid muscle, into the interior jugular. Blood flowed through his hollow fangs directly into his veins, filling the emptiness in him. Draining whatever years remained in the man, converting them into borrowed time for an immortal. Henry fed until the thrashing stopped, until there was nothing left in the driver's veins. Empty sewer tunnels, a few puddles on the stone. Henry dropped the dead, heartless husk of a man and collapsed against the side of the barn, closing his eyes and feeling the warmth run through him, feeling the world spin slowly around, the way it does when the wine finally catches up with you, and you smile because you're drunk, and being drunk was all you wanted out of the night.

They say that certain foods taste better in New York City than anywhere else in the world. That it has something to do with the water. I wouldn't know, not having had the pleasure of eating real food in nearly five hundred years, but I don't doubt that it's true. There's something about the way blood tastes in New York City. It's unlike any blood anywhere else in the world. It would take a vampire with a far more discerning palate to describe it better than that. All I know is, I know it when I taste it.

He kept his eyes closed and listened to the sounds of the dark city. The carriage wheels rolling over the cobblestones of Canal Street. The seagulls perched on the masts of ships in the harbor. The crickets in the overgrown weeds of the driver's yard. The shire horse shifting in his stall. The blood filled every cell, every sinew. Soaking into him the way a first rain soaks into the cracks of the desert clay, replenishing and exciting him. Making some parts of him softer, and others hard.

The fact is that some vampires—male and female alike—become sexually aroused during and after the act of feeding. I mean, physically aroused. And of course they do. After all, when we feed, our veins, capillaries, arteries—everything is inundated with massive amounts of blood. Empty spaces become full. Porous tissue expands. This is more noticeable with the males, given that the part of them that becomes engorged is rather larger than the female counterparts. I don't know what you'd call it, medically. Or if such a term even exists. But among vampires it's known as "ballooning." It's a stupid name, and I wish to God there was a better one. But there you have it. I'm a ballooner. I balloon when I feed. I make no secret of it.

When Henry felt ready, he rose, threw the bridle on the old shire horse, and led it out of the barn. He walked it back to Broadway, his erection tucked into the waistband of his trousers, so as not to shock those women of stringent morals or entice those of low character. He turned north, toward home, pulling the horse behind him. They hadn't walked long when Henry saw two young boys coming down Broadway in the opposite direction, neither older than eight.

They were pulling a two-wheeled handcart. A bootblack's cart, I think, though I don't remember for sure. But I remember the two of them perfectly—each boy pulling on one of the handles, dragging that damned cart with all their might. Ragged clothes and ill-fitting shoes. Their worn soles providing no traction on the stone street. It was all they could do to keep the cart from tipping backward and lifting them in the air. *If you're willing to listen, every so often, life—or God or the Universe or whatever you prefer to call it—lets us know that it's paying attention.*

"Here," said Henry, handing the older boy the horse's reins. "Perhaps he can help."

The boys looked up at the well-dressed gentleman and his white shire horse, their jaws hanging slack. *It's a trick. He's playing a trick on us.*

"It's not a trick," said Henry, answering their thoughts. "I assure you. It so happens that this horse is in need of a good home. And you two, without question, are in need of a good horse."

Henry gave them a small salute and carried on his way. But he'd taken only a few steps up Broadway, when—*how could I have forgotten?*—he turned back.

"Oh, just one condition," he said. "Call him Alistair."

Henry looked up, as he always did when approaching the Union Headquarters. His eyes were drawn heavenward by the Gothic spire of Trinity Church across the street. At 281 feet, it was still the tallest structure in New York, and a beacon for distant ships trying to find their way to port.

Two churches had stood on the same ground before. The first, finished in 1698, had been destroyed in a fire when the British invaded New York. The second, finished in 1790, was torn down after being weakened by heavy snows during the winter of 1838. The third, and current, church had been consecrated in 1846, this time complete with its grand spire and a subterranean passageway in its catacombs, locked behind a brass gate, which none but a chosen few knew existed.

It was a way to sneak in and out of the Union Headquarters undetected, or, in the case of an attack, slip away. Few people would've dared ask questions about a locked gate in a church basement.

The circumstances of the passageway's construction—particularly how the Union convinced the clergy to let them build it—are unknown. Though it's doubtful they mentioned the fact that they were vampires.

They know, thought Henry. *They know about Abe, and they're going to kill me.*

It was all he could think as he sat in the grand ballroom of the Union—a two-tiered affair with thirty-foot ceilings, its dark wooden floors polished to a glossy finish, reflecting the painstakingly painted ceiling and the gilded railings of the second level. Years earlier, Abraham Lincoln had stood in the center of the same room and thought it the most splendid he'd ever seen.

> It was excessive in an age of excess. Every cushion was embroidered with gold thread, every rug imported from exotic lands. A crystal chandelier by Waterford, shaped like a glorious sunburst. A silver Tiffany tea service[3] neatly laid out on a Boulle[4] cabinet. At one end of the room sat an absurdly large fireplace, its hearth as tall as a man, its white marble mantel exquisitely carved with a scene depicting Christ the shepherd leading a flock of sheep over a mountain. I suppose this was meant to represent us. We, the vampire shepherds, guarding our human flock. We, the all-powerful and anointed, suffering in their stead. The saviors of mankind, cursed to live forever, so that others may find peace...It's a wonder they didn't build a huge crucifix with a vampire Jesus suffering on the cross.

On either side of the fireplace hung floor-to-ceiling red velvet drapes, suggesting that there were

---

3. This particular tea service dates to 1845. Members of the Union were so impressed with its craftsmanship that when the Civil War broke out, they arranged for Tiffany & Co. to be the supplier of swords to the Union Army.
4. André-Charles Boulle (1642–1732) was master cabinetmaker to King Louis XIV.

windows of equal size behind them. But this wasn't the case. Even though older vampires—those like Henry, who'd passed their first century—could build up a tolerance to sunlight, they didn't go out of their way to seek it out. In fact, when the drapes were removed, they revealed a pair of massive rectangular mirrors—twenty-six feet high by thirteen feet wide, in exquisitely carved frames, painted gold, naturally. They were, at the time, the largest mirrors in North America. And since there'd been no factory capable of making mirrors of such size anywhere in America, the Union had built one, two blocks away, and imported master artisans from Venice—then the mirror-making capital of the world.

It was all a joke. One giant, outrageously expensive joke. Like the silver tea service and the sun-shaped chandelier, the mirrors were there to poke a little fun at some of the old vampire myths. But make no mistake—they were also there because vampires are incredibly, sometimes *insufferably* vain creatures. In this case, there was the vanity of the extravagance itself—*look at what we can afford!*—combined with the vanity of admiring their own gold-framed reflections. They found it gratifying, I suppose. Staring at themselves, eternal and unchanging. Personally, I found it depressing. My reflection was a reminder of how I appeared to others. My skin a ghostly shade. My face barely more than a boy's, but with ancient, world-weary eyes.

Henry had been summoned by Adam Plantagenet, one of the founders of the Union of Vampires, and to anyone's knowledge, the oldest vampire on earth.

Christened Adam FitzRoy in 1305, he'd been the bastard son of King Edward II of England, grandson of Edward Longshanks, and half brother of Edward III, who would go on to rule England for fifty years. Adam may have been a bastard, but he was a noble bastard, and therefore he'd spent his life in relative comfort behind castle walls. But unlike his half brothers and half sisters, who would become kings, queens, and earls, Adam was shunted aside. Placed in the full-time care of a tutor who, at first, saw to his lessons and meals, then eventually to his every waking hour, tasked with keeping Adam out of the sight and mind of his father, the king. Adam, not surprisingly, grew to become a depressed and lonely child, and the tutor grew sympathetic to his plight. Grew to love him as a son. This tutor (whose name is lost to history, since Adam swore never to reveal it) sensed greatness in the boy. Yes, he was a bastard. But he was a *king's* bastard. There was royal blood in his veins, by God, and the tutor was determined to cultivate it.

Adam couldn't inherit titles or lands, but he could *earn* them—with his mind and with his sword. At the urging of his tutor, he devoted himself to becoming a warrior, squiring for one of his father's knights, in hope that, once he'd proved himself in battle, the king might bestow a knighthood upon him, making Adam a nobleman in his own right. Making the king proud to call him his son.

But it wasn't to be.

Adam fell in battle during his father's disastrous campaign against Robert the Bruce in Scotland. Mortally wounded, the seventeen-year-old squire was carted back to the king's tent so that his father might look upon him one last time. But the king refused him an audience. "I have no son by that name," he is reported to have said before sending Adam away to die of his wounds among the rabble.

In the end, it was the tutor—more of a father to Adam than his own had ever been—who'd been unable to bear the thought of his death. The tutor, who'd seen kings come and go since before the House of Wessex united England centuries earlier. Who'd looked into a bastard's eyes and seen purpose behind them.

And so he'd granted the boy eternal life and continued to tutor him: teaching Adam how to feed without being discovered. How to build up a tolerance to sunlight. How to master his vampire senses. Most of all, he'd taught him that vampires needn't be evil. That they could use their powers to defend the weak, rather than prey upon them. That they could feed on what the tutor called "the sick and the wicked," while sparing the innocent.

It was an idea that would give rise to a new sect of vampires. A Union, founded on the belief that men and vampires were equal. That the living had a right to life and to dominion over the light, and vampires over the darkness. It was, in a way, an early form of democracy. Preached by a tutor to the immortal bastard of a king, passed on to living men who would perfect the idea of "life, liberty, and the pursuit of happiness" and use it to break with another king hundreds of years later. The world was a strange place.

More than five hundred years had passed since Adam Plantagenet had been made immortal. He'd outlived his royal siblings by hundreds of years, while acquiring more power and wealth than they could've dreamt of. And his father, King Edward II? The man Adam had been so desperate to impress? Just two years after refusing his dying bastard son an audience, Edward was deposed. Betrayed by his wife, the queen, who raised an army against him and had him imprisoned. He died at Berkeley Castle, held down by two men while a third forced a red-hot poker into his rectum, burning him alive from the inside out. The king who'd refused his dying son was dead, and the dying son was immortal. Karma was a bitch.

Though the Union had no official leader, it was

commonly understood that, as he was the oldest of them, the honor belonged to Adam if it belonged to anyone. And like all Union vampires, Henry felt a sense of patronage to the old man. When Adam called for him, he came, even if no specific reason was given.

> I struggled to banish all thoughts of Abraham Lincoln from my mind. *He'll know.* The thought filled me with dread on the carriage ride to the Union, and it kept repeating itself: *He'll know what you did, Henry, and it will be the end of you.*[5]

As far as the Union and the rest of the world were concerned, Abraham Lincoln had gone to his eternal rest on April 15th, 1865, and stayed there. Henry had never shared the events of that week in Springfield

---

5. Research into the "telepathic" abilities of vampires has so far been inconclusive. Vampires themselves have long insisted that they can communicate without words in close proximity to one another, even "see the future" or divine details of a stranger's past life by merely "reading their mind." The science behind these claims is dubious, and the studies have been limited (vampires being hesitant to have their brains dissected in the name of science). Some scientists support the claims. Others have suggested that vampires are merely able to perceive minute physical cues—twitches of the eyes, changes in respiration, etc., that they perceive as a kind of "wordless language." In the 1950s, the CIA carried out a series of experiments into the telepathic abilities of vampires codenamed MKULTRA.

with anyone and determined that he never would—
for sharing them almost certainly would have meant
his death.

> Vampires don't do rules. It isn't in our nature. Try
> getting a few dozen powerful, independent, and
> immortal killers together and see what you can
> get them to agree to.

As such, the Union didn't have many rules. In fact,
it had only three:

A vampire will respect and protect the dominion
of humans over the earth.
A vampire will not feed upon the innocent
or the young.
A vampire will make no other vampire.

The punishment for breaking any of them was
severe, but special severity was reserved for any Union
member who broke the third. The world had quite
enough vampires already, thank you very much. Too
many, in fact. And when too many vampires settled in
one place, bad things happened, as recent American
history had proven. The slave trade that sparked the
Civil War had been controlled by Southern vampires
who had grown too rich and too comfortable. With
slavery, they had finally found a sustainable method of
feeding on human blood. Vampires possessed of such

cruelty could never be allowed to concentrate such power again.

"Our kind have all but abandoned America," said Adam, his back pressed into the red velvet upholstery of a high-backed chair. His posture perfect. "They return to the lands of their birth, while the living flock here in droves. We get reports almost daily, you know. Dispatches from our Union brothers abroad and our living allies. They come from every corner of the civilized world—Europe, Asia, South America. Daily reports, right here, in this very building, traveling over a wire no thicker than my fist. Can you believe it?"

"An age of miracles, indeed."

Henry looked around as Adam spoke. The last time he had been in this room, the Civil War had been raging. The ballroom had been alive with rows of telegraph operators, click-clicking away at their desks. There'd been maps on the walls, the comings and goings of sympathetic humans. But the war was long over. The enemy had been scattered to the four winds, and now the room was vast and empty, save for the two of them and a butler who hovered in the doorway at the opposite end. Every pop of the fire echoed off the hard, polished surfaces, adding to the feeling that they were ants in a canyon.

"A wire, stretched across an ocean," said Adam.

"Words, *thoughts*, traveling across it in an instant. Did you ever think such a thing possible?"

I was an old man myself, yet I felt like a child in his company, nodding politely as his grandfather prattled on about trivial nonsense, telling the same three stories, over and over. He reminded me of those living men, those warriors whose glory has long since faded. You've seen them—the ancient lords and admirals who get carted out for parades or memorial dedications in their dress uniforms, so weighed down with ribbons and medals they can barely stand. That was Adam, only he had the smooth, porcelain-white face of a seventeen-year-old boy. A shock of red hair. It's a strange thing to hear ancient thoughts come out of such a young face.

"My ambassadors in Europe have made great use of this new telegraph device. Communications are brisk, and because of that my views always have a seat at the table, even when that table is halfway around the world."

My dread—the fear that I'd been called to answer for my sin of making Abe—began to lift. Was Adam going to make me an ambassador?

"Alas, my friend," said Adam, guessing Henry's thoughts. "That's not the kind of job I have to offer you."

He rose and gestured for me to follow. We walked
out of the grand ballroom, down a narrow, twisting flight of stone steps to a corridor below—still
lit by torches in those days. My dread returned.
I couldn't help but feel like a mouse following
a cat.

Henry followed Adam through a heavy wooden
door and into a small, candlelit library, its floor-to-
ceiling wooden shelves and leather-bound volumes
framed by cold stone walls. In the center of the room,
neatly placed on a table, were five wooden boxes, each
ornately hand carved, and each roughly the size of a
large hat box.

"Three months ago," said Adam, "the telegraphs
began to go silent, one by one, and the boxes you see
before you began to arrive. One after the other. Each
accompanied by a note, written in the same hand."

Adam took a white card from his pocket and
handed it to Henry:

No more Americans.

Regards,

A. Grander VIII

With his eyes, Adam urged me to open the first
box, and against my better judgment, I did.

Inside was the severed head of Elias Corwyn, the Union's emissary in Spain. The skin had been peeled from his face, leaving only muscle, and his fangs had been pried out and shoved into his eyes. My stomach clenched at the thought of what was in the next four boxes.

"Spain, Germany, France, Italy, England," said Adam. "All of our ambassadors murdered. Their heads severed and sent here, each one more horrific than the last."

Henry opened the next box. This second head was locked in an eternal scream. Its eyes were missing, the sockets around them blackened. But the rest of the face was otherwise pristine.

"Michael Burakow," said Adam. "Terrible. What could do such a thing?"

I knew what could do such a thing. I'd seen such contraptions in the war. "Fire masks" they were called, black masks that covered the vampire's face completely, except for the eyes, which were then exposed to the harsh sun. The light burned through the sockets and roasted the brain inside the skull. It was the apex of cruelty, but it showed imagination.

"The man who did this is deranged," said Adam, shaking his head.

"Who is this Grander?" asked Henry. "I've never heard of him."

"That's what I need you to find out. Such affront to the Union cannot stand. And a man capable of this"—he motioned toward the boxes—"is capable of much, much more."

Adam handed Henry an envelope containing the names of the murdered ambassadors, their addresses, and their known associates. There was also a ticket for passage aboard the RMS *Umbria*, departing the next evening.

"Go to Europe, Henry. Find this 'Grander' and put an end to him."

THREE

★ ★ ★

The Actor's Assistant
1563 / 1888

We shall not cease from exploration
And the end of all our exploring
Will be to arrive where we started
And know the place for the first time.

—*T.S. Eliot*

Henry Ogden Sturges was born on the second day of March, 1563, five years into the reign of Elizabeth I. Son of Edmund Sturges, a wherryman, and Abigail, who kept house and worked as a seamstress on occasion. He was christened Henry, not after the queen's late father, Henry VIII, but after one of Edmund's brothers, who had died at the age of five.

Henry was the third of four children, but the only one to survive infancy. The first two boys had been stillborn. The fourth, a girl, died before the age of one month.

> I have no memory of her, or of my parents' grief. In all likelihood, they shed a tear, built her a box, and buried her in the yard—thankful that it had only been a girl. Such were the times.

They lived in the parish of Putney.[1] It was an ancient place even then, having been settled by Saxons some five hundred years earlier. Like all things English, it had a damp, rugged charm.

Edmund made his living ferrying passengers back and forth across the Thames in a skiff—a long, narrow rowboat that could hold up to eight paying customers at a time.

> It was a good trade, and a well-regulated one, unusual in those days. Unlike, say, blacksmiths or stable hands, watermen needed a license to operate skiffs on the river—sometimes in teams of two, or sometimes, as in my father's case, alone, rowing with two small sculls.

When Henry was ten, he joined his father as an apprentice, studying the ever-shifting currents of the

---

1. Then part of Surrey, but now part of Wandsworth, in Greater London.

Thames, keeping the skiff clean, and collecting fares from paying passengers.

It was in Westminster, on the other side of the river, that young Henry Sturges caught his first glimpses of a larger world. On those rare days off, he and his father would row across, tie up the small boat, and walk the narrow streets of London, moving to the side to make way for the occasional well-appointed carriage or well-dressed aristocrat. On occasion, they might even see a lord or lady walking through town, all puff and garters and fur and capes. Women in their heavily embroidered Spanish farthingales, men in their high stockings and feathered hats, their torsos pulled tight by doublets and their necks encircled by ridiculous white lace collars.

> I suppose those collars had the effect of framing their faces in elegance, but to me it always looked as if their severed heads were being served up on white platters.

The clothes were both elegant and uncomfortable, but then, so were the times. Books could be printed and bound in beautiful leather volumes, but few could afford or even read them. England had a new queen, but her ascension to the throne had come in the midst of much controversy and bloodshed, and there were some who believed her reign illegitimate. Many thought a woman unfit to lead.

But for the Sturges family, those concerns seemed a world away, even if they were just across the river.

We were the working class, adorned with dull burlap coats. We tied sashes around our waists to keep our itchy trousers from falling down.

Henry had few memories of his living years. The images had become blotted after his vampire transformation, and when he tried to summon them, it was as if his nose was pressed against a canvas, looking at splotches of colored paint and trying to guess at the shape of the whole. But one incident still stood out sharply in his memory.

There was a simple boy who lived in a house near ours. I say "simple," because that's what he would've been called back then. That is, if you felt like being polite. If you didn't, you would've called him "mad," or an "idiot." He was still a boy, perhaps a year or two younger than I was. I'm not sure what he would've been called now. "Autistic," perhaps. He didn't say much. Rocked back and forth when he sat. He was prone to fits, I remember. Terrible, red-faced fits. Foaming at the mouth. Screaming and pulling out clumps of his own hair. But then, he was also a quiet, gentle child. Sitting out in front of his house for hours on end when the weather was warm enough. I'd pass him on my way to or from the river. "Henry, Henry, Henry," he would say as I passed. Always like that. Always in threes. "Henry, Henry, Henry." But never looking up. Never looking me in the eye. I took a liking to him and, insomuch as he was able to, he took a liking to me.

Eventually, Henry began taking the boy for rides on the river, paddling his father's skiff in the back while the boy sat silently near the bow, his hands folded in his lap, watching the water lap up against the sides of the hull. Feeling the gentle rocking from side to side.

He found it peaceful, I suppose. I did, too, not having any brothers or sisters of my own to share such moments with. So much time has passed, so many things have happened since then, that I don't even remember the boy's name anymore. Christ, not even his name. But for a time, long ago, we were companions. He enjoyed my company, and I enjoyed his, even though he wasn't much for conversation. I believe—I can't be sure about this, since it was so long ago—but I believe that I loved him the way I would've loved a brother, if I'd had one.

One day, after taking the boy on one of their gentle sojourns down the river, Henry pulled the skiff ashore, stepped onto the muddy bank of Putney Parish, and held the boat steady while the simple boy stepped out.

The boat lurched and he slipped. I reached out, instinctively, and put a hand on his shoulder to steady him, and he changed, instantly, violently. It suddenly dawned on me—*I've never touched him. Not once.* Before I knew what was happening, he'd gone wild. He turned his head toward my arm and bit into it the way a lion bites an antelope. I remember feeling his teeth clamping down on my flesh and tearing it away. I remember the shock of looking down at my arm and seeing the perfect, bloody impression of his top and bottom teeth. I can still see that wild, absent look in his eyes. The red of my blood on his lips. It's one of the few memories of my living years that has stayed with me over the centuries. My mother's and father's faces are lost to me. My own reflection as a boy, lost. But those wild eyes and blood-soaked lips...I've never forgotten them, and I never will.

The crossing was uneventful. The *Umbria* reached Liverpool in seven days, three hours, and twenty-two minutes. From Liverpool it was straight on to London by carriage. And so it was that Henry Sturges returned to the city of his birth for the first time in nearly three hundred years.

He may have carried an American passport, but Henry was an Englishman by birth, and he was returning to the seat of an empire at its height. This was the London of Dickens. Of naval conquests and African colonies. Queen Victoria was still in her forties, and only halfway through a reign of nearly sixty-four years—not yet the dour, matronly figure she would be remembered as, though she was a large woman, and not an inch over five feet tall. She wore only black—her beloved Albert having died in 1861—and she had survived no fewer than seven assassination attempts, the most recent occurring in 1882, just six years before Henry's arrival. In each case, her would-be assassins either missed their target or had their pistols misfire. This unbelievable streak of good luck only added to Victoria's already sizable legend and, in the eyes of the public, provided proof of God's favor and Britain's invincibility.

London was a dense, soot-filled city of some six million souls in 1888, with its newly reconstructed Palace of Westminster and its Elizabeth Tower, which would become famous as Big Ben. Construction on Tower Bridge[2] had been going on for only two years and wouldn't be completed for another six. It was a city in which one could experience the marvels of the

---

2. Better known as "London Bridge" to all but Londoners themselves.

age. The Crystal Palace, then the largest collection of plate glass seen anywhere on earth. The Metropolitan Railway, the world's first subway, which used steam engines pulling wooden carriages to ferry passengers in three classes of service. Incandescent lights, which had first begun to pop up as novelties at exhibitions and were now moving into the homes of the wealthy.

> Of the all the wonders, [electric light] excited me the most. There have been a few times—just a handful, really—when I've known, instantly, that the world would never be the same. When I could almost see the long-assumed future disappear before my eyes. Seeing my first electric light was one of those moments. I'll never forget it. New York, in the fall of 1880, in the Mercantile Safe Deposit Company. The whole interior had been redone with electric lights to demonstrate the new technology. People would stand in line to get into that bank and see the miracle of light without flame. I went night after night, marveling at this strange, constant light that didn't flicker. But while it excited to me to think of a world where night could be vanquished by the flip of a switch, it also frightened me. The same way that the first DNA tests and surveillance cameras frightened me. I didn't know what this new electric world would look like. I only knew it would be a more difficult place to be a vampire.

There were all the usual hassles and lies. The hassles—living out of a hotel room while I looked for a home; presenting letters of credit to the bank to pay for it...The lies—"Yes, yes, I'm in the textile business." "Oh, you're very kind to offer, but I'm afraid I won't be able to make it quite so early in the morning." It's always the same. The same hassles, the same lies.

Grander's trail was already cold, and Henry knew he couldn't afford to waste any time. On his arrival in London, he hastened to the nearest of the addresses Adam had given him—the home of the Union's ambassador in England, Tobias Forge. Of the five decapitated vampires, Forge had been the hardest to recognize. His head had been burned beyond recognition, like a cut of meat left roasting for days over a campfire, until all that remained was a blackened lump of carbon in the crude shape of a human head. But when Henry arrived, he found that, like Mr. Forge's head, the entire building had burned to a charred husk some five months earlier. Inquiries about an "A. Grander VIII" were met with puzzled stares and more than a few mutterings of "bloody Yank."

I'd lost [my accent]. It's funny—I was an Englishman, or at least I thought I was, but the centuries had coarsened the queen out of my speech. I sounded like an American now. I'll admit...part of me mourned the loss of that last piece of my old identity.

Henry's investigation, scarcely begun, had already reached a dead end. Left without a lead in a city he no longer knew, he decided to reacquaint himself with London and her culture. If nothing else, perhaps it would hasten the return of his accent.

He attended the opening of a production of his favorite of all Shakespeare's works, *Macbeth*, at the Lyceum Theatre, starring the crown jewel of the English theater, Henry Irving.

You have to understand, Irving was as big a celebrity as a man could be in the nineteenth century. He was, by far, the most famous actor in the world at the time, and had been for years. He could play anything, but he really excelled at villains. In those days, most actors played villains as cackling and cartoonish. Big, over-the-top movements, stroking their glued -on beards, shaking their fists in the air as they shouted soliloquies to the back row. But Irving...Irving could knock you over with a feather. He was all about subtlety. All about playing the truth, not the exaggeration. And keep in mind, this is almost a century before

Strasberg.[3] Stanislavsky[4] was still in his twenties. People give them all the credit, but Irving was already doing it.

When the curtain rose on Irving that night, the audience applauded at the mere sight of him, as was customary. But Henry was too astonished to clap. Irving had already knocked him over with a feather. Just not in the way Henry had expected.

He was a vampire. Henry Irving, the world's greatest actor, was a goddamned vampire. I knew it immediately, before he'd even said a word. It's a skill you develop. A million tiny, almost molecular subtleties you learn to recognize over time. The same way a human might catch a glimpse of a man on the street and know—somehow instinctively know—that he's troubled or dangerous.

He had an ageless quality about him, his eyes slightly sunken, his face narrow and dour, and his frame slender. It was impossible to know his true skin color, as he was caked in makeup,

---

3. Lee Strasberg (1901–1982), acting teacher, founder of the Group Theatre, and director of the Actors Studio.
4. Konstantin Stanislavsky (1863–1938), author of *An Actor Prepares*, which laid the groundwork for the method approach to acting. He was an advocate of "spiritual realism" in performance, and his methods became popular among a generation of post–World War II actors, including Marlon Brando, James Dean, and Dustin Hoffman.

but I didn't need to see. I knew. His mannerisms were subtle. Elegant. I recall him seeming to glide across the stage, the audience breathless in anticipation of his every word.

Here was an answer to the mystery of his greatness. The mystery of how he seemed to perform Shakespeare so well, as if he understood every word on an instinctive level. As if he was speaking in his own words and not reciting those of a man who'd died more than 250 years before. Here's why he was so much better than his contemporaries: he'd simply had more time to rehearse.

Vampire actors were nothing new. Another one famously murdered my friend in Ford's Theater. Show business has always been littered with them and remains littered with them even today. The profession seems to draw them in. It appeals to their vanity. It's another one of those little jokes, I guess. A creature that's supposed to shrink into the shadows, flaunting itself in the bright lights.

In a way, every vampire becomes an actor. It's necessary to our survival. If we don't possess a natural charisma, we learn to do a serviceable imitation of being charismatic. We learn to improvise our way through awkward conversations: "What's the matter? You haven't touched your food." Or, "Why can't a man like you find a nice girl and settle down?" We play a variety of roles throughout our long careers. Changing our names, our settings, our costumes. Changing our appearance to blend in with the times and places we find ourselves in. Learning new phrases and languages the way professional actors learn lines.

The play hadn't even ended before Henry made up his mind. He had to meet Irving. Not only to confirm his suspicions, for they hardly needed confirmation, but also to pick his brain.

Here was the world's greatest Shakespearean, and here I was, not ten yards from him, watching him perform my favorite of all Shakespeare's plays. But as he performed that night, all I could think about was the role his immortality had played in it all. Had he known Shakespeare? My God...*was* he Shakespeare? Was the Bard a bloodsucker? Was that why I was so infatuated with his works? Had they been speaking to me on a deeper level than I'd ever realized? My mind sifted though the collected works, looking for clues to support the theory: Richard III, the twisted, conniving, and powerful villain, haunted by the ghosts of his victims...Lear, the old and outdated king, whose legacy turns to dust before his eyes...The treacherous Iago, doomed to live out the rest of his days in pain and silence. And everywhere, ghosts and magic, talk of "blood" and "curses."

Henry shuffled out of his seat before the final curtain ("an unforgivable breach of etiquette, I know") and made his way to an alley beside the theater. He tapped the head of his cane on the stage door. Moments later, a young stagehand opened it.

"Who're you?"

Henry reached a leather-gloved hand into his coat, pulled out a card, and presented it to the stagehand.

"I should like to pay my respects to Mr. Irving."

The stagehand looked at the card. It was black with raised white type:

H. Sturges

Importer of Fine Textiles

No. 2 Chester Square[5]

Belgravia, London

"But...," said the stagehand, "he's doin' a show right now."

"So I noticed, whilst sitting in your theater these

---

5. Today, visitors to No. 2 Chester Square will see a circular blue plaque out front identifying it as the former residence of Matthew Arnold (1822–1888), famed English poet and critic. Arnold died suddenly, just prior to Henry's arrival in London. Henry rented the house from Arnold's widow.

past three hours. Tell me, when I said I should like to pay my respects, did you take my meaning as 'this very moment'?"

The stagehand looked at Henry blankly.

"Wait here," he said at last, and closed the door. When it opened again, less than a minute later, Henry was met by a tall, forty-year-old Irishman. Smartly dressed. Barrel-chested, with a reddish brown beard and suspicious eyes. He looked like the sort of man who routinely punched holes in walls when he didn't get his way. He also looked like the kind of man who would run into a burning building to save a kitten. Henry liked him immediately.

"Mr. Irving doesn't receive callers after a show," said the Irishman.

Ah, thought Henry. *You're his Renfield, then.*

Vampires often employ humans to act as fronts. Professional secret keepers who double as their direct link to the present. In the community, as it were, they're known as "Renfields." Who knows why. Perhaps the first human to serve a vampire was named Renfield or was from a place called Renfield. But that's what they're called. The practice is tolerated but frowned upon by some, the conventional wisdom being that the fewer humans who know the fact of our existence, the better. These human employees are called many things: "personal assistants," "associates," "confidants."

I've never hired one, personally. Not that I fault those who do. But in my opinion, Renfields create a barrier between the vampire and the world. Another shadow to hide in. If anyone's going to act as my direct link to the present, shouldn't it be me?

"Very well," said Henry. "Then I'll call on him tomorrow, before the show."

"Mr. Irving doesn't receive callers before the show, either."

"Well, when does Mr. Irving receive callers?"

"Mr. Irving isn't in the habit of receiving callers."

"Ah, I see. Well…you might've mentioned that straightaway and saved us both the time."

"Look, Mr.—"

"Sturges. It's right there on the card."

"I have a theater to run. Now, if you'll excuse me…"

The Irishman began to close the stage door in Henry's face. Henry stuck the end of his cane out and stopped it from closing all the way.

"I'll be happy to," said Henry, "if you'll answer just one question."

"What is it?"

"How long have you been his Renfield?"

The Irishman's face flushed bright red.

I thought so.

"Let's try this again, shall we? Now, I'm a great admirer of Mr. Irving's, and I should very much like a few moments with him…if, of course, it wouldn't be too much of an inconvenience. I realize what a busy creature he is."

He extended a hand. "Henry Sturges."

The actor's assistant looked at Henry's hand a moment, then shook it.

"Bram Stoker."

Stoker first met the great Henry Irving a decade earlier, when he'd been toiling away as a theater critic in Dublin and working, with little success, on his own short stories.

Bram Stoker follows his boss, famed actor and vampire Henry Irving, to a waiting carriage outside the Lyceum Theatre in London. This is the only known photograph of Irving wearing dark glasses.

In 1876, he wrote a rave review of Irving's *Hamlet* for the *Dublin Evening Mail*. Irving, who always read his reviews, had been flattered by its effusive praise—but more important, he'd been impressed by the quality of its prose. He sent for the young critic, and the two met in Dublin. Irving needed someone to run his Lyceum back in London. Someone smart, energetic, and ambitious to write the adverts, keep the staff in line, and—most of all—keep the house full.

> Stoker later told me how nervous he'd been at that first meeting and how Irving attempted to put him at ease by doing the one thing he did best: performing. He asked Stoker to name his favorite poet. Any poet would suffice.
>
> Stoker, so nervous that all the moisture had left his mouth and moved to his palms, grasped at names in his mind like a drowning man grasping for a rope. The words "Thomas Hood" finally escaped his lips.
>
> The way Stoker tells it, no sooner had he said the name than Irving proceeded to recite Hood's "The Dream of Eugene Aram" from memory. And not just recite it, but perform it with an intensity and elegance that sent chills through Stoker's body.

"The Dream of Eugene Aram" offers fictional insight into a factual murder. The real Eugene Aram

(1704–1759) was an English schoolmaster who gained notoriety after the disappearance of his friend Daniel Clark in North Yorkshire. It was widely thought that Aram, whose wife had been having an affair with Clark, had had something to do with the disappearance. But with no evidence to support their suspicion, the authorities did nothing. Aram moved to London, where, as the poem explores, he lived with the guilt of his crime for the next fifteen years.[6] An excerpt:

> *And how the sprites of injur'd men*
> *Shriek upward from the sod,—*
> *Aye, how the ghostly hand will point*
> *To shew the burial clod:*
> *And unknown facts of guilty acts*
> *Are seen in dreams from God!*
>
> *He told how murderers walk the earth*
> *Beneath the curse of Cain,—*
> *With crimson clouds before their eyes,*
> *And flames about their brain:*
> *For blood has left upon their souls*
> *Its everlasting stain!*

---

6. In 1759, Clark's remains were found, leading to Aram's arrest and, later that year, his execution.

When Irving was done, Stoker had been "mesmerized," he said. He accepted the job on the spot, partly because it would afford him time to work on his stories during the day, and partly because his association with Irving would afford him access to levels of London society that were otherwise off limits to a theater critic. But mostly, he took the job because, after that meeting, he'd been too frightened not to.

Stoker hurriedly married his sweetheart, Florence, an Irish beauty who'd once been courted (halfheartedly, one presumes) by Oscar Wilde. Together the young couple moved from Dublin to London, Stoker working on his stories till midday and attending to the Lyceum and Irving's affairs till midnight and beyond.

> I'm not sure when he first began to suspect that there was something strange about his boss, or if Irving just revealed it from the start. But by the time we met, Bram Stoker knew that Henry Irving was a vampire. That much I'm sure of. Part of his job in managing the Lyceum was keeping the secret—politely declining dinner invitations on Irving's behalf, protecting his privacy above all. Whether he ever procured victims for Irving, I don't know. I remember trying to broach the subject with him once and seeing that big Irish head flush bright red. "What sort of damned-fool

question is that?" he asked. I suppose that was as good an answer as any.

Henry got his audience with the jewel of England's stage. He and Irving sat in the actor's parlor one Sunday evening, Stoker waiting in an adjacent room.

I found him dull, to be honest. He didn't want to talk about Shakespeare. His interpretations of the text. Whether he'd personally known Shakespeare, whether Shakespeare had been one of us—not even the characters he'd played. Basically, all the good stuff was off limits. He didn't want to talk about being a vampire, either. How he'd become one, what insights the condition gave him into his craft, how he felt about killing or world affairs or anything. I raised subject after subject. I gave him every opening, and he refused to engage.

I've had this experience with other actors. Some of them are perfectly charming and engaging in person, but many of them are self-serious or withdrawn or insufferably dull. They're often lost without a role to play. When they're unable to escape the existential terror of who they really are, or squeeze snugly into someone else's skin. I asked [Irving] if he'd heard of anyone named "Grander." He hadn't, so I promptly offered my thanks and left. It's quite possible that I left that meeting knowing less about Henry Irving than I had before it.

His encounter with Irving had been brief and unmemorable. But Henry's relationship with the actor's assistant would prove far more lasting and rewarding. Bram and Florence soon became part of Henry's exceedingly small social circle. They passed most of that summer of 1888 together. Florence didn't mind the company. It was nice to see Bram spending time away from the theater and with someone other than Mr. Irving (whom, though she wouldn't dare say so to her husband or anyone else, she found strangely unnerving and didn't much care for). Henry was charming and well mannered, though she worried about how skinny he was and wished he'd eat more. She was determined to fix him up with a nice girl.

We passed many a night at the Stokers' kitchen table. I remember laughter. Lots of it. And those accents. [Henry laughs.] Those Irish accents. Bram's big, booming voice. And Florence... so sharp. What a lively, beautiful woman. Very unlike the picture you probably have in your mind of women in those days. She'd been an actress herself, and she still had an actress's grace. We would talk and laugh, the three of us. Eventually Florence would turn in, and Bram and I would lower our voices and tell each other stories into the early morning hours, most of them about vampires. He was especially fascinated by stories of Abe and the war. I told him everything—our first meeting, training Abe as a vampire hunter, Jeff Davis and his cabal of vampires, tracking John Wilkes Booth to a tobacco barn in Virginia and exacting vengeance for my fallen friend. Of course Stoker wanted the bloody details, and reluctantly I obliged. I told him that I'd held Booth across my knees, like a father whipping a child, as the farm burned all around us. I told him that I'd removed Booth's vertebrae, one by one. I told him that they'd popped like the corks off champagne bottles. Blood and spinal fluid splashed onto my face, but I did not drink a drop of John Wilkes Booth. The thought of his vileness coursing through me was anathema. The only thing I left out was Springfield. That was the one secret I would take to my grave.

August 30th, 1888, was just another Thursday night. Henry and Bram sat at the small kitchen table, sharing stories, laughing, and talking about the troubles of the world well into the night....

Neither man with any inkling of what horrors sunrise would bring.

FOUR

★ ★ ★

The Tall Man
1888

Do not all passions require victims?
—*Marquis de Sade*

Polly Nichols had five mouths to feed, by God.

She was forty-three years old but was told she looked at least ten years younger—though a few strands of gray had begun to appear in her chestnut-brown hair, and five babies had changed the shape of her bosom and left lines in the loose flesh around her middle. None of the men seemed to mind, though. It was all the same to them when the lights went out. Something warm and different. That's all they wanted.

Polly knew what she was. But she didn't like being called that word. It was an ugly word, it was, and she'd been born better. The pretty, petite daughter of a London locksmith, christened "Mary Ann" but called "Polly" since she could well remember. It had been a rough home, what with her father's drinking, but whose home wasn't rough? Besides, there'd been love there, and as angry as he got, Father never laid a hand on a one of them. Not on her mother, her sisters, or Polly—which was more than she could say for Nasty Will.

She'd known William Nichols from the neighborhood since both of them were little children. "Nasty Will," they'd called him. And he *was* a naughty, nasty boy. Spitting and fighting and saying things that had no business coming out of a Christian's mouth. But where the other girls had kept their distance, Polly had been strangely attracted by it all. When she was twelve, she'd let Will take a peek under her dress. When she was fifteen, she'd let him put a hand on one of her breasts and keep it there a full ten seconds. When she was nineteen, she'd borne him a son— seven months to the day after their wedding, a fact that the neighborhood gossips didn't miss. But Polly and Will hadn't cared about all the talk. They had a son. They named him Edward, because it seemed a proper name for a boy, and he was their joy. The children kept coming, one every couple of years. Those were the good times, when the babies were small and Polly's skin was radiant and Will still looked at her that certain way on certain nights. The days before he discovered the comforts of other women, and she the comfort of drink.

Yes, she'd been known to enjoy a drink or two. Was it such a sin? Was it reason for Will to take her babies away? To run off with that woman and tell those damnable lies?

The things she'd sacrificed for those children. Working as a servant for those liars, the Cowdrys, who'd thrown her out on the street after accusing her of stealing money and clothing. Yes, maybe she'd nicked a shilling or two from the dresser top when she cleaned, not that they'd miss it, the rich bastards. But she'd never stolen a stitch of that woman's ugly clothing, let her be struck down if it be untrue.

She'd slept on stone in Trafalgar Square. And yes, she'd given her body to those men who would pay to have it. They called her a mollisher. A dollymop. They judged her and turned their backs. But what did they know? She had five little mouths to feed. And who was going to do it—her husband? She'd given him everything. And what had the rotten bastard done? Left her for a nurse. The very nurse who'd delivered their fifth child. Taken her babies from her and told a bunch of stinking lies.

If you'd asked Polly what she was doing on the streets that night, looking fetching in her new bonnet, that's what she would've told you. "I've got five mouths to feed."

He seemed nice enough, this one. She'd met him in the Frying Pan.[1] The same shithole she met all of them in. She'd had no choice but to come to the pub that night, having been turned away from the lodging house for want of a fourpence. *No choice, no, sir.* She told herself this, though chances were she would've found an excuse to go to the pub whether she'd been turned away or not. She hadn't had enough money for a bed, but she'd had that new bonnet. And in a shithole pub, a new bonnet was as good as gold to the woman who wore it right.

He was tall, this one. Very tall, with kind eyes and a clean-shaven face. He hadn't given his name at the pub, or maybe he had. Polly couldn't remember, to be honest. He'd been pouring drinks down her like she was on fire. *I'll call him the Tall Man,* she thought. He'd bought her another drink and another and another. He'd complimented her eyes. Her face. Told her what a lovely bonnet she had. *I knew that bonnet would pay for itself.* He'd put his fingers in her, right there, under the table. Told her he wanted to split her open and taste her.

"Well then, why don'tcha," Polly had said, taking the Tall Man's fingers and putting them in her mouth.

---

1. A pub on Thrawl Street, Whitechapel.

It was nearly three in the morning when Polly found herself stumbling along Buck's Row,[2] a dark and narrow cobbled street of brick warehouses on the right and modest working-class terraced houses on the left, the Tall Man beside her, smoking his pipe. The windows of the houses were dark. Most of the poor rabble had to be up for work in two hours.

Where were they going again? Bloody hell, she'd forgotten. His place, most likely. Or a rented room, if he was the married type, which most of them were. Polly knew it was a sin. Sometimes, if you must know, she felt no better than the nurse Will had run off with. But she wasn't out here on the streets because she liked it. She didn't want to hurt no one. She just wanted to see her five babies again.

They passed the Board School on the north side of the street, the tallest building in sight. Five stories of brick and glass, surrounded by a six-foot wall. Polly thought of the fortunate children sleeping inside. Dressed in their smart uniforms, learning their lessons. *My Edward'll go there someday. He'll go there, and his brothers, too. When I get back on my feet, that's where I'll send 'em.* It was a nice thought. One of the last Polly Nichols ever had.

They walked until the brick wall that bordered the schoolyard gave way to an unpaved drive. The Tall Man stopped. His pipe had gone out. He took it from

---

2. Since renamed Durward Street.

his mouth, tapped away the ash and dottle, and put it in his coat pocket. It was particularly dark on this part of the street, but Polly could make out the closed gates of Mr. Brown's stable yard. She knew those gates well enough. Mr. Brown was a regular customer, and Polly had crossed those gates on many a night, usually when Mrs. Brown was off playing whist with her sisters.

She turned back to the Tall Man and was surprised to find his face very close to her own. Much closer than it had been a moment ago.

"Do you know what I am?" he asked.

"Sure I do, love," said Polly, tracing a finger from his chest down to his belt buckle. "You're a big, strong beast, and I'm a helpless little lass."

"Do you know what this is?"

"Yes…"

The Tall Man grinned.

"You have no idea, do you? You have no idea what's happening."

Polly could feel him through his trousers. He was, as she'd heard another unfortunate woman say, "harder than a loaf of day-old bread."

"Sure I do, dear," said Polly. "It's *already* happening."

"Yes… it is."

He smiled at her. Polly knew this because she could see his teeth in the dark. She smiled back.

"We're not goin' to a boardinghouse, are we?" said Polly.

The Tall Man let a nervous little laugh escape his lips—barely more than an exhale.

"No," he said. "No, we aren't."

"You wanna do it right here, don'tcha."

"Yes..."

"Do it, then," she said, grabbing hold of him over his pants. "Do it right here."

The Tall Man pushed her backward, and she fell to the pavement, landing hard enough to scrape her back bloody, though she would never know it. "Careful, love," said Polly with a laugh. *Oh, to be drunk and properly prigged and paid when it's done.* It wasn't all bad, this life.

He knelt in front of her, hiked her dress up, and ripped the buttons of her drawers open. *Now he takes me,* thought Polly. *Now he hammers my nail for a minute or two. Three at the most. And then he pours into me and collapses on top of me like a sack of grain. Poof goes the pipe, and off he goes to his wife, leaving pretty Polly and her blue bonnet to pray the blood comes on time.*

But none of that happened. Instead, the Tall Man grabbed a fistful of Polly's hair with his right hand—*Too hard! Too hard, he's hurting me!*—yanked her head back, elongating her neck, and cut her throat in two swift, powerful strokes, severing all but her spine.

Polly didn't feel it. She was drunk, sure. But even if she'd been as sober as a judge, she wouldn't have seen his left arm move the way it did. So quick, it was like he hadn't moved at all. She didn't feel any pain, either.

Not at first. Only the strange sensation of needing to take a breath but not being able to. He was thrusting his left arm down at her, again and again, while holding her hair in his right. There was no flash of silver. No knife. Not that she could see. *How is his arm moving so fast?*

The pain came. A pain she could feel deep inside, as if he was dragging the blade of a knife along her bones, separating them from the muscle, one strand at a time. Pulling fingernails out over every inch of her body. It was a pain she'd known five times before, when her babies had come, and she'd felt that tearing and breaking and bleeding. When she'd been sure there was something wrong. *It can't possibly hurt this much.* When she'd been sure that her body would never be able to put itself back together. *But it won't, Polly,* she thought. *Not this time, love.*

Light-headed… Too much to drink…

The Tall Man was pulling something from her stomach. Polly thought of the midwife, pulling her babies out. Covered in blood, the umbilical trailing out behind them. But there was no baby this time. Only the cord and the blood.

My insides… he's pulling my insides out…

The thoughts no longer belonged to her. They were somewhere else now, along with the pain. With no muscle or flesh left to support it, Polly's head tilted back, lifting her eyes to the stars. It hung there, held in place by the stem of her exposed spine, a ripe apple hanging from the end of a branch. Her pretty new bonnet—*It'll pay for itself*—slipped back over her brown hair as the life poured from the gash in her throat, spilling onto the damp street. The lights growing dim and the sounds distant. She had a thought. A lovely thought of her Edward in that school uniform. What a handsome figure he would cut! What a fine student he would be! She had another thought, this one of her five babies in a small boat, holding on to one another in turbulent red waters. And then they were gone. Lost over the edge of the world.

So ended the forty-three years of Polly Nichols.

Henry woke to pounding from downstairs.

Someone's at the front door.

He glanced over at the clock on his dresser. Six fifty-five in the morning. He'd gone to bed only an hour earlier. He put his head back on the pillow and let the pounding continue. *They'll give up and go away soon enough,* he thought.

They didn't.

"Damn it!"

He threw on a shirt and went downstairs, reminding himself along the way that he really needed to get around to hiring a maid. Leaving New York in such a hurry had whipped up a whirlwind of loose ends that Henry was still trying to sort through.

He opened the front door, shielding his eyes from the morning light. Three men in suits and bowler hats were on the other side, chains hanging from their pocket watches and gloomy expressions hanging from their faces. They all looked to be in their forties, and they all had fantastic mustaches. As annoyed as he was, Henry had to grant them that. *Fantastic mustaches.* He'd always preferred to keep his face clean shaven, even when whiskers were the fashion. He'd been twenty-five when he became a vampire. His beard had still been a splotchy and sparse one. Just as a man stops aging when he becomes a vampire, so does his beard stop thickening.

The shortest of the men stepped forward. He had a high-pitched voice that didn't fit his gruff, broad-shouldered appearance.

"Henry Sturges?"

"Yes."

"Frederick Abberline, Scotland Yard. These are my associates, Inspector Moore and Inspector Andrews."

Understand, I was prepared for this. Every vampire with half a brain prepares for the day the police show up at his front door. I'd decided long before that I would be cooperative and courteous when they finally came. If asked to "go downtown" for questioning, I would gladly oblige. I've never understood those vampires who panic at the first hint of suspicion. Who kill detectives on their doorsteps and become fugitives. Why? Let them question you. Let them put you in hand- cuffs. Let them lock you in a cage if they want to. So what? What cage can hold you? What sentence can't you outlive?

Remember, there were no forensics in those days. No databases or photo IDs. Provided you had the money, assuming a new identity and changing your address were relatively easy.

"Mr. Sturges, are you acquainted with a Mary Ann Nichols? Sometimes called Polly?"

Am I? I don't believe so. I haven't fed on any women here.

"No. Why?"

"Mr. Sturges, were you in Whitechapel last night?"

I don't think so. Then again, I'm not sure exactly where Whitechapel is.

"No. What's all this about?"

They're frightened of me.

"Mr. Sturges…a woman was murdered last night. On Buck's Row."

"I'm sorry to hear that. But what does it have to do with me?"

"You're absolutely *sure* you don't know a Polly Nichols?"

"I just told you I didn't, sir!"

Henry collected himself. "Look, gentlemen," he continued, "it's very early, and I've had very little sleep. Now, I'm happy to cooperate in any way I can, if you'll only tell me what any of this has to do with me."

One of the other inspectors, Andrews, stepped forward. He was taller and leaner than Abberline, his thick brown mustache connected to muttonchops.

"Mr. Sturges, your card was found among the victim's possessions."

Andrews held something black aloft between his thumb and forefinger. He flicked it, like a magician displaying a jack of clubs and asking *Is this your card?* Henry wondered if the inspector had practiced this maneuver. Nevertheless, in this case, it *was* Henry's card. White lettering on black stock. Unmistakable.

> I was more intrigued than surprised. Whatever fate had befallen this "Polly," I knew I wasn't directly responsible for it. I hadn't killed any women since arriving in London, or in recent memory, for that matter. But I *had* handed out a number of cards. I sifted through names, faces, trying to remember exactly whom I'd given them to. A haberdasher in Mayfair. A furniture maker in Buckinghamshire. A coachman or two. And Irving. Henry Irving. *That* was the name that jumped out in front.

The third inspector, Moore, was next to speak. His was the thinnest and least impressive of the mustaches.

"You say you've had very little sleep. Am I to take your meaning that you were out late?"

"Yes," said Henry. "Dining with friends, all of whom would swear to the same, if that's what you're driving at."

Moore barely concealed his disappointment. The lead inspector, Abberline, stepped forward again.

"I can see that we've inconvenienced you, Mr. Sturges. Please forgive us. Perhaps we can make arrangements to sit later in the day, when you've had ample time to prepare yourself?"

I didn't appreciate the insinuation that I needed time to "prepare." *Oh yes, you're so clever, Inspector. You've caught me off guard. How will I ever keep my story straight?*

Henry made arrangements to meet the inspectors that afternoon. He dressed quickly and set off on foot, well aware that Scotland Yard would likely have placed a tail on him.

I saw him almost immediately. It was Andrews— one of the men who'd been at my door. From my house, I made my way east, toward the river, then cut over to Parliament Square. He followed, taking care to keep his distance but doing a poor job of it. I diverted into the Westminster Bridge[3] station, where I bought a third-class ticket and waited on the platform for the next train. Andrews bought a ticket, too. When the train arrived, the conductors stepped onto the platform and opened the coach doors. I presented my ticket and stepped aboard a third-class coach, making sure I sat nearest the door. Andrews presented his ticket and stepped into another third-class coach, behind mine. There were no automatic doors back then; the conductors simply called out that all were aboard and shut each of the coach doors before climbing aboard themselves. I waited for the train to begin moving, then, just before it entered the tunnel ahead, I opened my coach door and jumped back onto the platform. The conductor nearest me yelled—I don't remember what, only that he was very upset. But not upset enough to stop the train. On it went, with Andrews still aboard. And what choice did he have? To jump off after me would've meant revealing himself.

---

3. Then part of London's original Circle Line, which began service in 1863 using steam-powered trains. The station consisted of two covered platforms above track level. It's since been moved deep below street level and extensively expanded and renovated, and is known simply as "Westminster."

Henry hurried back to the street and hailed a hansom cab.

"Eighteen Leonard's Terrace, in Chelsea," he told the driver.

He had to see Stoker at once.

"I'm not asking him that," said Stoker.

"He's one of the few men I've given a card to in London," said Henry. "And as far as I know, the only vampire. If it was him, I need to know."

"I'm telling you, it wasn't."

"Stoker, I was with you all night. You can't account for his—"

"I've known him ten years!" said Stoker, his face flushing red. "And I know what he is. But in those ten years, I've not seen him make a single error! Not one! Especially one so careless as dropping a bloody calling card! Nor have I seen him do anything remotely as vulgar as lay with a whore. If it were his desire, which, might I add, I've never known it to be, there are a thousand actresses in this city alone who would weep with joy at having their petals plucked by the great Henry Irving!"

Stoker's breathing steadied, and his face began to drain back to its normal hue.

"Well...," said Henry, "someone killed the poor girl and left my card on her body, whether intentionally or not. And I should very much like to know who and why."

"I know someone who may be able to help. A friend, visiting from Portsmouth."

"Oh? Is he a lawman?"

"A physician."

"Christ, Stoker, the girl's already dead. We don't need a physician. We need a detective."

"He's not an ordinary physician."

"How do you mean?"

"He has a rather . . . curious mind."

Arthur Conan Doyle walked with purpose.

He always did, even if he had no purpose other than walking itself. He'd been "born with boundless energy," his mother often said. An excitement that required constant exercise. In addition to running a medical practice and writing stories, Doyle was a cricketer, golfer, and goalkeeper for an amateur football club. He had a round face and cheerful eyes, and had it not been for his thick brown mustache, he might have passed for a teenager. His wife, Louisa, was expecting their first child. Some men cowered in the face of becoming fathers for the first time. Doyle was already looking forward to getting Louisa pregnant again.

After years of unsuccessfully submitting stories to various magazines, he'd just published his first novel, *A Study in Scarlet*, which featured a gifted detective named Sherlock Holmes and his friend

Dr. John Watson.[4] As a doctor and a detective novelist, Doyle had a keen investigative mind. He'd learned to develop it while in medical school, where he studied beside fellow authors Robert Louis Stevenson and J. M. Barrie. But it was one of his professors at the University of Edinburgh Medical School, Dr. Joseph Bell, who'd most impressed the young Doyle. Dr. Bell, or "Joe," as his students called him, was a Scot known for his keen powers of deduction.

Doyle had a friend in Scotland Yard who knew the details of the Polly Nichols murder. Nichols was a prostitute, and the current thinking was that she'd been killed by a client—an all too common occurrence. Whitechapel was a rough part of London, especially for those women who walked the streets after dark. Official estimates put the number of prostitutes in Whitechapel at more than a thousand, and vicious attacks and murders were commonplace. Doyle learned that, in addition to Nichols, Scotland Yard was also looking at another recent murder, and trying to determine if they were dealing with the same killer.

"The woman in question was Martha Tabram," said Doyle. "Aged thirty-nine. A prostitute, like the Nichols woman. Roughly the same height, though a good deal heavier. She was found stabbed to death in Whitechapel three weeks ago."

---

4. The novel appeared as part of a collection, *Beeton's Christmas Annual,* in 1887. Doyle received £25 for all the rights.

"On the street?" asked Henry.

"In a tenement stairwell. She was stabbed thirty-nine times."

"Good Lord," said Stoker.

"Scotland Yard thinks it's the same killer," said Doyle.

"Do you?" asked Henry.

Doyle shook his head. "Too clumsy. Too savage. One doesn't stab a woman thirty-nine times unless one of two things is true: one, the murderer was caught up in the throes of anger, which means the victim was familiar to him. A lover, perhaps. Unlikely, given that our victim, by the very nature of her trade, would have had many lovers. The second possibility is more likely—that the murderer was not in control of his senses and that this murder was not planned. The facts, gentlemen: he killed her in a tenement stairwell, where they could have easily been discovered, had another tenant come home or peeked his head out the door. Two, he stabbed her repeatedly in the torso but left the throat untouched, giving her ample time to scream, as the majority of her wounds were not instantly fatal. No... the man who stabbed Martha Tabram was careless. But the man who killed Nichols... he was in complete control, from the choice of victim to the location of the murder to its execution. See here..."

Doyle slid his journal across the table for Henry and Stoker to see. He'd copied down every detail of

Literary titans and erstwhile Ripper investigators Arthur Conan Doyle and Bram Stoker pose together in a previously unreleased photograph from the private collection of Henry Sturges.

the Scotland Yard reports, including drawings and diagrams.

"Her throat was severed to the spine in two swift strokes. Like this..." Doyle demonstrated, moving his right arm back and forth across Henry's throat in level, precise strokes. "Then he repositions his body and makes three deep, successive wounds across the abdomen and genital area, before disemboweling her."

"A madman," said Stoker.

"A very strong madman with a very sharp blade," said Doyle. "To make such severe wounds in single strokes."

A chilling thought bounced around my skull as Doyle spoke. The brutality, the precision, the wallowing in gore and detail; I wondered, *Could it be Grander?* But then why murder common streetwalkers? Unless, of course, the *real* target was the man who would get the blame. The man who'd been sent to London to find him. Was this Grander's way of warning me off?

"There was ash and a small amount of pipe tobacco found at the scene, quite near the body."

"Oh, a pipe smoker," said Henry. "Well, that narrows it down."

"Sometimes," said Doyle, "there is nothing so significant as a trifle."

"Well, trifle or not," said Stoker, "it doesn't get us any closer to finding out why Henry's card ended up on that woman's body."

Doyle turned to Henry. "There is, of course, one possibility that we haven't discussed."

"Oh?" said Henry. "And what's that?"

"That you are, in fact, the killer, and that you left your card on the victim—whether intentionally or not."

"Are you mad?" asked Stoker. "He came to us. He's the reason we're investigating this in the first place."

"Precisely what a clever murderer might do to deflect suspicion. If we're to conduct a thorough investigation, we must consider every possibility—no matter how unlikely."

Doyle noticed Henry glaring at him.

"Even those that are...extremely unlikely," said Doyle.

"Is there anything else in the report?" asked Henry.

"Nothing definitive, though Scotland Yard seems strangely certain that the killer is a foreigner. A theory they base entirely on the statement of one witness who claims to have seen the victim with a 'dark, shabbily dressed foreign type' an hour before her murder. There is, however, one detail that puzzles me. See here—at the top of the Inquest Testimony, it states that her torso was riddled in lacerations. Yet here, at the bottom of the same page, the coroner states, 'No blood was found on the breast, either of the body or the clothes.' If her throat was indeed cut with the severity described earlier...what happened to all of the blood? In his own notes, Abberline states that, for all of the woman's injuries, there was not blood enough to fill two wineglasses at the site. Strange, given the severity and location of the wounds. It's almost as if it was... collected."[5]

---

5. Observations of Dr. Rees Ralph Llewellyn upon arrival at Buck's Row at four a.m. on the morning of August 31st. After only a brief examination of the body he pronounced Polly Nichols dead. He noted that there was a wineglass and a half of blood in the gutter at her side but claimed that he had no doubt that she had been killed where she lay. Inquest testimony as reported in the *Times*: "Five teeth were missing, and there was a slight laceration of the tongue. There was a bruise running along the lower part of the jaw on the right side of the face. That might have been caused by a blow from a fist or pressure from a thumb. There was a circular bruise on the left side of the face which also might

Stoker and Henry exchanged a glance. It was brief, but enough for both men to acknowledge—*Let's keep that part to ourselves.*

"Still," Doyle continued, "one thing is clear. Unless apprehended, our murderer is likely to strike again."

Henry sat in a small room in Scotland Yard, watching Inspector Abberline pace back and forth. It was a small, windowless room in the middle of a lower floor, a precursor to the interrogation rooms that would become ubiquitous in detective films fifty years later—ash-gray walls, a wooden table in its

---

have been inflicted by the pressure of the fingers. On the left side of the neck, about 1 inch below the jaw, there was an incision about 4 inches in length, and ran from a point immediately below the ear. On the same side, but an inch below, and commencing about 1 inch in front of it, was a circular incision, which terminated at a point about 3 inches below the right jaw. That incision completely severed all the tissues down to the vertebrae. The large vessels of the neck on both sides were severed. The incision was about 8 inches in length. The cuts must have been caused by a long-bladed knife, moderately sharp, and used with great violence. No blood was found on the breast, either of the body or the clothes. There were no injuries about the body until just about the lower part of the abdomen. Two or three inches from the left side was a wound running in a jagged manner. The wound was a very deep one, and the tissues were cut through. There were several incisions running across the abdomen. There were three or four similar cuts running downward, on the right side, all of which had been caused by a knife which had been used violently and downward. The injuries were from left to right and might have been done by a left handed person. All the injuries had been caused by the same instrument."

center, a single light hanging over the suspect's head. Henry had been there for more than three hours, answering the same questions, over and over. Deflecting accusations. Inspectors Moore and Andrews were there, too, both men slouched in stiff wooden chairs against the wall. They looked bored beyond comprehension.

The killer had indeed struck again, just as Doyle had predicted. Polly Nichols had been killed on August 31st. A little more than a week later, on September 7th, the body of Annie Chapman was found in the backyard of 29 Hanbury Street, Spitalfields, just after sunrise.

Like Nichols, Chapman was an East End prostitute. And like Nichols, her throat had been cut in two deep gashes, her stomach sliced open, and her entrails pulled out. But there were a pair of key differences. One, Chapman's uterus had been removed. And two, the white letters "H" and the "S" on the "Hanbury Street" sign had been smeared over with blood, though this detail was kept out of the papers at the request of the investigators. Abberline had almost screamed when he'd seen those two letters. He felt as if he was being mocked, and he had a pretty good idea of who was doing the mocking.

Once again, he and his colleagues knocked on Henry's front door in the early hours, and once again, an aggravated Henry answered it. This time, Abberline wasn't willing to wait until later in the day. He took Henry directly to Scotland Yard, intent on keeping him there until he confessed.

It was a time-honored policeman's tactic—wear the suspect down. Aggravate him. Do anything in your power to make him slip up or lose his temper.

But Henry wasn't taking the bait, and now it was Abberline who was growing aggravated—rolling and lighting his brown cigarettes with increasing frequency. Pacing back and forth, beads of sweat visible on his lip, just above his splendid mustache.

As [Abberline] grew more impatient, I quietly grew more paranoid. Whoever he was, [Grander had] possessed the resources to track down and assassinate five of the Union's top men in Europe. Surely he knew I was here in England looking for him. Was I being set up? Had Grander infiltrated Scotland Yard?

"Let's start from the beginning, Mr. Sturges."

"Very well."

"You say you were home all night."

"You know that I was. You had two men posted across the street from my front door."

Abberline flushed red but recovered quickly.

"Well, if I *did* have men posted there, and if you were aware of them, then it stands to reason that you might have evaded them somehow. Taken another route out of your home."

"Mr. Abberline—"

"*Inspector* Abberline."

"Forgive me. *Inspector* Abberline, do you mean to suggest that—with the full knowledge that I was under your suspicion and under your watchful eye— I crept out of my house like a spirit, committed a ghastly murder on the other side of London, and then crept back in, all without being noticed? Perhaps you think me able to change form at will or render myself otherwise undetectable to the naked eye."

"Do you know what I think, Mr. Sturges? I think you know more about these murders than you've let on."

> On this point he was technically correct, but see-
> ing that I was, in fact, innocent, I thought it best
> to keep that information to myself.

"Perhaps," Abberline continued, "you committed them yourself, or perhaps you're merely an accomplice. But I've learned to trust my instincts over the years, sir, and my instincts tell me you are holding back."

"Mr. Abberline, if I were the killer you're looking for, would I be here right now, answering your questions? Don't you think I would have fled at the first hint of suspicion?"

"It is my experience that guilty men are often the most confident in the face of questioning. And you, Mr. Sturges, have an unnerving confidence about you."

It was an interesting observation. And maybe I did. We don't really know how we're perceived by others.

"If you aren't the killer, Mr. Sturges, then why did you make such a desperate attempt to evade our man on the train? Hmm? Why such desperation to disguise your movements?"

"Perhaps the issue is not that I evaded him, but how easily I did so."

"Now, look here!" cried Andrews, standing up.

Abberline turned and gestured to Andrews—*steady, steady*. Andrews settled down and took his seat. Abberline turned back. Crept closer to Henry... almost nose to nose.

"Mr. Sturges...I *am* going to catch you, if it takes me the rest of my life. And I am going to see you hang."

From the front page of the *Evening News*, Monday, October 1st, 1888:

THE WHITECHAPEL HORRORS

HORRIBLE MURDER OF A WOMAN
NEAR COMMERCIAL ROAD

Another Woman Murdered and Mutilated in Aldgate

One Victim Identified

Blood Stained Postcard from "Jack the Ripper"

Two more ghastly tragedies were, yesterday, added to the appalling list of crimes with which the East-end of London has been associated during the last few months; and there is every reason to believe that the whole series is the work of one man. The first of the two murders was committed in a yard turning out of Berner-street. The body was discovered by a Russian Jew named Diemschitz, about one o'clock yesterday morning, on his return from the neighbourhood of Sydenham, where he had been selling cheap jewellery. He drove into the yard, which is situated next to a working man's club, of which he is steward, and noticed that his pony shied at something which was lying in a heap in a corner of the yard. Having fetched out a friend from the club, he looked more closely into the matter, and then found a woman lying on the ground, dead, with her throat cut clean to the vertebrae. The body was quite warm, and blood was still flowing freely from the throat, so it is pretty certain that the murder must have been committed within a very few minutes of the time when Diemschitz discovered the body. Indeed, all the facts go to show that it was the arrival of Diemschitz in his trap which disturbed the murderer, and we may safely assume that, but for this disturbance, the miscreant would have proceeded to mutilate the body in a similar way to that in which he mutilated the bodies of the two unfortunate women, Mary Anne Nichols and Annie Chapman. The wound in the throat is almost identical with the throat wounds of the other victims—a savage cut severing the jugular and carotids, and going clean down to the vertebrae. It bears, if we may be permitted to use the phrase, the trademark of the man who has so infamously distinguished himself before, and leaves no room for doubt that the three murders were committed by one and the same person.

Having been disturbed in his first attempt, yesterday morning, the murderer seems to have made his way towards the City, and to have met

another "unfortunate," whom he induced
to go with him to Mitre Square, a
secluded spot, lying off Aldgate, and
principally occupied by warehouses.
He took her to the south-western corner of the square, and there cut her
throat, quite in his horribly regula-
tive way, and then proceeded to disem-
bowl her. He must have been extremely
quick at his work, for every portion
of the police beat in which Mitre
Square is included, is patrolled every
ten minutes or quarter of an hour,
the City beats being much shorter
than those of the Metropolitan Police.
Police-constable Watkins 881 passed
through the square at about 1:30 or
1:35, and is quite certain that it was
then in its normal condition. Within
a quarter of an hour he patrolled it
again, and then found a woman lying
in the corner with her throat cut from
ear to ear. On closer examination he
found that her clothes had been raised
up to her chest, and that the lower
portion of the body had been ripped
completely open from the pelvis to the
sternum, and disemboweled, just as
were Mrs. Nichols and Annie Chapman.
Indeed, this last murder is in its
main features an almost exact repro-
duction of the horrible tragedies of

Buck's-row and Hanbury Street, and, humanly speaking, it is absolutely certain that it also was committed by the same man. There were certain deviations from the murderer's ordinary plan, but they are not inexplicable, or very significant. He gashed her face in several places, but there is evidence to show that the woman at the last moment suspected his design, and struggled with him, and it is not improbable that he stabbed her in the face before cutting her throat and committing the other atrocities.

This brief summary of the facts connected with the two tragedies which startled London, yesterday, brings us then face-to-face with the almost indubitable fact that there exists somewhere in the East-end, at this moment, a fiend in human shape.

Abberline was furious.

He held a written report in his hands. It was a report he'd demanded on his desk every morning since the investigation had begun. A summary of the previous night's surveillance. He read it again, just to be sure:

The subject left his house before dark, which we took note of being somewhat unusual. His coach

was waiting, and drove him to Chelsea—we
following discreetly in our own carriage. The
subject's coach stopped at No. 18 Leonard's
Terrace, where he picked up a burly man of
about forty, with reddish hair and a beard.
The two rode to Rules Restaurant in Covent
Garden, making no stops along the way. There
they were met by another man—closer in age
to the subject, though shorter, and possessing
brown hair and whiskers. It was a few minutes
past eight o'clock when they arrived. Despite the
restaurant being quite full with the Saturday
night crowd, and despite others waiting in line,
the subject and his companions were seated
straightaway at one of the better tables, which
happened to be at a large window that faced
Maiden Lane. We were quite able to see the
subject and his companions from the street. The
three sat, talking intensely at times, for nearly
four hours. When their dinner was concluded,
the shorter man left the restaurant and walked
on Maiden Lane, at which point we lost sight
of him. The other two drove off in the subject's
coach. We followed, never losing sight of the
target. The carriage dropped the bearded man at
No. 18 Leonard's Terrace at half past midnight,
making no stops between, then proceeded
directly to the subject's home. We observed the
subject enter his home at five minutes past one in

the morning. We remained until five. The subject did not appear again.

Faithfully submitted on this day, 30th September, 1888,

W. Andrews
H. Moore.

Henry Sturges couldn't be the Ripper. Not unless he had wings.

Elizabeth Stride's body had been found at one in the morning—five minutes before Henry Sturges had walked in his front door, halfway across the city. The body of Catherine Eddowes was found shortly thereafter. Abberline sent for Andrews and Moore, had them roused from their beds and brought before him to verify everything in the report. Were they absolutely certain? Perhaps they lost sight of Sturges without realizing it. Perhaps he was able to slip away during that four-hour dinner. No, they'd said. They were certain. They would swear by every word in the report.

Doyle and Stoker were holed up in Henry's parlor, poring over the Scotland Yard reports. Proposing theories. Arguing, much like they'd done when they'd dined at Rules the night before, discussing the Nichols and Chapman murders in detail. They'd made a list of every business card Henry could remember giving out and divided the task of following up with each recipient among the three of them. While these follow-ups continued, Doyle was also busy analyzing the new postmortems and crime scene reports from Scotland Yard, working on a sketch of the killer. Based on the force and angle of the wounds on all four victims, he'd concluded that the killer was a tall man and probably left-handed. This theory seemed to be corroborated by a new discovery at the scene of the Stride murder— one that the investigators had once again taken care to keep out of the paper: a set of footprints in the mud of the yard leading away from the woman's body. They were roughly size fourteen, an almost unheard-of size that would help narrow the search. There was no doubt in Doyle's mind that their killer was tall and strong, nor was there any doubt that he was clever and cautious, and possibly trained in anatomy, given the swiftness and cleanliness with which he removed his victims' innards.

"What can we infer from the fabric found clutched in Ms. Stride's right hand?" asked Doyle, looking pointedly at Henry.

"What?" asked Stoker. "There's no mention of any such fabric in the report."

"Not in the official report, no," said Doyle. "Scotland Yard is playing its cards close to the chest. But I have here a sample of the fabric in question. It's velveted herringbone, of English origin and of exceedingly high quality, probably torn from a gentle-man's topcoat."

"You mean the Ripper's topcoat," said Henry. "And meanwhile your friends at the Yard busy themselves trying to pin the murder on me. Wouldn't their time be better spent calling on every suit maker in London who sells such fabric?"

"Oh, I doubt that would help, unless you want to arrest every well-dressed man in the city," said Doyle. "What we can deduce, however, is that this killer goes about his murderous business in his finest garments."

Stoker wasn't following.

Doyle sighed. "Meaning he doesn't dress to fit in with his surroundings. He doesn't care if anyone notices him. He simply doesn't care."

It was the blood that baffled Doyle. The amounts found at the scene were never consistent with the severity of the wounds.

"Both Stride's and Eddowes's throats were cut in the same gruesome manner," said Doyle. "Right down to the spine. Stride's abdomen was intact, but Eddowes was disemboweled, and one of her kidneys was miss-ing. Yet again, Phillips[6] makes mention of there being an unusually small amount of dried blood near the area of the wounds. He even inquires as to whether anyone at the scene might have erred in cleaning the

---

6. Dr. George Bagster Phillips (1835–1897) was the police surgeon and performed the autopsies of three of the Ripper's "Canonical Five" victims.

blood from the victims. But the investigators assured him that the bodies were exactly as found."

"What if he's collecting it?" asked Stoker. Didn't one of the letters[7] say as much? That he'd collected some of the blood in bottles?"

"Indeed, but I doubt very much that those letters were from the real killer."

"Oh?" said Stoker.

"Our killer left Ms. Stride mostly intact," said Doyle. "Why?"

"I don't know. Perhaps he fancied her more than the others."

"Because he was interrupted," said Henry.

"Exactly. Stride was the first of the two women to be killed, yet her injuries were less extensive, and the scene of her death is the only one to include discernible footprints—an unusual oversight by a capable killer. It stands to reason that someone happened along during the murder. Perhaps this person was drawn by some noise related to the deed itself, or perhaps they

---

7. During the autumn and winter of 1888, hundreds of letters were sent to police and newspapers claiming to be from the killer. Though most were dismissed as hoaxes, a few contained details that would have been hard for the public to know and prompted further investigation. The most infamous of these is the "From Hell" letter, delivered to the head of the Whitechapel Vigilance Committee along with a human kidney, possibly belonging to Catherine Eddows. Here, Stoker is referencing the "Dear Boss" letter, which includes the line: "I saved some of the proper red stuff in a ginger beer bottle over the last job to write with but it went thick like glue and I can't use it."

merely wandered onto the scene by chance. Whatever the reason, the killer retreated rather than risk capture, and struck again when it was safe to do so—this time savaging Ms. Eddows in his usual manner, later in the evening. In any case, he's demonstrated an ability to control his urges until it's safe to indulge them. Not the sort of man who creates needless risk by writing letters and taunting policemen."

"I've hunted murderers before," said Henry. "Even the best of them get caught sooner or later."

"I beg to differ," said Doyle. "Famous murderers are only famous *because* they get caught. The best killers are those whose names we shall never know."

The Tall Man was delighted.

The city was paralyzed, on the verge of full-blown panic. The police were having fits. And to think, it had all begun by chance. To think, it had been just another day in London. The Tall Man's soles had worn thin, and he'd paid a visit to his cordwainer[8] on High Street, to place an order for a new pair of brogans, just as he'd done a hundred times before. It was hard finding good-quality, comfortable shoes in a size fourteen, as almost no one had feet that large—especially when the average height was five feet seven inches. While in the shop that day, the Tall Man happened to notice

---

8. A craftsman who makes fine leather shoes and boots.

a rather distinctive calling card on the cordwainer's workbench. Distinctive, for it was made of black stock with white lettering. But when the Tall Man took a closer look, he nearly gasped aloud.

H. Sturges

Importer of Fine Textiles

No. 2 Chester Square

Belgravia, London

It couldn't be him . . . could it?

It was foolish. Who could say that the "H" stood for "Henry"? It might well have been "Harry" or "Horace" or a hundred other common men's names. And even if it was "Henry Sturges," there were probably a thousand men in England with that name. And yet it nagged at the Tall Man. Nagged at him enough to ask the tailor to describe the man who'd left that card. He wanted to know. He *had* to know.

The Tall Man wasn't the least bit religious, but he'd come to believe in a kind of Cosmic Wheel. There were undeniable connections between certain individuals. And there was such a thing as fate. Oh, he believed it with every part of his being. You could keep your Christ and your Buddha and whatever superstitious man-made nonsense you liked, but there was no denying the existence of fate.

And so he'd waited that night, just down the street

from the address on that card. He'd waited until night fell, and then some more, until the front door of No. 2 had opened and Henry bloody Sturges had walked out.

There he was, after all they'd been through together.

After all those years. Life was funny sometimes, wasn't it? The Tall Man had been tempted, *oh so tempted*, to walk right up to him. To surprise him right there, that night, on the street. To see the look on Henry's face before he choked the wretched life out of him. But where was the fun in that? Why not make him squirm first? Make him dangle like a marionette on the end of a string? They'd parted under such unpleasant circumstances, after all. Wasn't the Tall Man owed his revenge?

And so the game had begun. Like others of his kind, he'd become skilled at picking victims who wouldn't be missed. Those whose disappearances or deaths would evoke little more than a shrug, a certificate, and a pile of fresh dirt. But here, the Tall Man had *wanted* to attract attention. He'd mingled with the whores of East London before, picking them up in pubs, taking them back to their lodging houses, and feeding on them. There were plenty of forgotten women to pick from, some new to town, some just passing through. But, as he was with most of his prey, he'd been careful to leave the appearance that the victim had succumbed to some sickness or unfortunate accident. Or he'd simply disposed of the bodies, digging a shallow grave on Jacob's

Island, tying rocks to their feet and throwing them in the Thames, or tossing them into the furnace of a brass foundry where he had a financial understanding with the owner. Though it wasn't always the most practical method of disposal, the Tall Man liked this last one the best. Not only because it destroyed every last shred of evidence, but also because he liked thinking of those ashes joining with molten metal, being poured into different molds—instruments, church bells, and the like. The Tall Man often smiled when he heard church bells ringing or a brass horn playing, thinking that perhaps the ashes of one or more of his victims were contributing to the beauty of the sound.

But this time, the point was to stir up a frenzy of suspicion and ensnare his old friend Henry Sturges plumb in the middle of it. Not that Henry was at risk of being thrown in the Tower of London or hanged from the end of a rope. No, far from it. The point was to make him uncomfortable. To make him desperate. Desperate enough to come looking. And when capable, determined old Henry Sturges finally found him (which he would, sooner or later, that capable boy), then the Tall Man would get to see the shock on old Henry's face, just for an instant, before he tore it off.

The Tall Man had been having a grand time, but it was getting too risky out in the open, with all those patrolmen and volunteers roaming the streets, hoping for their chance to catch the Ripper.

The Ripper.

It was a fine name. He hadn't counted on receiving a name at all, or on causing such a sensation. But some lunatic had taken it upon himself to write a letter to a newspaper, taunting the police, and calling himself "Jack the Ripper." It added to the mystique of the thing. Added to the fun. It was fun, playing games with the living. It excited him, seeing how helpless they were in his grasp. Take this one before him... Mary. He'd been at her for hours, courting her, luring her in... falling in love with her.

You had to love them. That was the key. You had to love them or it ruined everything.

Mary... She'd been easy to fall in love with. Far easier than any of the others. The Tall Man had loved her the moment he saw her. She was lovely. Just lovely. A tall girl, about twenty-five years old, with fair skin, faint freckles on her cheeks and nose, and auburn hair, which she wore pulled back in a ponytail. She was slender but buxom, with wide hips and large breasts. A blue-eyed Irish beauty. How such a pretty girl ended up selling herself on the streets of East London, the Tall Man neither knew nor cared. She was here with him now, and he loved her. That was all that mattered.

He told her to undress and lay upon the bed. She did so with no fuss, unbuttoning the top of her dress and pulling it down over her shoulders. Down the length of her body, onto the floor. Her pubic hair was the same auburn, and her breasts, full and covered with gooseflesh, held their shape as she settled on her back.

You've never nursed a child, thought the Tall Man, *but there's a child in you now. Right now, as you lay there naked. I can hear its little heart beating with yours. I can see the extra blood in your body widening every one of those beautiful veins. Those veins, so easy to make out beneath your porcelain skin.*

The Tall Man couldn't wait to taste that blood. To hear those two heartbeats speed up to a rousing symphony, then slow to a funeral dirge. But first he had to make everything perfect. Just as a chef has to peel and then dice his ingredients before the real cooking begins. Before he can taste the delectable results. The ingredients were spread out before him. He had to make her comfortable. He had to love her and put his mouth on her. He had to feel her warmth so that he could better appreciate the cold when it came.

She was drunk, poor girl. The whole world must've seemed a pinwheel to her, lying there naked and warm on the sheets. She'd been singing a song as they'd walked from the pub to her room at 13 Miller's Court. A relatively new song, called "A Violet from Mother's Grave."

Father and mother they have passed away.
Sister and brother now lay beneath the clay;
But while life does remain, to cheer me I'll retain
This small violet I plucked from mother's grave.

She had a bright, clear voice. Good pitch. The Tall Man wondered what other future might've awaited her had circumstances been different. Perhaps, with her looks and voice, she would have found a home on the stage. *Oh, but she is. This is her stage, right here. And though she doesn't know it, she'll be famous come morning.*

"Are you cold, dear?" the Tall Man asked, rubbing his cold hand along the gooseflesh of her breast. "Or are you frightened?"

"What's there to be frightened of? This ain't my first time bein' naked with a man, love."

"I meant on account of the recent...incidents in Whitechapel."

"Ah, you mean the Ripper. The whole city's gone mad, 'asn't it," she said. "It's all anybody'll talk about."

"And you...are you not interested in the Ripper?"

"Interested, sure. But I 'aven't lost my wits, 'ave I? Another one'a the girls—'er name's Mary like mine— she says, 'Aren't you scared, Mary? Shouldn't we be careful?' But I says, 'Mary, there's 'undreds of us girls workin' out 'ere, and only one Ripper. What's the chances you or I's gonna be the one 'e picks? Besides, what other choice we 'ave, stop workin' and starve to death? Well then, we're dead anyway, ain't we. My roommate, 'e's a better reader, reads all the newspapers to me. And I've got a good idea of who 'e is, the Ripper."

"Do you, now...And who is he?"

"'E's a little man, sure as I'm lyin' here. Short and funny lookin', I'd wager."

"Oh? What makes you say so?"

"It's always the short ones and funny-lookin' ones who turn out mad. Them and the ones with the little peckers. Been laughed at by the girls since they was little. Got a grudge against 'em. So this one—this Ripper—'e gets it in his head 'e'll teach 'em a lesson. Carve a few of 'em up."

"Yes," he said. "It makes perfect sense when you put it like that."

The Tall Man beamed. It was all too perfect. The presence of the cosmic wheel was undeniable.

"Sing that song again," he said. "The one you sang on the way over. The one about the violet."

Mary began to sing, softly, as he moved his hands over her body.

Well I remember my dear old mother's smile,
As she used to greet me when I returned from toil;
Always knitting in the old arm chair.
Father used to sit and read for all us children there.

His fingers reached her neck. He closed his hand on her throat, gently at first...feeling her vocal cords vibrate as she sang.

But now all is silent around the good old home,
They all have left me in sorrow here to roam;
While life does remain, in memoriam I'll retain
This small violet I plucked from mother's grave.

He began to squeeze. The singing stopped. She thought he was being playful at first, but as the squeeze grew tighter, the drunken look fell off her face. The light from her eyes. She began to struggle, grabbing hold of his wrist and trying to push his arm away. Trying to roll off the bed to escape his grasp. The Tall Man held her in place, calmly, effortlessly. He watched her porcelain skin turn that beautiful shade of purple as he squeezed harder. *She knows. She knows it now.* It was so easy, so perfect.

"Hundreds of girls," he said. "What were the odds you would be the one I picked?"

Dark went his eyes, down came his fangs, and out came those razor-sharp claws. He wanted her to see him. He wanted her to know what he was while she still had some fight left in her. He drew his hand back like a painter about to make a decisive stroke across his canvas—*that's exactly what this is...it's my art*—and opened a gash in her throat. She spilled forth, and he put his mouth on her. Drinking her. When he'd had his fill, he set about the work of dismantling her beauty, piece by piece. Of sculpting her into a shape that pleased him.

From the notes of Dr. Thomas Bond, who performed the postmortem with Dr. George Bagster Phillips:

The whole of the surface of the abdomen and thighs was removed and the abdominal cavity emptied. The breasts were cut off, the arms mutilated by several jagged wounds and the face hacked beyond recognition of the features. The tissues of the neck were severed down to the bone. The uterus, kidneys and one breast had been placed under the head, along with the nose, the other breast placed by the right foot, the liver between the feet, the intestines by the right side and the spleen by the left side of the body. The flaps removed from the abdomen and thighs were on a table. The bed clothing at the right corner was saturated with blood, and on the floor beneath was a pool of blood covering about two feet square. The wall by the right side of the bed and in a line with the neck was marked by blood which had struck it in several places. The face was gashed in all directions, the nose, cheeks, eyebrows, and ears being partly removed. The lips were blanched and cut by several incisions running obliquely down to the chin. There were also numerous cuts extending irregularly across all the features. The neck was cut through the skin and other tissues right down to the vertebrae, the fifth and sixth being deeply notched. Both breasts were more or less removed by circular incisions, the muscle down to the ribs being attached to the breasts . . . The skin and tissues of the abdomen from the costal arch to the pubes were removed in three large flaps. The left calf showed a long gash through skin and tissues to the deep muscles and reaching from the knee to five inches above the ankle. Both arms and forearms had extensive jagged wounds. The right thumb showed a small superficial incision about one inch long. The lower part of the lung was broken and torn away. The left lung was intact. It was adherent at the apex and there were a few adhesions over the side. The pericardium was open below and the heart absent.

Henry woke to pounding on his front door again.

He was livid. He knew it was Abberline. There had been another murder, no doubt, and Abberline and his two pets had come to harass him again with their fine facial hair. He dressed and hurried down the stairs, silently vowing to hire a maid before week's end. But when he swung the door open, his temper already raised, it was Doyle waiting on the other side.

"I know who the Ripper is," he said.

To both writers and detectives, nothing is ever without meaning. Every moment is fraught with significance. Every trivial dinner conversation or miscellaneous fact is filed away internally. Doyle's mind was a vast library of carefully organized bits of ephemera waiting to be brought down from the shelf, dusted off, and put to use.

A month earlier, Doyle had purchased a dinner of fish and chips, which came wrapped in the traditional newspaper. As he ate, he glanced at the newsprint in his hands and learned of a new machine for making a different type of shoe. Later known as the Goodyear Welt Sewing Machine, it was invented by Charles Goodyear Jr., son of the famous inventor of the process of vulcanizing rubber. The welt sewing machines made shoes faster, cheaper, and better. They also left a distinct mark on the back of the heel.

A mark that was on the Ripper's footprints.

The image had buried itself in Doyle's mind, waiting to be awakened. Now, with a mouthful of fish and chips, it came hurtling out of the darkness of his subconscious, its significance suddenly revealed. The newspaper article mentioned that there were only two cordwainers in London with these new machines. One specialized in women's shoes, which left only—

Doyle left his uneaten meal and rushed to Cole's Fine Men's Shoes.

> He spoke to the cordwainer, who remembered seeing my card when I'd gone in and ordered a pair of boots—Oxfords, Balmoral cut. Usually, he affixed the customers' calling cards to the soles of their unfinished shoes, so he would know whom to contact when they were finished. But somehow, he'd lost mine.

"Very unusual indeed," said Cole. "I pride myself on being organized."

He led Doyle over to see the boots he was making for Henry. And that's when Doyle saw them. A pair of brogans, nearly finished . . . the biggest pair of brogans he'd ever seen.

"What size are those, if I may?" asked Doyle.

"Fourteens, those are, sir. I've only made one bigger pair in all my life."

Doyle didn't know *why* the man with size-fourteen feet had taken Henry's card, but he knew in that moment that he had.

"And who, if I may, are those shoes for?"

Henry told the coachman to hurry. But it was a weekday morning, and the streets were packed with pedestrians. If the coachman went any faster, he was liable to kill someone.

Henry got out and ran, taking care not to run faster than a human could, lest he draw attention. A cheetah moving at a snail's pace, so as not to offend the snails.

He ran, his body not tiring, his breath not quickening, his heartbeat nonexistent, until he reached the address Doyle had looked up. Doyle, who had insisted they go straight to the police. But Henry knew that if Doyle was right—if the Ripper *was* who he thought he was—they would be sending those policemen to their deaths.

Henry could smell another creature on the other side of the door. He could sense the presence of another vampire, reaching into his mind as he reached back. *He knows me,* thought Henry. *Whoever this vampire is, he knows me.* There was something so familiar about that mind...flashes of shared experiences.

Henry reached the door and found it ajar. He pushed it open, slowly. Doyle was right.

> It was him.
> It was impossible, but there he was, sitting on the edge of a bed against the opposite wall, facing the door. Expecting me. There he was...one leg crossed over the other. He sat there, looking at me, as if this were just another other social call. It was an absurd sight. I'll never forget it.

"Hello, Henry," said the Tall Man.

> He hadn't changed a bit. He was tall and balding. His face pockmarked; his eyes kind. He looked exactly as he had in Roanoke, all those centuries ago.

It was the man who had taken his love. The man who had taken his life.

The man who had made him a vampire.

FIVE

★ ★ ★

Good Devil

He that falls into sin is a man; that grieves at it, is a saint; that boasteth of it, is a devil.

—*Thomas Fuller*

God had delivered them to a virgin shore.

Henry Sturges stepped out of the rowboat and stood on the sand of the New World, young and alive. A blacksmith's apprentice. A runaway. A young man of solid build and handsome features, with long, dark hair that ran to the middle of his back and which he almost always wore in a ponytail.

It was July 22nd, 1587. A Wednesday afternoon, in the humid height of a North American summer. A storm was approaching, kicking up onshore winds that only heightened the drama of their already dramatic arrival. The ship that had borne Henry and 116 other English souls across the ocean, the *Lyon*, was anchored just off the coast. They'd landed on the northernmost tip of Roanoke Island, part of a two-hundred-mile string of barrier islands that make up the Outer Banks of present-day North Carolina, just a few miles south of Kitty Hawk, where the Wright Brothers would fly the world's first motorized airplane 316 years later. The *Mayflower* wouldn't land at Plymouth Rock for another thirty-five years.

Henry fell to his knees, letting the ocean wash over his legs, his long hair whipping beneath gray skies. He kissed the rocky beach—its stones in shades of black and gray, like the gathering storm clouds above, polished smooth over the eons by the motion of the sea they'd just crossed. He kissed the stones a second time, then, with sand and salt water still on his face, he rose and kissed his bride, Edeva.

> She was a beautiful girl—let me start there. Blond hair. Brown eyes speckled with amber. Tall and delicate with a lightly freckled nose and perfect teeth, which in those days was nothing short of a miracle. She was—and I say this with all respect to the other women I've loved—the most beautiful, the most *physically* beautiful woman I've ever known. But it was more than that. It was ... she was also my *first* love. The only innocent love I suppose I ever had. We were only a day apart in age. That's true, by the way. Absolutely true.

She was, as Henry had said to her on their wedding day, his "heart" and his "hope."

Henry and Edeva had known each other for less than a year by the time they first set foot in America. They had met the previous August, around the time John White, an artist and adventurer, was mounting an expedition to the New World. It was to be financed by his patron, Sir Walter Raleigh, and White needed not just a crew, but the seeds of a new society as well. He'd put out a call for "sturdy, married English men and their wives, to establish a colony, for the glory of Her Majesty, the Queen, and the kingdom."

Edeva's father hadn't approved of his daughter marrying a man of my stature. He wasn't rich by any means—not an aristocrat or anything of the sort—but he was a well-respected merchant, and she was his only daughter, and a stunning one at that. You can't blame the poor man for having high hopes. Higher than seeing her run off with a wherryman's son, anyway.

I don't remember exactly how we heard of the expedition. Word of mouth, most likely. Looking back, it seems a little extreme. Why not run away to Scotland or France? Why risk everything to go off into the unknown? But we were madly in love and young. And big decisions come easily when you're young.

To the young lovers, here was an answer to their prayers. A way for them to be together. To have a life together, on their own terms.

> We got married right away. A small ceremony, at home. My parents served as witnesses. Edeva's parents weren't able to attend the wedding, mainly due to the fact that they didn't know it was taking place. If they had, I'm sure they would've done everything in their power to stop it.

On May 1st, 1587, Henry bid his parents farewell, not knowing if he would ever see them again. A week later, he and Edeva boarded the *Lyon* at Plymouth and embarked on a ten-week voyage across the Atlantic.

Hers were the warm fingers entwined in his on the cold and uncertain nights, both of them shivering beneath the sheets during their treacherous crossing. Both of them young, and in wretched, undying love that would assuredly last until the end of time, because all love was eternal and theirs above all.

> It was a miserable crossing; that much I remember. [Captain and colonial governor John] White and [ship's navigator Simon] Fernandez didn't agree on anything. Fernandez resented having an aristocrat for a captain, and White resented having a degenerate sailor questioning his every command. It didn't help that the voyage was

an especially difficult one, marred by a pair of strange deaths.[1]

The first days at Roanoke passed with excitement and uncertainty. A search party was sent to look for the fifteen English soldiers who'd been left behind on the previous expedition, charged with keeping watch over the fort, but no sign of them was found, other than a single skeleton that may or may not have been one of the men in question. Abandoned buildings were rebuilt; relations with the local Algonquin[2] tribes—most notably the Croatans—reestablished; a perimeter fence made of logs with sharpened points at the top was put up, turning their encampment into a fort, just in case relations with the natives soured.

A week after the colonists arrived, that's exactly what happened. An Englishman named George Howe was found facedown in the shallow waters of Albemarle Sound, some two miles from the fort. He'd

---

1. The first death occurred on Sunday, May 24th, when a ship's mate named Blum (or Bloom) fell from the crow's nest and broke his neck. The second occurred on Tuesday, June 30th, when a sixteen-year-old passenger named Elizabeth Barrington disappeared during a storm. She was presumed to have fallen overboard and drowned.
2. The Algonquin Peoples were a loosely connected nation of more than a hundred tribes, all speaking a version of the Algonquin language. Their combined population numbered as high as one hundred thousand at the time of the Roanoke Colonies.

been fishing for crabs with a small forked stick, alone. There were sixteen small puncture wounds in his body—presumably from Indian arrows, though none were found at the scene. His head had been crushed by forceful blows. When the search party found him, there were crows perched around him, eating pieces of his brain.

Indian attacks were a constant concern, but nothing frightened the Roanoke settlers more than sickness. It was a New World in every sense: new people carrying new diseases; new foods and vegetation testing their tender English constitutions. Their lodgings were damp and cold, and their diet supplemented by fish, crab, and vegetation gathered from the surrounding wilderness. Something as simple as a bout of food poisoning or influenza could wipe out the whole colony in a matter of days, if left unchecked.

On August 18th, Henry and the others were in good spirits, rejoicing at the arrival of the colony's first baby, Virginia Dare—Captain John White's granddaughter. She was the first English child born in the New World and, like her mother, possessed a shock of red hair.

It was all too perfect. "Virginia Dare." "Virginia," for our "Virgin Queen," and "Dare," which is exactly what we were there to do. To dare and tame this vast wilderness. To dare! To conquer, for England!

The Roanoke colonists gather to celebrate the baptism of Virginia Dare, the first English child born in the New World. The highlighted figure is the only rendering of a pre-vampire Henry Sturges, then twenty-five years old, to ever exist.

Only two weeks after his granddaughter's birth, and one month after making landfall, Governor John White set sail for England, to arrange for the delivery of supplies and reinforcements. He would return within six months, it was promised, with ships stuffed to bursting with salted beef, grain, and, most important, more able-bodied men to aide in building and defending the new settlement.

In fact, it would be three years before John White set foot on Roanoke Island again.

Thomas Crowley loved to laugh.

"A good laugh," he often said, "is a powerful tonic." And as a doctor, he knew what he was talking about. Over the years, he'd observed that those patients who were possessed of a "cheerful disposition" often recovered more quickly than those of a "dour character." Laughter, he believed, could even mean the difference between life and death.

He was a tall and kindly man of fifty-six, bald headed, with a curtain of graying hair that fell over his neck. His face was kind, and his cheeks bore the scars of a childhood bout with acne. Thomas Crowley was a skilled physician, to be sure, but unlike the humorless, bloodletting butchers of the day, he possessed what would today be called a "pleasing bedside manner." Nothing made him happier than helping a patient lift his or her spirits with a good laugh.

Crowley had, naturally, attended the birth of the New World's first English child, Virginia Dare. Unlike other physicians of his stature, who would have had a nurse or midwife assist him with the menial details, Crowley insisted on doing everything himself—including the collection and disposal of the large quantities of blood and afterbirth. However, unlike other physicians of *any* stature, he'd consumed the blood while no one was looking.

Like his fellow colonists, Crowley had risked everything to come to the New World. But it wasn't the glory of England that had compelled him to cross an ocean or, like the pilgrims who would follow decades later, religious freedom. It was food. London may have been home to millions of humans, but it was also home to thousands of vampires, all of them competing for victims in the same seedy alleys, it seemed. The New World, while dangerous, represented an opportunity for an enterprising vampire. A hundred colonists would soon become a thousand. Then ten thousand.

There had been some tense moments during the crossing. He'd managed to subsist on rats (always plentiful aboard a ship) for two weeks before the hunger had compelled him to kill the poor lookout and throw him from the crow's nest. With a fresh supply of human blood, Crowley had been able to go another three weeks, topping himself off with the occasional rat, before the hunger had come again, and he'd taken the dear girl during a storm.

Two strange deaths on a single crossing wasn't unheard of, but if a third member of the passengers or crew was to go missing or meet with a freak accident, well, who could say? And what would he do if the finger of suspicion was cast at him? Kill the lot of them? Crowley was a fine doctor, but he knew nothing of sailing a ship. He imagined himself alone in the middle of the Atlantic. Adrift. Bored.

Hungry. If a storm didn't sink him, he would surely starve to death.

So it had filled him with joy when the cries of "Land!" had gone up. And it had been with thanks to God that he'd set foot on the shores of the New World. With the exception of George Howe—a slipup early on in his stay—Crowley had managed to get by on an all-animal-blood diet at first. He found that if he fed twice as often (every week, instead of twice a month), and if he avoided rodents, fish, and reptiles in favor of deer and wild game, he could mitigate the ill effects that usually accompanied such a diet—namely, lethargy and mild aches.

But three months, though nothing in the face of eternity, was a long time to feel run down, and Crowley had begun to crave human blood again. But how to acquire it? That was the issue. There were barely more than a hundred of them in colony, packed tightly together behind the walls of their little fort. If people began disappearing every two weeks, the suspicion would be intolerable. Crowley supposed he could sneak off and snare a native every so often—a woman or child walking in the woods. But relations with the Indians were fragile as it was. Even if no bodies were found, the disappearances would undoubtedly raise suspicion, possibly even lead to war.

It was Ambrose Viccars, the portly carpenter, who'd given Dr. Crowley the idea. He'd come in with a stubborn fever, nothing out of the ordinary. After examining him, Crowley recommend bloodletting, by the far the most common—and as most physicians of the time believed, the most effective—means of battling ailments.[3] The cause of the fever was undoubtedly some contaminant in the patient's blood, and how better to remove the contaminants than by removing a volume of blood and letting the patient's body replenish it with a fresh, untainted supply? It also happened to be a *wonderful* way for a vampire physician to get his hands on a meal, without having to go through the trouble of killing. But there were challenges. The blood had to be consumed quickly after leaving the patient's body, or it lost its replenishing properties. If left sitting too long, this "old blood" could even make the vampire sick.

Crowley had been supplementing his animal-blood diet with the occasional bowl of patients' blood, but unlike in London, where he might see upward of a hundred patients a week and bleed fifty, in Roanoke he had occasion to open the veins of only one or two adults a week, at best. Hardly enough to get by on.

---

3. The practice of bloodletting dates back more than two thousand years and remained popular until the late 1800s. Some historians believe its origins were tied to female menstruation, which was thought to be the body's way of purging bad "humors," or maladies, from the blood. Bloodletting was used to treat a wide variety of conditions, from the common cold to cancer to, ironically, blood loss as the result of a wound.

"We'll have to breathe a vein," said Crowley, reaching for his lancet.[4] Viccars knew the drill and rolled up his right sleeve as Crowley brought a white measuring bowl over and sat beside him. Crowley tied off Viccars's arm with a tourniquet, then, holding the lancet's blade between his thumb and forefinger, carefully dragged the pointed blade down the length of a protruding vein. The blood began to pour forth immediately, and Crowley turned the arm over so that it flowed directly into the white bowl. Some physicians liked to bleed their patients to the point of fainting, but Crowley took a more scientific approach. He took the patient's height and weight into consideration, for one. He also considered what kind of ailment he was bleeding them for. For a man of Viccars's size, with a fever, he would remove about four gills[5] of blood every four hours until he saw an improvement. If he didn't see any improvement, he might supplement the treatment by inducing vomiting or urination to further cleanse the body of poisons.

It would have been another routine bloodletting, had Viccars not asked:

"How much new blood doth the body produce in, say, a day's time?"

---

4. A folding straight razor with protruding points (or "teeth") along the blade, used to open veins.
5. About twenty ounces, or 590 milliliters.

"More than enough to replenish that which I take now, I assure you."

"It excites the mind," said Viccars, the blood flowing from his arm, "to think that, were a man bled slowly enough, and he be otherwise in good health, that he could bleed forever."

Crowley nearly spilled the bowl resting on his lap. *Could it be that simple?* After years—*decades*—spent treating patients, opening their veins, stealing sips of their lukewarm blood, how had it never occurred to him? *Bleed a man until he loses consciousness. Then feed on him in intervals, draining him near the point of death, but not too close. No, let him recover. Let his body make more blood. Keep him warm and fed until he's near the point of waking. Then feed again. Keep him balanced atop the fence that divides the living world from the dead.*

"Yes," said Crowley, looking at the blood coming in rivulets from Viccars's arm. "I suppose . . . if one could devise a way of bleeding a man more slowly than his blood replenished itself."

It was just a seed of an idea. A single cell, you could say. But it divided quickly, growing in Crowley's mind until he could think of little else.

Ananias Dare was fighting for his life, the poor soul.

"I'm sorry," said Crowley to Dare's wife, Eleanor. "But there is little we can do but wait and beg God for His divine mercies."

Eleanor Dare sat by her unconscious husband's side, the infant Virginia on her lap. In addition to her shock of wavy red hair, the little girl possessed, as was written at the time, a fair complexion and "angelic features." She passed the time by playing with one of Crowley's tools, a pestle for grinding herbs—far too young to understand the severity of the situation.

"I believe the disease a native one," Crowley said. "I must admit—and it shames me to do so—that it is beyond my skill."

"You're a good man," said Eleanor. "God will grant you the wisdom to help my husband. I know it."

No, he won't, madam. I'm afraid the devil's beaten Him to it.

It had been a dreadful six months for the colony. In all, twenty-two of them—sixteen men, four women, and two children, ages thirteen and nine—had succumbed to the strange illness. Crowley's little ruse had proved trickier than he'd anticipated. Keeping men alive for weeks on end, slowly draining and sucking their blood, was harder than it sounded. For one, the wounds had to be small enough to remain hidden, lest any of the colonists ask where they came from. Then there was infection—an inevitable result of opening and reopening the same wounds over and over. And once an infection took hold, they were as good as dead, whether Crowley liked it or not.

Then there was the constant supervision. The worry that the patient might suddenly bolt awake and run screaming and bleeding into the night. Dealing with the ever-present relatives sobbing and praying by the bedside. Having to forcefully but politely usher them out so he could feed. The stress of it all nearly drove Crowley mad.

Such a chore, this killing. Such a chore.

No, it was better they die in the end. Easier for all involved. Crowley refined his method, "treating" each of his patients for a week or so, gradually weakening them, until—always in the dead of night, when no one was around—he drained them until their hearts gave out. The news was broken, a few tears shed, and then the bodies were covered and carried out into the woods. Buried with little fuss, as was the puritanical way. Crowley hadn't felt so strong, so *full*, in a long time. He'd considered pulling back, yes. There were only so many colonists to go around. But the ships would arrive from England any day now, doubling or tripling the size of the colony overnight. No, he would keep on feasting until the reinforcements came.

But they didn't come.

Weeks passed with no sails on the horizon. The colonists grew restless, wondering if, perhaps, some terrible fate had befallen their governor on his way back to England. Or on his return journey. Even wondering if the queen had undergone a change of heart and decided to let them rot on the other side of the world. Wondering when the "strange illness" would strike next and whether it would be their turn. Crowley had seen this sort of quiet panic before. He'd seen it as a young vampire during the Black Death, when all of Europe was gripped in fear. Patients vomiting blood on their deathbeds, just days after showing no symptoms at all. The tips of their fingers black and falling off. Tumors the size of eggs on their armpits and necks, oozing pus.

Ananias Dare had come to him complaining of an upset stomach. Crowley had prescribed a mixture of the usual herbs, telling Ananias to steep them in hot water and drink the resulting tea three times daily. But by nightfall the same day, Ananias had grown violently ill. So ill that two men had to carry him to Crowley's structure. The grim-faced doctor had examined poor Ananias Dare and, with a heavy heart, shared his diagnosis with Eleanor and a few of the colony's remaining elders: it was the strange illness that had befallen the others. He left out the bit about how he'd mixed a trace amount of hemlock in with the other herbs he'd prescribed.

He'd been bleeding Ananias out for three days and nights, carefully, slowly, as he had with the others. A plague had befallen the poor people of Fort Raleigh, God bless and keep them. And though he struggled mightily to diagnose and treat this strange plague, Dr. Crowley had been unsuccessful. Unlike his fellow colonists, who were crammed into outbuildings three and four families apiece, Crowley had a structure all to himself, in which he both worked and slept. One of the many advantages to being a physician, and a very necessary part of being a vampire.

Like the other worried spouses before her, Eleanor Dare sat diligently beside her unconscious husband, praying for his recovery. Crowley had gently urged her, as he had the spouses before her, to return home and get some sleep when night fell. "No use in the both of you falling ill, dear," he'd said. "Tend to your precious little one," he'd said.

But Eleanor hadn't been able to sleep tonight. Not with her poor Ananias fighting for his life within shouting distance. *What if he's already passed? What if he's in heaven, flying with the angels, and the good doctor is sparing me the sad news till morning?* So she'd risen, lifted her sleeping Virginia in her arms, covering her with a blanket, and walked through the cold toward Crowley's structure, resigned to spend the rest of the night in silent prayer, her daughter in her arms.

But when she'd crossed the threshold, every part of her had gone as cold as if she'd been stripped bare and left to the frozen night. There was the good doctor, his mouth affixed to Ananias's neck. Only it *wasn't* the doctor, but some beast wearing the doctor's clothes— a beast with fangs planted firmly in her husband's skin, locked on with primal force, the way an ant's jaws remain locked on, even after you pull the rest of its body away and sever its head.

"My God...," she'd whispered, without thinking.

Crowley withdrew his fangs and saw Eleanor in the

doorway, Virginia asleep in her arms. His eyes were as black as those of the shark she'd watched a sailor pull aboard at Bermuda. Eleanor knew she was looking into the eyes of the devil himself.

"Eleanor..."

Crowley walked away from the bed and its lantern and into darkness. When he crossed into the light of another lantern, his features were perfectly normal again.

"Eleanor, I wasn't expecting you at this hour. You look troubled, dear. Is everything all right?"

"You...you were—your face was..."

"Was what, dear?"

She didn't answer.

"There, there," he said, putting a hand on her shoulder. "Look at you. You've driven yourself to fits with worry. Precisely why I urged you to rest."

Eleanor supposed he was right. *What a silly thing to imagine,* she told herself. *A doctor, biting a man's neck.* She shuffled Virginia in her arms, instinctively pulling her closer to her chest, without realizing she'd even done so. *A trick of the light—that's all it was.* She might have gone on believing this, and things might have turned out differently for the Roanoke Colony, had Eleanor not noticed the blood on the front of Crowley's shirt—directly below his chin.

Crowley saw her eyes dart down to his shirt and knew the game was over. Their eyes met again, and they held there a moment, each waiting for the other to make the first move.

"Of course you're right, sir," said Eleanor. "I... I've driven myself to fits. Best I go and get some sleep."

She pulled away, but Crowley's hand shot out and grabbed her arm.

"If only," began Crowley, "you had listened when I gave you that very advice not two hours ago."

"Please," said Eleanor. "Let me go."

"Whose care, madam?"

"What?"

"Whose care shall I place your precious daughter in?"

"Let *go*!"

"Someday, when she comes of age, perhaps I shall tell her of her mother... and what a dangerous thing it is to go wandering in the dark..."

Crowley took his vampire form—the whites of his eyes disappearing behind a black cloud; his hollow, off-white fangs punching through holes in his gums like they were spring-loaded. Claws doing the same atop each of his fingernails—each one bone hard and razor sharp. All of this in the time it took Eleanor to take in a single, sharp breath.

Eleanor screamed. Crowley cut her throat with a single stroke of his claws, nearly severing her head. All at once the blood ran out of her head and down the front of her dress, and she collapsed, already flying with the angels before her body even came to rest. Crowley snatched baby Virginia from her arms as she fell, saving her from a ghastly knock. The noise of her mother's scream had woken her, and her sharp cries filled the night, her breath visible against the crisp winter air.

The men will come now, thought Crowley.

No bother. *It was an Indian,* he thought. Who would possibly doubt it? Yes, he would simply tell them that Eleanor had come to check on her husband, and while visiting, they'd seen a savage sneaking about the fort outside. Eleanor had gone to investigate, and the savage had cut her ear to ear before running off. *Yes, they'll believe that. Why wouldn't they?*

He could hear them rustling. He could even hear them whispering to one another: "Sounded like it came from—" "Savages! Keep the children qui—" "—woman's voice, I'm certain."

The men came—four of them at first, swords and crossbows in hand. They found Dr. Crowley outside his structure, little Virginia in his arms, and a grim expression on his pockmarked face. What appeared to be Eleanor Dare was slumped on the threshold behind him, a pool of blood spreading quickly as her heart beat its last.

"Savages," said Crowley. "Wake the others at once."

But the men didn't move. They just stood there, staring at him. Crowley found this odd, to say the least.

"What the devil are you lot staring at? We've been attacked! Wake the others at once!"

Only now did Crowley hear the arrhythmic

footsteps on the threshold behind him. He turned and at once realized that the men hadn't been looking at *him*.

They'd been looking at Ananias Dare.

Somehow, despite being drained of his blood for three days and three nights, poor Ananias had risen from his deathbed, blood still running from the twin bite marks in his neck. As pale as a ghost. He was unable to speak, but he staggered forward, reaching out for his crying baby girl with one hand...and pointing at Crowley with the other. The other men understood.

"Put the child down!" the biggest of the men yelled.

"Listen here," said Crowley, turning back to them, "I don't know what lunacy this is, but if you don't wake the others, we'll all be—"

The big man raised his sword and started forward. "I said put the baby down, or I'll run you through!"

Crowley had to laugh. It had seemed like such a good plan. Now he would have to kill them. *All* of them. What then? Crowley supposed he would wait for the ships to arrive. What story would he tell them? It didn't matter. There was time to sort all of that out. Right now, he had to put an end to this madness.

His vampire form exploded across his face. The men recoiled, the way Crowley had seen a thousand brave men recoil the moment they'd realized they'd followed their puffed-up chests into a butcher's shop. He flashed his fangs, sending them staggering backward, then—with the crying Virginia still tucked under one arm—turned around and whipped a clawed hand across Ananias's face, taking most of the skin and muscle off, leaving a fairly clean cross section of the human head, which, as a doctor, Crowley found rather interesting.

Seeing this, two of the big, brave men turned and ran. The other two stood their ground, paralyzed by fear. Crowley set Virginia on the ground just outside his door, making sure she remained covered by the blanket her dear mother had wrapped her in. Crowley suspected that he would need both of his hands for the next few minutes. He began with the two men nearest him, advancing on them almost too quickly for their eyes to perceive, and killing them—one by driving a fist into his eye socket, caving half of his face in and driving fragments of skull into his brain; the other by wrapping an arm around his neck and pulling upward until his head separated from his body, popping off and taking a small section of spinal cord with it. Crowley held the head aloft by its hair, studying it as the blood ran out, the eyes still darting around. With the spine hanging out, it reminded Crowley of a fish on a plate, the body picked clean but the head intact, the eyes staring blankly back at you. Crowley let some of the blood drip into his mouth, then dropped the head on the ground, wound up, and gave it a swift kick, sending it over the wall of the fort and into the dark woods.

Such a chore, such a chore...

And now the calamity. The colonists rising and hurriedly dressing. Men telling their women to stay as they answered the cries of alarm with their pistols and their puffed-up chests—each of them going bravely, valiantly to their graves.

Run, Thomas. Run away, and start anew, as you have so many times before. There's no point in killing all of them.

But there *was* a point, and Crowley knew it. His secret was out. If he let any of them live, even a handful of them, they would wait for the ships to arrive, and when they did, they would scurry aboard like rats off a sinking continent and sail back to England with tales of monsters on their tongues. "Thomas Crowley! Yes, the doctor! Fangs in his mouth! Eyes black as soot!" And Crowley couldn't have that. The older vampires would frown upon it. "Clumsy," they would call him. No...he'd killed some of them. Now he'd have to kill all of them. Kill all of them and then figure out his next move. It was settled.

Jack Barrington—*sound as a pound, that one; never once came to me with any complaints*—charged at him with a sword, which Crowley promptly snatched away and swung at him with more force and speed than any human being had ever swung a sword. The blade cut Barrington from hip to hip—a loud *crack!* as it shattered plates of bone, tearing him clean in half. The upper Barrington landed on his back, still quite alive. He cried out like a child—"Oh! Oh! Oh!"—and propped himself up with his hands to get a better look at the entrails spilling out of him.

And here was young Mr. Sturges, having just witnessed sound Mr. Barrington's unfortunate end, and in plain view of the various heads and torsos that now orbited the monstrous Crowley. He stood his ground. He did not charge (*wise*). His hands did not shake (*commendable*). He leveled his pistol and fired it, and the ball found its mark in the center of Crowley's chest. This, of course, had no effect whatsoever, but Crowley noted that young Sturges *was* the only man to approach the situation with a degree of caution, and the only with sense enough to keep his distance. Crowley had always liked the Sturges boy. He'd liked both of them—he and that wife of his, Edeva. *And she's with child, too, God bless her.* What a shame, all around.

Henry was surprised to see his target unaffected by the bullet in his chest, yes. But rather than stand there like an idiot and load his pistol, he did the sensible thing. He ran away.

Crowley could hear the Sturges boy and his young wife rustling in the dark, distant woods. Every footfall. Every snapping twig. He could hear their labored breaths as they ran harder than they had in their lives. *They're running for the coast,* Crowley thought. *They don't know why. They're just going on instinct, the poor dears, God bless them and keep them. They think that if they can just make it to the coast, Providence will deliver them.*

Crowley gained on them as easily as a sure-footed man gains on a wobbling toddler. So easily that, for a moment, he lost track of their footsteps, until he realized that he'd passed them entirely. *All the better.* He waited as their footfalls and breaths grew nearer. Waited until he could see them in the dark, running hand in hand, the girl trying to keep pace, the boy dragging her along. Crowley kept his eyes trained on them, shuffling himself quietly into their path and taking a position behind a tree.

Henry never saw it coming. One moment, he was running full speed. The next, he was on his back, his head swimming with stars like the sky above. Crowley had sprung from hiding as they passed and swung an arm at Henry's throat. But his aim was slightly off, and rather than sever Henry's head as he'd intended, Crowley had merely crushed his windpipe and knocked him onto his back. Crowley remedied his mistake by balling a fist and punching Henry in the center of his chest, breaking his sternum and collapsing one of his lungs.

With Henry convulsing on the ground, gasping for air, Crowley turned his attention to Edeva. She'd also lost her footing but managed to get her hands in front of her, tearing up the flesh on her palms but protecting her belly. He walked calmly toward her and grabbed her by the ankles. She kicked and dug her fingernails into the dirt—"No! No, please!"—trying to free herself as Crowley dragged her over the dead leaves and frozen ground. He stopped, spread his feet slightly, hunched his shoulders a bit, then spun 180 degrees, like an ancient Greek discus thrower, lifting Edeva off the ground by her ankles and swinging her torso into a tree trunk, the way a woodsman might swing an ax.

The muffled sound of bones breaking inside a bag of skin. Not the dramatic cracking sound Crowley had expected, but a dull, anticlimactic *thump*, like a bag of grain tossed off the deck of a ship and onto the docks. He let Edeva fall to the ground, slivers of bark embedded in her face. Blood pouring from her broken nose and running from the corners of her mouth— just moments ago home to a set of perfect teeth, most of which were now broken or missing. The force of the blow had knocked her out cold—*merciful God be thanked*—but she was beginning to come around again. Beginning to moan, as the nerves began to wake up and relay the bad news to her brain. Crowley couldn't stand to see her suffer. *A woman in her condition.* He grabbed her ankles and swung her again, her face pointed away from the tree. There was a sharper sound as she hit the trunk this time. A cracking sound.

So many, nearly *all* of the images from my living years are gone. The faces, the moments of those first twenty-five years. The sickness of vampirism changes our bodies down to the molecule, to the neuron. It installs a new operating system and reboots us, erasing all but the most essential lines of code from our previous versions. But *her* face, Edeva's face...I *forced* myself to remember it. I accessed it from the first day I was made a vampire and every day after. I clung to it as if I was clinging to that last part of me that was human. In a way, I guess I was. But her voice...[A long pause]...Her voice is gone. Sometimes—even today, I'll hear a piece of music, a woman singing, and I'll think of her. I'll wonder if that was what she sounded like. But I don't remember. [Another pause.] Jesus...

This time there was no moaning when she fell to the ground. *There we are...second one broke her back, God bless her.*

The end would come soon for mother and child. And for the Sturges boy, too. He was on his back beside his wife, thick, bright-red blood foaming from his mouth. *Let them die together, as a family,* thought Crowley. *Afford them that small dignity.* Besides, there were dozens of men, women, and children yet to kill, and time was short. With the unpleasantness behind him, Crowley ran back toward the fort, leaving Henry and Edeva to die in each other's arms.

Such a chore.

Funny thing was, the killing had been the easy part. It had been the digging that had worn the good doctor out. Each body had to be dragged hundreds of yards from the fort, lest any of the future settlers stumble upon an assortment of human bones while digging a new well or tilling a garden. There were more than a hundred dead, in all. Crowley figured the trench would have to be just under six feet wide to make room for the tallest of the colonists, and no less than four feet deep to ensure that a rainstorm didn't reveal his secret. If he buried them on their sides, he could probably get away with making the trench seventy feet long. Still, that meant excavating nearly seventeen hundred cubic feet of earth, dragging more than a hundred corpses into the resulting ditch, and covering it all over again. All with nothing more than a spade and his own two hands.

Daylight had broken by the time Crowley finished the dragging and digging. The arranging and covering over would have to wait. It had been a long night, and he was eager to sleep awhile before resuming his work. Before he returned to his bed, there were two more bodies to pick up. The ones he'd killed the farthest from the settlement, almost in sight of the coast.

Crowley retraced his steps to where he'd left Henry and Edeva. The smell of death led him in the general direction, and when he was close enough, a tiny hummingbird heartbeat took him the rest of the way. A faint heartbeat, still there in its mother's cold belly. *You're a strong one,* thought Crowley as he neared the site. *God bless you. Go now…go to your rest, little angel.* There was the tree he'd hidden behind as they'd approached. There was Edeva's body, frozen and quiet.

But Henry was gone.

Crowley followed a trail of red droplets all the way back to the fort. There he found Henry—broken and barely standing, able to lift only one of his arms—leaning awkwardly against a tree, using a knife to carve something into its bark:

"CRO—"

Now, that's a clever boy. He was trying to identify his murderer with what little time he had left.[6] Crowley was amazed. You had to hand it to him. *He's a tough one. Brave.*

"You look a mess."

Henry spun around, startled by the voice behind him. Even now, with his body shattered, he held the knife out and came at Crowley, staggering forward, on the verge of toppling over with each step. Crowley might've laughed at the pathetic sight, had it not been for the hatred in Henry's eyes. The determination. *Yes, there's a killer in you, boy. I see it plainly upon your face. Oh, the joy of cultivating a killer. Raising him up like a son, teaching him the beauty, the artistry of it.*

---

6. Historians have long assumed the "CRO" found carved into a tree at the Roanoke site was short for "Croatan," the Indian tribe with which the colonists had established contact upon their arrival, taking it to mean that the Lost Colony of Roanoke was either attacked and destroyed by the Croatan or, faced with starvation, decided to join them.

Once again, the cell of an idea began to divide in Crowley's mind:

The others had panicked at the sight of him. Their hands shaking as he glared with his black marble eyes and hissed at them with those hollow razors. But Henry's aim had been true. Yes, he'd killed the boy's pregnant wife, and Henry would doubtless hold a grudge against him for that, but it would pass, as all things pass. Once Henry realized what a gift he'd been given, it would pass. No, he would spare the boy. Turn him. Teach him.

And poor Virginia. How could he feed on her? This poor, orphaned child whose birth he'd attended with his own hands? The first English soul born in the New World?

No, it would be too cruel. More than cruel—it would be *treasonous*. Crowley would take her. Yes, he would take the child, too. He would look after her. Care for her. And when she was old enough to bleed, he would lay with her.

She would be his companion.

His lover.

Like all vampires before him, Henry was suffering through the worst, and last, sickness of his life.

I dreamt of metal. Using tongs to hold a raw bar of iron in a forge, rolling it evenly in the flame until it began to glow red. Taking it out of the flame and placing it on the anvil. Bringing my hammer down hard—again, again, again—gradually flattening it out...taking it from a raw, useless piece of scrap, and turning it into something sharp and beautiful. A weapon. Heating it, cooling it, striking it into the perfect shape; the perfect balance. Sharpening it so that it would draw blood if a man merely tapped the pad of his finger against the blade. Polishing it until it shone brightly.

He drifted in and out of consciousness, his nightmares indistinguishable from reality. There were periods of movement. The moonlit forest floor passing below as he (*flew?*) was carried over a (*monster's?*) man's shoulder. There were periods of rest and darkness. The cries of a child in the faraway nothing. There were lullabies that made Henry yearn for home. Yearn for his mother to cradle him and dry his brow and tell him it had all been a dream. Tell him that he was still in good old Putney, still just a lowborn boy with limited prospects. He became other people, the way you can only in a dream. Saw the world through their eyes.

Suddenly he was his mother, mourning the death of her stillborn sons and her baby girl. *And now, on top of all my sorrow, my only son leaves me and runs off to the New World. Why, Henry? Why have you done this to your poor mother?* He was his father, ferrying passengers across the Thames, resigned to his meager lot in life. He was Charon, ferrying the damned across the Styx, in the hopeless and eternal darkness of hell. He was the simple boy with wild eyes, drawing blood with his teeth. Lashing out. He was Edeva, dying on the ground. He was the unborn child in his wife's belly, shrouded in darkness...the faint, muffled vibrations of the great unknown growing ever fainter as the great nothingness came to reclaim it.

Henry would never know if the child had been a boy or a girl. He would never see its face or hold it or sing it a lullaby. He wondered—and hated himself for wondering—how long it had lived inside its mother's belly after she'd died. A minute? An hour? Was it still alive, even now, its tiny heart struggling to beat? *Why did I drag her away? Why did I drag her from the safety and comfort of home to come here? She was reluctant, I could tell. She was afraid, but I urged her on. I told her it would be better for both of us.*

His heart and his hope were gone. Edeva's was just another face flittering away from his grasp, as the darkness closed in around him and his mind was twisted into something else. His DNA forming new chromosomes inside his cells, those cells dividing and carrying out their new instructions—making calcium harden into new shapes in his mouth; making muscle fibers grow in new places and in new configurations. Making his bones grow denser; changing the physical characteristics of his inner eyes, his rods and cones and receptors hundreds of times more sensitive; and reconfiguring his *neurons* to handle his new heightened senses. Perhaps, even, to communicate without any of them.

Three days had passed since the massacre. It was dark. Virginia had finally fallen asleep, and Henry had finally woken up. Crowley watched the new vampire—*his* vampire—begin to come around. The length of the transformation varied, but on average, it took three days. After that, the fever broke and the vampire emerged from the fog and into a clarity no living man could comprehend.

It's hard to describe. Imagine you've only ever seen the world through an old black-and-white television set. Eleven inches across, broadcast over the airwaves in two fuzzy dimensions. A slightly buzzy sound farting out of its little speaker. Add to this the fact that you've been nearsighted your whole life but haven't realized it. So not only are you looking at a narrow, noisy image, but it's out of focus. Everything you've ever experienced, every kiss or sunset or adventure, has come through that fuzzy little screen and speaker. To you, it's as beautiful as the world can be. Nothing could ever be more magical or real, because you don't know any better. *That's* what it is to be human.

Now imagine you wake up one day, and someone's replaced that little black-and-white set with a 3-D IMAX screen, eighty feet high; replaced that little speaker with digital surround sound. Imagine experiencing color for the first time. Crystal clarity and three-dimensional sight and sound for the first time. Imagine having your senses expanded beyond what you ever considered possible. The curtains pulled back on a world you never could have imagined in the static of your little black-and-white mind. That's what it is to be a vampire.

Henry was amazed upon awakening, as nearly all vampires are. He staggered out of Crowley's structure and lay on his back in the center of the fort, looking up at the Milky Way through the clean, crisp winter air, which carried distant perfumes of plant and animal life to his nostrils over impossible distances. He reached his hand out to run his fingers through the stars and nebulae above, which seemed so close... so *real*.

It's a birth in every sense. You're an infant in those first moments... taking in light and sound when all you've ever known is darkness and silence. I was overwhelmed by the raw amount of information coming through my senses... that big, crisp, 3-D world, those sounds coming from every direction—the beating of a moth's wings. It was all my brain could handle. It took a while—I'm not sure how long, an hour...two maybe—before I began to remember little things about myself: my name, where I was...what had happened.

Crowley sat in the dark, watching his creation emerge from its cocoon. What a gift he'd given him! How many men, after all, could say that they'd stood at heaven's gates, only to return to earth with the strength of Samson and the longevity of God Himself? Henry sat up and looked at Crowley blankly. *He doesn't remember me,* thought Crowley. *Not yet.*

The anger came, of course. It took a few more hours of Henry wandering around the empty fort, marveling at the detail he could make out in the darkness, staring at his hands in wonder, as if he'd dropped a tab of sixteenth-century acid. Crowley sat on a stool just outside the door of his structure, smoking a pipe under the stars as Virginia slept inside. He saw the memories creep over Henry's face. The little flashes of horror. Images of headless Englishmen and useless pistols. Of running. Of poor Edeva, *God bless her and send her swiftly to the angels.* And finally—*here it comes*—the image of the man responsible for all of it.

"You...," he said.

Henry took his vampire form for the first time, fangs punching through his virgin gums, staining his teeth with the blood that still ran in his veins. He ran at Crowley, intent on tearing off his limbs. But Crowley didn't so much as flinch.

> He just sat there on his stool, smoking that pipe as I came at him. And when I was an arm's length away, up came his leg. He braced his back against the structure and kicked me in the chest, sending me flying backward, sliding across the dirt, and landing in a heap against one of the other buildings.

Henry was still weak from the ordeal of his transformation. His senses still foggy. *He won't know his true strength until he feeds.* No matter. Crowley would weather the anger, and when it subsided, the lessons would begin. The lessons *he* was never fortunate enough to have had, *his* maker having run off as if the whole thing had been a cruel joke. *Surprise! I've made you a bloodthirsty demon; go and sort the rest out yourself!* Crowley had always been quite fond of jokes, but there was nothing funny about that.

"Why?" muttered Henry.

The sun had risen outside. After walking for hours through the bitter night, Crowley had found a small recessed cave—barely more than an overhang—in a line of granite that cut through the frostbitten woods like a giant zipper, holding two halves of the earth together. As the stars had begun to fade, he'd torn branches off the larger trees and uprooted the trunks of smaller ones entirely, arranging them against the rock and then laying a pair of heavy blankets over them to construct a makeshift shelter that kept the light out and the warmth in. The cold didn't bother Crowley or Henry much, but little Virginia was susceptible, so Crowley had made a small fire inside their temporary home. There the three of them sat, lit only by the glow of the flame. Crowley and Henry had given Virginia their coats. She slept on top of one and used the other as a blanket.

> The night after I came around, Crowley had marched us out of the fort to the shore. He loaded us into a canoe and paddled us across the sound to the mainland.[7] From there we marched through the wilderness when it was dark and rested by day, in caves if we were lucky enough to find one, or in makeshift shelters that Crowley constructed. He was taking us inland. Searching for prey.

"Why *what*? Why did I kill everyone? Why did I make you a vampire? Why didn't I just leave you to die? Please, Henry. You're being terribly vague."

---

7. The colonists had made this trip before to visit and trade with the Croatan and other Virginia Algonquin tribes. It's roughly a three-mile trip across the present-day Croatan Sound.

"Virginia…why did you bring her?"

"You're weak, Henry. You must feed."

"I would forfeit my own rather than take the life of an innocent."

"Oh no, you wouldn't. Stop that; you're being absurd."

"I cannot kill as callously as you do."

"Of course you can. You've done it a thousand times."

Henry didn't know what Crowley meant. "I've never killed anyone," he said.

"I take it you're a laborer's son? You'll forgive the assumption; it's simply—you don't strike me as an educated man. Bright, certainly. Bright, yes, but not learned. Certainly not a yeoman or a gentleman. Your father had a trade, probably owned a muddy little parcel, is that it?"

Henry didn't respond.

"Tell me, Henry Sturges, he of the labor class, he of the poor rabble—how many chickens' necks have you broken with your bare hands? How many rabbits have you skinned without a second thought? Dozens? *Hundreds?* And did you weep for them? And on those blessed occasions when there was meat at your table, did you weep as you tore the warm flesh of cattle or goat between your teeth? As you bit into the strands of muscle, letting those juices— the juices of salty, roasted blood—run down your throat?"

Again, Henry said nothing.

"You fed," said Crowley, "because it was in your nature to feed. Because it was your right as granted by the Heavenly Father."

"You *dare* evoke the name of God to excuse what you are?"

" 'But whosoever drinketh of the water that I shall give him, shall never be more athirst: but the water that I shall give him, shall be in him a well of water, springing up into everlasting life.'[8] Have you not drunk the water, Henry? Has it not granted you eternal life? I've laid the gift at your feet. All that remains is the acceptance and the thanks."

"You would have me thank you . . . for making me *this*?"

"Do you think suffering is exclusive to men? To be human is to be *inhumane*, dear boy. When you butcher a pig, does it not shriek? When you wrestle it to the ground and cut its throat, does it not bleed?"

"That's different."

"Ask the pig if it's different."

Henry turned away. *Enough of this.* Why? Why waste his breath talking to this monster?

"Did you have a trade in London?" asked Crowley.

Henry said nothing. He was done talking. Angry with himself for engaging the monster in the first place. *You should be ashamed of yourself,* he thought.

---

8. John 4:14.

Conversing with the man who killed your wife…your unborn child. The monster inside is trying to make you forget. Trying to get ahold of you.

"Oh, come now—*you're* the one who started the conversation. Did you have a trade, or were you just a mud-caked lowborn boy, butchering pigs and breaking necks and cutting into bloody flesh while congratulating yourself for being a saint?"

Henry turned back toward Crowley.

"I was a blacksmith's apprentice."

"Ah…hammering horseshoes and nails, cutting firewood and sweeping floors, while your master sat on his ass." Crowley laughed at the thought of it.

"It's better than cannibalism," said Henry.

"It isn't cannibalism, Henry, because we are no longer human. Tell me, young Apprentice Sturges— did you ever make a sword?"

"Of course."

"Of course. Of *course* you made swords, because that's what blacksmiths' apprentices do. I would wager you made *dozens* of swords, and being a man who takes his labors seriously, I would wager that they were as sharp and true as any sword crafted by English hands. And did you ever wonder, Apprentice Sturges, what *became* of those swords after they left your anvil? Did you ever consider the possibility that your work would be used to butcher men on the fields of battle? To take the heads of women accused of witchcraft?"

Again, Henry said nothing.

"Tell me," said Crowley, "who is the guilty party in this equation? The sword? Its maker?"

"The one who wields it."

Crowley smiled. *Exactly.*

"*We* are the swords, Henry. Shaped by our maker, with but one purpose—to kill men and feed upon their blood. And no less a swordsman than *God* wields us, for if He did not wish us to be, why would He have forged us in the first place?"

"Who says God was the one who forged us?"

"And if it was the devil? What then—have we any less right to exist? You have to *free* yourself, Henry. Free yourself by letting go of those old myths. Those human notions of right and wrong. You are not a man anymore. You are something *more*."

After wandering in the wilderness for days and finding nothing but more wilderness, Henry, who'd been granted eternal life, was growing close to death.

> I refused to feed. It's common for new vampires, especially those who were made against their will, as I was. Not to mention the fact that my maker had just killed my wife and unborn child and virtually every English soul in the New World. I wasn't feeling cooperative.

Night after night, Crowley tried to teach me how to be a vampire. Making me watch as he fed on the blood of animals. Demonstrating how he used his heightened senses of hearing and smell to track them and his speed and strength to chase them down. Wildcats, deer, rodents...they were poor substitutes for human blood, but then, there were no humans to be found. Not yet. For all we knew, ours were the only white faces on the continent.

Virginia sat atop Henry's shoulders, her chin resting on his head, her red hair intertwined with his black hair as they followed Crowley through the dark, untouched wilderness. The job of carrying her had fallen to Henry, simply because Virginia still recoiled at the very *sight* of Thomas Crowley and cried out when he so much as touched her arm or smiled cheerfully at her.

Human evolution has seen to it that children have short memories. Otherwise, we'd all be traumatized for life, when every loud noise or funny face has the power to terrify us. Virginia seemed to get better as the days went on. I was glad to see it, but I was also slightly heartbroken, because she would never remember her mother's or father's face. The love they'd felt for her.

But as the days passed and Henry grew weaker from hunger, carrying her for long periods of time became too difficult.

When I couldn't tend to her anymore, Crowley saw to it that she was kept warm and fed. He sang to her when she cried. The sick fuck *sang* to her. The same creature who'd killed her mother and father—torn them apart as she'd watched, screaming—now sang to quiet her when she cried.

I was starving to death. My strength was leaving me. You have to understand—blood is the only nutrient a vampire's body will accept. You can't put food in our bellies and expect our motors to run. It doesn't work that way, and I knew it, intuitively, even then. But I refused to accept it. I was grieving for myself, and the first stage of grief is denial. I ate berries. I ate the meat of the animals Crowley killed. I ate the bark off of trees and drank water from streams, only to have it all come back up in spectacular, projectile fashion. I was starving, but food and water made me sick.

Crowley kept us marching inland, night after night. I knew what he was doing. What he was looking for. And I knew what he was going to do when he found it. I became obsessed with running away. Running off into the woods; getting away from him.

But Henry couldn't run.

How could I leave her? How could I leave a baby with a monster? And even if we could escape—how would Virginia and I survive? I was too weak to carry her, let alone provide for her. Besides, I knew next to nothing about being a vampire, and while Crowley was a terrible man, he was a willing teacher.

One morning Crowley ventured out into the light, leaving Virginia and me in the dark of our shelter. When he returned to the fort at sunset, he was carrying a native man in his arms. The man was unconscious but breathing. I could hear his breath, hear his heart beating, all the way across the room. I remember the way he brought the body over, laid it in front of me like an offering at an altar. Half of the native's face was caved in. Blood had dried in his eye sockets, so thick that I didn't know whether his eyes were even there anymore, or whether Crowley had ripped them out for some reason, which wouldn't have made any sense. *Why rip the poor man's eyes out? Haven't you done enough to him already?* In a way, I hoped he *had* ripped them out. I couldn't stand the thought of him looking back at me, even in death. Worse, the thought of those eyes suddenly popping open. Looking at me. Begging me not to kill him.

The Henry of the civilized world—the wher-ryman's son, the good boy who loved his simple neighbor—was giving way to Henry the vampire. *The monster.*

I laugh whenever I see it portrayed in movies—how effortless they make it look. Even *romantic.* But really, just for a second, try to imagine bit-ing into human flesh the way you bite into a chicken leg, clamping down on it the way your cavemen ancestors did eons ago. Now imagine that chicken leg thrashing around, trying to pull away, screaming as you hold it still enough to find an artery with your teeth. Imagine holding it there as you suck the blood out of its body. Not in the five seconds it takes on television, *but for the better part of a minute*—longer if you're less experienced.

I tried to fight against it. Tried to keep my eyes from turning, my fangs from falling. But I was weak. Running on instinct, reflexes. Try telling a starving vampire to control himself when there's warm blood on his lips. You'd have as much luck telling a burning man not to scream.

Though there were no tears, Henry cried as he fed. As the blood flowed through his fangs and into his veins, filling him with a warm peace he'd never known, while at the same time filling him with a deep sense of grief. Grief for *himself.* For what might have been. He took the body in his arms as the man's heartbeat slowed; wrapped his arms around it, squeezed it the way a child squeezes a juice box, coaxing out every last delicious drop. The world was revealed in full.

> Suddenly I understood what he'd been talking about. "Freeing yourself" and "to be human is to be inhumane" and all of that. It wasn't that all my grief suddenly fell away or that I suddenly relished the thought of killing people. It wasn't like I forgave Crowley, either. I didn't. I still hated him, and I hated myself for what I was doing. But I *understood.* The possibilities. The advantages. It was that first high. The one that addicts spend the rest of their lives chasing but never catching.

With their veins full of human blood, the vampires took turns carrying Virginia back to the fort at Roanoke.

It had to be tonight.

Henry knew it. He hadn't the slightest idea how he was going to pull it off, but it had to be tonight, while he was still full. While he had the strength and the courage. Before the monster inside strengthened its hold. *Stay with your maker,* the monster would say.

Learn from him. You could do great things together, you two. A whole New World, all to yourselves.

Thinking about it now, it was foolish. Even if I did manage to escape, I had no idea where I was going. There were no other colonies in America. No towns or roads. And even if I managed to keep us alive, who knew when the next ship would come? It might be months. They might never come at all. Plus, Crowley could move in daylight. I couldn't. That meant that for eleven hours a day, from sunrise at seven to sunset at six, I was a sitting duck. Just waiting there in whatever darkness I'd managed to find, waiting for him to come and sniff me out. Follow the trail of bread crumbs I'd probably left without even knowing it.

Crowley was snoring. Henry had been waiting all day, too nervous to sleep. It would be dark soon. Crowley would be getting up from his winter's nap. Henry had been observing him for three weeks now. He had a knack for rising precisely at sunset. But when he slept deeply, snoring away as he did now, he often slept up to an hour longer. Henry's plan was simple: wait until it was dark enough for him to venture outside, scoop Virginia up in his arms, sneak away quietly while Crowley slept, and then run as fast as he could to God knew where. That was it. That was the extent of the plan.

I waited until the light [through the curtains] was almost gone. I watched him awhile longer, making sure he was sound asleep, then rose slowly and crept to where Virginia was sleeping. I scooped her up, blanket and all, thinking *please don't wake up, please don't wake up.* I crept toward the door and I was most of the way out when I heard something moving.

"I would rather you didn't," said Crowley. Henry spun around, startled. Crowley was standing, holding something compact in his right hand, leveled at Henry. He pulled the trigger, and the flint of his wheel-lock tinderbox snapped closed on a piece of steel, creating a small spark, which lit the sliver of dry bark loaded in its pan. Crowley used the resulting flame to light a candle and walked toward Henry, who pulled Virginia close, just as her mother had done in the last moments of her life.

"Think, Henry. Where will you go? How will you care for yourself? For her?"

Henry tried to back away. Crowley grabbed his wrist and held tight.

"Henry...if you do this, you'll force me to hurt you. Please...I'd like for all of us to be agreeable. A family. Come. Set the child down and let us forget this folly."

It happened so fast Henry didn't even feel it. His eyes clouding over in darkness. His fangs descending.

I raised a fist in anger for the first time in my life and struck Crowley in the face with everything I had. The tall son of a bitch flew clear across the structure and hit the other wall, cracking its wooden planks. The candle flew out of his hand and landed on the floor, igniting a small fire that began to climb the wall. The suddenness of it surprised him, I think. The power of it. I know the feel of it surprised *me*. I'd never felt my body move like that before. That quickly. If it had been a living man, my fist would've gone right though his skull.

But Crowley wasn't a living man. By the time he'd found his feet again, he'd also taken his vampire form—his limbs tensing, ready to pounce. Little Virginia was awake in Henry's arms. Screaming. The monster was back. The black-eyed monster with the big teeth who'd hurt her mommy and daddy.

I'd never really been in a fight before that. I'd wrestled with other boys growing up. Maybe shoved and been shoved in return, but never a fight. Never closed fists, let alone fists with razor-sharp claws. It's a strange thing to hit someone with the intent to hurt them. Even stranger when you mean to *kill* them. I'm not sure you're ever quite the same after. I'm not sure you can ever go back.

Faced with the vampire Crowley, Henry once again decided to run. To where, he didn't know. Right now all that mattered was protecting Virginia.

I had a few steps' head start, but Crowley was taller and had a longer gait. And though I was, outwardly, much younger, I learned that a vampire's outward age is irrelevant.

Henry ran as fast as he could, trying to keep the baby steady in his arms. He was fast—as fast as a horse in full gallop, it seemed. But Crowley was faster, and once again, the monster was gaining. Henry approached the wall of the fort, twenty feet high, wooden spikes at its top. He might've taken the leap if he hadn't been carrying Virginia in his arms. What if he didn't clear it? She might be impaled or crushed to death. Henry pulled up at the last second, and Crowley pounced.

He grabbed the baby and tried to pull her away. In that split second, the story of Solomon and the two mothers flashed before my eyes. I had to make a decision: let her go or hold on and risk having Virginia torn in half?

Henry let go. Crowley set Virginia down and attacked—leaping at Henry with his claws extended, gnashing his fangs. Night was falling quickly now, the dark blue of the sky becoming black.

I'd been given the keys to a race car, and I had no idea how to drive it. Crowley, on the other hand, was a master. But it's like I used to say to Abe when he was young: all the technique in the world doesn't amount to anything without passion. Without anger. To Crowley, I was just an obstacle that needed to be dealt with. But me— I was fighting the motherfucker who'd killed the love of my life. My unborn child. My friends. The man who'd left me to die, before he'd decided that death was too merciful.

Yes, thought Crowley. *There's that hatred. That's why I chose you, don't you see? Can you hear me in there, boy? Don't you understand how much I can teach you? How wonderful it can be?*

Crowley's structure was completely engulfed, the flames climbing higher than the fort's outer wall. The two vampires fought in its light, punching and clawing at each other with animal power and savagery, seeming to defy the laws of physics as they leapt across absurd distances. Human beings with the power-to-weight ratios of insects. But Henry was on his heels—up against a bigger, more experienced opponent. And unlike Crowley, Henry was battling *fear.*

I'd seen his vampire face only once before, on the night he killed Edeva. But that had been for only a moment, and at a distance. Now he was right on top of me. This demon, gnashing its teeth at me. Black eyes staring into my black eyes. I'd never been so close to something so terrifying. There were no movies or television shows to prepare me for anything like that face. The closest thing I'd ever seen to it were the gargoyles on Westminster Abbey.

The fire had already jumped from Crowley's structure to a pair of adjoining ones. The fort was built out of timber, crude constructions covered in bark and grass. Fire had been a constant concern among the colonists, and it was easy to see why. If left to burn, the whole fort would be gone in a matter of minutes. But the fire also gave Henry a way to level the playing field.

I knew that if I was going to have any chance, I had to keep him close. Grab on and grapple with him. So I did. I wrapped my arms around his middle and tried to wrestle him to the ground. He dragged his claws across my back, ripping my shirt to shreds and opening deep gashes along my spine, but I held on. He bit a chunk of skin off the back of my neck, but I held on. I held on, and I started pushing him toward his structure. Toward the flames. He started to feel the heat on his back and dug his boots into the dirt—but I kept pushing. Crowley didn't want to die. That was his weakness. Me, I didn't really care whether I lived or died. That was my strength. I was willing to go right into that fire with him.

Virginia was crying on the ground somewhere behind them. It wouldn't be long before the fire spread to where she was. *Live,* thought Henry. *You have to live, or she'll die.* Henry lowered his head, wrapped his arms around Crowley's middle, and surged forward with so much force that for a moment, Crowley's feet were lifted clear off the ground.

We were right up against the wall of [Crowley's] structure. Right on the edge of the flames. The heat was incredible. Enough to singe the hairs on my arms, blister my skin. The hot air whooshing at us, making our hair blow like we were standing in front of a fan. I held him in a bear hug, even as he pounded his fists into my back, trying to get me to let go. But I wasn't going to. Even if I burned with him.

Crowley's clothes caught fire. Feeling the flames lick up his back, he pushed back harder than before. "You'll kill us...both!" he grunted.

He pushed back as hard as he could, grunting, but I pushed harder. The sleeves of my shirt burned away, but I held on. The skin on my arms turned red in the flames. Began to blacken. The pain was incredible, but I was only a passenger in my body at that point. I would've held him there until there was nothing left of my arms but two charred bones. I've seen my share of burning bodies since that night, and I can tell you—the smell is something you never forget. The smell of hair and skin cooking. The smell so thick you can taste it on your tongue. *It's just a meat, like any other,* some people say. But steaks don't have fresh blood pumping through them when you throw them on the grill. The blood—that's the smell you remember. Gets in the back of your throat and chokes you. And the screams. The screams of the burning are unlike any sound I've heard human beings make. Thomas Crowley made that sound just before I let go of him.

It had been Virginia's sharp cries that had brought Henry back to his senses. *Live,* he thought, and let Crowley go. Crowley fell to the dirt, the whole of his upper body engulfed. He rose to his feet, blinded by the flames—*his eyes have probably cooked away*—and staggered off, marching blindly into the wall of fire, screaming the unmistakable screams of the burning.

He would burn, and the fort with him. *Good.* Henry didn't like the fort, anyway. It was full of shadows. And now the good doctor was one of them.

Virginia had finally fallen asleep. Henry cradled her, his back against a large piece of driftwood on the rocky beach. The gashes on his back and the burns on his arms had already healed beneath the long white sleeves of his shirt—the only article he'd bothered to take from the burning fort. The sun had long since dipped below the western wild, making it safe for the young vampire to venture out, though the last of the pale daylight hung stubbornly in the summer sky. He looked down at the sleeping girl in his arms, not yet a year old. Now solely his responsibility.

> I don't know how to describe it. There was a passage in one of [Abraham Lincoln's] journals,[9] something about the first time he held Robert. I don't remember exactly what he said, but it was about that indescribable feeling of being responsible for something so helpless. The knowledge that you would do anything—sacrifice anything, commit any atrocity—to protect it from the slightest harm. I think I fell in love with her. That's really the only way I know how to describe

---

9. From an entry dated August 14th, 1843: "I shall happily trade every ounce of my own happiness for his. My own accomplishments for his. Please, Lord, let no harm come to him. Let no misfortune befall him. If ever you require one to punish, I beg you—let it be me."

it. I mean, have you ever held a sleeping infant in your arms? Looked down at that little being who so desperately needs you, so unconditionally loves you?

It was the near dark that humans have to squint to see in, but to Henry, every crashing wave and grain of sand shone brightly. They'd slept on this beach for three nights. Rather, Virginia had slept while Henry stood guard, the rhythmic sound of the ocean soothing her. Henry hadn't rested more than a few hours in the past week. Finding dark places to stay by day, foraging food and fresh water for Virginia after dark, and standing watch over her when she finally stopped crying out for her mother and fell asleep, exhausted. Each wave pushing one of those smooth black or gray stones up from the ocean depths, a fraction of an inch closer to the shore.

Eternity.

Henry tried not to think about it. There was no telling whether he'd survive the next few days. It was presumptuous to ponder the decades and centuries. Still, sitting there in the dark, with only his thoughts to keep him company, it was hard not to wonder how long his own journey to shore would take, or if he'd ever get there at all. How the currents would shape him. Would he resemble anything of his human self when he arrived?

Someone's approaching.

There was some rustling in the high grass near the beach. Too faint for human ears to pick up. And a scent on the wind. I wasn't sure what it was, but instinct told me that it was alive and that I should be afraid of it.

It's Crowley, thought Henry. *He survived. Somehow, he survived and tracked us here.* Henry was suddenly panicked by the thought. So panicked that he was actually relieved to see that it was a group of four men and not one. Henry stood slowly, taking care not to make any noise as he lifted Virginia in his arms. The quartet approached. They'd already spotted Henry, thanks to his white shirt and the last of the blue dusk.

They were natives. I knew from the way they were dressed, but I didn't know which tribe they belonged to. They could tell from my clothes that I was English—and they probably wondered what the hell I was doing out there on my own, sitting on a beach with a baby. I could've run, and chances are they never would've caught me. But I didn't. The truth is, I think I *wanted* to give myself over to them. I wanted company, even the company of strangers who didn't speak my language. I wanted help.

The natives stopped a good fifty yards down the beach and considered the Englishman. They wore long coats made from dark animal hides, some with fur-lined collars and feathered tassels. Leather boots, laced up to their knees. Each had a different weapon— one carried a bow and a quiver of arrows, one a long wooden staff, and one a decorative war club. The fourth held a large tomahawk, its blade made from stone, the edge sharp enough to shave with.

> They were turning their heads and speaking to one another in whispers. I could hear them clearly, but it didn't matter, since I couldn't understand a word. I'm sure they were deciding what to do—whether to approach me, kill me, or just ignore me and move on.

They decided to approach. Henry stood his ground, pulling the sleeping infant close to his body. The natives stopped, no more than ten feet separating the two sides. Both parties stood there, staring at each other. No words. No sound, other than the ocean lapping against the shore.

> They whispered to one another some more. Again, I had no idea what they were saying, but it was clear that something about me was causing them concern. I noticed them gripping their weapons more tightly. Examining me more closely.

"Re'apoke...," said the one with the tomahawk.

"Re'apoke...," repeated the others, in unison.

"English," said Henry, pointing to himself with his free hand.

I'm not sure what I was hoping to accomplish by that. Surely they already knew I was English, but it was killing me, just standing there, being looked over. One of the natives—the one with the tomahawk—started to come forward, his eyes glued to my face. I turned my body so Virginia was behind me and balled up a fist, as if to say, *That's close enough.* But he kept coming, step by step, looking at me with a sort of fascination.

"Re'apoke...," he whispered, and drew his tomahawk upward to strike. Henry's eyes went black, his fangs descended—he had no control over this, it was simple instinct—and he swung a clawed hand at the native.

I missed him. Not because I was off target, but because he moved out of the way faster than I could strike. And in that dumbfounded moment, as I regained my balance, wondering how in the hell he'd done it—*whoosh!*—I looked down and saw the fletching of an arrow jutting out of my neck.

Henry staggered backward. He laid Virginia on the sand, yanked the arrow from his throat, and charged at the natives, intent on tearing them apart before they could harm the baby. *They have no idea,* he thought. *They think I'm just some lost Englishman that they can kill for sport, but they have no idea how wrong they are.*

Except that the natives seemed to have *every* idea what Henry was capable of and how to protect themselves against it. The four men spread out, forming a square, and kept Henry in the center. When he charged at the native with the decorative club, he was struck from behind with a long staff. When he spun and charged at the long staff, another arrow plunged into his body. He'd never seen men fight with such speed and skill.

I was sure they were vampires. I'd grown up in England, remember, where warriors put on fifty-pound metal suits and rode around on horseback, trying to knock each other over with long poles. But these men—they had an answer for everything I threw at them. Almost like they were toying with me. And the strangest thing was, despite my eyes and fangs and claws, they seemed to fight without fear... *like men who'd faced vampires before.*

I had arrows jutting out of my chest and legs. I'd been clubbed over the head so hard that my skin had split open to the skull. There were gashes in my hands and face from that tomahawk. It started to dawn on me that I was going to lose. If I kept fighting them, I was going to lose, and Virginia would be left to their mercy. The only choice I had—the only choice for *her*—was to surrender. To throw myself at their mercy and fight another day.

Henry knelt on the ground and threw his hands up, the borrowed blood of his first feeding running down his arms from the gashes in his hands. The natives closed in, cautiously, barking orders in a language he didn't speak. But Henry got the message: "Try anything stupid, and we'll finish you."

So concluded Henry's first encounter with vampire hunters.

He and Virginia were taken to a large Indian village[10] at the mouth of a river, arriving just as dawn began to break. Henry had been gagged. The battle club's wooden handle shoved between his teeth, pulled tight behind his head with rope. Another rope had been placed around his neck and tied to the long staff, so

---

10. Werowocomoco (*whero-wo-ko-mo-ko*), a fifty-acre site that served as the political center of the Virginia Algonquins. The village was home to more than a thousand people.

that he could be led at a safe distance. As an extra precaution, his hands had been tied behind his back and
attached to another length of rope, which was held by
a second native. The warrior who'd given up his battle
club as a bit held baby Virginia in his arms. From the
confidence with which he held her, and the subtle,
almost subconscious noises and motions he used to
soothe her, it was clear this wasn't his first time holding an infant. Henry prayed it also meant he wasn't
planning on harming her.

Colonist John White's depiction of an Algonquin village, circa 1585.
Henry and Virginia would have met a similar sight upon their arrival in
Werowocomoco.

Years later, the leader of another English expedition, Captain John Smith, would describe his first meeting with Powhatan, supreme chief of the Algonquin People:

> Their Emperour proudly lying uppon a
> Bedstead a foote high, upon tenne or twelve
> Mattes, richly hung with manie Chaynes of
> great Pearles about his necke, and covered
> with a great Covering of [raccoon skins]. At
> heade sat a woman, at his feete another; on
> each side sitting uppon a Matte upon the
> ground, were raunged his chiefe men on each
> side of the fire, tenne in a ranke, and behinde
> them as many yong women, each a great
> Chaine of white Beades over their shoulders,
> their heades painted in redde: and [he] with such
> a grave and Majesticall countenance, as [drove]
> me into admiration to see such state in a naked
> [savage].

Henry's introduction to the "Algonquin emperor" was similar. On arriving in Werowocomoco, he was led through a hanging animal skin and into the great chief's *yehakin*.[11] Narrow, perhaps twenty feet across,

---

11. A longhouse, usually made with timber frames, lashed together with strips of bark. The frames were then covered in sheets of bark, leaves, and grass. The biggest longhouses could reach more than three hundred feet in length and were typically twenty feet in width.

but incredibly long. *It has to be fifty yards,* Henry thought. *More, perhaps.* He was led past women and children, huddled together on either side of them, some on woven mats or rugs, some on the bare earth. Small fires burned everywhere, the smoke rising toward small holes in the thatched grass roof. At the far end, a man of about fifty sat on a raised platform, a large fire burning in front of him, around which sat only men—some warriors, others wizened elders. A few looked older than any men Henry had ever seen.

Henry was presented. Words he didn't understand were spoken between his captors and one of the elders, who sat near Powhatan. The elder then passed this information to the chief. Henry tried to read their expressions. A translator was summoned. He'd picked up a rudimentary grasp of English from the previous settlers.

"He says you are . . . re'apoke."

There's that word again. It was the same word the four natives had whispered to one another when they'd first seen Henry on the beach.

"I don't know," said Henry. "What is"—he tried his best with the pronunciation—"re'apoke?"

"Devil," said the translator.

"Devil." I had so many questions. How had the four natives fought like that? Why hadn't they been afraid of me? And why did they have a word for what I was?

The chief spoke again.

"He wants to know," said the translator, "are you good re'apoke or bad re'apoke?"

You'd think it would be an easy decision. When someone asks you, "Are you a good devil or a bad devil?," you say "Good," right? But in that instant, while they were waiting for my answer, I thought, *Well, if I say "good," what if they take it as a sign of weakness and decide to kill me? But then again, if I say "bad," they'll probably kill me anyway. Wouldn't a "bad" devil lie and say he was "good"? Who knows what their concept of "good" and "bad" even is?*

"Good," said Henry at last.

The chief understood this without the translator's help. He spoke again.

"He says that he believes you. He says that he sees your heart is good."

How does he "see"? What nonsense is this?

"He offers choice," said the translator.

"What choice?"

"You give yourself or die."

"'Give' myself?"

More words were exchanged between the translator and the chief.

"You fight or die," said the translator.

"Fight who?"

The translator didn't seem to understand this, so Henry turned to the chief and shrugged his shoulders. *Fight who?* This time it was the chief himself who spoke:

"Monacan."

The Algonquins were at war with a small collection of Virginia tribes, the Monacan, that refused to pledge their loyalty to Chief Powhatan. They were more of a nuisance than a real threat—too small in number to have any real chance of overthrowing the chief, but also too small to fight conventionally. They were constantly on the move, attacking Algonquin hunting parties and satellite villages and then retreating into the wild before Powhatan's warriors could track them down and strike en masse.

As it happened, Powhatan had, that very day, received word from his scouts that the Monacan chief was camped with some of his warriors and their families upriver. I suppose he was going to send a war party out. Try to cut the head off the snake that had been biting at his ankles. But here I come, a vampire—a "good devil"—delivered on a silver platter. Here was a way for him to test me and strike a blow at his enemies at the same time.

"He says you go Monacans in the night," said the translator. "He says you kill all the Monacan. If you do this, you and your child will be welcome. If you do not do this, you die."

"No," said Henry.

The translator understood but hesitated to pass along the answer to Powhatan. He didn't have to. The great chief could tell what Henry had said by the look on his translator's face.

"Whoever the Monacan are, I won't kill 'all' of them," said Henry. "Not the women and children."

The translator related this to the great chief, who considered it a moment, then nodded.

"Monto'ac re'apoke," said the chief.

Good devil.

The bit was back in Henry's mouth. His hands were tied behind his back again, and he was being led along by rope. The four natives who'd found him on the beach and captured him now led him upriver through the night.

> Little Virginia was back in Werowocomoco, being held as ransom, essentially. If I failed to do what Powhatan had asked, or if I simply ran away the minute my hands were untied, there was no question what would happen to her.

One of Henry's captors carried a rolled-up calfskin on his back. When the sun began to rise on the first morning of their long march, the natives cut several long branches from the trees and lashed them together, placing Henry beneath them and covering the frame with the calfskin to keep the light off his skin.

> I longed to talk to them. To ask them where they'd learned these things. Where they'd encountered other vampires. But we didn't speak each other's language, and even if we had, I got the feeling that they weren't interested in communicating with me. I was an animal.

They reached the camp[12] on the second night, where a hundred or so Monacans—thirty of whom were able-bodied men—made their homes in teepees instead of longhouses. It was all designed to be picked up and moved at a moment's notice.

Henry's bonds were cut. The bit taken out of his mouth. One of the foursome pointed in the direction of the camp and nodded. *Go. Now. Kill.*

Henry crept out of the trees and into the small clearing where the Monacans had made camp on the river. He saw as clearly as if it had been midday, thanks to a nearly full moon and a clear winter sky. A large fire burned at the center of the camp, around which a number of the men, young and old alike, had gathered to

---

12. Likely Massinacak, on the James River, near present-day Richmond, Virginia.

eat and talk. Most of the women and children looked to be asleep. *Good,* thought Henry. Better to have them out in the open, rather than go stalking from teepee to teepee, killing fathers in front of their sons.

I couldn't decide how to begin. Should I run at them, screaming? Should I make animal noises and lure them into the dark? Should I jump over their heads, land in the middle of their fire, and scare the shit out of them?

In the end, Henry just walked up to the fire and stood there, waiting for someone to notice that their camp had been invaded by a lone Englishman. It didn't take long.

One of them turned, saw me there, and—I swear this is true—did a double take. He started yelling, and in a second they were all on their feet, all the warriors, spitting food out of their mouths and reaching for their weapons. They came at me with bows and axes. But they were nothing like the men on the beach. Whatever experiences or secrets had allowed the Algonquin to fight me so effectively—with grace, without fear—the Monacan didn't possess them. They were brave men, sure. Strong. But they were ordinary men. They'd never faced a monster. I was a giant being attacked by children armed with toys.

I didn't use my claws and teeth at first. Why would I? I'd been a vampire all of two weeks. I was still thinking like a human and still fighting like one—balling up my fists and punching them, kicking them. And down they went, my punches ten times faster and harder than theirs. But I didn't realize the cruelty of what I was doing.

Before long, the ground was covered with dying men. Men with their skulls shattered, their insides hemorrhaging. Moaning and coughing up blood. Henry had broken them, but he hadn't killed them.

By being *human*, I was actually being *inhumane*. My hesitation to embrace my new abilities was causing needless suffering. Once you cross that moral threshold—once you decide to kill a man who hasn't threatened or wronged you—better to do it quickly, or whatever moral high ground you're standing on gets washed away by their blood.

Henry could hear the screams of the women, gathering up their children and running off into the night. He looked down at the five little knives on each of his hands. *Better to do it quickly.*

I often think of the first soldiers to leave the trenches of World War I, lined up in neat rows, expecting a battle like every battle that had come before, only to be slaughtered by the first machine gun. A new miracle of death. That's what I was to those brave men.

I began to cry as I slaughtered them. Dry sobbing[13], the hallmark of a vampire's grief. I suppose it was the guilt of taking the lives, especially those of men who hadn't wronged me. The fact that they'd met such an unfair, inglorious death. But mostly, it was the fact that the last of me was dying with them.

I crushed skulls like overripe fruit. I tore jugulars from screaming throats. I ripped open rib cages like rusty-hinged doors. Limbs, torn from their sockets. Flesh, ripped away like paper. Bones, snapped like sticks. Once or twice I slipped in the outpouring of entrails.

You ask me when I became a vampire. I'm not sure. Was it the day I drank Crowley's blood? Was it three days after that, when my fever broke and I saw the world through my new eyes for the first time? Part of me will always think it was that night. The night I first took human lives with my own hands. The night I first embraced what I'd become.

The hunting party returned to Werowocomoco before sunrise, Henry's face and clothes still caked in

---

13. Though they do cry, vampires are incapable of producing tears.

blood. His eyes in their human form, but wild. He walked the length of the great chief's *yehakin*, carrying two dark bundles—one in each hand. Powhatan's warriors stood and blocked Henry's path with their weapons. *That's close enough.* The chief spoke, and the warriors parted to let him pass. None of them taking their eyes off Henry, lest the *re'apoke* try anything stupid.

Henry approached the raised platform and laid the bundles at Powhatan's feet.

They were the scalps of thirty men.

The chief considered the tribute, then repeated: "Monto'ac re'apoke..."

"Dear boy...you haven't aged a day," said Thomas Crowley.

Henry could hardly move. The shock of seeing his maker, alive, all these centuries later had rendered him speechless and paralyzed. It was exactly the reaction Crowley had been hoping for. Oh, it'd been no small feat, killing all those women in such a ghastly fashion, leaving little clues for his dear old friend, but this moment—seeing Henry standing there in the doorway, mouth agape, truly shocked and helpless...this moment made all the trouble worth it.

"You...," said Henry.

Crowley laughed. The big, thunderous belly laugh that Henry had heard in his nightmares.

"'You'?" he said. "Is that all you have to say? Oh, but don't tell me you've forgotten my name, now. Granted, it's been what—three hundred years? But Henry, after all we went through together...it would break my tender heart if you'd forgotten."

"I remember your name...and what you did to me."

"What I *did* to you is the only reason you're still here. Imagine the shock, Henry! Imagine the shock of seeing your name on a calling card on a cordwainer's countertop. 'It couldn't be,' I told myself. 'It couldn't *possibly* be the *same* Henry Sturges.' But I had to know, you see. I had to be sure. And imagine, dear boy, the shock upon seeing you walk out of No. 2 Chester Square. The miracle of it. The same man, still going by the same name."

"But you've changed *your* name, haven't you?"

"Changed my name? I don't follow."

"Grander...it's you, isn't it?"

Crowley's eyes narrowed, then widened with delight. "You think *I'm* Grander?" Another booming belly laugh. "Oh, delightful! Oh, that is absolutely delightful, Henry!"

"But you *are* the Ripper. This game, this *ruse*, is how you planned on getting back at me?"

Crowley laughed again.

"Get back at you? Henry, if I'd meant you harm, I would have harmed you. I was merely having a bit of fun; that's all."

"You call sending a whole city into panic 'fun'? Tearing four women apart 'fun'?"

"Five women. They haven't found the last one yet. And yes, I do consider it fun. Have you lost your sense of humor? Good Lord, Henry, they're just humans."

"So were we, once."

"Oh, don't tell me you're one of *those*."

Crowley hunched his shoulders. The air let out of his balloon.

"I must admit," he continued, "this is not going at all how I'd hoped. Aren't you the least bit happy to see me? Aren't you going to ask how I've been? How I managed to survive after you tried to burn me alive and abandoned me on that savage continent?"

"No."

"Good heavens, the anger! I can hardly breathe through it, Henry! I thought you might have gained a bit of perspective by now. I thought we might sit down and share a laugh. Catch up on three centuries of stories. Of travels, philosophy, music. I thought both of us might benefit from having a kindred spirit in London."

"Share a laugh? With you? Are you mad? You killed my wife and child! You condemned me to walk the earth as a monster! If I should live to see *time itself* run off the end of the tracks, I shall never forgive you for what you did!"

"I gave you everlasting life, dear boy. I liberated you from weakness and sickness and death! And I daresay, if anyone should be angry, it's *me*! I kept you sheltered and safe. I fed you, cared for you. And in return, you betrayed me. Burned me alive! Left me for dead and ran off with our dear child."

"A child whose parents you murdered."

"What choice did I have? I'd been discovered."

"You didn't have to kill them, Crowley. You didn't have to slaughter dozens of women and children."

"I spared you, didn't I? And little Virginia?"

Crowley's eyes lit up at the mention of her name.

"Whatever became of our dear child?" he asked. "God bless her and keep her...Please, if nothing else, I must know that. I can't tell you how often I've found my thoughts drifting to that angelic face. Those red ringlets. Oh, that dear child. There are stories[14]— you've heard them, no doubt—stories of her living in the wild, bedding down with Indians. Nonsense, of course, but they do serve to stir the imagination. I *must* know. Surely you understand how curious I've been. How long did you manage to keep her alive? And yourself! How on earth did you ever manage to keep yourself alive? Tell me...I promise I won't think any less of you, but tell me, did you feed on her?"

---

14. By 1888, there had been at least one popular novel pondering the fate of Virginia Dare: Cornelia Tuthill's *Virginia Dare, or A Colony of Roanoke*, in which Virginia survives the Lost Colony and marries a member of the Jamestown Colony. In 1892, author E.A.B. Shackleford published *Virginia Dare: A Romance of the Sixteenth Century*, in which the titular Virginia befriends Pocahontas.

"I would've starved before I laid a hand on her."

"Indeed, noble Henry, indeed. But surely she didn't grow old. Surely hunger or sickness took her quickly. Tell me, did you weep as you dug a little hole in the earth for her?"

I could feel Crowley poking around in my thoughts, searching for a clue, a memory. I tried to keep my mind empty, but he was as skilled a reader as any vampire I've known, and try as I might, I couldn't keep the images from playing back. Flashes of Virginia as a baby, a little girl...

"She lived," said Crowley, "and you loved her, as a father loves a daughter."

"Enough..."

There was ten-year-old Virginia, skin and bones and knobby knees, topped with red hair that fell in curls to the middle of her back...playing with her Algonquin brothers and sisters in the perfect and tranquil light of those halcyon days. There was Virginia the teenager, the freckles on her nose fading away, taking long walks by herself—"I need to be alone, you don't understand, just leave me alone, please, Father"—as the winter gave way to spring. There was Virginia the young woman, the awkwardness gone, but a new awkwardness. Both aware of it, both feeling it, a pair of magnets in orbit, attracted one minute, repulsed the next...

"My God...," said Crowley. "You *fucked* her."

"Watch your tongue!"

"Her 'savior'! Her 'knight'! Not even the long-suffering *Saint Henry* could keep his hands off her! Ha!"

"Shut your mouth..."

"The stench draws you in, doesn't it? Even in the youngest of them. That delicious stench, and subtle gestures, oh, I know them well. Tell me, did you wait until she bled? Or did her perfume intoxicate you?"

"You were wrong to play this game," said Henry, reaching a hand into his coat pocket. "You were wrong to bring me here. You've brought about your end."

"You forget, boy...I walked the earth for two centuries before your mother opened her legs and squeezed you out. I *made* you...I hand-fed you your first meal when you were but a helpless infant."

"I'm not so helpless anymore."

Henry drew his hand out of his pocket and struck it against his belt buckle. The tightly bound bundle of matches sparked into a brilliant white phosphorous flame, blinding Crowley's sensitive vampire eyes.

It was a trick I'd learned from Abe, back in his early hunting days, when he came up with the idea for his "martyrs."[15]

---

15. The name Abraham Lincoln gave to his crude, homemade matches. He had studied the work of English chemist John Walker, who had

When the flame died out, Henry was *gone*. Absorbed into the ether like a spirit, in the instant it had taken Crowley's eyes to adjust. Before he had time to turn his head and look for Henry in the shadows, Crowley felt a bolt of pain shoot through the whole right side of his body. He looked down and watched his right arm fall to the carpet, severed just below the shoulder. The blood of a dead whore spilling out of it. He stared at the arm, farther away from him than it had been in nearly five hundred years— *no, that's not right, that can't be*—then turned around. There was Henry, standing in front of the hearth, holding the bent fire poker he'd just swung with all his might.

"Look what you've done," said Crowley.

Henry swung again. This time Crowley was ready—bringing his left arm up to shield himself. The poker left a deep gash where it met Crowley's forearm but didn't go clean though. However, without his right arm there to balance him, Crowley stumbled and fell backward from the force of the blow, landing in a seated position. Henry took the opportunity to strike again—bringing the poker down with both

---

perfected a method of making friction matches (which he called "congreves") by dipping small wooden sticks in a mixture of stibnite, potassium chlorate, gum, and starch. When the sticks dried, Abe bundled them together, twenty at a time, using glue. They were incredibly unstable, sometimes lighting by themselves in his pocket, or not lighting at all when he needed them to.

hands and splitting the top of Crowley's skull clean open.

> I had to use force to pull [the poker] out of his head, and when I did, I could see clear down to the middle of his brain. I panicked—*please, don't let him be dead, not yet.* I kicked myself for doing it too quickly. See, it wasn't enough that Crowley had to die. He had to *suffer*, just like the colonists at Roanoke had suffered. Just like the Whitechapel victims had suffered. And, I suppose, as selfish and dramatic as it sounds, to suffer like *I'd* suffered.

Crowley had fallen backward onto the carpet. He was helpless, but he was still alive. It was good enough for Henry. He dragged Crowley over to the fireplace by his shirt collar, grabbed a fistful of gray hair on the back of his neck, and held his face in the flames of a civilized fireplace, just as he'd once held it in the flames of a doomed colony. Crowley began to scream, though in his condition his "screams" were more like moans. *The moans of an animal in terrible pain, which hasn't the words to express its suffering.* The skin began to slough off Crowley's face, dripping like candle wax onto the iron grate. His body began to thrash, but Henry held on. This time, he wouldn't let go until the screaming stopped.

To be human is to be inhumane.

He lied, of course.

I decided to keep the truth from Doyle and Stoker. Stoker might have known that I was a vampire, but he didn't need to know about Thomas Crowley or Virginia Dare. When we met up at my house later that night, I told both of them that I'd scared off the Ripper, whoever he was, when I'd arrived. I'd knocked on the door, I said, and gotten no answer. But I'd heard a window open around the back of the house, and run around the side just in time to see a tall figure jump over the wall of the back garden. To tell them otherwise would have meant opening myself up to too many questions. Questions of who Crowley was, or how he and I had known each other. Or why he'd singled me out in the first place. We agreed to turn the information over to Scotland Yard and let them investigate the mysterious man with the size-fourteen shoes. I was confident they'd never find him, seeing as I'd hauled a bag of his charred bones and rocks to the river's edge and tossed it in before sunrise.

"Well," said Stoker, rising from his chair at the close of a long evening, "we shall just have to remain diligent and pray that the devil has had his fill."

"Yes," said Henry. "I suppose we shall."

"And I suppose we should be thankful, too," said Stoker. "If it was, in fact, the Ripper's home, and he'd been there to greet you, who knows what might have happened? My God, Henry, rushing headlong into a situation like that by yourself! In retrospect it seems sheer madness!"

"A shame," said Doyle, taking his coat from a rack by the door, "that you weren't able to get a better look at the scoundrel. It might've provided a critical clue as to his identity."

"Indeed," said Henry.

"But," said Doyle, "allow me to second the sentiment of my good friend, in giving thanks that no harm befell you."

Henry showed his appreciation with a slight bow. Doyle grabbed his cane and reached for the door but hesitated.

"Oh, Henry," said Doyle. "One last thing... Why, in all this time, have you never told me that you are a vampire?"

I was paralyzed. Shocked to my core. Stoker tried to fill the vacuum that had been left by Doyle's words. But all he could come up with was—

"Are you mad? 'Vampires'? Good heavens, Doyle, what on earth are you talking about?"

"Oh, come off it, Stoker. You've known it all along. After all, I would expect you to recognize a vampire, having worked closely with one for so long."

Now it was Stoker who was shocked.

"My suspicions began," said Doyle, "when I noticed the two of you sharing a concerned look upon my mentioning a lack of blood at the scene of the Nichols murder. I thought little of it at the time but made note of it."

"But...," said Henry, "how—"

"Elementary, my dear Sturges. You claim to be in the textile business, as advertised on your calling card, yet when I erroneously referred to the fabric found at the scene of Ms. Stride's murder as 'velveted herring-bone,' you made no attempt to correct me, despite the fact that no such fabric exists—something any textile importer would surely know. Now, this in itself was no reason to suspect you of anything other than a tendency toward politeness. But as you had shown no such tendency in any of our *other* interactions, one could assume that you were, in fact, ignorant of the particulars of different fabrics. Hardly believable for a man who makes his living from them. It was therefore reasonable to assume that you wished to keep your *true* profession a secret. Furthermore, you recently hired a butler, a maid, and a coachman—but not a cook. A strange omission for a man who clearly has the means. Again, one might assume that you prefer to take your meals out, yet I have never heard you make mention of doing so, nor voice any opinions, favorable or otherwise, of a single restaurant. And on those occasions when we have dined together at Mr. Stoker's or elsewhere, you have merely made a show of eating—pushing food around your plate, taking small sips of wine and letting the liquid trickle back into your glass. I also noticed that, before shaking hands with others, you make a habit of rubbing your hands quickly together, as if they are in need of warming, even on the hottest of days. You're also in the habit of wearing dark glasses when outdoors, no matter how clouded over the sky. And, if given the choice, you always choose to sit farthest from windows during the day but make no such distinction after dark."

These were illusions I'd practiced and perfected over *hundreds* of years. And he'd picked up on them. All of them. It was remarkable.

"And you took all of that and decided that I was a vampire? Don't you think that's a bit…far-fetched?"

"When you have eliminated the impossible," said Doyle, "whatever remains, however improbable, must be the truth."

He turned for the door but stopped. Turned back.

"Oh, and, Henry—you needn't worry about me sharing this information with another soul. I value your friendship far too much to betray your trust. To say nothing of my own life. Besides . . . you've given me a great deal to write about."

SIX

★ ★ ★

Electric Company

Heaven for climate, Hell for company.

—*Mark Twain*

Strange, thought Adam. *I wasn't expecting any callers.*

Though "Union Headquarters" was its official name (a rather uninspired one, Adam thought, but such was the American way), the building at the south end of Broadway was really little more than a glorified private residence, Adam being its sole permanent occupant. Its king, he liked to think, though he kept such thoughts to himself as they were, again, decidedly un-American. And the grand ballroom on its ground floor was his court. And there he'd been on Friday, November 25th, 1898, reading a newspaper by the light of the fire. News of the terrible rainstorms that had blown their way up the coast earlier in the week, bombarding New England with hurricane-force winds, sinking or destroying half the Massachusetts fishing fleet, and sending a steamship, the SS *Portland*, to the bottom with all 192 souls aboard.

"Terrible, terrible," Adam had muttered to himself as he read the news. Humans had such brief lives as it was, making their untimely ends all the more tragic.

His peace was interrupted by footsteps echoing through the ballroom. Adam looked up from his paper. The hall was dark, save for the light from the fireplace behind him. But with his vampire eyes he could make out the details in the shadows. He saw three hooded figures approach. Two of them were broad-shouldered brutes of men, but the foremost, while tall, had a youthful, almost radiant face. A face that Adam didn't recognize. They were all vampires; he was certain of it. But he'd never met them ... and that frightened him.

"Hello, Adam," said the foremost of them.

"Who are you? How did you get in here?"

The youthful vampire smiled and came forward. "Incredible. It's really you. Forgive me if I seem amused. I admit, you aren't at all what I expected. I'd pictured you ... older."

They mean to kill me.

"How dare you enter this building."

"You can understand why I would've had this picture in my mind," said the youthful vampire. "The Union itself is such an old institution. A relic, really.

Fitting that you should have a tunnel connecting your little social club to a church, isn't it. A bunch of old priests, clinging to a book of woefully outdated scripture. Preaching the doctrine of brotherhood between vampire and man. It would only stand to reason that such an institution would have a wizened old fool for its figurehead. But then, you *are* an old fool, aren't you, Adam? Under that boyish face of yours, you're nothing but a weak old fool who's ashamed of his race."

"You seem to have me at a disadvantage," said Adam.

"Indeed."

"You know who I am, yet I don't recall ever meeting you before."

"Oh, but we have met, in a sense. I sent you a gift. Well, five gifts, to be precise. And in return, you sent one of your pets to try and hunt me down, *tsk, tsk.*"

Adam suddenly felt as if his body had been plunged into ice water.

"You...," he whispered. "*You're* Grander?"

"You seem surprised. You were expecting a royal, perhaps? A pampered old bastard such as yourself?"

Adam rose. *Enough of this.* He may have been an old fool, but he was still a powerful vampire. And these three would soon regret ever laying eyes upon him.

"Have you gone through all of this trouble to come here and spout insults at me?"

"No. I've come to kill you. But you already knew that from poking around in my head, you naughty old dog."

Adam tried to hide his surprise. He'd always been a skilled reader. So skilled that even other vampires were usually unaware of his presence in their mind. This Grander was more powerful than he'd thought.

"Others have tried," said Adam. "I've scattered their ashes on every continent."

Grander laughed heartily.

"Listen to yourself! You even *speak* like a relic!"

"Do you think," said Adam, undeterred, "that in my seven centuries, I've not met a hundred of you? Those who would kill me for my love of mankind? You needn't ask what became of them, for I'm standing here before you now."

"They didn't have my patience. Or my vision."

"If you're so sure of yourself, then why did you bring them?" Adam indicated the two brutes behind the youthful vampire.

"Because I wanted witnesses. I wanted them to see the end of a weak old age."

"Kill me, and the Union will never rest until they find you. You'll start a war."

"Oh, my dear old man ... I'm counting on it."

Those were the last words Adam Plantagenet ever heard.

Another century was over, and another friend was gone. On November 26th, 1898, Henry had received a telegram in London. It consisted of just a few lines:

```
GA92 8=NEWYORK 442P 26NOV 1898

MR H STURGES NO 2 CHESTER SQ LDN

OUR OLDEST NON-WESTERN FRIEND
ABOVE GONE TOO SOON. REQUEST YOU
HASTEN TO HIS HOUSE TO SHORE UP
FOUNDATION. CABLE REPLY.
```

"Our oldest non-Western friend above." *"Our oldest Union friend,"* Adam Plantagenet. "Gone too soon." *Murdered.* (It was safe to assume he hadn't taken his own life, and he certainly hadn't died of natural causes.) "Hasten to his house." *Get your ass back to Union Headquarters.* "Shore up foundation." *We've been attacked, and we're afraid it might happen again.*

Adam Plantagenet, the oldest vampire in existence as far as anyone knew, was dead. Murdered in the headquarters of the Union, which he'd founded centuries earlier.

It was Grander. I was *sure* of it. No other vampire had the strength or the audacity.

I'd spent nearly ten years searching Europe
for the mysterious "A. Grander VIII." Ten years,
without so much as a glimpse of the man. Always
whispers, but nothing solid. He was vapor.
Rumor. And now he'd killed an old friend.

Henry had attended countless funerals, but this was
the first time he'd ever watched a vampire's coffin lowered into the frozen earth. There were perhaps fifty
mourners in all, not a single one of them human. All
the same, the collars of their winter coats were turned
up, and their shoulders shrugged to ward off the cold.
A steady snow had begun to fall as their procession of
carriages and wagons had wound its way through the
Bronx, to St. Raymond's Cemetery, which would one
day be the final resting place for tens of thousands of
New Yorkers but was then home to only a few lonely
graves. Until recently, the cemetery had been farmland, an eighty-acre swath of flat green to the south of
St. Joseph's School for the Deaf.

It was this school, not the cemetery, that was the
reason for their trek to the Bronx. St. Joseph's had been
Adam Plantagenet's pet cause, and he'd given liberally
to see that its students—most of them orphans, like
him—received the best and kindest care available.

The burial service was so close to the school building that Henry could make out the faces of the
children pressed to the windows, looking on as their

anonymous patron was laid to rest. The world was freshly and perfectly white, the snowflakes falling steadily. Henry marveled at the silence of it. All that snow, millions of tons of frozen water, falling to earth without a sound. He thought of the children in those windows. How even the heaviest rainstorm would sound no different to them than the soft blanketing of a first snowfall.

When Adam's coffin hit bottom and the straps were pulled free, Henry stepped forward and said a few words, as he'd been asked to do:[1]

"Adam Plantagenet may not have been human, but he was a lover of humanity. He believed that vampire and man could coexist, and to that end, he founded our brotherhood. I think it fitting that he goes to his rest in sight of the school he gave so liberally to, and believed so fervently in. A school where those who have been born into unenviable stations, who have been cast out by those who were supposed to love them, as Adam was cast out by *his* loved ones, can find their place, and thrive."

I stayed behind as the other mourners dispersed. I wanted one last moment alone with Adam. I couldn't help feeling that I had failed him, that

---

1. This is one of the few instances where we have the exact words spoken by Henry at the time. The slip of paper had somehow survived the decades. The ink still bears the blotches where flakes of snow landed on the paper as he read.

his death had been partly my doing. If I'd been more committed, more diligent in my search for Grander, he'd still be alive. I approached the lip of grave, mulling over an apology that would come too late.

That's when I saw the man on horseback.

Bundled against the cold, his face obscured by a scarf, the rider was staring straight at me from across the cemetery. We were alone among the gravestones.

I knew at once it was Grander, come to witness the fruits of his dark labor.

Henry sprang into motion as Grander turned his horse and galloped away, speeding out of the cemetery gates with snow crunching under the hooves of his mount.

Henry was fast, but he couldn't outrun a horse—not in the snow, anyway. He sprinted into the street and saw a mounted policeman giving directions. Henry grabbed the man and pulled him from his saddle, hurling him to the street with far more force than he'd intended. He mounted the unfamiliar beast, and the chase was on.

Grander rode west toward the river with Henry hot on his heels. He paid pedestrians no heed, knocking them violently aside as his mount snorted in the frigid air. The icy wind slashed at Henry's bare face, his horse struggling to keep its balance on the wet cobblestones.

I could see the Bronx River up ahead, covered in snow. I wondered whether Grander would turn north toward Van Cortlandt Park or south toward Rikers Island.

He did neither. Grander urged his animal off the street, down the embankment, and straight across the frozen river. The ice groaned in protest at the sudden burden, but held.

Henry had no choice but to follow. Gritting his teeth, he kicked his horse's side and followed in the tracks left by Grander's beast. The ice was already veined with cracks and fissures, but new fractures announced themselves in sharp, staccato fury. Henry's horse whickered nervously.

People on the street were staring and shouting now, yelling at Henry to get off the ice, warning him that it wasn't safe.

I know it isn't safe, you idiots, he thought. *I'm not out here on a pleasure ride.*

Grander pulled up on his reins. He turned back, waiting to see if Henry would follow through with the pursuit.

I couldn't stop. Not now. Not after being so close. I urged the horse on, people shouting behind me. Grander waiting ahead. The horse took a few steps forward, then—*bang!* A gunshot. That's what it sounded like. A loud crack, followed by the sensation of weightlessness.

Horse and rider plunged into the frozen river. The animal panicked as it fell, twisting its body and driving Henry into the ice at an unfortunate angle.

Its weight forced me down, under the ice. We both sank like stones. The water went red as pain shot up my body. I looked down and saw my shinbone protruding from my leg, jagged and broken, the wound coughing blood. The pain was phenomenal, but somehow I swam back to the surface. I clawed my way onto the shoreline and looked behind me.

Grander was still there. Watching. It was hard to know, since his face was covered, but Henry would've sworn he saw a smile, just before he turned and rode away across the frozen river.

All told, Henry had spent a decade in London. In vampire terms, barely enough time to unpack his suitcase. He'd thought of Abe often—especially in the spring of 1890, when he learned that Abe's only grandson, Abraham "Jack" Lincoln, had died at the age of sixteen, less than a mile from Henry's home in London, where his father, Robert Todd Lincoln, was serving as the American ambassador. The cause of young Jack's death was reported as "blood poisoning"—a vague diagnosis that caused Henry no small concern. Europe was still rife with expatriate vampires who might have seen Abraham Lincoln's grandson as a prize. But Henry never got the chance to examine Jack's body, as it was hurried back to the States to be entombed in Springfield (where his grandfather was supposedly interred). From a letter to Bram Stoker, dated March 15th, 1890:

> [Abraham Lincoln] buried a mother, a sister, a brother, and two of his own boys in life. And now he buries a grandson—his namesake, his legacy, in death. The fields of his future progeny are being slowly salted.

For his part, the experience of working with Henry to catch the Ripper had inspired Stoker's imagination.[2] Nine years after Whitechapel's summer of terror, he published a fictional account of a vampire who comes to London, only to be pursued by a great hunter of the dead. *Dracula* was written in epistolary fashion,

---

2. It's long been theorized that Stoker was inspired to write *Dracula* after meeting a Hungarian writer named Ármin Vámbéry, who regaled Stoker with wild tales of the Carpathian Mountains. In reality, it was Stoker's experiences with Henry Irving and Henry Sturges that led him to begin the work.

that is, as a collection of diary entries, newspaper clippings, letters, and telegrams, presented as fact. And, in truth, there were many facts hidden away in Stoker's masterpiece. For instance, the novel's climax was likely the result of a trip that Henry took to Asia in 1894. He traveled by way of Istanbul, taking the new Orient Express—a four-day, three-night journey. An excerpt from a letter sent by Henry to Stoker, from Peking,[3] on his arrival:

> Consider the plight of this lonely vessel, racing
> through vast expanses of the untamed and terrible
> wild. The dark mountains with their treacherous
> passes looming on all sides, in direct opposition
> to the opulence of the interior. The drama seems
> inherent.[4]

Dracula was an instant sensation. Yet for all his newfound money and fame, Stoker remained at the Lyceum, acting as both theater manager and Renfield to the great Henry Irving. He'd long hoped that Irving, with his dramatic, sweeping gestures, gentlemanly mannerisms, and specialty in playing villain roles, would play Dracula in the stage adaptation of

---

3. Now Beijing.
4. Stoker took the advice, using the Orient Express in the climax of *Dracula*, in which Van Helsing and his posse ride the famous train in a race to Transylvania.

his novel. However, when the play was mounted at the Lyceum in 1897, Irving refused to appear in it.

> He was insulted, I think. Put off by the fact that Stoker had borrowed so liberally in creating the character of Dracula. And like other vampires at the time, he was probably upset that the novel had created something of a vampire hysteria in the culture, and given millions of humans an insight into the customs and mannerisms of our kind. But what really pissed Irving off, in my opinion—the real reason he refused to do the play—was that his assistant, his employee, had achieved a fame comparable to or likely even greater than his own.

Toward the end of his life, Stoker, who had been suffering from ill health, wrote one last letter to Henry Sturges, dated August 1st, 1911:

> My Dear Sturges,
> Well, old friend, we come to the end of the play.
>   Doyle will no doubt be remembered for [creating Sherlock] Holmes. But his adventures with you and I in that strange Autumn of 1888 added ingredients to his tales that never would have existed without you,[5] just as it gave rise to

---

5. The clearest example comes in one of his Sherlock Holmes stories, "The Adventure of the Sussex Vampire" (1926).

the book I shall be remembered for. For this, and for your constant friendship, I leave you with a full heart, and a fondness greater today than ever in these three and twenty years.

It gives me some comfort knowing that those memories will live on in your head for all time. Spare a thought for your old friend once in a while, will you?

Yours Sincerely,

Stoker died less than a year later, in London.

★ ★ ★

It was impossible to get into Union Headquarters without being heard. Since the days of the Civil War, when the Union had helped the North win, making numerous human and vampire enemies in the process, the building had been a veritable fortress. The ground-floor windows were covered by iron shutters, which had been locked since anyone could remember. The boiler room was cemented off from the rest of the basement level, so that coalmen could make deliveries and tend to the furnace without gaining access to the rest of the building. With the exception of a pair of two-inch-thick cast-iron doors in the first-floor lobby, which were always locked, there was no way into the building from the street.

That is, except for the tunnel. Whoever had killed Adam had known about the tunnel that ran underground between the Union Headquarters and Trinity Church on the other side of Broadway. A tunnel designed, ironically, as a means of escape, in the event that the headquarters were attacked. And whose existence was supposed to be revealed only to those who had sworn an oath of loyalty to the institution. Someone had broken that oath, and Adam had paid with his life.

Henry was back in the Union's grand ballroom, in the country of his vampire birth. The compound fracture in his leg had been bothering him. Usually, a broken bone would've taken a matter of hours for his vampire body to mend, but it had been splintered badly and set incorrectly, leaving him with a noticeable limp. Henry desired nothing more than to resume the hunt for Grander, but to do so while recovering would be to invite death.

Adam's portrait had been placed on an easel at the far end of the ballroom, the black lacquer finish of its frame reflecting the fire burning in the oversize hearth behind it. Dozens of red and white roses had been arranged around it, in honor of the Houses of York and Lancaster—the two branches of the Plantagenet line, which fought each other for control of England in the Wars of the Roses. Henry was admiring the arrangement and wondering just how in the hell they'd managed to find such beautiful flowers in the dead of winter, when a squeaky little voice shook him from his thoughts:

"Are you Henry Sturges?" it asked.

Only that's not at all how it sounded. It was more like, "A'yu E'nry Stuh-jess?" An annoying, high-pitched, nasal voice, rendered even more annoying by its thick Cockney accent.

Henry looked over—or rather *down*—at the stout frame of William Duell, a boy of about sixteen, his round face covered in freckles, his hair reddish brown and unkempt. His ill-fitting brown suit looked itchy and worn, and he looked more like an eager newsboy than a vampire.

"And you are?"

"Name's Duell. I'm to be your bah'yguard."

"You?"

"Yeah, me. What of it?"

"I wasn't aware I was in need of a bodyguard," said Henry.

Duell looked at Henry's bandaged leg and snorted. "Well, you are, and I'm 'im."

With Adam Plantagenet gone, the Union had been left with something of a leadership gap, even though, officially speaking, it didn't have a leader.

A few of the older crowd—the five-hundred-and-up club—got together and decided to invoke some ancient bylaw that none of us had ever heard of. Some of us, those who had been around long enough to make a few enemies, would be paired up with "bodyguards" for the time being, and the headquarters would be placed under guard around the clock. I found the whole thing a little absurd, to be honest. I couldn't help feeling like we were playing right into the hands of whoever had killed Adam—walking around vigilant and afraid, locking ourselves up in the safety of our cells.

"Someone thinks you're 'igh and migh'y enough for someone else to wanna kill," said Duell. "So 'til they says otherwise, I'm to be your shadow."

Duell may not have looked the part of the bodyguard, but he played it to the hilt. True to his word, he was at Henry's side around the clock, ever vigilant. Two days after Adam's funeral, the two walked down Fifth Avenue, both wearing dark glasses to ward off the late afternoon sun. They were headed back to Henry's home on Park Avenue and had decided to take the Sixth Street elevated railway rather than walk.

"You was around for the war, then?" asked Duell.

"I've been around for many wars."

"The last one, I mean. North and South."

"Yes."

"And was they this worked up? Pairing us off and locking us away? Never seen 'em as worked up as this," said Duell. "Not since I was made."

"No, I haven't seen them 'this worked up.' But then, I've never seen anyone get into the headquarters uninvited, either. When *were* you made, if I may?"

"Born 1701, died 1717."

" 'Died.' There's that damnable word again. You do realize we're not actually *dead*, don't you?"

"You take me for an idiot? Course I know that."

"I don't mean to be rude; it's simply a term I don't care for."

"Oh, well, it's good ya don't *mean* to be rude."

"All the same, you do very well in the light for one so new."

"I'm a 'undred and bloody ninety-nine years old!"

"Relatively new."

"Age ain't got nuffin to do with 'ow you 'andle the sun, anyways. 'A century,' they tell you. 'A century before you can wander about during the day.' *Bollocks.* I did it in a quarter of the time."

"Impossible."

"Like 'ell it is. Just 'ave to be willing to get a little burned is all."

Henry was taken aback. "You allowed yourself to burn?"

"Said I did, didn't I? What, you never tried it when you was new? Never 'eld your arm out a window to see how long you could stand the pain?"

"I can't say that I did."

"See? That's the problem. Most vampires is proper types. They get old and rich and proper, and who do they choose to make immortal? Them 'umans that remind 'em of themselves. Other proper types. Don't see too many cottagers with an extra pair of teeth, do you?"

"No, I suppose you don't."

"It's no wonder we're always gettin' mistaken for queers. Look at us—a bunch'a proper men, never growin' old, 'angin' about in the dark, bitin' other men on the neck. They don't fear us 'cause we got claws and fangs; they fear us 'cause they think we're comin' after their sons."

Duell made himself laugh. It was a high-pitched, nasally laugh, and Henry found it deeply annoying.

"They fear us," said Henry, "because we're an affront to nature."

"Oh now, don't start that rubbish."

"It was *man* whom God invited into the Garden of Eden. *Man* whom He created as part of nature. Where in the Bible does it say anything about vampires?"

"Oh, *Christ*. Come off it, you dowdy cunt. 'Garden of Eden.' First off, you ought'a be ashamed of yourself, goin' around, quotin' the Bible like it's full of facts. Three 'undred odd years old, still believes in those fairy tales. Second off, there's plenty in your Bible about us: people risin' from the dead, miracles and what, drinkin' Jesus's blood, 'oh, drink this and have everlasting life.' Are you daft? You think bein' a vampire's an 'affront to nature'? Fine. You go on and think it. But for the love'a your Mother Mary and all your made-up saints, leave me out'a your misery."

Henry was taken aback, to say the least.

"I pity you," said Henry at last. "You'll never know what you are."

"Save your pity. I know *exactly* what I am. You 'ate bein' a vampire. Me? I think it's right fun."

" 'Fun'? You jest."

"Know what I did when I was 'uman? Mucked stalls for a bloke my father owed money to. Up before the sun I was, six days a week, shoveling 'orse shit to pay off a debt that wasn't even mine. I 'ated bein' 'uman, I did. 'Ated the work. 'Ated bein' sick and tired and aching. 'Ated knowin' that I'd probably never see thirty-five. A 'uman life's over in a blink. Can't squeeze but a few drops out of it, see. Then along comes a bloke, says, ' 'Ere, drink this.' Next thing I know I can see in the dark and run fast as a dog. Best bloody thing that ever 'appened to me. Sleep all day, strong as ten men, get to live forever? What's not to like?"

"How about the fact that we're murderers? The fact that everyone we know and love will pass to dust before our eyes? That we're confined to the shadows of the world?"

"I been with over two thousand women. You know that? That's not braggin', neither. That's a plain and simple truth, that is. Young ones, old ones, skinny ones, fat ones. Light ones, dark ones, in-between ones. Ones that's been with a hundred men, ones that's been with none. Yeah, some of 'em was ugly, but some of 'em was about the most beautiful things you ever saw. I been with 'em in every part of the world, and I done things with 'em no living man could imagine. And you wanna know somethin'? Now that I think about it, I done most'a them things in the dark, on a bed, with the shades pulled shut. The shadows of the world is just fine, thanks."

Henry was, once again, stunned into silence.

"Perspective," said Duell. "That's your problem, 'tis. I'm a vampire. I love killin', I love fuckin', and I love watching the world go by. *That's* what I am. Question is, what the 'ell are *you*?"

Henry was relieved when they reached the elevated train platform, where common decency required Duell to be somewhat less salacious and annoying. Both sides of the platform were packed with rush-hour commuters—most of them men in dark suits and bowlers, with a few women in long skirts and flowered hats. Henry and Duell had arrived just in time. A train was approaching.

The tracks were nearly even with the platform in those days. At some stations, you actually had to step up to climb aboard a train. And there were no electrified tracks, either. When there was no train, you could walk from one side of the

platform to the other, almost as easily as crossing the street. The trains were smaller, of course.
Typically three passenger cars, pulled along at
twenty or thirty miles an hour by a small steam
locomotive. That doesn't sound fast by today's
standards, but it was fast enough to turn a person
into a mess.[6]

Duell saw it first. One of the faceless mob of men
in dark suits and bowlers had tripped on a rail tie running between the platforms and badly twisted his
ankle. Unfortunately, he'd fallen directly in the path
of the approaching train.

"Betch'a a dollar 'e don't make it," said Duell.

Henry watched the man try to get back to his feet.
A few people on either side of the platform saw him
struggling, but none of them made any effort to help
him—too concerned with their own safety.

He was thirty or so, bushy mustache, still holding
on to his cane with one hand while he tried to get
to his feet. He knew it was going to happen. He
could see the mathematics of it. The poor bastard
had walked into an equation with no solution,
and he knew it. I remember watching him brace
right before the locomotive struck him. A natural

---

6. By 1900, on average, two people a day were struck and killed by
trains in New York City alone.

thing. A beautiful, human thing. As if bracing himself against ninety tons of iron would make any difference. It's strange, the little things that stick in your mind. The sight of that man facing certain death, but bracing himself for it anyway.

He braced, and a moment later, he exploded, knocked to the tracks by the front of the locomotive and cut from his crotch to the top of his skull by its wheels. His assorted organs and liquids spilled out onto the wooden platform as the train squealed to a halt. People screamed, fainted, and got sick on both sides of the platform.

Henry watched the train's engineer step down onto the tracks and look at the front of the locomotive, more concerned with his equipment than the remains of the poor soul who now lay in two pieces on the platform. For the unlucky commuter, the journey was over. But the city moved on. Mostly oblivious.

I wrote this man's story in my mind, as I always do when I witness an untimely death. I imagined he had a young family somewhere in the city. A pretty young wife and three children—none of them older than five. They lived in a cramped third-floor walk-up. It wasn't much, but they made do. Right now, his wife was telling the kids to calm down and wash up. Father would be home soon, and she'd have his dinner hot and ready for him on the table. They would kiss, then say a prayer, and he would bounce their youngest on his knee while they ate. Then off to bed with the three, and Father would light a lamp by his chair and read the paper while he smoked his pipe. His wife would sit across from him, sewing a small pair of trousers for their son, who had a knack for finding new and exciting ways to rip them. Except none of that would happen. Not tonight. Not ever. The knock at the door would come, and there would be the policeman. And just like that, that young wife would be a widow. Mother of three, without a penny to her name. Just like that. One twisted ankle.

"Ha!" cried Duell. "Ha, there! There's *exactly* what I was gettin' at! You see 'ow bad they got it? One minute you're walkin' from 'ere to there, gettin' on with your stupid little existence, the next—"

Duell clapped his hands loudly—*bang!*

"'uman life don't amount to *nothing*," he said. "It's an ant fartin' into a 'urricane, it is."

Henry turned and walked toward the stairs to the street. There was no point in waiting for another train. The line would be shut down for at least an hour, while some unfortunate city employee dealt with the mess. Duell followed.

"If you have such little regard for human life," said Henry, "why did you pledge yourself to the Union?"

Duell paused. It was a good question, and one that William Duell, being the sound sleeper that he was, didn't have an easy answer to.

"When I was wee," he said, "my father used ta tell me I was a useless little runt. I was the only boy who made it past bein' a baby, see. 'Is only son, and he used ta take a switch to me every chance 'e had, the bastard. Beat the skin right off'a my back, 'e did, more times than I could count. Fear. That's what it was from sunup to sunset. Fear I'd walk in on 'im at the wrong time. Say the wrong thing. And it wasn't just 'im, neither. Boys in my village, they picked on me on account of my bein' small, too. You'd think they might'a shown me a little mercy, seein' what was happenin' to me at home. But boys ain't like that. Boys, when they see blood on your back, they jump right on top and beat you some more."

"I'm sorry," said Henry.

"'S'all right," said Duell. "They're all long dead, and I'm still fightin' and fuckin'."

An ant farting into a hurricane. It was a crude, simple metaphor from a crude, simple vampire. But as much as Henry hated to admit it . . . Duell was right.

Delmonico's was widely considered New York City's finest restaurant and, more important, the "it" place to see and be seen by the city's most glamorous and illustrious. Its menu had been called "one of the great

American innovations," because, for the first time in the nation's history, its patrons could order food à la carte, as opposed to prix fixe, where one had to choose from predetermined multicourse meals with little room for substitution. The menu was a sensation, for it was seen as emblematic of the American spirit: independence, the freedom to choose, to determine one's own destiny—even if that destiny was a bowl of Manhattan clam chowder.

Henry Sturges had sampled every item on Delmonico's revolutionary menu. That is to say, he'd ordered every item and pushed it around his plate for an hour or so before paying the bill. It was a small price to pay for the atmosphere.

> On any given night, you might see [Theodore] Roosevelt, Gilbert and Sullivan, Lillian Russell, a European prince, an emperor... All the barons of the day were there: Carnegie, Morgan, Rockefeller, the Vanderbilts, the Astors. I watched them sip their cream of artichoke soup and gnash steak between their teeth; I eavesdropped on their conversations from across the room. Sometimes, if they were close enough, I even wandered around in their thoughts. I can admit it now, since there's a statute of limitations on insider trading, but I picked up more than a few stock tips this way and made myself quite a bit of money.

Henry began dining at Delmonico's so frequently that a table was kept permanently reserved for him. It was a small table in the corner, where he and his young associate, Mr. Duell, were always welcome. But for all his wealth, and all the energy and opulence of his surroundings, Henry began to feel like a ghost ship, endlessly adrift, doomed to never make port.

> The world was getting ready for the twentieth century. A century of trains and electricity and photographs and who knew what else. There was excitement everywhere, and why not? For the vast majority of human beings alive in 1899, this would be the one and only time they got to ring in a new century. For me, it would be the fourth. I thought often of something Emily Dickinson had written in a letter decades earlier: "My friends are my estate."[7]

The warmth and conversation of the Stokers' kitchen was an ocean away. The rambling elder statesman of the Union was in the ground. And Henry's old friend, maybe the closest friend he'd ever had, was gone.

---

7. It's a matter of record that Emily Dickinson was a recluse during the last fifteen years of her life, choosing to speak to visitors through doors rather than face-to-face, even skipping her beloved father's funeral for fear of being seen. Locally, this was attributed to her being an eccentric. In reality, she had been made immortal by a lover, Kate Scott Turner, in the late 1850s.

So it was that Henry and Duell once again found themselves at their corner table, surrounded by the well-whiskered gentry, pushing food around their plates to the ever-present murmur of conversation and the music of the string quartet that always played on Thursday evenings.

Henry heard the foreigner before he saw him.

"It is not *hot*!"

The murmurs and strings abruptly stopped.

He was a slender, dark-haired man of about forty, with a well-groomed mustache and an expensive gray wool suit. He spoke with a thick Eastern European accent in a high-pitched voice that cut through the air and made the foreigner's waiter tilt back on his heels so far that Henry thought he might topple over.

"Hot! You understand 'hot'?"

"Of course, sir," said the waiter. "My sincere apol—"

"No! I think you do *not* understand! You have read Gibbs's laws of thermodynamics, yes? You are familiar with Le Chatelier's principle, yes? Perhaps *then* you understand! Here—a lesson for you! You heat the soup with energy..."

The foreigner lifted the tea light from his table and held the flame under the bowl of soup in the waiter's hands. All eyes were on his table now.

"Like this...then the energy excites the molecules in the soup, and it becomes hot! I will not pay for this! No, no, no!"

"I'll pay for it," said Henry, "if he'll shut up."

The foreigner froze and whipped his head around, like a prairie dog who'd just caught the scent of a predator. He looked in the direction of the voice.

"Who says this?" asked the foreigner. "Who is the man who wishes to silence me?"

Duell put his napkin on the table and slid his chair out, but Henry put a hand out—*sit down; it's all right.*

"I am," said Henry. "And who is the man who won't be silent?"

A smile crept over the foreigner's face. He helped himself to a seat at Henry's table, all memories of lukewarm soup suddenly distant. Seeing his chance, the maître d' waved his hands urgently at the string quartet, which began to play again. With the spectacle over and the dining room once again filled with music, the other patrons resumed their chatter.

"I like you," said the foreigner, squinting his eyes, as if studying Henry's face. "Too many Americans, they do not say what they truly think, think, think."

"I'm an Englishman."

"An Englishman? But you sound like an American!" cried the foreigner, louder than anything he'd yelled at the waiter, pounding his fist on the table. "Then it is an even *greater* miracle! That an Englishman would put aside his civility to stand on principle! Please, English American, I must know your name. I must befriend you. You will be my friend."

"You want me to toss this bloke out on his ear?" asked Duell.

Henry looked the foreigner over. He was mad, to be sure. But Henry sensed no malice. Just pure, frenetic energy. "Henry Sturges," he said at last. "My associate, Mr. Duell."

Henry extended his hand, but the foreigner didn't shake it.

"Sturges and Duell; one is young, one is younger! You will be my guests! I will test things on you, yes? You will be honored, yes? I am Nikola Tesla. But surely you recognized me."

Tesla leaned back, awaiting some outpouring of awe.

"What in the 'ell is 'e on about?" asked Duell.

When Henry and Duell arrived at Tesla's lab at 46 East Houston Street, they found themselves on another planet. A strange planet of machinery and wires, the smell of kerosene pervasive. The hum of motors constant.

> It's funny. Most people probably picture [Tesla's] lab as a dark, foreboding kind of place. But it was actually very bright, lit by electric fixtures in the ceiling. White walls. Very sparse and clean, with a black iron spiral staircase in the center, leading

up to his private quarters. In all the time I spent at the Houston Street lab, I never once saw Tesla climb those stairs. He was always down in the lab. Always working.

Nikola Tesla didn't sleep more than two hours a night. He was never known to have any romantic relationships, believing that chastity, not necessity, was the mother of invention. He suffered from terrible OCD. Besides his aversion to shaking hands, Tesla was obsessed with the number three, having to repeat certain actions—even words—three times.

Born in Serbia in 1856, he'd gained notoriety as a rival to Thomas Edison and would be considered the underdog in that rivalry for the rest of his life.

When I met him, he was at the height of his genius and fame. He was crazy, sure, but he had more money than he could spend, and he still had his vitality.[8]

Tesla came to America in 1884, virtually penniless, and used his credentials to get a job working for Edison. The American inventor recognized the talent in the young Serb and offered him the task of working

---

8. Tesla was in his mid-forties when he first met Henry in New York. Decades later, his money and vitality gone, he would famously fall in love with a pigeon and claim to have received a transmission from Mars.

on his DC (direct current) generators. After examining the machines, Tesla told Edison that he could radically improve their power and efficiency. Edison told Tesla, "If you can do that, then there's $50,000 in it for you."[9]

And so Tesla had slaved away for months, obsessed, completely retooling Edison's design. When he unveiled the results, Edison was impressed but told Tesla that he'd only been joking about the bonus. Tesla quit on the spot, vowing to himself that he would crush Edison. And he very nearly did.

In 1886, Tesla went into business for himself—but it wasn't Edison's DC power he was working on. Unlike Edison, who thought that direct current was the way forward, Tesla believed that the future belonged to AC—or alternating current.[10] He perfected his design for a powerful, efficient AC generator and licensed his patents to the Westinghouse Company, casting himself in direct opposition to Edison's General Electric and making him a rich man

---

9. Equivalent to more than fifty years' pay for Tesla, who was making $18 a week at the time.

10. Edison's DC (direct current) system relied on each neighborhood (or in some cases, each home or building) having its own, smaller generator. To Edison, the advantage was safety—less risk of fire and less risk of death by electrocution, as the system peaked at one hundred volts. Edison also saw DC as a way to democratize electric power. With no all-powerful, central manufacturers providing power to whole cities, there would be no mass blackouts, and the price of generating electricity would remain low.

overnight. But Tesla poured nearly every penny back into his research—creating elaborate experiments and working on concepts that other engineers and scientists found strange, or even mad, such as the wireless transmission of electricity.

> It's funny how a man's personality is reflected in his work. Where Edison's direct current was steadier but weaker, Tesla's alternating current was more powerful but more dangerous, too. His own current ran in peaks and valleys, and in great doses, it could prove dangerous.

Edison, perhaps fueled by feelings of betrayal by his former employee, fought viciously against AC power, waging what would be called "the War of Currents." Edison arranged for public demonstrations of the dangers of high-voltage electricity, going so far as to electrocute dogs and horses. In 1903, he electrocuted a thirty-six-year-old circus elephant named Topsy, who'd killed one of her trainers after he'd burned her with a cigar.[11]

Lately, Tesla had been obsessed with capturing images of the "invisible," using vacuum tubes to capture rudimentary X-ray photographs.

---

11. Topsy had been scheduled to be hanged, but the ASPCA deemed hanging "too cruel" a method of execution.

"See inside a body?" asked Henry. "Without opening it?"

"And from a distance," said Tesla.

He showed Duell and me one of his X-ray photographs, which he was still calling "shadowgraphs." It was [a picture] of a man's foot inside a boot. There were the bones of his ankle, and his heel. There were the eyelets holding the laces of his boot in place, and the nails holding his boot heel to the rest of the sole—but the shoe and skin and muscle were invisible. You have no idea what a breathtaking sight this was. We were sure it had to be some kind of elaborate hoax. Some kind of painting, maybe.

"This...," said Henry. "This is real?"

"Yes, yes, yes!"

"It's bloody magic," said Duell.

"*No!* Not magic! No, no, no! Science, boy! *Science!*"

"You needn't be so damned *loud*," said a voice from the top of the stairs.

"You will excuse this," said Tesla to Henry and Duell. "There is a man staying with me from out of town, and he is a *very rude old bastard.*"

A man of about sixty-five came down the stairs, carefully holding the rail, nursing an injured foot. He had an excess of wavy white hair—the very last whispers of dark brown still visible at the roots. His eyebrows nearly as bushy as the mustache that bridged his dimpled cheeks. His eyes were mischievous and alive, like a child's, and had a way of looking *into* you when they looked at you.

"Well, if you dislike me so much, you ought to quit inviting me to stay with you."

"You must be joking," Henry muttered to himself.

> I'd never met him, but I recognized him immediately, from seeing his photographs in the paper— a relatively new phenomenon in those days. In fact, come to think, he might have been the first celebrity I recognized on sight.

Mark Twain and Nikola Tesla had begun their friendship as mutual admirers. As a young man in Serbia, Tesla had read some of Twain's works while recovering from an illness and claimed that the power of the American's words had actually helped save his life. Twain had become interested in Tesla's work after reading about him in the early 1890s, and when the two met on the New York party circuit, they'd hit it off. But their mutual admiration had quickly given way to what Twain described as "fond disdain."

> One was from the American South, one from Serbia. One was a family man; the other had never been married or shown any interest in women. But they were both towering geniuses

Mark Twain and Nikola Tesla in the lab. The two geniuses had a tempestuous friendship, which Twain described as "fond disdain."

whose faces and names carried a sort of burden. They were two of the first true American celebrities. Not many people knew what it was like to be famous, and I think that for all their differences, they always had that. That mutual respect for what the other had sacrificed in the name of his work.

Henry had been a fan of Twain's writing for years, particularly of *Huckleberry Finn*:

I'd read it so many times that I could quote whole passages of it from memory. There's one I remember, even now:

"The stars were shining, and the leaves rustled in the woods ever so mournful; and I heard an owl, away off, who-whooing about somebody that was dead, and a whippowill and a dog crying about somebody that was going to die; and the wind was trying to whisper something to me, and I couldn't make out what it was, and so it made the cold shivers run over me. Then away out in the woods I heard that kind of a sound that a ghost makes when it wants to tell about something that's on its mind and can't make itself understood, and so can't rest easy in its grave, and has to go about that way every night grieving."

Twain extended his hand. "Sam Clemens," he said. "Pleased to make your acquaintance, Mr.—"

"Sturges," said Henry. "Henry Sturges, and the pleasure is all mine, sir. I'm a great admirer of your work."

"Well," said Twain, "that makes one of us."

He held my hand longer than I expected and looked at me with those eyes—eyes that, and I know this is an overused expression, but in this case it's the right one—eyes that twinkled. I noticed him do the same thing when I introduced Duell. He looked at us like a schoolboy with a secret. I considered trying to read his thoughts, to see why his eyes twinkled the way they did, but then scolded myself. Lifting stock tips from J. P. Morgan was one thing. But this was Mark Twain. How dare I invade his privacy?

"And where did you and our friend Mr. Tesla meet?" asked Twain.

"At Delmonico's."

"Ah, of course. Helluva steak they have there, isn't it."

"Yes."

"'E was makin' a fuss over 'is soup," said Duell, pointing to Tesla.

"I was," said Tesla, smiling. "Very funny, very funny, very funny. Mr. Sturges told me to shut my mouth. I loved this. We are friends now."

"And did you know Mr. Sturges and Mr. Duell are vampires?" asked Twain.

He said it so matter-of-factly, without the slightest hint of fear or accusation. This was the kind of confidence born of being one of the most famous men on earth.

"Know?" asked Tesla. "Of course I know this, you blustering old fool! Why do you insult my intelligence? Vampires, yes, yes, yes."

It was clear that Tesla hadn't known. That he hadn't, in fact, had the *slightest idea* that his new friends were vampires. He suddenly seemed less interested in showing them his inventions and more interested in keeping an eye on them.

Twain winked at Henry. "Don't be alarmed, Mr. Sturges. Some of my closest friends are dead."

There's that damnable word again. This time Henry kept his mouth shut. Scolding William Duell and scolding Mark Twain were two very different things.

"We ought not to discriminate against them on that account," said Twain, "since sooner or later we all end up afflicted with the same condition."

The foursome of Tesla, Twain, Sturges, and Duell passed much of 1901 together, congregating in Tesla's lab and dining at Delmonico's—where Twain amused himself by telling the waiters to "bring Mr. Sturges's and Mr. Duell's plates back to the kitchen, as they clearly can't tolerate a mere mouthful of it." There were no other attacks on the Union Headquarters or on any of its members. All the same, the Union kept its war footing, and Henry remained under Duell's watch.

> I'd grown to like [Duell]. He was ribald and loud, and he certainly wasn't an intellectual. But he was intelligent in his own salty way, and more than that, he had good intentions, even if he often fell short

of displaying them. You know the saying "possession is nine-tenths of the law"? In my experience, intentions are nine-tenths of a man's character.

Tesla divided his time between his lab on Houston Street and a new facility he was building on Long Island called Wardenclyffe. The centerpiece of this new facility, built largely with J. P. Morgan's money, was a huge metal tower that rose 187 feet from the center of the brick laboratory and was topped by a metal dome that vaguely resembled a flying saucer. Tesla planned to use the tower to beam energy wirelessly across the Atlantic and claimed that he had already proved the concept on a smaller scale. When not overseeing Wardenclyffe's construction, Tesla carried on with various experiments at his Houston Street lab, often using one of his frequent guests as test subjects. He took an X-ray of Henry's head and hands and studied the anatomical differences between the bone structures of humans and vampires. For the first time, Henry could see the physical changes that his body had undergone over those three days at Roanoke. His old bones thickening and new bones—claws—growing beneath the skin of his fingers. The retracted fangs that rested behind his face.

This was, I think, the beginning of a change in my thinking. The change from believing, like most vampires, that our condition had some kind of "magical" component, that it was a kind of "curse," to wondering if maybe—*maybe*—it was rooted in the physical. That it was just another ailment, passed from person to person through the blood, no different than, say, the HIV virus, or hepatitis.

Tesla was also interested in the physiological differences between vampires and humans and was determined to make a scientific study of them. He quizzed Henry endlessly on a variety of intimate subjects, taking notes and mumbling to himself while pulling at strands of his black hair with his free hand.

"Do vampires...do they use the water closet?" asked Tesla.

"Well, we don't eat or drink, so..."

"Yes, yes, yes, I see, and...can you make love to a woman?"

"Yes."

"Ah, ah, ah, and when you finish making love, do you...?" Tesla mimed a miniature explosion—*poof!*—with his hands. Henry found it amusing that such an unabashed man was embarrassed by something so natural.

"Forgive me," said Henry. "I'm not sure what you mean."

"You understand," said Tesla, turning red, and mimed his little explosion again.

"Do we disappear?" asked Henry.

"No! Do you—" Tesla repeated the gesture, this time with an accompanying moan that sounded to Henry less like unbridled pleasure and more like the gravelly bleating of a large sheep.

"Yes," said Henry, laughing at Tesla. "Yes, we do."

"Ah, yes, yes, yes. But then, why—"

"Why can't we have children?" said Henry.

It was a question all vampires pondered sooner or later. Henry himself had spent countless hours wondering if there was some deeper meaning behind the barrenness.

> It had never occurred to me that there might be some medical reason behind it. I'd always assumed it was just another part of the "curse" of being a vampire. That somehow, some cosmic trade-off had been worked out at the dawn of time. "Okay, you get to live forever, but you don't get to create life. All you can do is borrow it from others." I'd been so close. That's the thing that really got me. I'd been so close to being a father, before a vampire, of all things, had taken that chance away. You understand why I thought— why I *had* to think—there was something bigger going on.

Tesla's experiments were interesting and often exciting, but it was Twain's company that Henry took the most pleasure from. He soaked up every minute of it, cherishing the chance to converse with one of his favorite writers and the great wit of his day.

Imagine having a chance to talk to Shakespeare or Voltaire. Actually, in point of fact, I *did* meet Voltaire in Paris at the very end of his life, but it was only for a few moments, and nothing substantive came out of it. I was fascinated by [Twain]. I was hundreds of years older than he was.[12] Yet to me, he seemed like an elder. Like he had all the answers. We talked about everything. His books, the philosophical and religious implications of vampirism, life and death, especially the death of his oldest daughter,[13] which he was still carrying on his old shoulders. We talked about Roanoke and Paris and the American Revolution—he had a million questions about that, especially about Ben [Franklin], some of which I could answer, some of which I couldn't. He wanted to know all about the Civil War and my friendship with Abe. He was especially interested in all that. He'd always considered Abe something of an idiot

---

12. Twain was in his sixties when he and Henry became acquainted.

13. Susy Clemens died of spinal meningitis in 1896, at the age of twenty-four, leaving Twain devastated. He had the following poem, adapted from the poem "Annette" by Robert Richardson, inscribed on her headstone: "Warm summer sun shine kindly here, / Warm southern wind blow softly here, / Green sod above, lie light, lie light—/ Good night, dear heart, good night, good night."

savant, I guess. Good at stringing words together, but not much else. It was hard for him to picture that caricature—that gangly man in ill-fitting trousers and an old top hat—fighting off vampires with an ax.

The Civil War had divided Mark Twain's household, as it had so many others. And it had divided Twain, too.

"I was still a young man during all that business," said Twain. "Tell you the truth, Henry, I didn't know whether I wanted to fight or not. Or for that matter, which side I wanted to fight for. We owned a slave, I'm not ashamed to admit. I'd grown up thinking it was the way of things. Nothing in the local papers or preached from the pulpit told me otherwise. I had friends, good men, all of them, who were tripping over each other to take up arms against the Yanks. Yet my own brother Orion had been a staunch Lincoln man. Knew him. Campaigned for him. I knew both sides would be in need of a good steamboat pilot, and by that time I daresay I was a pretty good one. But which way to point the bow, you understand? North or south?"

In the end, Mark Twain ended up fighting for both sides. In 1861, he joined a local Missouri militia loyal to the Confederacy, but the small force disbanded after only two weeks, when they got word that a Union detachment had been ordered to hunt them down.[14] At roughly the same time, Abraham Lincoln appointed Twain's brother Orion secretary to the Territory of Nevada. Having failed in his brief career as a rebel, Mark Twain decided to point his bow not north or south, but west—joining his brother in Nevada and working as his assistant during the war.

"I came to respect Lincoln mightily," said Twain. "Read all about the man. He lost his mama when he was nine. I lost my daddy when I was eleven. He worked the Mississippi, as did I. We both wandered here and there, doing this and that, trying to make something out of nothing. And the man could turn a phrase, by God. He had a wit. Most people don't remember that. He was a helluva witty fellow."

"He had a wit," said Henry. "But I wouldn't describe him as 'witty.' To be perfectly honest, he had a rather gloomy disposition."

"Oh, Henry, Henry—the wittiest pens are usually wielded by the gloomiest hands," said Twain. "Surely you know that. A man can be whip smart and witty and caught up in the gale of life, chatting up roomfuls of people and making them laugh till their teeth damn near fall out, and at the same time, he can be the world's loneliest, most miserable creature."

Twain paused. His wise eyes suddenly fogged over, somewhere else.

---

14. Twain wrote a fictionalized account of his experiences in the doomed regiment in "The Private History of a Campaign That Failed" (1885).

"I had a brother named Henry, you know," he said after a while.

"Had?"

"He was the youngest of the seven of us. I was the second youngest. He and I...we were about as close as brothers could get. Folks sometimes thought we were twins, on account of his being big for his age and me small. Died when he was twenty, working on the river. Boiler went."

"A boiler explosion...Well, he never knew what hit him, I suppose."

"I'd like to think so," said Twain. "I'd like to think that it was just like *that*." Twain snapped his fingers. "I like to think that one minute, he was asleep in his bunk, young, his lungs full'a air, dreamin' of a pretty girl. That he woke up drinking out of a golden chalice. But that's not the way it happened."

Twain hesitated. He'd told the story a hundred times. He'd even written about it. But each time brought those old feelings back—the pain as fresh as it had been all those years ago.

"It was me who drug him down there in the first place," he said. "I'd been working on the *Pennsylvania*[15] a year or so as a cub pilot, and I was itching to move on. Me and the pilot, Bill Brown, we didn't get

---

15. Built in 1854, the *Pennsylvania* was a side-wheel steamer, 247 feet long and 32 feet wide, capable of carrying nearly five hundred tons of passengers and cargo up and down the Mississippi River. Her twin engines were powered by five high-pressure boilers.

on so well, to put it mildly, and I wanted out. But before I left, I got Henry a job on the boat as a mud clerk.[16] Henry was a likeable fellow and got on well with the crew, with one exception."

"Bill Brown."

"He'd be damned if any brother of mine was going to get ahead on his boat. One day, he laid into Henry for something or other and gave him a good slap across the mouth. Now Henry, being the agreeable type, stood there and took it."

"But you?"

"I knocked the spit out of the wretch's mouth. Knocked him to the floor and then kept on knocking him till I had to be pulled off. The captain didn't like Brown much, either, but all the same, he couldn't well tolerate cub pilots beating pilots on his boat, and that was the end of me and the *Pennsylvania*. I took another boat upriver. A few days later, Henry was gone.

"Sunday, June eighteen, one-eight-five-seven anno Domini. Dead of night. Steaming upstream, just outside of Memphis. Four hundred and fifty souls aboard, most of 'em asleep, including Henry. But the engineer, he was awake. He and the two ladies he was keeping company with, trying to stoke a different sort of fire. I say 'ladies,' of course, the same way I would

---

16. A nonsalaried, entry-level position on a riverboat, a mud clerk was so named because he often had to go ashore to run errands for the officers at each of the boat's stops.

use 'gentleman' to describe the engineer. Anyway, the pressure built up in those five big cast-iron boilers, until one of 'em—only God knows which one—couldn't hold on anymore. The first one blew and took the other four with it, and there went the whole front of the boat in a shower of burning splinters. Henry woke up in the air. Flying through the dark like a comet, his skin on fire, his lungs full of boiling steam, cooking him from the inside and out. By the time he landed in the Mississippi, he was a dead man. Not straightaway, mind you—he somehow managed to swim back in the dark to what was left of the *Pennsylvania*. Somehow, he found the strength to pull a few passengers out of the water, the fire beginning to spread, before he dragged himself ashore and collapsed."

"A hero's death."

"Might've been. But he didn't die just then," said Twain. "If he had, I s'pose it would've been easier. No, he lay on that muddy shore, that burned and boiled mud clerk, wearing only a soaking nightshirt as the sun came up and beat down on him. It was hours before the *Kate Frisbee* came and scooped him up. Fifteen hours in all before he was in Memphis getting his wounds dressed. He held on another two weeks—waking just enough to look around, but never speaking. As far as I know the last words he ever spoke were before he went to bed on the *Pennsylvania*. I hurried to Memphis as soon as I got word, of course. Sat next to him day and night, praying for a miracle, in part because I wanted Henry to live, even if he would spend the rest of his life covered in burns, taking only shallow breaths. But I also wanted him to live—and it shames me to tell you this—because I knew that I would never forgive myself if he didn't. Imagine that. Wanting someone you love to suffer, just to spare yourself a little guilt.

"There were others," Twain continued. "Other victims of the tragedy, in beds lining both walls of the ward. Moaning, crying out in pain day and night. It was a noise I won't forget should I live to see the end of time. It was hell, listening to them. An insufferable hell, though nothing compared to their suffering, I know. The doctor, a man by the name of Peyton—the best physician in Memphis—he looked after Henry and the others. He did his damnedest, God bless him. He'd been giving him morphine for the pain. An eighth of a grain to help him sleep through the night. Well, one night, Henry was squirming more than usual. Grunting, obviously in terrible pain. Dr. Peyton had already given him his morphine for the night. I'd been there when he gave it to him. But he was still in pain, you understand. Terrible pain, and all I could do was watch. Later that night, one of Peyton's medical students came by to check on Henry. Saw how much pain he was in. The student asked me if he'd been given morphine."

"And you said he hadn't."

"I'd gone from praying for a miracle to praying for

the end, see. Whether it was the morphine or not, I don't know. But Henry died the next morning, and that's that."

"And you never forgave yourself."

"You can call it dumb luck, or you can believe it was written in the stars. But you can't argue with facts. And the fact is, I brought him to that boat, and I left him there. I got to grow old; he didn't. Under those circumstances, it wouldn't be fair if I didn't use at least a pinch of my life blaming myself, would it?"

"Perhaps," said Henry, "the 'miracle' had already occurred."

"How so?"

"Well...if your brother had never come aboard, you never would've had the fight with Bill Brown and had to leave. And if you hadn't left, chances are *you* would've been killed when those boilers went. And if that had happened, well—not only would I have been denied the pleasure of your company, but countless others would have been denied the pleasure of your words. If your brother hadn't been on that boat, the world would have been the poorer for it."

"That's a nice thought, Henry. I thank you for it. But an old man deserves his sorrows, and I won't be denied mine."

An old man. The words stirred something in Henry. Visions of an enduring friendship with an endlessly fascinating man. The thought of a hundred more *Huckleberry Finns*, each one more entertaining and enlightening than the last. Yes, the Union strictly forbade the making of vampires. But Twain was worth the risk, just as Abe had been. When Henry broached the subject, however, Twain laughed him off.

"What?" said Twain. "You mean become a bloodsucking heathen like you? No, thank you, sir. I'll be sweating plenty as it is when I get my turn in front of Saint Peter, but if I play my cards right and don't allow myself to become too corrupted by your pleasurable company, I may still have a fighting chance of getting past him."

"Think of the stories you could write."

"Who says they'd be any good?"

"Think of the wonders you would live to see."

Twain indicated the laboratory around them. "My grandfather couldn't have imagined a world of locomotives and steamships. This, right here? This is the electric future *my* father never could have imagined. What happens after I kick off, well...that'll be a future *I* couldn't have imagined, and rightly so. It's none of my business. No matter how long you live, there'll always be a future just beyond your reach. It's as true for me as it was for my brother. Always has been, always will be, until God strikes the tent and takes the circus to the next town. Hell, I wish we could all be born at the age of eighty and work our way back to eighteen, too. But that's not the way the plans were drawn up.

"A fear of death," Twain continued, "follows from

the fear of *life*. A man who lives fully is prepared to die at any time."

Henry was thunderstruck.

> In one sentence, this man—this *mortal*—had diagnosed the disease that had been ailing me for nearly forty years.
>
> What had I done with myself since Abe died? Pushed expensive food around my plate...bought expensive homes...dressed in expensive clothes. Would I have become involved [in the Jack the Ripper case] if my calling card hadn't been found on the first victim? Would I have cared if Thomas Crowley hadn't forced me into caring? I doubted it.
>
> How had I lived? What had I felt? Those words—"A man who lives fully is prepared to die at any time"—rang in my head like few words ever had. They shamed me. They shamed me, and, in time, they changed me.

In many ways, they also changed the course of the next century.

The idea had come to Henry in a dream.

> It was night. I was walking through a vast, empty church. Walking down the center aisle, pews on

either side of me. There was a terrible storm raging outside. Thunderclaps every few seconds, right on top of the roof. Flashes of lightning making the stained-glass windows glow as bright as day for a second or two at a time. A pair of candles burned on the altar ahead of me, the only light, except for those intermittent flashes. Between the two candles, in the center of the altar, sat a gold crucifix—huge and heavy and ornate. The figure of Christ upon it, flickering in the warm light, his arms outstretched, head hung low, eyes closed. I climbed the four steps to the altar and stood there, admiring the beauty of the crucifix. Not the beauty of the craftsmanship, you understand, but the beauty of the meaning. A man suffering for his convictions. Giving his blood so others might live.

Something said, *Go on, Henry. Touch it.* The way that voice always does in a dream. So I did. I reached out and touched the crucifix, and the instant my finger made contact, there was a flash of lightning, a crack of thunder outside. A terrible shock went through me, every muscle in my body tensing. The pain was...incredible. Like having your fingernails ripped off, only over every square inch of your body. The flash of lightning passed; the stained glass went dark again. So did the candles—the flames blown out by the rush of displaced air. I brought my finger close to my eyes, expecting to find it charred beyond recognition, but it was fine. As if nothing had happened. Another thunderclap and flash of lightning. I looked back up at the crucifix as the light flickered through the stained-glass windows. The eyes of the little Christ were open and looking at me. When I woke up, I had it. The whole thing, fully formed.

It took some convincing, but Henry got the Union elders to let a famous human inventor—and an even *more* famous human author—into the heart of American vampiredom.

Tesla had designed an electrified gate, which would be placed in the tunnel between Trinity Church and the Union building. He'd also built a system of electric locks for the heavy iron doors that had been installed on the first floor and in the lobby, which could be controlled from a central console. No door could be opened without the console's input. And if one of the doors was forced, it would trigger an alarm bell. The Union Headquarters was receiving, in essence, the world's first electronic security system. To power it, Tesla would have to install a generator, which would have to be kept fueled and running twenty-four hours a day. It was a huge, expensive undertaking—

But as I explained to some of those who resisted the idea, no more expensive than building a factory and importing craftsmen for the sole purpose of making a pair of gigantic mirrors.

The installation took nearly three weeks of almost round-the-clock work. Tesla, as was his custom, barely slept or ate. The sounds of hammering and of his frequent cursing could be heard echoing through the building at all hours. Just as Henry had been, the vampires were enamored of Twain and excited to have a celebrity of his caliber around. Where the Union Headquarters were usually a place to be avoided unless official business called, suddenly every vampire within a fifty-mile radius of New York City had a reason to drop by.

Twain didn't mind the attention—in fact, I think he loved it. He held court in the grand ballroom, telling stories of his life as only he could. How he'd first learned of vampires as a young man on the Mississippi; how they'd had been something of an open secret in the South in those days. He offered his perspective on the relationship between vampire and man, joking that "any good Christian ought to love vampires, for who needs prayer more desperately than a sinner?" He even joked that he was, in fact, a "union man" himself, having joined the Printer's Union as a teenager.

The Union vampires ate up every word of it. It was a bizarre sight, the old man with his shock of gray hair and push-broom mustache, sitting at the head of a semicircle of immortals, who hung on his every word like children being read a story at bedtime. And yet it seemed perfectly natural. He also listened in rapt fascination as the others told him firsthand accounts of figures and events he'd read about only in books.

When Tesla's work was complete, the Union Headquarters, at 100 Broadway, officially (but secretly) became the most secure building in the United States.

With the new system in place, and with no attacks having occurred in the past nine months, the elders relaxed their security measures. High-value targets such as Henry would no longer be required to be under guard, which meant that William Duell could finally sail back to England and his life of killing and fucking.

I'd always thought I'd be happy to be rid of [Duell]. But it was a bittersweet parting. I wasn't going to miss his nasally voice or having him around at all hours, but I'd come to appreciate his unique perspective on being a vampire, and even his wit, as it were. Time had taught me to treat every parting as a final parting. So when he offered me a hand, I pulled him in for a hug instead. He went along with it, not really embracing me in return, but not pushing me away, either. I released him. He stood there and looked at me like I'd asked him to marry me.

"Fuck off," said Duell, and walked away.
Henry smiled. He couldn't have said it better.

SEVEN

★ ★ ★

Diplomacy

No bastard ever won a war by dying for his
country.
You won it by making the other poor, dumb
bastard die for *his* country.

—*General George S. Patton*

The anarchist was nervous, of course, this being
the first time he'd ever done such a thing. But he
would do it because the cause was important. Because
he'd heard the rallying cries of Goldman[1] and others. He was an American, and he was proud of being
an American. So proud that it gave him great pain
to see his beloved country in such a state. A vast gulf
separating the immensely wealthy from the desperately poor. Children working their fingers to the bone
in soot-covered factories. Working endless hours for

---

1. Emma Goldman (1869–1940) was a Russian-born anarchist and
political activist.

meager wages, sacrificing their innocence, and often their lives, to make the rich even richer.

Leon Czolgosz knew their pain firsthand. When he was just ten years old, he'd taken a job at the American Steel and Wire Company in Detroit, working sixteen hours a day in the noise and heat and coal smoke of the factory floor, eating a crust of bread for his dinner, and sleeping in the crowded bunkhouses on factory grounds.

And that son of a bitch McKinley. Friend to the rich. Friend to the factory. But enemy of the common

Leon Czolgosz in 1900, a year before dying in the electric chair for the assassination of President William McKinley.

man.[2] The fact that he'd been elected to a second term showed just how blind the voters were. How corrupt this so-called democracy really was.

But the beautiful woman had shown him a way.

He'd met her in Cleveland, earlier that year. She'd come to him after one of the meetings. Leon had risen to speak for the first time that night. He'd told the assembled anarchists his story. How he'd lost his job in the Panic of '93. How his family had turned its back on him after he rejected their poisonous Catholic dogma. Most of all, he'd told them about the anger. The anger that had been building in him for years now. He felt like a boiler, he'd said. Growing hotter by the minute. Ready to explode.

"It took bravery to speak tonight," the beautiful woman had said. "My friends and I are looking for brave men like you."

She'd shown Leon and the others how beautiful the future could be, if only there were men brave enough to claim it. The future didn't belong to governments or companies or even the church—it belonged to the people. It was high time that men like Leon Czolgosz took their lives into their own hands. High time they overthrew the greedy, corrupt governments of the world. Abolished the banks and dragged the tycoons from their temples of wealth. It was time the common

---

2. McKinley had, in fact, often sided with striking workers in labor disputes.

man put that wealth back in his *own* pocket and shared it with his brothers. The beautiful woman had shown them a vision of a world without nations. A world of peace and prosperity for all.

Leon was no fool. He knew that the enemy wouldn't let go of his power without a fight. He knew that peace was attainable only through violence, and that there had to be sacrifices to achieve the world the beautiful woman had described. And he was prepared to make that sacrifice.

Leon shuffled forward in line. An organ was playing Bach, the bright notes of its pipes blending into chords that echoed through the Temple of Music at the Pan-American Exhibition in Buffalo, New York. It was an especially hot early September day, and many of those in line carried fans or handkerchiefs to dab their brows and wipe their hands. One couldn't well shake the hand of the president of the United States with sweaty palms. Leon carried a white handkerchief in his right hand, a .32-caliber revolver hidden beneath it. He'd bought the gun a few days earlier for $4.50, using the money that the beautiful woman and her friends had sent.

They'd sent money to others, too. The man who'd stabbed French president Sadi Carnot to death in 1894. The bomber who'd struck Chicago's Haymarket Square in 1886. The gunman who shot and killed Umberto I, king of Italy, in 1900. Nameless individuals who had toppled kings. Pennies that had altered the course of history. *The meek inheriting the earth,* Leon thought.

There were only a few more greeters in line ahead of him. He watched McKinley take a red carnation[3] off of his lapel and hand it to a little girl. It would be his turn soon. His turn to alter the course of history.

Perhaps his would be the first shot fired in a war.

Henry arrived in Washington, D.C., on October 29th, 1901. The day Leon Czolgosz was executed by electric chair for assassinating President William McKinley. The telegram had arrived the previous morning:

```
WASHDC 617A 28OCT 1901

MR H STURGES 603 PARK AVE NEW
YORK NY

SEC STATE JOHN HAY URGENTLY REQUESTS
MEETING. TOMORROW IF POSSIBLE.
DISCRETION CRUCIAL. CABLE REPLY
TO CONFIRM.
```

---

3. McKinley almost always wore a red carnation on his lapel, believing that it brought him good luck. When greeted by twelve-year-old Myrtle Ledger, the president's face lit up. He knelt down and said, "I must give this flower to another little flower." Moments after giving her his lucky carnation, he was shot.

Henry had first met Secretary of State John Hay decades earlier, when he was Abraham Lincoln's baby-faced twenty-two-year-old personal secretary. Now in his sixties, his baby face obscured by a graying beard, Hay was his nation's highest-ranking diplomat and the man charged with advising the president on all vampire-related matters.

The two had last seen each other four years earlier, in London, shortly after Hay's appointment as ambassador to Great Britain. They'd corresponded semifrequently over the years, beginning not long after Lincoln's assassination, when Hay and his fellow presidential secretary, John Nicolay, began an exhaustive, decade-long process of writing the first major biography of their late beloved boss. Henry had filled in some of the missing details of Abe's childhood and clarified a few of Nicolay's and Hay's questions, but he wasn't much use, as most of the stories he had to tell had to be left out of any "official" biography of the late president. Still, he and Hay had always been bonded by a shared love of "the Ancient," as Lincoln's secretaries used to call him.

It was a crisp, clear Tuesday afternoon as Henry and Hay walked from the State, War, and Navy Building[4] across the street to the White House, accompanied by one of Hay's aides and a Washington, D.C., policeman—a precaution that had been ordered for

---

4. Now the Eisenhower Executive Office Building.

all cabinet members by the new president, Theodore Roosevelt.

> Hay had warned me to say nothing of vampires in front of our companions. Few on his staff—only his closest aides—were aware of that part of his job.

It was a policy that had begun while Hay was still a young man, under William Seward—Abraham Lincoln's secretary of state and a vampire hunter in his own right. In the wake of the Civil War, with stories of "vampire soldiers" running rampant among the returning Union soldiers, a concerted effort was made to discredit the growing notion that vampires were more than myth, mostly to prevent panic. With the shooting war over, Seward waged a propaganda war, meant to reassure the public that this talk of "vampires" was nothing more than wild stories. Chief among his tools were the newspapers, in which Seward planted front-page stories and editorials, such as the one that ran in the *Boston Post* in early 1866:

RAVEN-WINGED LIES

```
In my duties as pastor I am often
called upon to comfort those who have
suffered some torment, whether it be
of mind, body or soul. Of late, those
```

members of my congregation who have sought my private counsel have come with fear in their hearts and rumors on their tongues. Rumors of "devils" and "demons" fighting for the South during the War. They ask me what the Bible says about such creatures. Whether they be fallen angels, or a sign of End Times. They worry that the South will gather itself and attack anew. I have addressed my flock, and now I feel it is my duty to address the good readers of this newspaper.

These stories, first whispered on the city streets, and now in my parish, are outright lies, dripping from the tongue of no less a sinner than the father of lies himself. They have infected even the most reasoned lips. I have sat with learned men, who repeat these stories of "savage men, whom bullets nor bayonets could fell." How such creatures were so roundly defeated by a force of merely ordinary men, it would especially please me to hear. It would further please me to know why such whimsy persists in the mind of the public, when it has been labeled as such by no less a Union soldier than Gen. [Ulysses S.] Grant himself. These lies, designed to terrorize the rightful victors, and

chase them from the conquered South,
have spread their raven wings on every
northern street corner. There is not
a threshold they have not crossed,
nor a family apartment they have not
entered.

I call on every good Christian to
condemn them, and to cast out the
darkness by lighting a candle of reason in his brother. If my prayers be
heard, I shall not be called upon to
chronicle so wide and profound a lie
again.

Rev. Daniel Tobin
Walpole, MA

At the same time that he was planting stories, Seward organized a reporting structure within the American government, specifying who would be privy to the truth about vampires: the president and his cabinet, the vice president, and the speaker of the house.[5] Within the State Department, only the

---

5. In the early 1930s, FDR amended this reporting structure to include the heads of the FBI and OSS (forerunner to the CIA). Today, nearly every Western nation has a similar structure in place. In Great Britain, for example, it includes the prime minister; as well as the speaker, leader, and shadows leader of the House of Commons; leader and lord speaker of the House of Lords; and the head of MI6. As a courtesy, the monarch is also briefed on vampire activity, even though there is no constitutional duty to do so.

secretary, the deputy secretary, and their top aides would have access to those presidential briefs that related to vampire activity "foreign and domestic."

"If I'd known I was being summoned to meet with the president," said Henry as he walked with Hay, "I would have worn a nicer suit."

"The president would prefer there be no record of this meeting. You understand, of course."

"Of course."

"And if memory serves, Henry, I don't recall you ever dressing formally to meet *another* president."

"Yes, well...I had a somewhat different relationship with that one."

"We all did," said Hay.

Hay's eyes began to tear up. He rubbed a gloved hand across his face, wiping them dry, and excused himself for becoming emotional. His old friend, Nicolay, had gone to his eternal rest just a month earlier, and he'd found himself "somewhat haunted" by Washington of late.

"Everywhere I turn, I see a street we ran down bearing urgent messages in the dead of night. Every time I have occasion to visit the White House, I picture the two of us sitting at those desks, working ourselves half to death, and I'm certain—sometimes, Henry, I'm certain that I hear him speaking in the next room. Certain that I catch a glimpse of him passing a doorway, hurrying with that long, strange stride of his."

They walked silently for a while, approaching the

South Lawn. Henry hadn't been to the White House in nearly fifty years, and the one before him, though familiar in many ways, seemed foreign. The grounds, once open to the public, were now surrounded by a fence[6] and protected by guards.

"Have you ever wondered," said Hay at last, "what might have been if he'd lived?"

"Hardly a day passes that I don't," said Henry.

"I cannot tell you how often I've longed to see him again," said Hay, "if only for a moment or two. How often I've craved his wisdom, his guidance. There have been heavy days, Henry, far too many heavy days, when I have craved that reassuring hand on my shoulder. Those nights he couldn't sleep, when he would wander into our office past midnight, pull up a chair, and tell us stories until the sun rose. Make us laugh. Make us forget the war. Make himself forget. That high and hearty laugh, Henry…do you remember it?"

> I did. And I'd longed for it. I'd longed for all of the same things. Grieved for him the same way. But my grief—my longing for my lost friend— had always been tinged with a layer of guilt. Unlike Hay, Abe and I hadn't parted as friends. But what could I have said—"Yes? Yes, I missed his company so much that I broke into his crypt,

---

6. Installed on the orders of President Rutherford B. Hayes in 1876.

stole his corpse, and made him immortal against his wishes?" That I'd listened to his screams as he burned himself alive? But that was my burden, and I had to bear it alone.

"Yes," said Henry. "I remember it well."
Hay rubbed a finger under his right eye again.
"Funny," he said. "I can still hear it so clearly...but it was a lifetime ago."
"For some," said Henry as they neared the White House. "And for some, it feels as if he could be waiting on the other side of those doors."
They reached the base of the South Portico. Henry paused and pulled down on his coat, making himself presentable.
"This new one, Roosevelt," said Henry. "Any words of advice?"
Hay smiled. "Hold on to your hat."

Teddy Roosevelt had been born into privilege in New York, a sickly, lonesome boy with dreams of far-off adventures and wild frontiers. Over time, he had willed himself into the picture of masculinity, becoming a boxer, a cowboy, and a big-game hunter. He'd served as a sheriff's deputy in the Dakotas, hunting down outlaws—an experience that he later credited with helping him serve as New York City's police commissioner. In 1897, President McKinley had appointed the thirty-eight-year-old Roosevelt assistant secretary of the navy, a post that he resigned a year later to fight in Cuba during the Spanish-American War. He became colonel of the famed Rough Riders—a cavalry unit he helped found by recruiting friends from the dusty plains of the Dakotas and the bricks of Manhattan brownstones alike.

Roosevelt made a name for himself during the war, becoming something of a national hero. On his return in 1898, buoyed by his image as a "scholarly soldier," he was elected governor of New York, promising to root out corruption. He proved so effective that the corrupt establishment sought a way to get rid of him, so that a more cooperative governor could be installed in his place. The opportunity presented itself in 1900, when President McKinley was campaigning for a second term. McKinley's first vice president, Garret Hobart, had died in office, and he was looking for a new running mate. The corrupt Republican machine put Roosevelt's name forward, and six months into his second term, McKinley was assassinated by Leon Czolgosz, and Teddy Roosevelt was sworn in as the twenty-sixth president of the United States. He was just forty-two years old when he took the oath. The youngest man to ever hold the office.

Hay and Henry were ushered to the second floor, while the policeman and Hay's aide waited downstairs. As they walked the wide second-floor hall toward the president's office, they passed a large painting of Abraham Lincoln.

> Not the Healy[7] one that became famous later on, but the portrait that William Cogswell had done. There was Abe, looking serious and presidential, standing with one hand on a chair back, and a rolled-up paper—the Emancipation Proclamation, probably—in the other. Looking down on us from a gilded frame. Maybe it was the nerves of meeting a new president, or the strange feeling of being back in the residence after so many years, but I let a little snort escape at the sight of the painting. It was so wrong—so opposed to what Abe would have wanted a portrait of himself to look like—that I had to laugh. Hay looked at me like I'd lost my mind, then realized that it was the painting that I was laughing at and laughed along with me. "Terrible, isn't it?" he said.

Hay stopped at the door to Roosevelt's office. "Aren't you coming in?" asked Henry.

"He wanted to meet you alone," said Hay. "Man to man, as it were. It's the way he prefers doing things."

---

7. George Peter Alexander Healy (1813–1894) was an American painter, and one of the most accomplished artists of his time. His contemplative portrait, *Abraham Lincoln* (1869), was purchased by Robert Todd Lincoln. It was donated to the White House in 1939, where it hangs in the State Dining Room today.

Hay lifted his thumb and index finger, mimed touching a brim, and shot Henry a smile. *Hold on to your hat.* The usher opened the office door, and Henry stepped in.

The president was standing on a bearskin rug in the center of his office, repeatedly bending over and touching his toes. Henry had seen Teddy Roosevelt before, across the dining room at Delmonico's and in the newspapers. But up close, he looked more like the caricatures in recent political cartoons. Neatly trimmed mustache. Gold pocket watch chain dangling from the vest of his three-piece suit. Pearly white teeth the size of tombstones. Spectacles clinging to the bridge of his nose. At five feet ten inches, he was taller than average but looked shorter because of his large head and round middle.

Everything about his appearance projected strength. Every fiber in him seemed to ache for contest and conflict. When he eventually died of a heart attack in his sleep in 1919, Vice President Thomas R. Marshall said, "Death had to take Roosevelt sleeping, for if he had been awake, there would have been a fight."

An usher closed the door behind Henry, leaving him alone with the president of the United States. No aides. No guards.

"Mr. Sturges," said Roosevelt, bending forward and exhaling, "I understand you're a man, if I may use the term, who can be reasoned with."

"I like to think—"

"I'll do the talking, Sturges."

He had no shortage of confidence—I'll give him that. He'd attained the office suddenly, and through an unlikely series of events. But unlikely president or not, it had taken him precisely four seconds to grow into the role.

"Mr. Hay speaks highly of you," Roosevelt continued, pausing occasionally to exhale or grunt from the strain of his exercise. "He says that of all the vampires he's ever met…you're the one he trusts above all others. To which I replied, 'Calling a vampire trustworthy…is about as big a compliment as calling a thief…honorable.'"

Roosevelt stood fully, his face flushed from the exertion. "I don't like cats, Sturges. Untrustworthy creatures. *Disloyal* creatures, sneaking around in the dark without making a sound. *Nine lives*, they say. Tell me, would you trust something that was still walking around after you'd killed it eight times? No, Sturges, cats are in league with the devil; make no mistake about it. And yet…I find myself in a predicament. You see, I've inherited a house that's overrun with mice."

His analogies were about as subtle as the rest of him.

Roosevelt in Africa, hunting some of the "bigger game" that he bragged to Henry about.

Roosevelt came forward. He looked Henry over, chewing on his bottom lip from the inside, a nervous habit.

"How old are you, Sturges?"

Henry raised his eyebrows and pointed to himself. *Is it my turn to speak?*

"Yes, yes," said Roosevelt. "Go on, go on."

"Three hundred and thirty-eight, sir."

"Bully!" cried Roosevelt, with a hearty laugh. "A man older than an oak tree! It fascinates me. It absolutely fascinates me! Tell me, Sturges, are you a fighting man?"

"When the fight is just."

"*All* fights are just, Sturges. All the great masterful races have been fighting races, you know. No triumph of peace is quite so great as the supreme triumph of war. That...," said Roosevelt, wagging a finger at Henry, "that is something your beloved Lincoln never understood. He was a timid man. Mark my words, if he had lived in a time of peace, no one would know his name."

I couldn't hold my tongue at hearing a friend slandered.

"A 'timid' man, sir? Perhaps you wouldn't have thought so if you'd seen him take the heads of countless vampires with his ax."

"A primitive weapon, for a primitive man! He was an unschooled woodsman, and I don't mind saying that he was unfit to hold the highest office in the land!"

"I apologize, sir," said Henry. "I didn't realize that you'd been personally acquainted with him."

Roosevelt glared at him through those little lenses, framed in perfect circles of gold wire. "I do not argue that he was a man of great will," said Roosevelt, "or that he accomplished great things. But he was not a gentleman."

"If he was not a gentleman," said Henry, "then no man is."

"You think you can intimidate me?" asked Roosevelt. "I've hunted bigger game than you, sir! Creatures with far bigger teeth and tougher hides!"

Roosevelt refused to break eye contact. Refused to blink. He chewed on his lip some more and squinted.

"Bully!" cried Roosevelt at last, breaking into laughter. "Good man, Sturges! Good man! Yes, that's what we need! A fighting man! A spirited man!"

> He perplexed me. He was so brash. So self-assured. Yet in time, I would learn that this was the same man who enjoyed curling up with Tolstoy. The same man who was so grief stricken over the death of his first love that he wrote "the light has gone out of my life" in his diary the day she died and never spoke of her again. He was a cowboy with the soul of a poet. To this day, he is the most *American* American I've ever met.

"Do you know what an 'anarchist' is, Mr. Sturges?"

"Of course."

The word "anarchist" was a staple on the front pages of 1901 newspapers. McKinley's assassin, Leon Czolgosz, had been a self-described anarchist, after all. It was an ideology on the rise, its fires stoked at rallies, where speakers decried the growing gap between the ultrarich and the desperately poor. Proposals were made for a world without leaders, without governments and armies. A world in which monarchs would be dragged from their palaces and their wealth distributed among the people equally.

"It's a poison," said Roosevelt. "A cancer that infects the minds of the desperate and the frightened and the just plain stupid. The king of Italy, murdered by an anarchist. The president of France, murdered by an anarchist. The president of the United States, murdered by an anarchist.[8] Unrest on the streets of Chicago. Tides of rebellion and civil war in China and Russia. Do you think it a coincidence? Do you think that this disease of discord has spread without a source? No, sir. Its seeds are being sown by your kind."

> According to [Roosevelt], the anarchist movements in Europe and the United States were, in fact, part of a "veiled vampire resurgence," with aims to overthrow governments that had become increasingly hostile toward vampires in the wake of the Civil War. With their numbers dwindling, these vampires had taken advantage of an existing movement, recruiting young, ideological, and easily manipulated minds to their cause. And not just in the United States.

---

8. Roosevelt would himself be shot by a would-be assassin while campaigning in 1912. The bullet entered his chest but failed to puncture any vital organs. Roosevelt, in typical fashion, refused to be taken to the hospital until he delivered his speech. He proceeded to speak for ninety minutes, blood dripping down his shirt.

The president added that among all the dispa-
rate anarchist movements, one name kept coming up. An invisible leader, pulling the strings of
chaos:

A. Grander VIII.

"He wishes to drive the world into war," said Roosevelt. "To destabilize it, so it's ripe for the picking.
His forces may be too small in number to do it with
an army of their own, but they're well on their way to
recruiting an army to do it in their stead. We must cut
this cancer out of the world body before it spreads any
further, Mr. Sturges. Before it infects America at the
dawn of her greatest century."

"They've tried to take America before. We ran
them out."

"Ran them out, yes. But you didn't *finish* them,
Sturges. There's a mile of difference between deport-
ing and destroying."

"All the same, they wouldn't dare attack America
again."

"They don't want America, Sturges. America is too
small a prize in their twisted view."

"With all due respect, sir, if they haven't the
strength to take America, how can they possibly take
the world?"

"Intrigue, Mr. Sturges. Foreign intrigue. They
mean to destabilize the governments of the world.
They mean to foster rebellion in the streets. They

mean to plunge us into darkness, and in that darkness, they mean to take their hold. My predecessors have lived by a policy of ignorance. Doing nothing because they were too afraid to do the *wrong* thing. Well, I shall not be ignorant of this threat! I shall not shrink from it and pray that it resolves itself! At San Juan Hill,[9] more of my men died from malaria than from bullets or machetes. I asked a doctor with our unit, a man named Gorgas,[10] how in the hell we could stop the disease from spreading. 'Easy,' he said. 'Just kill every mosquito in the swamp.'"

> At first I thought he was testing me again. Saying something absurd to see what kind of reaction it elicited. But his expression never changed, and I realized that he was deadly serious.

"I'm going to kill every bloodsucking mosquito in the swamp, and you're going to help me do it."

"You're talking about war."

"A war? No...No, wars are fought on battlefields, with rifles and horses. If I could declare war on this enemy, I'd do it this very minute; then I'd march out

---

9. In Cuba, the site of the Rough Riders' greatest victory in battle.

10. Dr. William Crawford Gorgas (1854–1920) was one of the first medical professionals to accept the fact that malaria was spread by mosquitoes. His sanitary programs during the construction of the Panama Canal are credited with saving thousands of lives. He would later be appointed surgeon general of the United States Army.

of this office and saddle up. No...This, sir, this is simple diplomacy. You'll be delivering personal messages, on behalf of the United States. Nothing more."

"And what message might I be delivering?"

"The same message Benjamin Franklin printed on the eve of America's Revolution: *Join or die.* America is going to give the vampires of this earth a choice: either they can join us, or they can die. But mankind will not live another hour in quiet fear."

"And I assume none of this will be officially sanctioned."

Roosevelt smiled. "No," he said. "You will receive no commendations for your service, beyond the thanks of a grateful president and the knowledge that you have served your nation proudly. But that's not to say you'll be alone, either. We'll share whatever intelligence we have. Give you access to our friends abroad."

"And access to a mortician, should I fail."

"Ha! That's the spirit!" cried Roosevelt. "Take the bull by the horns, and do it with a smile on your face. Far better it is to dare mighty things, to win glorious triumphs, even though checkered by failure, than to take rank with those poor spirits who neither enjoy much nor suffer much, because they live in the gray twilight that knows not victory or defeat."

It was a rousing sentiment, but I couldn't help feeling like the army dog who's patted on the back as he's sent off to walk through a minefield.

"When compared with the suppression of this vampire agenda," Roosevelt continued, "every other question sinks into insignificance. To destroy this invisible government, to dissolve the unholy alliance of your kind, is the first task of the statesmanship of the day, and you, sir, are to be my newest statesman."

"An honor, sir, to be sure. But why me? What you're asking is the very purpose of the Union and the sworn duty of its members."

"Ha!" shouted Roosevelt. "And a fine job you've done of it! Sitting idly, drifting off as the enemy marched through your front door and assassinated *your* president. You and your 'Union.' You call yourselves patriots! Congratulate yourselves for standing up for the North in the war! Yet you live somewhere outside the margins of citizenship—loyal to your little brotherhood before your country. Addicted to soft living and averse to your patriotic duty! Well, I won't tolerate it! I won't tolerate any sort of damned fifty-fifty allegiances! Either you're an American and nothing else, from your boots to your hat, or you're not an American at all!"

"What you ask is too much for one man."

"That's why I didn't ask a man to do it."

A fair point, thought Henry.

"Do you love this country?" asked Roosevelt.

"I have loved her since before she was born."

"Then serve her."

"Are you asking me to betray my oath to the Union, sir?"

"I'm not 'asking' you anything. A man's obedience to his country isn't asked as a favor; it's demanded! And if that means choosing sides between the needs of your country and the needs of your social club, well, then you'd damned well better make the right choice, or I'll have you stuffed and mounted!"

Roosevelt's face had turned bright red again. This time, he wasn't testing Henry's mettle. This time, his anger was sincere.

"Look me in the eye, Sturges. Tell me...are you an American or aren't you?"

"I am."

"Well, I am the *president* of the United States of America. And from this moment forward, you work for *me*."

EIGHT

★ ★ ★

The Mystic

War means an ugly mob-madness, crucifying
the truth tellers, choking the artists,
sidetracking reforms, revolutions, and the
working of social forces.

—John Reed

SECRET INTELLIGENCE SERVICE
Memorandum

CLASSIFIED
Date: November 26th, 1916

To: Secretary of State Robert Lansing
From: Director, SIS
Subject: Possible withdrawal of
Russian troops

It has come to our attention that
TN2[1] is currently considering a

---

1. Tsar Nicholas II (1868–1918).

complete withdrawal of Russian
forces. The result of such a
withdrawal would prove disastrous
to Britain and France, as it would
allow the Germans to abandon the
eastern front and redouble their
attacks on our lines in the West.
As we have seen at Verdun, our
forces are able to fight the Germans
to a stalemate, at best. We believe
the judgment of TN2 has become
compromised, and that he has fallen
under the influence of ███████████,
who, as we have stated in previous
communications, we believe to be
a ████████████. Upon consultation
with ████████████, PMG[2] urges you
to consider sending your asset,
████████████, to rendezvous with ours,
to coordinate and enact a solution
to this problem as expediently as
they are able.

C^3

2. Prime Minister David Lloyd George (1863–1945).
3. This signature belonged to Captain Sir George Mansfield Smith-Cumming, the founding director of what is known today as MI6. He abbreviated his long name by simply signing "C" on documents in green ink. The abbreviation evolved into a code name for "chief," and all subsequent directors of MI6 have since signed documents in this manner.

Russia was the last place Henry wanted to spend Christmas. And judging by the hardscrabble faces on the streets of Petrograd,[4] it was the last place the Russians wanted spend *their* Christmas, too. Now, instead of enjoying a good book at home, by the light of an electric lamp (powered by Tesla's AC current, naturally), he was freezing in the heart of the Russian Empire, standing on the snowy banks of the Neva River, which had frozen over. Russia had been electrified since 1886, and Petrograd had become something of a national showroom for incandescent light, with buildings and streetlamps eschewing their gas lines in favor of electric cables and strings of bulbs glowing in crisscrossing patterns above the city's main streets and marketplaces. But now, with a war on, power was being rationed, and the streets were dark enough to see the stars slipping away, as a wall of dark clouds moved in from the ocean to the west. Henry watched them roll in. It would snow soon.

"This is absurd, absurd, absurd," said a voice beside him.

Nikola Tesla stood shivering just to Henry's left. The two of them surrounded by snowdrifts on a dark street, in a city they'd never been to, waiting for men they'd never met.

---

4. Present-day St. Petersburg.

Twain had ridden off on his comet[5] and left me to deal with Tesla by myself, the bastard.

I wish I could say [Twain] and I had seen a lot of each other in those last ten years, or that we'd written each other diligently. I wish I could say that we'd gotten into more adventures together, or traveled the world righting wrongs. But the truth is, other than a few [letters] here and there, and one brief visit to his home in Connecticut, I didn't see Twain much after that year in New York. Life is often like that. We write the fantasy of what will be in our heads, and more often than not, reality falls short of our wild expectations. But I was grateful, all the same. Just as it's better to have loved and lost than to have never loved before, it was better to have spent a year with one of your heroes than not.

Tesla had just turned sixty. No longer a young man but, to Henry's consternation, still young enough to find himself in trouble.

---

5. In 1909, Twain said, "I came in with Halley's Comet in 1835. It is coming again next year, and I expect to go out with it. It will be the greatest disappointment of my life if I don't go out with Halley's Comet. The Almighty has said, no doubt: 'Now here are these two unaccountable freaks; they came in together, they must go out together.'" His prediction was accurate—Twain died of a heart attack on April 21, 1910, in Redding, Connecticut, one day after the comet's closest approach, as if there to carry him off into eternity.

I'd invited [Tesla] along as a translator. He spoke a little Russian—just enough for us to get by without drawing too much attention. Really, I think I just hated the idea of spending Christmas in Russia alone and wanted a familiar face around—even if it was Tesla's face. I remember him being excited when I confided the details of my mission. He insisted on bringing one of his inventions along. Something he'd been working on but hadn't tested in the field yet. But once we arrived in Petrograd, all he wanted to do was drink and play cards and drink some more. It was like the proximity to his homeland had awakened the young man in him. He was a brilliant inventor, but good God Almighty, he was a terrible spy.

Henry Sturges had become an unofficial one-man branch of the United States government, and he'd spent the first decade of the twentieth century as something of an errand boy to presidents—first Roosevelt, then Taft, and now Woodrow Wilson. His "diplomatic missions" had been innocuous, for the most part: helping the White House assess the numbers of those "friendly" vampires living within its borders; traveling abroad to gather information about possible "problem vampires." On occasion, though, Henry was dispatched to send a "message" to one of these problem vampires on behalf of the president of the United States.

> The irony wasn't lost on me. I'd spent much of the nineteenth century sending a future president out to hunt vampires. Now, in the twentieth century, presidents were sending *me* out on the same errands. But where Abe and I had been trying to prevent an overthrow of the United States, the threat was less direct this time, and the enemy almost impossible to identify. As [Theodore] Roosevelt had said, it was a war that was being fought slowly, unfolding in dark alleys and sitting parlors.
>
> Hiding somewhere in that murk, moving chessmen on a checkered board, was Grander. Between us were pawns and knights and bishops, each of them manipulated by his invisible hand. Most didn't even know they were part of the game.

In 1914, Henry's "missions" suddenly took on a new urgency, when Archduke Franz Ferdinand, heir to the Austro-Hungarian throne, and his wife, Sophie, were assassinated by a young Serbian radical named Gavrilo Princip in Sarajevo. As a result of the assassination, Austria-Hungary declared war on Serbia, which led Russia to move against Austria-Hungary, which led Germany to move against Russia, which led to the First World War.

Princip had succeeded in doing what Leon Czol-gosz had dreamed of—he'd fired a shot that started a war.

President Wilson opposed direct American involve-ment in the Great War, which was raging in Europe. However, he *did* agree to send Henry on a crucial errand in the winter of 1916. Though he was English by birth, it can be argued that Henry Sturges was the first American soldier to enter World War I.

It was Christmas Eve, but Petrograd seemed devoid of joy. Henry thought the Russians a largely joyless people. It wasn't just the rationing of light, either. The previous year, with more than a million and a half of its troops already dead, and with millions more freez-ing and starving due to poor supply lines, the Rus-sians had been forced to give up their occupation of Warsaw and fall back, in what became known as "the Great Retreat." Humiliated, the tsar had dismissed his generals and taken direct control of the army. But many suspected that the tsar wasn't even in control of his *faculties*, let alone his army. There were rumors that another man was pulling the strings behind the scenes. A man who possessed strange abilities.

These rumors had reached the tsar's first cousin, King George V of England, who ordered his intel-ligence service to investigate. The more they learned about the tsar's mysterious shaman, the more unnerved MI6 became. There were multiple accounts of his having performed "impossible" acts: healing the sick, reading minds, even emerging unscathed from an assassination attempt that "no mortal could have survived."[6] And if these sources were to be believed, this man had put the tsar and his family under some kind of spell.

His name was Grigory Yefimovich Rasputin.

Rasputin was a wandering monk, traveling from village to village, offering his services as a faith healer. His past was a patchwork of myth and mystery. Some said he'd been born in remote Siberia and raised his own family before abandoning them to pursue his calling. Others said he was an orphan, delivered to the doorstep of a monastery in the Ural Mountains, and that he'd bewildered the monks with his abilities from a young age.

A self-purported "mystic," Rasputin claimed that he could pray away many common ailments and see visions of the future. He seems to have made his living doing just that, wandering from village to village at

---

6. In the summer of 1914, a woman named Khioniya Guseva, follower of one of Rasputin's faith-healing rivals, attacked him with a knife, slicing him across the belly so severely that his entrails spilled out. Guseva is said to have exclaimed, "I have killed the Antichrist!" as Rasputin fell to the ground, bleeding profusely. He was rushed away to receive medical attention, but there is no record of his ever having seen a doctor. He was seen by few people for nearly two months. When he reemerged in Petrograd, he bore no signs that he had ever been injured. Rasputin told others that he had "healed himself, as he had healed others."

the turn of the twentieth century, presenting himself to the local priest or mayor, setting up a temporary "clinic," and accepting donations in return for his services. It was said that he could walk for "days on end, without want of food or rest." In 1903, whether by chance or by design, his wanderings brought him to Russia's capital city. A city obsessed with the occult, as many cities were at the turn of the century.

It was not publicly known at the time, but the tsar's youngest child and only son, Alexei, had been born with hemophilia—a common disease among European royalty, due to the frequent intermarriages of first and second cousins. Young Alexei was given to fits of vomiting. His joints ached horribly. There was often blood in his urine. Once, when he was three, he had fallen off the back of a toy wagon that one of his sisters had been pulling. The next day, his entire body was swollen and covered in black bruises that lasted for weeks.

Not even the tsar's personal army of doctors could help poor Alexei, and he was given long odds of surviving childhood. Desperate, Tsarina Alexandra ignored her royal advisers (and her husband's skepticism) and sent for a mystic to heal her son. Rasputin had already gained a reputation among the elite during visits to Kiev and Petrograd. After meeting with Rasputin, the tsarina declared herself impressed and invited him into the royal household.

Rasputin *was* able to give Alexei some relief, but it was only temporary. After a day or two of feeling fit, Alexei would succumb to fatigue again, followed by more pain and bleeding. Rasputin insisted that he could "cure" the young grand duke, but to do so, he would have to be alone with him for several days. At first, the tsar refused. He wasn't going to send his only son off with some relative stranger, no matter what "powers" he seemed to possess. But when Alexei took a turn for the worse, Alexandra begged her husband to let Rasputin try. The tsar relented, and when Rasputin returned with the young grand duke four days later, Alexei Romanov seemed miraculously healed. The mystic had cemented his place in the royal household.

Of the many vampires who meddled in world affairs in the twentieth century, few were more famous or more successful in their aims than Rasputin. Posing as a faith healer, mystic, and spiritual adviser, he would eventually gain the trust of Russia's tsar and almost single-handedly bring about the fall of the Romanov dynasty.

But while Rasputin was working in secret to undermine the tsar, it seems that he wasn't working on his own behalf. In the summer of 1916, the head of MI6, a man with the incredibly English-sounding name Captain Sir George Mansfield Smith-Cumming, sent a secret cable to Tsar Nicholas II on behalf of King George.

```
BELIEVE ██████████⁷ WORKING IN
CONCERT WITH KAISER. HAVE EVIDENCE
TO SUPPORT. REQUEST MEETING IN
PERSON.
```

It was unclear what a Russian mystic and the German government could have in common, or how they could have run across each other in the first place. But it hardly mattered. By then, Rasputin had cast his spell and secured his hold on the Romanovs and those around them. King George's cable never reached the tsar.

Henry and Tesla waited for their contacts to arrive, Tesla grumbling and shivering and Henry carrying a newspaper under his left arm—the signal that had been prearranged. It was well after ten p.m., and Henry's newspaper was soaked through from the snow that had begun to fall, when two men in long black coats came walking across the bridge and stopped a few feet away.

There was no CIA to speak of in 1916. The army and navy had their own intelligence-gathering units, but they weren't espionage services in the way we think of them today. The British, however, had recently formed the Directorate of Military

---

7. Rasputin.

Intelligence, Section Six, or MI6, for short, and had agents operating in every corner of Europe.

> And so naturally, I'd expected our contacts to be Brits. I was surprised when the first man spoke with a thick Russian accent. I was even more surprised when he gave his name: "Prince Felix Yusupov."

The Russian prince was then twenty-nine years old. Like many members of the royal family, he'd grown concerned by Rasputin's influence over his uncle, the tsar. The other man introduced himself as Grand Duke Dmitri Pavlovich, twenty-five years old and the tsar's cousin. Both were handsome, both dressed in their military officers' uniforms, over which they wore heavy fur coats, with fur hats upon their heads.

> Yusupov had that "royal demeanor"—I guess you could call it swagger, or arrogance. He'd studied at Oxford, and had a solid grasp of English, which he spoke with a less pronounced accent than the grand duke.

It had been a mutual friend from his Oxford days who'd first reached out to Yusupov about working for MI6. Yusupov had jumped at the chance, excited by the prospect of being a spy, and recruited his cousin the grand duke. Together, they'd spent nearly two years trying to root out German spies in Russia's high society, and they'd proven effective at gathering information and passing it on to MI6 agents. But they'd never carried out a murder.

Henry introduced himself, then introduced Tesla, who didn't offer a hand, and said, through chattering teeth, "U nikh yest' chasy v Rossii?" *Do they have clocks in Russia?*

Both of them were clearly surprised that *the* Nikola Tesla was standing before them.

"Mr. Tesla is a close friend," said Henry. "He's come to be my translator, but I'm the one who will be helping you with your problem."

"I appreciate that you have come to help," said Yusupov, "but we do not need this help. We have a plan. A very good plan. The grand duke and I, we are able to carry this plan out by ourselves."

Yusupov laid it all out for us. (It was clear he'd rehearsed this presentation, and it was even clearer that he was pleased with himself for thinking it all up.) First, Yusupov would send word that his wife, the beautiful twenty-one-year-old princess, was eager to speak with Rasputin concerning strange, erotic dreams she'd been having. Felix knew Rasputin was a man of few weaknesses, but women—especially young, married ones plagued by repressed erotic desires—were one of them. Once Rasputin arrived at the palace (and with the princess safely miles away in another residence), Yusupov and Pavlovich would stall him while feeding him pastries and wine that had been laced with cyanide. When he died of poisoning, they would burn his clothing, take his body to the river, and toss it in. Ta-da—no more Rasputin. The royals would finally be free from his spell, they would both be hailed as heroes, and the Russian Empire would enjoy a thousand years of uninterrupted glory.

"With all due respect," said Henry, "your plan has no hope of success."

"I know why you say this," said the prince. "Rasputin has survived assassination before, yes. He is very strong and can heal himself, yes. I know all of this. But this is why we will use enough cyanide to kill five men."

"Indeed, indeed. But you may as well use enough cyanide to kill a hundred men, for I doubt very much that he'll accept your offer of wine and pastries."

The prince and the grand duke looked at him, confused.

"Come," said Henry. "Let's find someplace warm where we can talk."

It took a few days of preparation, but by the evening of December 29th, the conspirators were ready for Rasputin. As night fell, they gathered in a large room in the basement of Yusupov Palace—a room chosen specifically for its distance from where the other royals would be sleeping. "A lovely room for a murder," as Henry told his accomplices when they'd first shown it to him. It had been a formal dining room prior to the palace's 1830s restoration and had more recently been used for storage. Its walls had once been covered by mirrors, now cracked and painted over, obscured by large pieces of furniture and art that had been piled against them, all covered by white cloths to protect them from the dust. A small table and several chairs had been set up in the center of the vast room. Above it, hanging from a high ceiling, was the sole source of light—a chandelier that had been converted to electricity. Nearly half of its forty bulbs were burned out, and the power was prone to fluctuations, the result being a dim and ever-flickering glow that tapered off into darkness near the edges of the room.

For a time, part of Yusupov Palace had been converted into a field hospital for wounded Russian soldiers. But the prince's mother, Zinaida, complained that "[the wounded solders'] crying out at all hours disturbed her sleep, and their blood stained her floors," so the hospital was moved elsewhere. But for all the hype about its grandeur, Henry found the inside "utilitarian and uninspired." It reminded him of virtually every other palace, château, or manor he'd ever had occasion to visit.

> There were all the usual touches: grandly carved stone staircases and long hallways, a private theater with red velvet curtains and gold leaf, ornate ceiling moldings, priceless works of art collected over the centuries through both legitimate and illegitimate means, but like most things Russian, it valued function over form.

After Prince Yusupov and Grand Duke Pavlovich had recovered from the initial shock of learning that Rasputin was an immortal (and after all the attendant questions about God and the universe and the meaning of it all that usually follow such a revelation had been addressed), Henry had given the prince and the grand duke a two-day crash course in vampire hunting.

> There wasn't much I could do in two days, so I focused on the basics, which amounted to: (1) don't get near the head, and (2) when in doubt, run away. They were royals, and they'd been trained in swordplay and shooting. Trained to be confident and brave their whole lives. Still, I wondered if they would be able to keep their cool when the

time came. I was especially worried about Pavlovich. When I'd shown them my vampire form—
in part to convince them that vampires were, in
fact, real, and in part to prepare them if Rasputin
showed his—Yusupov had let out a little yelp and
jumped back but quickly recovered. Pavlovich,
however (and I feel comfortable saying this only
because he's long dead), had pissed himself in
spectacular fashion.

Henry had assumed that it would fall to him to kill
Rasputin. That was, after all, why the Americans had
sent their "asset," as the memos so warmly referred
to him.

My plan began exactly as Yusupov's had—the
prince would send word to Rasputin on behalf
of his wife. Rasputin would travel to the palace
to meet with her.

Only, in this version of events, Rasputin would never
arrive. En route, his coach would be ambushed by a
small group of radicals—the Bolsheviks,[8] no doubt—
and Rasputin would be attacked and beheaded in the
street.

---

8. An offshoot of the Russian Social Democratic Labor Party, founded
by Vladimir Lenin and others to represent the country's revolutionary
working class. It would later become the Communist Party of the Soviet
Union, following the October Revolution the following year.

But Yusupov was opposed to this approach. He didn't want Rasputin's death to have any political connotations. Things were shaky enough for the royals as it was without some foreign vampire assassin stirring up tensions between the tsar and the Bolsheviks. Yusupov was adamant—Rasputin had to disappear without a trace, leaving everyone perplexed and no one to blame.

It was Tesla who came up with an alternative plan.

> He brought up the possibility of using [his weapon] to kill Rasputin.

While Tesla had certainly done his share of drinking and playing cards on the trip, he'd also found time to tinker with his latest invention—which Henry would later describe as looking like "a cross between a satellite dish and an espresso machine." The "dish" part of Tesla's device (which Tesla called a "teleforce weapon"[9]) resembled a briefcase, with handles on two

---

9. Toward the end of his life, Tesla spoke publicly of a "teleforce" weapon, which could be used to wipe out entire fleets or battalions over great distances. The press dubbed it "Tesla's Death Ray," and wild stories were written imagining all of its uses. In many ways, it was the forerunner of the "ray guns" that became popular in the science fiction of the 1940s and '50s. In describing it, Tesla said, "[It would] send concentrated beams of particles through the free air, of such tremendous energy that they will bring down a fleet of 10,000 enemy airplanes at a distance of 200 miles from a defending nation's border and will cause armies to drop dead in their tracks." When asked how long it would

sides instead of one, and covered not with leather but with copper plating, fastened with hundreds of tiny rivets. This copper briefcase[10] was attached by bundled wires to a large, boxy pack that Tesla strapped to his back; the pack was also covered in riveted copper plating and was built around what looked to Henry like a large vacuum tube[11] surrounded by a thick metal ring. There were several small pressure gauges on the side of the backpack, none of which made any sense to Henry, but all of which, based on the way Tesla constantly fussed over their readings, seemed very important.

> [Tesla] claimed that his device could kill anything he aimed it at, up to a distance of thirty meters. We were doubtful, to say the least. You have to understand, this was a sixty-year-old man wearing a funny-looking box on his back, holding a flat piece of copper between his hands. He was asking us to bet our lives on what looked like a parlor trick. So he offered us a demonstration. He asked Yusupov to have some uncooked meat sent down, which he set on the table in the center of the room.

---

take before such a weapon was practical, he answered, "But it is not an experiment...I have built, demonstrated and used it. Only a little time will pass before I can give it to the world."

10. A transmitter.

11. This was, in fact, an early version of a split-anode magnetron tube—a device used to produce microwaves.

There were no batteries capable of powering such a weapon at the time, which meant that it had to be kept plugged in, via a thirty-foot cord that Tesla had rigged up. This ruled out an ambush on the streets of Petrograd. But there was another problem. Tesla's weapon ran on alternating current, but the palace's generator was one of Edison's direct-current models.

After cursing the stupidity of the Russians for investing in "the inferior electricity of an inferior man," he went to work—scrambling to make a transformer out of whatever he could find lying around. When he finally got it working and switched it on, all the needles on the backpack's gauges jumped and a *hum* filled the room. The backpack started to emit a low vibration that you could feel in your bones and made the hairs on your arms stand up. And a smell—that electrical smell of charged air before a storm.

Tesla told us to get behind him—which we were more than happy to do—and pointed the little copper briefcase at the table, some twenty or thirty feet away. He closed one eye, lining it up the way a rifleman lines up his gun barrel, and squeezed a button on one of the briefcase handles. I'd expected some kind of flash of light or sparks to come shooting out of it, like the experiments he'd shown Twain and me in his lab. But there was nothing like that—just that low vibration and a crackling sound as the raw meat began to smoke, cracking, popping. Cooking before our eyes.

Henry and his fellow conspirators had never seen a microwave oven or a radar. They'd never watched television or even imagined such a thing possible. To them, the idea of energy being beamed, invisibly, across a room, was simply magic. Yet here it was, a piece of raw steak sizzling and smoking by itself on a bare plate. No flame. No damage to the plate or the table.

> [Tesla] went bug-eyed, as if he was surprised the thing was actually working. The rest of us, we were...I don't know—shocked? Amazed? More than anything, we were excited, because we knew we had our answer.

The new plan was quickly drawn up: Rasputin would arrive at around eight in the evening, expecting an audience (and who knows what else) with the beautiful young Princess Irina to discuss her "strange and erotic" dreams. Rasputin would be led down to the basement dining room, where the table would be set in the center.

> I would remain hidden, just off the old dining room, in a basement kitchen, ready to rush in if

things went to hell. Yusupov would greet Rasputin and tell him to wait while he fetched [Princess]
Irina. Once Yusupov disappeared, Pavlovich
would enter and tell Rasputin that he'd arranged
a surprise for him: a personal demonstration by
the one and only Nikola Tesla, who just so happened to be visiting Petrograd from America.

Pavlovich would introduce Tesla, who would give
Rasputin a demonstration of his latest invention, an
"electrical mind reader."

We knew this would pique Rasputin's curiosity,
as he was a connoisseur of all things occult.

Tesla would strap on his boxy copper backpack, flip
it on, and aim the handheld plate at Rasputin's head.
Once the switch was thrown, Tesla estimated it would
take "between five and ten seconds" for the blood and
water in Rasputin's brain to boil.

If it all went right, we would kill a powerful vampire without firing a shot or spilling a drop of blood.
     But then, nothing went right that evening.
Absolutely nothing.

They'd expected him at eight, but it was well past ten
o'clock, and there was still no sign of him.

The conspirators were gathered at the table in the center of the basement dining room, beneath the dim light of its dying chandelier. Tesla's device was on the table in front of them, covered by a white table-cloth. A gramophone blared out a scratchy recording of "Yankee Doodle Boy."[12] A small detail that Henry couldn't deny himself.

> I'd seen a copy of it in Yusupov's record collection while we were rehearsing our plan, and I insisted we have it playing when [Rasputin] walked in. The others were dead set against it. They thought it might tip him off to the plot—namely, the fact that there were Americans lurking in the palace. But honestly, what were the chances of him making that connection? It was a popular tune at the time. Besides, if you can't have a little fun when you're carrying out an assassination, then what's the point?

It was nearly midnight before Rasputin showed up. His motor carriage sputtered through the palace gates and up its round drive to a covered entrance.

He was already in a foul mood by the time he reached the palace. He hadn't fed in nearly two weeks

---

12. Popularly known as "Yankee Doodle Dandy," the song hails from the 1904 Broadway show *Little Johnny Jones*, the first musical written by legendary composer George M. Cohan—considered one of the founding fathers of American musical theater.

due to the demands of his schedule, and his temperament always soured when his blood ran thin. Plus, it had been a thoroughly annoying evening, what with his German contacts keeping him for hours, requesting assurances, making demands. *Idiots. Brutes.* Had they no appreciation for the precariousness of his situation? Did they think it was easy, keeping the leaders of an empire under your spell? Still, even a vampire of Rasputin's power had to show patience and respect given whom these Germans represented. They'd come bearing a note:

Grigory,

These men are my personal represent at ives. They speak for me, and T hey are aut horized T o negot iat e on my behalf. I urge you T ake T hem seriously.

A. Grander VIII

The mysterious Mr. Grander. Eighth of his name. The faceless, all-seeing, all-knowing vampire of all vampires. It had been his idea to have Rasputin ingratiate himself with the Romanovs. His idea to exploit the tsarina's weakness for her beloved Alexei and her desperation to believe in the occult. If you believed the rumors, the whole war had been his idea.

On most occasions, Rasputin wore a black body-length gown that gave one the impression that he was floating as he walked. But tonight he was dressed in a blue embroidered silk shirt, his long dark hair pulled back. His bushy beard making his long face all the longer. At six feet four inches, he was uncommonly tall, and there was not, as one contemporary newspaper account described, "an ill-placed morsel of fat on him. His entire body is sinew and skin; everything about his appearance is long and muscular."

Through a crack in the kitchen door, Henry could see Rasputin walk down the long hall that led to the dining room, led by one of the Yusupovs' butlers.

A chill went through my body as I saw him approach. He was exactly the same height, the same build [as Abraham Lincoln]. But there was a grace about him that Abe had never possessed. Abe had always seemed a little awkward in his body. But Rasputin had learned how to control that big vessel. Which is strange, given that he had small feet for such a big man.

And his eyes. Those dark, haunted eyes. People often comment on them. Their intensity when he stares into the camera. But something no one ever comments on—and you can go back and check

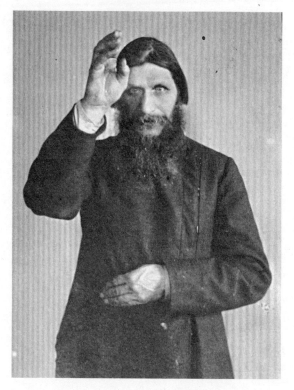

Many photos exist of Rasputin and his famously intense eyes, but this is the only known photograph where a hint of his fangs appears just below his mustache.

this—*Rasputin is always in sharp focus.*[13] In every picture taken of him, even if other faces are blurred, Rasputin's face is *always in focus*, and his

13. The plates used by photographers of the day often required long exposures to absorb enough light for an image. This meant that the camera shutter would have to remain open for several seconds or more. If anyone in the picture moved during that time, they would become blurred in the final image. To be in perfect, sharp focus in *dozens* of known images was almost unheard of and possible only if the subject (Rasputin) was able to keep himself perfectly—*unnaturally*—still.

eyes are always locked, unblinking, right on the camera. They had a hypnotic quality, as if he was peering into your soul, even if he caught sight of you for only a second. It was easy to imagine someone being taken in by them. Especially a human.

Just as they'd rehearsed, Pavlovich cranked up the Victrola and dropped the needle as Rasputin and the butler neared. The cracks and pops gave way to the first tinny notes of "Yankee Doodle Boy":

I'm a Yankee Doodle Dandy,
A Yankee Doodle, do or die;
A real live nephew of my Uncle Sam,
Born on the Fourth of July.

Rasputin was disappointed, but not the least bit surprised, to find the prince and the grand duke—*conspirators, the both of them, and when I finally prove it, I'll attend to them personally*—waiting for him in their military uniforms. Rasputin had smelled them from the end of the hall. There were other smells down here, too. Some familiar, some...foreign.

I've got a Yankee Doodle sweetheart,
She's my Yankee Doodle joy...

"Togda eto proch'!" barked Rasputin, looking at the Victrola. *Turn that off!*

Yusupov gave a nod to Pavlovich, who slunk over and lifted the needle.

"Gde ona?" asked Rasputin. *Where is she?*

"Grigory!" said Yusupov, laughing. "Not even a 'hello' for the man whose wife you wish to meet with?"

"Where is she," Rasputin repeated, "and why are we down here in this dungeon?"

"We love it down here!" said Yusupov. "We're here all the time, drinking, playing music, playing cards. We can make all the noise we want, and Mother doesn't complain. Irina was with us until, oh, not even twenty minutes ago. She grew tired of waiting and went up to bed. But," said Yusupov, seeing Rasputin's face darken (if such a thing was even possible) at the prospect of having his time wasted, "fear not. I shall go and fetch her. She is very eager to spend some time with you...alone."

The dangling "alone" was enough to calm Rasputin.

"A moment," said Yusupov, "if you please."

He left, disappearing down the same hall that Rasputin had just crossed. The butler followed, sliding two large doors closed behind them, shutting Rasputin in with Pavlovich. Just the two of them in the dim and flickering light of the chandelier.

Pavlovich was scared out of his wits. I could see it on his face. I could *smell* it, and I'm sure Rasputin could, too. But I didn't flinch. I could only go in as a last resort. I knew that the second I burst through the door, the fight would be on, and all hope of our quiet little assassination would be out the window. Besides, everything was going as we'd planned. All Pavlovich had to do was hold himself together long enough to introduce Tesla.

Grand Duke Pavlovich (who had never felt quite big enough to fill his outsize title) had always been nervous around Rasputin—and that was *before* he'd known that he was a vampire. Rasputin, therefore, thought nothing of the fact that he was nervous now. A fact that likely saved Pavlovich's life.

"So," said Pavlovich, his mouth bone-dry, "would you care to...sit?"

"No," said Rasputin.

"I, uh..."

Rasputin considered Pavlovich with those impossible, hypnotic eyes.

"I have something for you," said Pavlovich. "A, uh, a surprise."

"I have no interest in your surprise," said Rasputin, walking in long, graceful strides toward the table in the center of the room. "Leave me. I prefer to wait for Irina alone."

"No," said Pavlovich.

Rasputin whipped around and glared at Pavlovich. *No?*

Pavlovich was doing everything but jump up and down and yell, "It's a trick! We've brought you here to kill you!" I watched through the crack in the door, filled with dread. Bracing myself to go in there and fight. I was probably a millimeter away from doing it when I heard the doors on the opposite side of the room slide open.

"I am here, here, here!" cried Tesla, bursting into the dining room.

Thank God, thought Henry. Seeing Pavlovich falter, Tesla had improvised, making an early entrance and taking the reins from the stuttering grand duke.

"Who is this?" asked Rasputin.

"This?" asked Pavlovich. "This! This is the surprise! Yes! This is, um, may I present to you—"

"You do not recognize the face of Nikola Tesla, Tesla, Tesla?" said the inventor with a sweeping, dramatic bow. "The master of lightning? A wielder of electricity, the likes of whom the world has not seen since Zeus threw thunderbolts from atop Mount Olympus?"

"You," said Rasputin, "are Nikola Tesla?"

It was like something out of vaudeville. It was an absolute farce, and I was sure that Rasputin was going to see right though it any second. But Tesla was just crazy enough to make it seem sane. He told Rasputin that he was making a tour of Russia, trying to convince cities and wealthy landowners to adopt his superior AC technology, and demonstrating some of his latest inventions in the process. While in Petrograd, he was honored to be the guest of the Yusupovs. And wouldn't you know it—they had insisted he demonstrate his newest, greatest marvel of science for the great Grigory Rasputin, whom they knew would appreciate it above all. In fact, it had been Princess Irina *herself* who had insisted on Rasputin.

"So," said Rasputin, when Tesla had finished his pitch, "the princess does not desire an audience with me...alone?"

"Of course she does, does, does!" said Tesla. "Don't be stupid! Yes, yes, yes, alone, she wants you, alone— but first, she *demands* that I demonstrate for you, personally, a marvel that will change the world!"

Tesla strode confidently to the table and with a flourish pulled the white tablecloth off his copper contraption.

"Behold!" said Tesla.

"What is it?" asked Rasputin.

"Sit, please. I will demonstrate."

"I will stand."

"*You will sit!*"

Rasputin was taken aback. It had been some time since anyone had given him an order. The two slender, famous figures just stood there a moment, seeing who would back down first.

Tesla had shoved all of his chips forward. Here was Rasputin—an impatient, arrogant, and intimidating figure. But rather than appease him, Tesla was fighting back by being even *more* impatient, arrogant, and intimidating. Barking at him like a parent at a misbehaving child. He'd walked into that room, sized up the situation, calculated the variables, and devised a solution. The only question was whether it would work or blow up in his face.

Rasputin sat down, his back to the door.

In that moment, I was reminded of why [Tesla] was the great man he was. A risk taker. A genius. Mad as a fucking hatter, yes, but a genius when it counted.

"Good," said Tesla. "Very good, now..."

Tesla attended to his device. Pavlovich had retreated into the corner, dabbing sweat from his brow, thoroughly relieved to be offstage.

"What," Tesla asked Rasputin, strapping on his boxy copper-plated backpack, "is the greatest frontier known to man?"

Rasputin said nothing. He was in no mood for games.

"The mind, mind, mind!" said Tesla. "The human mind, with its secrets! Its desires! Imagine—what if it were possible to peer into the mind of any man, across vast distances? To know his darkest secrets, his innermost desires, as effortlessly as knowing the color of his eyes? To control him as easily as a child controls a toy doll? The man who wielded such power would be able to conquer nations from the comfort of his armchair!"

"What is that . . . thing?" asked Rasputin, pointing to the device.

"Only the greatest invention the world has ever seen."

"Yes . . . but what does it do?"

"Nothing short of a miracle. Just as Marconi's radio waves transmit sound across an ocean, my device transmits thoughts across vast distances. Linking two minds together as if they were one."

Rasputin's own thoughts were suddenly aflutter with schemes of every size. If Tesla could penetrate his vampire mind—if he could control him like he said—then *any* mind was within reach. Rasputin imagined himself using Tesla's device to strengthen his stranglehold on the royal family. Perhaps he might even control the mind of the elusive Mr. Grander, whoever he was. Perhaps it would be Rasputin who would assume control of the world's remaining vampires. Steer the course of world events.

Tesla switched the pack on. The needles on its various gauges jumped to life, and the low electrical hum once again filled the room. That vibration in the air. That electric smell. Tesla held the transmitter by the handles and leveled it at Rasputin's head, aiming carefully. Rasputin looked somewhat concerned at having the device aimed at him but continued to sit obediently.

I couldn't believe it. It was going to be easier than we'd imagined. He was just going to sit there and let himself be roasted.

Tesla's hands began to shake as the gravity of what he was about to do sank in. Cooking a piece of meat was one thing, but he'd never taken a life. He'd never seen a man die, now that he thought of it. Why had this burden fallen to him? He was a scientist, not a soldier! But as nervous as he was, Tesla knew it was too late to turn back. He steadied himself, narrowed his eyes, and squeezed the button on the briefcase handle.

The electrical hum disappeared, along with the tingling vibration in the air. The needles on all of Tesla's gauges dropped to zero.

His pack went dead.

[Tesla] just stood there a moment, not sure what had happened.

"Uh, a moment, please," said Tesla, taking the pack off and examining it. Tesla flipped a switch on the pack, and it—*pop!*—emitted a large spark and a plume of black smoke, which rolled up into the old chandelier above.

"This is your 'miracle'?" Rasputin said, laughing.

"Goddamn Edison and his goddamned direct current...," mumbled Tesla, examining the device.

I can't describe the tension. Again—should I rush in? Should I let it play out? While Tesla was trying like hell to get the thing working, I saw something on the other side of the dining room. It was Yusupov. He was standing in the doorway, peering in. He had a pistol in his hand.

Yusupov knew he couldn't keep Rasputin waiting for Irina much longer. Tesla had had his chance, and he'd failed. It was up to him now. Yusupov walked into the dining room, his heart pounding, the pistol hanging by his right side. Rasputin had his back to the door, still distracted by the smoke rising from Tesla's device. Thrown off by the remaining static charge in the air, the lingering smell. He didn't sense Yusupov creeping up behind him.

No, Yusupov, thought Henry. *No, goddamn you... not yet.*

Pavlovich could see it unfold, too. He began to tremble as Yusupov neared Rasputin...pressed the revolver into his back. "Vo imya tsarya!" he cried. *In the name of the tsar!*

No, Yusupov…no…

Yusupov pulled the trigger. The bullet went clean through Rasputin's chest, shattering a china pitcher on the table in front of him, ricocheting off the wall at the far end of the room and whizzing past Tesla's head, very nearly killing him.

Rasputin didn't flinch in the slightest. He pushed his chair out from the table and looked down at his chest. The conspirators stood there, frozen. The smoke still trailing from the barrel of Yusupov's pistol.

"Shit…," Henry muttered.

Rasputin turned and looked at Yusupov. Then over at Pavlovich. Then finally at Tesla—the copper pack still smoking in his hands.

"Predateli!" he cried. *Traitors!*

His fangs and claws appeared, and his face took its vampire form. This time, there was no hesitation on Henry's part. He burst into the dining room—all claws and fangs. Rasputin turned around and grabbed Yusupov by the throat, squeezing his windpipe to the breaking point. Henry lunged at Rasputin, knocking him off Yusupov before he could fully strangle him.

> I was in the fight of my life. He was an incredible specimen. So much bigger and stronger. So much faster and more precise. It took me all of three seconds to realize that I was outmatched, and it took everything I had just to keep him from taking my head off.

Yusupov rolled on the floor, gasping for breath. Tesla, meanwhile, continued to fiddle with his pack, trying different combinations of switches and dials.

Every few tries, he would get it to power on, only to have it sputter out a second later. I could hear it—*power up, sputter out, power up, sputter out*— as I fought with [Rasputin]. He had massive hands, absolutely massive, and they were all bone. It felt like being punched with bowling balls.

Rasputin struck Henry in the mouth with a closed fist, so hard that Henry's own fangs tore clean through his upper lip, coating his teeth with blood.

I tried to hit back, but he wrapped me up in his arms—a bear hug—squeezing me the way a boa constrictor squeezes a mammal. My face fully enveloped in that beard. My ribs on the verge of shattering under the pressure. My God, he was strong. I managed to head-butt him—my forehead only came up to his chin, but it was enough to make him loosen his grip for an instant and let me break away.

"Shoot him!" yelled Henry to Tesla, as the two fought their way around the dining room, grappling, throwing each other into walls with such force that the plaster crumbled and the crystals of the old chandelier rattled as the ceiling shook with each impact.

Tesla managed to power up the device again. He leveled the transmitter at Rasputin and pressed the button on the handle. Nothing.

"Shoot him, Tesla!"

"Stop your yelling! Your yelling does not help, help, help!"

Yusupov had managed to sit up. He held his pistol, trying to get a clean shot at Rasputin without hitting Henry. But the two vampires were so close together, moving with such speed, that it was almost impossible. Pavlovich, meanwhile, had fallen back on the second rule of vampire hunting: *When in doubt, run away.* He ran into the kitchen, locked himself in a pantry, and curled up in a ball on the floor, muttering prayers.

Rasputin drew a huge fist back and hit Henry in the jaw, sending him backward into a wall, shattering one of the old painted-over mirrors.

If I'd been a human, my head would have come clean off. As it was, the force of it was enough to give me tunnel vision—take me right to the edge of blacking out. I hadn't experienced that sensation, that fogginess and ringing in the ears, since I'd become a vampire. It's the hardest I've ever been hit in my life.

Henry would later learn that Rasputin had spent time in monasteries *outside* Russia as well—namely, those in China, where he'd learned a style of fighting unlike anything in the West. A form of fighting particularly suited to his long limbs and wiry build and made all the more effective by his superhuman speed and strength. The force of Rasputin's uppercut had split Henry's chin to the bone and sent blood spilling down the front of his shirt.

"Shoot him, Tesla, goddamn you!"

Tesla stopped fidgeting with his switches and dials and gave the pack a swift smack on the side. The needles on its gauges jumped back to life, and its electrical hum returned. Tesla leveled the transmitter at Rasputin and squeezed the button on one of its handles. A quick succession of *pops* echoed through the room.

> For a second, I thought someone had fired a machine gun. But it was just a few of the chandelier's remaining bulbs exploding from some kind of electrical feedback.

This time the device held up. The remaining chandelier lights dimmed, and the low electrical hum grew louder than ever as Tesla kept the transmitter pointed at Rasputin, who still had Henry in his grasp.

> I felt an incredible sensation take hold of my body. A sensation I can only describe as like

being strapped in an electric chair—the current making my muscles tense and my limbs contort at unnatural angles. Making my eyes bulge halfway out of their sockets. It lasted for only a fraction of a second, before Rasputin freed me from his grasp and I fell out of the path of the beam— but that fraction of a second was enough to burn the sensation into my brain forever.

Rasputin froze—every muscle in his body locking up as a flood of microwaves flowed through him, exciting the hundreds of trillions of atoms in his body. Boiling the blood in his heart, his veins, and his organs. Boiling the cranial fluid around his brain and superheating the air in his lungs. Cooking him from the inside out.

He grabbed his head and tried to scream, but no sound came out. His eyes, those dead eyes, were suddenly alive and popping out of his skull. I can't imagine how painful it must have been. Worse than being burned. And the sounds—the sounds of that low electric hum and the pops and cracks and hisses of the fluid in his body boiling, his flesh cooking. Those sounds were worse than the screams of the burning.

Rasputin's body changed shape, swelling as the blood in his veins vaporized and built up pockets of steam beneath his skin. His already massive hands grew bigger, his narrow neck widening, ballooning up absurdly, reminding Henry of the spring peepers he'd seen in the South, then bursting—the mix of blood and water and bile spilling onto the dirty carpet with an accompanying *hiss*.

Tesla's weapon suddenly sparked, then—*pop!*— shorted itself out, giving Tesla an electrical jolt that made him yell out and drop the weapon to the floor. The glass on the pack's gauges cracked, and thick black smoke began to rise from the glass tube in its center. Free from the beam, Rasputin also dropped, smoking, to the floor, and lay still. His body continued to pop and whistle as pockets of air and fluid made their way to the surface and burst though his skin.

Henry sat against the wall, the gash on his chin already healing. Yusupov struggled to his feet, still light-headed after being nearly choked to death. He walked a few feet across the dining room to where Rasputin lay still, on his back. His left eye had par- tially popped out of his skull, and it dangled upon his high cheekbone. His smoldering clothes had fallen away as ash.

"Be careful," said Henry.

Yusupov put the barrel of his pistol against Raspu- tin's forehead.

"Yusupov, be careful! He might still be—"

Yusupov pulled the trigger, shooting Rasputin through the brain for good measure. Rasputin's head jumped up off the carpet as the bullet exited, then lay still as the report echoed off the walls of the dining room and down the marble hallways of the palace. Yusupov collapsed into a seated position beside Rasputin's body, sweating buckets, his chest heaving.

"We must hurry," said Yusupov. "The noise...people will be coming soon."

"Did you see?" cried Tesla, examining his copper pack. "Did you see it? Ha! It works! It works! It works!"

Yusupov looked around the dining room.

"Where is Dmitri?" he asked.

Before Henry could answer, Rasputin's eyes darted open and he bolted upright, his pupils cloudy white. He lunged toward Yusupov and took a blind swipe with his claws, just missing the prince's face, and ripping one of the epaulets off his uniform instead. Rasputin's vocal cords had cooked along with the rest of him, and the sound he made as he thrashed and stabbed at Yusupov sounded to Henry more like the squeal of a pig in the slaughterhouse than the cries of a man.

Despite being blind and deaf and having his brain partially liquefied in his skull, he managed to get ahold of the prince's hair with one hand and was drawing the other back to deliver a death blow, when a hand came out of the dark of the dining room and grabbed the top of Rasputin's head. Henry held him still just long enough to drive a claw through each of

Rasputin's eyes and into what remained of his brain. The mystic's body bent back as if a final jolt of electricity had just coursed through him. He gave a long, raspy wheeze, then collapsed again.

Silence, save for Yusupov's rapid breaths.

"I told you," said Henry. "Stay away from the head."

Henry and the others rolled Rasputin's naked body up in a carpet and loaded him into the back of Grand Duke Pavlovich's car.

> We couldn't throw him in the Moika [River]. It was right across the street from the scene of the crime, and as stupid as we'd all been that night, we weren't *that* stupid. We drove the body a short way to the Neva River and backed the car up to a dark section of its banks. I walked down to the river's edge to stomp a hole in the ice, so we could slip [Rasputin's body] beneath it and be done with this nightmare. It was either just before or after I gave the first stomp—I can't remember, honestly—that I heard the yelling back by the car.

Henry turned and saw the carpet unraveled on the ground and a naked Rasputin running away into the dark as Yusupov and Pavlovich chased after him. Tesla was leaning against the motorcar, smoking a cigarette.

He looked at Henry, shrugged his shoulders, and took another drag of his cigarette. He was done participating in this farce.

"Shit...," Henry sighed, and took off running.

The next day, the tsarina ordered the city searched for her beloved Rasputin. She feared (correctly, as it turned out) the worst—that the jealous, treasonous members of her own royal family had conspired against him. That they'd had her dear prophet, her dear son's savior, murdered. She suspected Yusupov at once. Yusupov and Pavlovich were placed under house arrest (albeit in a palace) while the police continued their search for Rasputin.

On the first day of 1917, the tsarina's fears were confirmed when divers pulled her mystic's frozen corpse from the Neva River. An autopsy specified that Rasputin had received "bullets to the forehead, back, and abdomen...trauma to the skull, chest, abdomen, and face...knife wounds[14] to the abdomen and heart..." His penis had also been severed.

> I'd run after Rasputin and tackled him to the ground, but he tossed me off. He was still fighting. Still *surviving*. He wrapped his gigantic hands around my skull and lifted me off the ground.

---

14. These were likely Henry's claw marks.

Then he squeezed. It felt like a bear trap had snapped around my skull. I kicked and thrashed, but he might as well have been a golem made of solid stone for all the good it did.

Rasputin would have crushed the life out of me if I hadn't glanced down and noticed his penis. It was enormous.[15] I reached out, wrapped my hands around it, and with all my strength ripped the thing right out of his body.

The fight went out of him after that.

And yet, after all that—after being shot at point-blank range in the forehead, bludgeoned, burned, and stabbed all over his body, and having his manhood ripped from between his legs, it had been *drowning* that had finally done Rasputin in. The doctors were mystified. *How could any man have survived such an assault long enough to drown?*

Many members of the Russian royal family were quietly overjoyed to see Rasputin go, as was a huge segment of the Russian population. *At last! The tsar would return to his senses! At last he would listen to his generals again!*

It wasn't to be. While Rasputin failed to deliver a Russian retreat for the elusive Mr. Grander, he succeeded in his greater goal—eroding the tsar's standing

---

15. Rasputin was reportedly so well-endowed that he caused women to faint upon orgasm.

with his people to the point that revolution became inevitable. Three months after Rasputin's murder, the tsar was forced to abdicate his throne by his own troops, setting in motion a chain of events that would set the stage for much of the coming bloodshed of the twentieth century.

Most of the Russian royals—including Yusupov and Pavlovich—grabbed what wealth they could carry and fled the country, seeking exile in France, Italy, and elsewhere. The tsar and his immediate family were held as captives as the revolution spread through Russia and a civil war broke out between the Bolsheviks' Red Army and the White Army, loyal to the tsar.

On the evening of July 17th, 1918, Tsar Nicolas, his wife, Alexandra, and their five children were roused from sleep in the middle of the night. They'd been held as prisoners by the Red Army for more than a year, shuttled from place to place, allowed few amenities, and denied contact with the other members of the royal family, including young Alexei Romanov. After getting dressed, they and four of their faithful servants were taken to a small basement room under the pretense that they were once again being moved.

But it was a lie.

Their jailer had just received an urgent telegram. The White Army was closing in on their position, and it had been decided that drastic measures were needed to ensure against the unthinkable: the rescue of the tsar and his restoration to the throne.

"Nikolai Alexandrovich, in view of the fact that your relatives are continuing their attack on Soviet Russia, the…Executive Committee has decided to execute you."

Before the words could even register, several guards raised their machine guns and opened fire. Tsar Nicholas, his wife, and their four servants died almost instantly. Alexei fell with them. But unbeknownst to the guards, the tsar's four daughters had sewn pounds of diamonds into their clothing for safekeeping and in doing so had created makeshift bulletproof vests. The girls fell in the hail of bullets, wounded but alive. Seeing them move, the guards came forward and stabbed them with bayonets, eliciting screams that could be heard half a mile from the house, then shot each girl through the back of the head. Finally, the room fell silent. The age of the tsars was over. The doors were opened to clear the room of gun smoke, and, in essence, clear the way for the rise of the Soviet Union.

The bodies were placed on a truck and driven into the nearby woods. The next morning, with loyalist forces closing in, the decision was made to remove the bodies and bury them deeper in the woods, where they were less likely to be found. A small detachment of Red Army forces returned to the grave site and uncovered the bodies. All of them were there.

All but young Alexei Romanov's.

For nearly a century, rumors have persisted that the Grand Duchess Anastasia, youngest of the tsar's daughters, somehow managed to escape that night. That she grew old under an assumed name.

But in truth, it was her baby brother, thirteen-year-old Alexei, who had escaped. The hemophiliac, whom the late Grigory Rasputin had cured by making him a vampire.

NINE

★ ★ ★

The Maker

I believe the power to make money is a gift of God...to be developed and used to the best of our ability for the good of mankind.

—*John D. Rockefeller*

Headquarters, Fifth Regiment,
Marine Corps, American E.F.
Germany, December 19th, 1918

From: Maj. Julius Turrill
To: Regimental Commander
Subject: Statement of First Lieutenant L. Greggs, substantiating recommendation for the Medal of Honor, case of Corporal ███████████████, USMC.

Corporal ████████████████ was a member of Sixty-Seventh Company, Fifth Marines. On the morning of June 6th, 1918, during the counterattack against the enemy in Belleau Wood, near Château-Thierry, our company was assigned the objective of taking and holding Hill 142, to the southern limit of the regimental sector. We fixed bayonets and advanced across a wheat field but came under heavy machine-gun and artillery fire almost immediately. Our losses were excessive, one of the first casualties being the company commander. We were able to retreat to a line of hastily dug trenches, but once there, the artillery fire and shelling only intensified. Several shells landed near our position without exploding. At first we thought that these were duds, but we soon realized that the Germans had switched from explosive shells to gas shells when we detected the smell of HS[1] in the air.

The shells had landed so close to the trench that the concentration of the gas quickly overwhelmed us. Even those men who were able to affix their masks quickly were overcome. At this time, Corporal ██████████, with no regard for his

---

1. Abbreviation for "hot stuff," a common nickname for mustard gas among World War I soldiers.

own safety, climbed out of the trench and
began picking the smoking five-nines[2]
up by hand, one at a time, and throwing
them back at the German positions. I
never saw a man pick up a smoking shell
with his bare hands, or throw them such
distances. It may seem impossible, but I
would swear on my honor as a Christian
that I saw him throw one shell at least
fifty yards. He continued to do this, even
as German machine-gun nests opened up
on him. Exposing his hands and arms to
the escaping gas in such concentrations
must have caused excruciating burns to
his skin, yet he continued picking them
up and throwing them back toward the
German positions. It was at this time that
I saw that Corporal ██████████████'s
gas mask had been damaged by gunfire.
Even as his mask failed him, the corporal
continued clearing the shells. When he
had finished, rather than retreat back
to the trench, he drew his revolver
and began to advance on the enemy's
position, firing his weapon. At this time,
I witnessed Corporal ████████████ fall

---

2. Common term for the 5.9-inch (150-millimeter) shells, each weighing more than one hundred pounds.

backward as a bullet struck the front of his helmet. Though injured, and clearly suffering the ill effects of the force of the blow, the corporal returned to his feet and continued his advance.

Seeing his bravery, the other men were inspired to pick up their rifles and follow suit. Upon the completion of our objective, Corporal ██████████████ refused to be evacuated and refused any treatment for his injuries. I believe that his courage, more than any factor, is responsible for taking Hill 142. Suffice it to say, neither I nor any of the members of my company would be alive today, had it not been for the courage and selflessness of Corporal ███████████████. I am sure that the statements of my fellow men will reflect the same sentiments.

Henry had returned to America a war hero, though few people knew his name or would ever know the feats of valor he'd carried out, both in uniform, on the front lines, and covertly, deep in enemy territory. Like millions of American men who'd served their country, he'd come home eager to forget the war.

The twenties were fully roaring. The stock market was booming, I was richer than ever, I was immortal, and thanks to men like Tesla, the night had become brighter and fuller of life than the day. We had signs glittering with thousands of lightbulbs. We had cars. We had jazz. We weren't Chicago, not quite, but New York was a respectable jazz mecca. We had [Duke] Ellington and [Louie] Armstrong. We had cigarette girls in short skirts and short haircuts doing the Charleston and the Black Bottom. You would get dressed up and go out to catch the new Broadway musical, or to one of the movie palaces—the Bunny in Brooklyn. The Audubon in Harlem. The Astoria in Queens.

Henry had just seen a new feature-length German import, *Nosferatu*—an expressionistic adaption of his old friend Stoker's novel *Dracula*.

I know it's considered a classic [now], but it bothered me. No. "Bothered," isn't strong enough. It *angered* me. The makeup was all wrong, for one thing. Two, no self-respecting vampire would go slinking around like that—a bug-eyed, over-emoting idiot, clasping his hands maniacally or tilting his head to the heavens every time he suffered a setback. The other people in the theater laughed every time [Max] Schreck was on-screen, mugging in that stupid makeup. I could hardly sit through it. In a way, it was the beginning of something I'd long feared: that vampires would become part of the popular culture. That people would be too busy worshiping them or imitating them or even laughing at them—and forget to fear them. Americans cast off the shackles of fear after World War I, but when you share the planet with an apex predator that is your better in every measurable way, a little fear is a healthy thing.

It was an early August morning in 1920, warm and cloudless. Henry was in the back of a chauffeured motorcar, on a twenty-five-mile trek upstate, the dappled light of the low sun glinting through the trees that lined the road. He wasn't accustomed to being out and about so early, but then, the man who'd sent the motorcar wasn't accustomed to waiting. Henry flipped through his morning paper as the car rattled along: the first commercially operated radio station in the country had begun broadcasting in Detroit. The Supreme Court had just unanimously upheld women's recently granted right to vote.

> Finally settling, for me, anyway, how America could go around calling itself a "democracy" while half of its citizens were barred from participating in it.

And another shooting. Always another shooting in the morning papers. One of Capone's men. Or

Schultz's. Or Luciano's. Prohibition was only two years old, and though it had so far failed to curb the nation's appetite for alcohol, it had succeeded wildly in giving rise to scores of clandestine distilleries and jumping speakeasies and ushering in the golden era of the American gangster. The new Thompson submachine gun, dubbed the "tommy gun," or the "Chicago organ grinder," tearing men apart like never before.

> But even death seemed like fun, like entertainment, in those days. There was an eagerness, you know? An eagerness to move on from the previous decade. Those years of war had been so joyless, so stagnant, that we were all about joy now. Joy and movement and sex. There was an infectious feeling of possibility everywhere. An optimism, especially in America. As if we could do anything. Build anything. Beat anyone.

No American embodied that conquering spirit more than John D. Rockefeller. He was the wealthiest human being who had ever lived, having amassed a fortune equal to more than $650 billion in today's money[3] through his monopolization of the oil industry. Henry had never met him, though they had mutual acquaintances. So it came as a surprise when

---

3. Rockefeller is generally considered to be the wealthiest person in history.

he'd received notice that Rockefeller wished to meet with him at once.

> I knew very little about him. What the papers printed, mostly. He was a deeply religious man. Never drank. Never smoked. Never swore, or even went to the theater. Anything that had the slightest hint of immorality.

Rockefeller was descended from ardent abolitionists and had given millions to establish black colleges in the South. He spent most of his time on the sprawling grounds of his Westchester County estate, moving markets and governments around the chessboard in his mind, pursuing his interests quietly and powerfully.

Lately, Rockefeller had become interested in death. Not his own. He was resigned to that, though still relatively fit and active for a man who was a few weeks from celebrating his eighty-first birthday and who would live to celebrate another sixteen after it. And he was secure enough in his faith and service (Rockefeller gave 10 percent of every dollar he earned to his church) that he expected rewards in heaven that would outshine even his seemingly impossible earthly blessings. He'd walked away from his oil empire at the age of fifty to focus on philanthropy, the pursuit of long life, and the perfection of his golf swing.

But after thirty years of semiretirement, and while

still in good health, Rockefeller could see the end on the horizon. There was a list of things he meant to accomplish with his remaining time. A list of "assurances," as he privately called them. Assurances that the good Lord would deem him worthy of his eternal rewards. That he would leave the world a better place than he'd found it.

> But there were other, less public assurances Rockefeller was after in his remaining years. And I was about to learn that I had a part to play in one of them.

Henry's motorcar passed through the gates of the Rockefeller compound before noon, winding up the long drive to a forty-room main house, called Kykuit (Dutch for "Lookout"), a Classical Revival–style villa that sat on a hill overlooking the Hudson River— about an hour's ride from where Henry would one day build his *own* upstate retreat. As manors went, Kykuit was relatively modest, especially considering it was the primary residence of the world's richest man. But if there was any mistaking the understated main house as a sign of the elder Rockefeller's modesty, the thirty-five-hundred-acre grounds that surrounded it—with their world-class golf course, sculpture gardens, and private cattle farm—more than made up for it. It was often said of Rockefeller's compound, "It's what God would have built, if only He'd had the money."

I was greeted by a butler and shown to the Japanese Garden, a short walk from the main house. Imagine being in upstate New York one moment, then rounding a corner and stepping back in time. Stepping halfway around the world, into feudal-era Kyoto. Cherry blossom trees, a carpet of moss on the ground, water flowing gently over terraced rocks. There was Rockefeller. Sitting on the porch of a teahouse built to resemble a Shinto temple, looking out at the still waters of a small koi pond. A blanket covering his lap. A napkin stuffed in his shirt collar.

"Mr. Sturges," said Rockefeller.

"Mr. Rockefeller," said Henry with a slight bow. "An honor."

"Yes, yes, all right." Rockefeller motioned for Henry to sit. The butler pulled a chair out for him, and Henry obliged.

"May I bring you some tea, sir?" asked the butler.

"Mr. Sturges doesn't drink tea," said Rockefeller, his eyes narrowing as he considered Henry up close. "Do you, Mr. Sturges?"

Henry paused a moment, considering Rockefeller right back.

"Indeed," said Henry. "Don't have the constitution for it, I'm afraid."

The butler gave a nod, clicked his heels, and left them.

An elderly John D. Rockefeller as he would have appeared on Henry's arrival at Kykuit. When adjusting his fortune for inflation, he remains the richest human being who ever lived.

"Well," said Henry, waiting until the butler was out of earshot, "it seems you know at least one thing about me."

"Oh, I know a great deal more than that," said Rockefeller, taking a sip of his tea. "Henry O. Sturges, born in England, March 2nd, 1563. Landed at Roanoke, July 27th, 1587. Friend to the American Revolution, present at the Battles of Trenton and Yorktown, staunch supporter of the North in its hour of need, adviser to presidents, a decorated soldier who distinguished himself in the trenches of the Great War, and member of the Union Brotherhood—a collective of vampires dedicated to preserving the freedom of man and his dominion over the earth."

It was unnerving, to say the least. Not so much that he knew I was a vampire—I'd been outed unexpectedly before, and there were plenty of powerful humans with ties to our world. But no one, other than myself, knew that much about my history. To put together such a complete picture of my life—my date of birth, the places I'd been, all of them under different assumed names—would have required a huge undertaking. It would've meant tracking down multiple sources, human and vampire alike. I couldn't imagine whom he'd talked to, or how he'd found them.

"It seems you have me at a disadvantage, sir."

"I have *everyone* at a disadvantage, Mr. Sturges."

Rockefeller pulled the napkin out of his shirt collar and set it down on the table.

"Lately," Rockefeller continued, "you've been something of a one-man branch of the Armed Services. Sneaking around Europe, intimidating and eliminating the enemies of the executive branch. I hear you're quite gifted."

Remember, the CIA wasn't created until 1947. The United States didn't have an organized foreign intelligence service, much less a group of trained soldiers able to execute operations on unfriendly—or even friendly—soil. We were still emerging from a long period of self-imposed isolationism, still reeling from the consequences of all those decades spent with our heads stuck in the sand.

Henry was a simple solution to complicated problems, the tip of America's secret spear. When Teddy Roosevelt uttered his immortal line, "Speak softly, and carry a big stick," he was talking about Henry Sturges. And he wasn't the only president who enjoyed wielding his secret weapon.

In 1919, President Woodrow Wilson and other world leaders had gathered in Paris to found the League of Nations—an international organization whose mission it was to promote and maintain world peace in the wake of the First World War.[4] Henry was invited along as an unofficial member of the American delegation. Having witnessed centuries of conflict, he was inspired by the prospect of such a peaceful covenant. But not everyone was as sure. And so, when each day's meetings were through, President Wilson put his unofficial emissary to work.

---

4. The League of Nations lasted until 1946, when it was replaced by the United Nations, which inherited numerous agencies, organizations, and philosophies founded by the League.

Denmark's chief negotiator found me very convincing, especially when I dangled him from the roof of the Grand Hotel. [V.K. Wellington] Koo, one of China's representatives, required a show of fangs and the threat of disembowelment before he acquiesced.

The League of Nations was agreed upon. But in the end, it was the Unites States who refused to join. Wilson won the Nobel Peace Prize for his efforts, but his own Congress didn't see the point of letting others have a vote in America's foreign affairs.

"With all due respect," said Henry to Rockefeller, "am I to sit here and listen while you rattle off my curriculum vitae, or is there some way I might be of service?"

"Oh, I don't require your help, Mr. Sturges... But you certainly require mine."

I was off balance. I still didn't understand why I was there—whether I'd been summoned because of *what* I was or *who* I was. But I understood why Rockefeller was Rockefeller. How this man—this *one* man—had been able to monopolize an entire industry and vanquish his fellow titans in the process. There wasn't a molecule of him willing to give ground or relinquish control. There was nothing in his tone to suggest that he was addressing a man three hundred years his elder.

A man who could rip him to ribbons in the blink
of an eye if so inspired.

"You and I," Rockefeller continued. "We're the last
of our respective breeds, Mr. Sturges. Gould is gone.
Field . . . Morgan . . . Carnegie,[5] gone."

I noticed a slight smile creep across his face at
the mention of Carnegie, the only one of his fellow robber barons to approach his level of absurd
wealth. The only one who'd ever given him a real
challenge.

"I outlived them all," said Rockefeller. "Just as
you've outlived every one of the great men you've
known in your time. Me, a titan who wishes to give
back some of the good fortune that God has bestowed
upon him. You, a monster—I use that term with the
greatest respect, of course."

"Of course."

"A monster, who wishes to redeem himself in the
eyes of our Heavenly Father. A vampire with a sense
of duty to his country. We're living pieces of history,
Mr. Sturges. Museum pieces in a world barreling out
of the past aboard a locomotive. Industry, modernity,

---

5. Jay Gould (1836–1892), railroads; Marshall Field (1834–1906),
retail; J. P. Morgan (1837–1913), finance; Andrew Carnegie (1835–
1919), steel.

electricity—these are the ways of the future. We old men in our castles...we're myths, and the world has little room left for us."

"Again, with admiration for the eloquence with which you're making your point, Mr. Rockefeller, these have been topics of conversation among my kind for the better part of a century. You'd be hard-pressed to find a vampire who doesn't feel as if our race is dwindling toward extinction, or that the world is becoming more unwelcoming to us."

"You'd be hard-pressed to find a vampire at all, Mr. Sturges. There aren't many of you left, it seems. Least of all in the United States. My men put the number somewhere between two and three hundred."

"Your 'men'?"

"With another thousand or so scattered around Europe, Asia, South America, and so on. That's some thirteen hundred vampires, worldwide. Why, during the Civil War, there were thousands of you in America alone."

"Yes, and we either ran them off or wiped them out."

" 'We.' The Union...yes. Ah, but even that venerable institution is on the verge of extinction, isn't it? I hear things haven't been the same since poor old Adam Plantagenet met his end."

"You've made your point, Mr. Rockefeller. And I'm impressed, truly. And quite grateful for the invitation to your magnificent home. But again—if you've brought me all the way here to discuss the details of my life, then perhaps I should come back better prepared."

Rockefeller's eyes narrowed again. His face struck Henry as gaunt, even sickly. His skin weather worn and sunburned from daily rounds of golf. But the eyes were still very much alive, as clear and sharp as the mind that operated behind them.

"Tell me," said Rockefeller, "what do you know about this vampire 'Grander'?"

> I was surprised to hear him mention that name. Until then, the name 'Grander' had been discussed only among my fellow Union vampires and a handful of high-ranking government officials. At the same time, it stood to reason that a man of Rockefeller's stature—a man who'd somehow put together my whole life story—would know his share of state secrets.

"Very little," said Henry. "No more than you, I suspect."

"What do they say? Who he is, what he wants."

"They say Grander wants to see America broken on the rack. And all who admire this nation, all who serve it, ground to dust. Vampires and humans both. I don't know his reasons."

"And as for who he is?"

"To tell you the truth, Mr. Rockefeller, I've begun to doubt whether he exists at all."

"Oh?"

"I've been looking for this 'Grander' for going on forty years. I've traveled halfway around the world, chasing shadows, and all I have to show for it are the stamps in my passport."

"Perhaps you've been looking in the wrong places."

"Perhaps. Or perhaps he's just a name given to a collective. Perhaps he's some kind of vampire bedtime story. Meant to frighten the rest of us from rounding up the last of the conspirators. Meant to keep us afraid."

"Oh, he exists, Mr. Sturges. He is as real as you and I. And he means to do exactly as you say: to lead others of your kind to victory against this great nation. To stand astride the corpse of America and spit in her face."

"Even if he *was* real, how could he possibly do it? Vampires are a dying breed, Mr. Rockefeller. You said so yourself."

"They may be few in number, but there's no overstating their ability to influence the weak and the desperate and the blind. To inspire men to take up arms against their fellow man, just as they did during the Civil War. 'Again, the devil taketh him unto an exceeding high mountain, and showeth him all the kingdoms of the world, and the glory of them; and he said unto him, All these things will I give thee,—'"

" '—if you thou wilt fall down and worship me.' Matthew four, verses eight and nine. Yes, Mr.

Rockefeller, men can be convinced to take up arms against their fellow man. But it's one thing to goad an already fractured nation to fight, and quite another to make an entire race enslave itself."

"It only takes one devoted man to conquer the world, Mr. Sturges...I should know."

Rockefeller reached into his coat pocket and pulled out a small, sealed white envelope. He placed in on the table beside his teacup.

"If the war taught us anything," he continued, "it's that one well-placed assassin can topple nations, kill millions. Even now, as we sit here on this beautiful spring day, Grander and those loyal to him are recruiting men to their cause. War, revolution, destabilization...those are his goals, and he means to achieve them. Unfortunately for him, my goals conflict with his."

"So what, then...you want me to find him?"

"That won't be necessary."

Rockefeller slid the envelope across the table. Henry stared at it, reluctant to touch it. *No,* he thought. *There's no way...*

"But," said Henry, looking at the envelope, "the Union has been looking for him. The United States government—"

"The United States government doesn't have my resources...or my insights."

Henry picked up the envelope, but he couldn't bring himself to open it.

It was someone I knew. Someone I'd been close to. It had to be. What other reason for the theatrics? Why else would he choose to reveal the name to *me* and not another vampire? I know it sounds strange, but I was frightened. Deeply. I imagine it's the way a patient feels waiting for the doctor to walk in with the results of their cancer test. That feeling that "my life is going to pivot drastically in one direction or another in the next few seconds, and no matter what, the person I was a minute ago will never exist again."

"A strange name, isn't it?" said Rockefeller as Henry stared at the envelope. "'A. Grander the Eighth.' I thought a good long while on that name. A pseudonym, to be sure. But why 'A. Grander'? There was always the possibility that it was simply plucked out of some vampire's imagination at random or invented because it sounded regal. But why 'the eighth'? Why not the seventh or the fourteenth? Or, perhaps it was a kind of statement: 'A grander future for vampires.' But then why the Roman numerals?"

I began to feel a kind of dread, as if my subconscious had already worked out what he was driving at and was waiting for the rest of my brain to catch up. Waiting, like a guest at a surprise party, to see the shock on my face when the lights came on.

"Then it occurred to me," said Rockefeller, "what if those weren't Roman numerals at all? What if the answer had been staring me in the face this whole time?"

I had to. I couldn't prolong it another second.

Henry picked up the envelope and opened it. There were two names, one above the other. Each twelve letters across.

The white men came, as Henry had always known they would.

It was the summer of 1607, the same year that Henry looked to the heavens and caught his first glimpse of the then unnamed Halley's Comet; just as he would again in 1682, the year the city of Philadelphia was founded; and 1759, when, in that same city, Henry helped found America's first life insurance company—a way of making restitution for another vampire's killing spree, which had left many destitute widows and orphans in its wake. In 1835, the comet's close approach would announce the birth of his future friend Mark Twain, and in 1910 it would return to announce his death.

But all this had yet to be written when the English landed that April.

They came aboard three ships: the *Susan Constant*, the *Godspeed*, and the *Discovery*, making landfall on the morning of April 26th at a spot they named "Cape Henry."[6]

> Not in my honor, unfortunately—but rather in the honor of the crown prince of England, Henry Frederick.

Three ships carrying 104 English men and boys, all led by a one-armed privateer named Captain Christopher Newport. They were tasked with doing what the settlers of Roanoke had failed to do: to create a permanent English presence in the New World, and their first step was establishing a fortified settlement, which they named James Fort,[7] in honor of their king.

> Word got back almost immediately. Word that white men had landed in three ships and made a fort. I remember an air of excitement in the village, some of it optimistic, some of it anxious, some of it belligerent. I was probably the

---

6. At the northernmost tip of present-day Virginia Beach.
7. Later Jamestown.

only member of the tribe who felt a kind of sadness on hearing the news. I remember having two thoughts, in quick succession. The first was, *Nothing will ever be the same.* The second was, *What will I do with Virginia?*

Henry and Virginia had been living among the Algonquins for seventeen years, mastering their language, adopting their customs. Virginia—known to all but Henry as Chepi (Algonquin for "Fairy," or "Ghost," on account of her white skin)—had grown into a beautiful young woman, nearly twenty years old, and still possessed of the same wavy red hair and fair complexion. Henry had been given the name Makkapitew, or "He Has Large Teeth."

Though it was unusual in a society that prided itself on sharing everything, Henry had been given his own small *yehakin*, as opposed to splitting one with a number of other families. While most of the longhouses were quite dark inside, extra care was taken to make sure no sunlight slipped into Henry's dwelling. He'd been a vampire for only seventeen years and was still extremely sensitive to its effects.

I was a shut-in by day, which made it hard for me to be much of a surrogate father [to Virginia]. And I think, to a degree, that I avoided her during those first years. Maybe it was the fact that she reminded me of everything that had happened.

Of losing Edeva and my own child. Of the future that had been stolen from us. The women of the tribe—they're the ones who raised her. Kept her clothed and fed. They're the ones who mothered her. Taught her the language, the customs. Taught her how to be a woman and a member of the tribe.

Henry quickly learned *his* place in the tribe, too. Chief Powhatan used his "good devil" liberally, trotting him out whenever conflicts arose with tribes outside his confederacy—the Monacans, whom Henry had been forced to attack as proof of his loyalty; the Occaneechi, the Saponi, the Tutelo—any number of smaller tribes that had aligned themselves to challenge the great chief's dominion over modern-day Virginia.

Typically, when there was some disagreement—usually over territory—Powhatan would send a message to the other tribe's chief. A warning. He would tell them that he could "command the old ghosts or demons" and so on, and that they'd better back down, or he'd send one to make trouble in their camp. Chiefs don't get to be chiefs by rolling over in the face of supernatural threats, and inevitably I'd have to kill a few warriors and make a big show of my claws and fangs in front of the terrified villagers. Problem solved.

It was difficult at first, killing those who hadn't wronged me. But you'd be surprised how quickly you push through that moral roadblock when you're starving, or when the alternative is banishment or worse.

In return for his occasional role as Powhatan's "demon," Henry and Virginia were accepted into the tribe. They were clothed and sheltered, taught a way of life that had evolved over thousands of years in the wilds of the New World. When there were no enemies to feed on, Henry survived on the blood of animals— mostly deer or foxes. In times of peace, he served as something of a glorified training dummy for the other warriors of the tribe. A sparring partner, used to keep their superior fighting skills sharp.

> One of the first questions I'd asked, naturally, was how they'd been able to beat me. How four living men had been able to subdue a vampire when they'd found Virginia and me on the beach that night.

The old men of the tribe told Henry tales of creatures—"ghost men"—who'd haunted the woods in the time of their ancestors.

> These "ghosts" or "devils" had killed many Algonquin, forcing them from their land and pushing them to the edge of extinction. The Algonquin men had developed techniques for

hunting and fighting them. And, if you believed the legend, they'd driven them out of their lands long before we ever landed at Roanoke. But the techniques had been passed down through the generations of their warriors, just in case they ever returned—even though no Algonquin had encountered a vampire in anyone's memory. At least until I showed up. As for who those first vampires were, or how they came to be, I have no idea. I'm not sure anyone will ever know.

But the skills Henry learned from his Algonquin brethren formed the basis of his own vampire-hunting techniques, which he would pass on to others, including Abe, in the centuries to come.

Almost as difficult as Henry's adjustment to playing the role of killer was his attempt at playing the role of surrogate father to Virginia. As she grew, he made an effort to be more involved—despite the fact that he remained a prisoner of the sun. He spent more time with her, taught her English. Not just how to speak the language, but how to *be* English. The manners. The dress. The religion.

It wasn't so much that I held on to some hope that we would return to England someday. It was more of a tribute to her parents. A feeling that they would have wanted their little girl to be raised a certain way. I suppose it also gave me some comfort, hearing someone else speaking my native tongue. A pretty white face framed by that wavy red hair. I suppose there was some of the old Englishman left in me. That sense of duty.

When Virginia was seven, she'd asked the question. The one Henry had been preparing for since the day he ran away from Crowley with the three-year-old in his arms.

We were sitting in my *yehakin*, the flaps closed to keep the sunlight out. Funny how a child will just accept those sorts of things, accept the fact that I was the only member of the tribe who never went outside during the day. I'm not sure how it came up, but I remember her looking at me, examining my face for a moment or two.

"Why do we look different from the others?" Virginia asked in Algonquin.

Henry poked at the fire with a stick, buying himself time as he worked out the right answer in his head.

"Why is our skin white," Virginia continued, "when everyone else's skin is brown? Why do I have orange hair with waves, when your hair and everyone else's hair is black, with no waves?"

"Well," said Henry in English, "you and I...we're from a different tribe."

"They speak the other tongue?" Virginia asked in her shaky English. "Like we speak?"

"Yes."

"We come from far?"

"Yes," said Henry. "From across the ocean."

Virginia looked away and narrowed her eyes—trying to work out how such a thing was even possible. *Across the ocean?* But there was nothing beyond the horizon. Nothing but the edge of the earth. She looked up at Henry again.

"You are my...?"

Virginia didn't know the English word.

"Nohsh?" she asked. *Father?*

This was the one I'd been dreading. I thought about my answer. Whether it was better to lie and tell her, *Yes, yes, I'm your father, now, hush, let's speak no more of it.* That certainly would've been the easier way out. But lying would have dishonored the memory of her real parents. Of the father who'd suffered at the hands of a murderer. Of the mother who'd died holding a baby in her arms. I felt that I owed *them* the truth, as much as Virginia—as hard as it was going to be for her to hear.

"No," said Henry, in English. "I'm not your father."

There was that look again. *How could it be, when we have the same skin? When we speak the other tongue? When you're the only person I ever remember holding me?*

"I have a . . . father? A mother?"

"Yes . . ."

"Across the ocean?"

"No . . . Your mother and father are in heaven."

There was that look again, as Virginia tried to work out what Henry had said.

"Heaven," said Henry again, and pointed a finger to the sky.

Virginia's expression darkened as the meaning sank in.

"They were taken from you," Henry continued. "Taken by a bad man."

"A bad man?"

"One of the ghost men, from long ago."

"A ghost man . . . ," said Virginia. "Like you."

It hadn't occurred to me that she might know what I was. I shouldn't have been so surprised. We were members of a close-knit tribe. [Virginia] spent her time with the women, and the women talked. But what shocked me even more than her knowing was the fact that she didn't seem to *care*. To her, I was just Makkapitew. Henry. The one who cared for her. The one with skin like her skin.

"The ghost man," said Virginia. "He is . . ."

Virginia couldn't find any of the English words she needed—"out there" or "still alive" or "in the woods." So she simply pointed toward the tree line that would have been visible, had they been outside Henry's dwelling.

"No," said Henry. "He's dead."

Dead. That was a word she knew.

"You," said Virginia, "you made him . . . dead?"

I nodded. Virginia looked at me with what—sadness? Adoration? I don't know. I couldn't tell. There was so much going on behind the eyes of so young a girl. But then, so much had happened to her at such a young age.

"You are my father," she whispered.

"No," Henry whispered back. "Your father is in—"

"You are my father." She came forward and put her arms around Henry's neck. Laid her head on his shoulder.

"You are my father," she whispered.

She kept repeating it . . . whispering it, over and over. "You are my father," in English. "You are my father." I put my arms around her and pulled her close. This went on awhile, before I was able to speak.

"I'm your father," Henry whispered.

Years had passed since that embrace. The English had returned to the New World, and the little girl had become a woman. As fluent in English as she was in Algonquin.

She was curious, especially when it came to all things English. She wanted to know everything about our "tribe." About the great cities across the ocean. And she was strong. She was tall for a girl, especially an Algonquin girl, and unusually skinny. To a European, she was striking. But to the Algonquin, she was just different. She'd been teased mercilessly as a little girl—teased about her hair, her skin. She'd even been beaten. But in all the years we lived among the tribe—and this is something you have to understand—in all those years of being teased and beaten, out in the daylight, where I couldn't protect her, Virginia never lost a fight. Not one. It wasn't that she was a better fighter than the other girls. Far from it. It was that she never *stopped* fighting. She never submitted or cried out or ran away. She punched and pulled and bit until the other girl had no choice but to give up.

In time, Virginia gained the respect of her Algonquin sisters. They'd welcomed her into their sorority, taught her how to weave mats, how to dry meat and berries for the winter and stretch furs to make warm clothing. When the great chief sired a daughter with one of his many wives, it was Virginia who had spent the most time caring for her. The baby was named Matoaka but would become famous for her nickname, which meant "Little Frolic"—Pocahontas.

> [Virginia] enjoyed holding her. Helping the women care for her, raise her, as was the custom. In time, Matoaka came to see her as something of a surrogate older sister. I've often wondered if being exposed to Virginia's white face, being around her and interacting with her as a family member from birth, was what led [Pocahontas] to fall in love with a white man later.

Captain John Smith almost hadn't made it to the New World. During the voyage from England, he'd been charged with planning a mutiny and placed under arrest by Captain Newport. Newport had considered executing him, going so far as to have a gallows constructed during a stopover in Bermuda. But Smith, ever the self-preservationist, had talked himself out of the noose, reminding the captain that the investors of the Virginia Company of London would be very upset indeed were one of their duly elected expedition leaders hanged without a fair trial. By the time they made landfall in Virginia, it seems Smith's transgressions had been forgiven.

> He wasn't the handsome, wide-eyed youth he's always portrayed as in movies. Yes, he was only twenty-seven, but his bushy beard already had flecks of gray in it, and his hair was already thinning. He had tired eyes and bad skin. But he was a leader. I'll give him that. In a landing party made up of overprivileged, work-averse English gentlemen, he was one of the few willing to get his hands dirty.

When the news of the landing reached him, Powhatan called a meeting of his trusted advisers. Henry wasn't a usual part of this group of elders and warriors, but he was invited the join them. He was "an English," after all, and might have special insights into the situation.

> I remember all of them sitting in the longhouse that night, smoking, discussing what to do. I held my tongue. I knew I would have only one chance to make my point, and I had to wait for exactly the right moment.

Powhatan told his advisers that he was eager to trade with the English, to ally himself with them before one of his enemies did. The white men could make metal tools to help them grow more food, metal swords to help them make war. In return, Powhatan would grant them good land. (Like the foolish English who had come before them, the new settlers had chosen swampy, mosquito-infested land to build their "James Fort" on.) Powhatan would help them adjust, help them survive.

> Remember, [Powhatan] was a king, a chief to thousands of men, women, warriors. It would have never occurred to him that he should fear a hundred white men.

The great chief called for a greeting party to go and make contact with the settlers, to welcome them, as he said, "with feasts and merrymaking," and to offer them everything that had been discussed. His advisers agreed.

> This was the moment I'd been waiting for. I rose and addressed the others. I told them that the English couldn't be trusted. That they would never see the Algonquin as equals. That they would take advantage of them. Use them until they were strong enough to enslave them. I warned them as best I could, and I was ignored.

Powhatan's decision was final. He would send the greeting party at first light.

"If you won't listen to me," said Henry, "at least let me go with them. I can help them. I know the English ways."

Powhatan refused.

"What will they do if they see a white face among my people?" he asked. "They will think *I* was responsible for the massacre at Roanoke. They will think that I took you and the girl captive. They'll make war on us."

I think [Powhatan] was more worried that his loyal vampire might be tempted to run off, back to England. But the truth was...I was more concerned than curious. Concerned for the safety of the Algonquin, the people I'd grown close to over time. More than anything, I was concerned about Virginia.

Powhatan had forbidden anyone other than the greeting party from visiting the fort—and the punishment for defying his decrees was severe.

But I knew Virginia. And I knew it was only a matter of time before her curiosity got the best of her. She would find a way to sneak off. To see more of her own kind up close. To hear white men—men from the tribe across the ocean—speaking her native tongue. And that terrified me. The thought of inviting the English into our lives. The thought of losing her...

The thought of another man being with her...

Virginia was sixteen when Henry first looked on her with different eyes. She'd grown into a woman by then, fertile and figured. Blue eyes—the same blue Henry had seen on his voyage across the ocean, when his ship had anchored in the electric shallows of the Caribbean. Those eyes, a contrast to her wavy orange hair and lightly freckled face. An accompaniment to her radiant smile and to the dimple on one cheek when she squinted and smirked playfully, as she often did.

> It was common for women of fifteen, even fourteen, to marry in those days, especially in the tribe. Many of the same little girls who'd once teased Virginia were wives and mothers by the age of sixteen.

It wasn't so much Virginia's age that gave Henry pangs of guilt, but all the years that had led her to that age. Years of rocking her to sleep. Bathing her. Comforting her. *Fathering* her. Hadn't she said it herself? "You are my father... You are my father." Yes, he *was*, in all but the biological sense. And Henry knew that he had a sacred responsibility to her. Not just to

Virginia, but to Ananias and Eleanor, her *real* father and mother.

> And yet, the thoughts came. She was so beautiful, so vibrant. She reminded me of home, I suppose. Appealed to that part of me that was still English. I chastised myself for being a sinner. I tried to get her out of my head any way I could. I made love to other women in the village (some of the unmarried Algonquin women saw me as a curiosity, I suppose, on account of my race, or my species, or both). I tried to banish Virginia from my mind by being with these women, but I only ended up picturing *her* in their place. Imagining what it would be like to be with her. Not just in my imagination, but to *be* with her. I couldn't help myself. A vampire is no more able to control those thoughts than a human is. No less susceptible to their influence.

It had been a dreadfully hot summer, with barely a breeze to break up the humid air. For weeks on end, the Algonquin had kept to the shade, sweating from standing still and seeking relief with frequent dips in the river. So it was a welcome sight when, one evening, dark clouds appeared in the east and a storm gathered over the ocean, promising a break from the stifling heat.

I had a fire going. I was alone, beneath a blanket—
a gift from one of my tribal dalliances—lying flat
on my back, listening to the droplets beat down
on the bark of my *yehakin*, counting the seconds
between the flashes of lightning and the thunderclaps so loud you could feel them rattle around
in your chest. With my vampire hearing, I could
almost pinpoint each strike, the sound of the tree
branches cracking or rainwater evaporating as
the bolts made contact with the earth.

The flap [of the *yehakin*] opened, and Virginia
came in—her clothes wet from running through
the village in the downpour. She'd come to me
before, as a small child, when the thunder and
lightning had frightened her. But I was surprised
to see her now. It had been years since she'd
sought me out for comfort.

Virginia hurried to where Henry lay on his back
and, without a word, slipped under the blanket with
him and curled up beside him, her face toward the
fire.

I didn't know what to do. Should I say something
to comfort her? Put an arm around her? She pressed
her back into me, the shape of her body conforming to
the shape of mine.

A succession of flashes appeared in the seams of the
bark walls. The thunderclaps followed just seconds

later, Virginia flinching with each one. The storm was getting closer. Almost on top of them. Virginia rolled over so that she was facing Henry, their noses almost touching.

She looked at me with those bright-blue eyes. There was no mistaking them. There was no mistaking why she'd come or what this was. It was the moment I'd been secretly fantasizing about. Praying would come and praying would never come. Now that it was here, I was frightened.

I wish I could say that I resisted. That I held firm to the so-called moral high ground. But love makes us do things that would repulse us under any other circumstances.

I rolled over and kissed her. I ripped her clothes from her. I put my mouth on her breasts, kissed her from her neck to her stomach. I tasted her. Slid into her. Came in her. A year's worth of bottled-up lust breaking open.

Henry and Virginia hardly left the *yehakin* over the next week.

I couldn't think of anything else but being beside her naked skin. Being inside her. Seeing her face flush red as she came. We barely spoke that first week. We just...fucked. I don't mean to be vulgar, but if I'm being honest, that's the only word that does it justice. We fucked, we sweated, we groaned, we collapsed, we started over. We drank each other until there wasn't a drop left in either of our bodies.

It was beautiful...and sinful. It was the same feeling I'd had when I'd tasted my first human blood. On one hand, I was disgusted with myself. I knew, in a moral sense, that what I was doing was a sin. Yet it felt so good...so much better than I'd imagined anything could feel, that I was filled with a warmth, with a joy, in spite of my guilt.

Henry and Virginia were careful to hide the affair from the Algonquin. Swearing each other to secrecy. Sneaking around in the dead of night.

Naturally, everyone in the tribe knew within a week.

The others thought it a good match. It was only natural, after all, that the two English should fall in love with each other, even if one of them was a *re'apoke*—a devil. Powhatan approved the union, and Henry and Virginia were promptly married in an Algonquin ceremony.

It was a good year. A happy year. So happy that I was able to put all thoughts of sin behind me.

Able to move on from mourning Edeva and the child I'd lost and focus on my new life with my new bride and, hopefully, new children. It was customary for Algonquin couples to get pregnant as quickly as possible. We tried—God knows we did. But nothing happened.

Many of the facts of my condition were still unknown to me, including my infertility. Immortality comes at a price, it seems. The only way we can reproduce is through blood and death.

In the spring of 1607, John Smith came to the New World, and Henry's happiness ended abruptly.

From the moment word of the landing reached us, I felt a sense of dread. A feeling that somehow, no matter what happened between the Algonquin and the English, things would never be the same between Virginia and me again.

As Henry had predicted, his young wife was overcome by curiosity. She was desperate to go to the fort. To see the English up close and meet more of her kind. But the great chief had spoken. She would have to wait.

On May 28th, 1607, Powhatan's greeting party left for James Fort, without Henry or Virginia. Two days later, it returned, grim faced and full of musket holes.

They'd shot at the Algonquin on sight. It seemed the English weren't interested in trading with the natives. They weren't taking any chances, not after the disappearance of the Roanoke Colony.

Powhatan was furious. If the English insisted on war, then he would give it to them. In the coming weeks, he sent raiding parties to attack the fort, setting off a series of skirmishes that claimed lives on both sides.[8] But despite having a "good devil" at his disposal, Powhatan refused to send Henry with them.

He was still afraid that I would run off or change allegiances if I got too close to my fellow Englishmen.

Under constant attack, and without the Indians to trade with, the English found themselves on the verge of ruin. Just a few short months after their arrival, 60 of the original 104 settlers were dead—some as the result of skirmishes with the natives, but most of starvation and disease. Eager to find better land to settle, Captain John Smith ventured inland alone. During his scout, an Algonquin hunting party happened

---

8. These became the first battles in what would be known as the Anglo-Powhatan Wars, a series of conflicts that would continue on and off for the next seventy years, until the Treaty of Middle Plantation (1677) established the first Indian reservations in America.

across him, took him prisoner, and brought him back
to Powhatan.

> This is the part everyone's always gotten wrong.
> The famous story of Pocahontas throwing herself
> on John Smith, begging her father to spare his
> life? The moment that's burned into the collective
> American memory?
> It never happened.

It was first light when John Smith was marched into
the village. Henry and Virginia were lying together,
alone in their *yehakin*, when a commotion roused
them from sleep.

> We heard voices. People yelling out, "They have
> the white chief!" and "Let us kill him," and so on.
> Virginia jumped out of bed and began to dress. I
> told her to wait, that we should find out what was
> happening before she went running off. It wasn't
> that I thought she was in any danger. In truth,
> it was my fear of having her see another English
> face up close, especially while I was trapped in
> the dark, helpless to follow her out in the sun-
> shine. I asked her to stay with me, but she left.
> She was too curious.

Smith was brought to the center of the village
and presented to Powhatan. Virginia was among the

Contrary to most historical accounts, it was Virginia Dare, not Pocahontas, who intervened in the execution of Captain John Smith—as evidenced by the hair color and fair complexion of the Algonquin girl in this rare illustration.

hundred or more Algonquin who had gathered to catch a glimpse of the "English chief." Pocahontas, then twelve years old, stood beside her father.

All I could do was listen as the men of the hunting party told Powhatan how they'd stumbled upon Smith while he was bathing in a creek, more than ten miles inland from the English fort. How they'd chased him as he ran through the woods.

Henry listened as Powhatan passed sentence: "He is a murderer of many Algonquin. He is a trespasser on Algonquin land. It is right that his blood should be spilled."

Cheers went up among the gathered. Powhatan gave a nod to the hunting party. Two of them held Smith down on the ground, while the other two drew clubs. They were going to beat his skull in.

Realizing that he'd just been sentenced to death, Smith spoke up as he was forced into the dirt: "I am the leader of my people! A representative of a mighty king! My death will bring severe consequences!"

Not understanding or caring about what the white man was saying, one of the hunting party drew back his club over Smith's head and prepared to strike.

"Stop!"

An orange mane pushed through the rows of black-haired onlookers.

It wasn't Pocahontas but *Virginia* who intervened on Smith's behalf. Virginia who threw herself on top of him and begged Powhatan to spare his life.[9] She was desperate to make peace between the Algonquin and the English.

---

9. Though Pocahontas did, in fact, become infatuated with John Smith later, there is no evidence that the two ever consummated their relationship. In fact, after Smith returned to England in 1609, Pocahontas married a *different* white settler, John Rolfe, after converting to Christianity and taking the name "Rebecca." Theirs was the first interracial marriage

On seeing another white face, Smith himself turned as white as a sheet. *How could it be? A white girl... here?*

"Get away from him!" yelled Powhatan. "He has killed many Algonquin. We will send his body back to their fort, and they will fear us."

"They will hate you!" said Virginia, speaking Algonquin. "And they will send more English to kill you."

The other members of the tribe were becoming agitated. They started yelling out, "Of course she cries for her own kind!" "Who cares what a white-faced girl thinks!" I was desperate to be out there with her. I couldn't remember ever feeling so helpless.

"You don't understand!" said Virginia, speaking Algonquin, "I share this man's color, but he is not like me. *You* are my tribe. *You* are my people. But if you let him live, he will be in your debt. He'll go and tell the other English of your mercy, and they will stop making war on us."

Us.

I had been wrong about Virginia's hunger for the company of other Englishmen. Yes, she was

---

in American history, and their son, Thomas Rolfe, would go on to sire countless descendants. Pocahontas, therefore, is the ancestor of some of the oldest families in America.

curious to see them, but only in the same way the rest of the tribe was. She wasn't looking for a place where she fit in. She'd already found that place.

Powhatan was a famously stubborn and decisive man. He wasn't used to being argued with, especially in front of others. But somehow, Virginia convinced him that sparing Smith was the right course of action.

To the astonishment of the tribe, Powhatan spared John Smith's life. He sent him back to James Fort with a warning: *Attack another Algonquin, or settle our lands without permission, and we'll drive you back into the sea.*

But rather than interpret Powhatan's mercy as a sign of strength and goodwill, Smith saw it as weakness.

The first thing he did was tell his fellow settlers that he'd been "face-to-face with the butchers of Roanoke" and that there were still "white prisoners" among the Algonquin.

Days later, Smith led a raiding party into one of the Algonquin satellite tribes. There, he and his men killed upward of seventy villagers, many of them women and children. They captured one of the lesser chief's wives and her children, fleeing with them in a boat downriver. During the voyage back to James Fort, their mother was forced to watch as the English threw her children over the side, leveled their muskets at the swimming children, and, as Smith recorded in his diary, "shot their braynes in the water." They waited until making landfall before executing the mother by sword.

Powhatan came to Henry's *yehakin* that night. The English had dishonored themselves, he said. Royal blood had been spilled. It was time for the good devil to make things right.

> He told me to go to James Fort and make war on them. To kill all the English. He told me that I would do as he commanded or Virginia and I would no longer be welcome among his people. He would consider us his "enemies" and send his warriors to hunt and kill us.

Henry was given until the next sundown to decide. With that, Powhatan left.

> There I was...caught between murdering fifty-odd Englishmen and being banished and marked for death by the people who'd been our family for nearly twenty years.

The way Henry saw it, there was only one option, one chance for all sides to emerge unscathed: he and

Virginia would surrender themselves to John Smith. Without the pretext of rescuing captured English prisoners, perhaps the settlers of James Fort would leave the Algonquin alone.

> It took some time for me to convince Virginia. She'd always been curious about the English, always wondered what it would be like to live among them. But now, faced with leaving behind the only family she'd ever known, she hesitated. But she also knew there was no other way. She loved her people so much, she was willing to give them up to keep them safe.

By the light of the stars, Henry and Virginia slipped out of the village and made their way to James Fort, where, standing in the torchlight of the walled compound's center, they presented themselves to John Smith.

> I spoke first, offering us up as tokens of goodwill. We would renounce our place in the tribe, I told him, and swear fealty to the Crown, on the condition that he left the Algonquin alone.

"If we give ourselves," asked Virginia in her oddly accented English, "will you make peace with them?"

Smith looked her over. "You care that much for these savages?"

"These 'savages' are my"—Virginia had to search for the right word—"family."

Smith considered her with a mixture of revulsion and disappointment, then turned to Henry. "Come, then," he said. "Let us make peace with your *family*."

Under cover of darkness, Smith and twenty mounted Englishmen rode in formation toward the village, rifles slung on their backs and swords at their sides. Henry and Virginia shared a horse toward the rear.

> I didn't think anything of [the guns and swords]. The English carried them everywhere outside the walls of the fort. We were going to end a war, after all. Not start one.

But when Smith and his men reached the outskirts of the sleeping village, Smith drew his sword, turned back, and ordered one of his men to hold Henry and Virginia at rifle point.

> At first I thought he was going to order us shot. But what he had in mind was much more cruel.

"Keep them here," Smith told the rifleman, his eyes on Henry and Virginia. "I want them to *see*."

He spurred his horse and rode into the village with the others.

Virginia's eyes grew wide. "What are they doing?" she asked Henry in Algonquin.

The English rode into the village with slashing blades and stamping hooves, slaughtering the unsuspecting villagers—some while they slept. Children ran screaming from their homes and were shot in the back. Women were beheaded where they stood. Tribal warriors struggled to mount a resistance, but the English slaughtered with impunity.

> Virginia watched it all, my arms wrapped around her. She tried to run into the gunfire and bloody mayhem. She would have preferred to die among her tribe, and she surely would have if I hadn't restrained her. I held her tightly as she struggled. Hot tears ran down her face.

"Liars! Murderers!" she wailed, over and over— struggling uselessly against Henry's grasp, until the horror of it rendered her too weak to move, too hoarse to scream.

> I saw no other choice. The English were going to do what they pleased. If I'd let her go, she would've been killed with the rest of them.

More than 150 Algonquin men, women, and children were butchered that night. Skulls were cleaved open. Pregnant women were impaled. Houses were set afire. The village holy man was murdered by Smith himself, his limbs hacked from his torso and piled atop his corpse like kindling for a bonfire.

When the English finally relented, the sides of their horses were stained red, and their swords were so spattered with clotted blood and viscera that they wouldn't fit into their scabbards.

Henry and Virginia were given a small cabin in the fort. Virginia lay on a mat against the wall, silently replaying the horrors she'd witnessed as the sun revealed the seams between the cabin's boards. Henry sat opposite her in a chair, staring at her back.

"I'm sorry," he said. "But, Virginia…had I let you go, they would have killed you, too."

> More silence. I don't know how long it was, a few minutes, maybe, an hour, but she rolled toward me, sudden and decisive. She stood and came to where I sat, her face just inches from mine. There was something…not entirely sane about the look in her eyes.

> "Make me, Henry…"

> I was startled by her words. Her conviction. Rage burned in her, and it made her strong. It tempered her, like steel.

"What I am...it's a *curse*, Virginia. I could never—"

"Make me as you are, and let us be together forever."

I had no words. In the years since Crowley had made me, it had never occurred to me that anyone would *want* to be a vampire. It had also—I know this sounds strange, but it's true—it had never occurred to me that Virginia might grow old without me. It came at me all at once...a vision of our future. She and I, forever childless. Living our little lie as her youth faded, year after year. I would watch her grow sick and old. I would bury her. Mourn her.

"Virginia..."

"I'll grow old, Henry. I'll grow old and you won't love me anymore."

She's right. The love might remain, but the passion...

"I could never stop loving you—"

"You will!" she cried. "And you'll leave me...and I'll be alone in the world."

I looked at her. At those eyes filled with tears. At her face, flushed red. I can't describe to you how beautiful she looked. How helpless I felt. I suppose I would've done anything she asked me in that moment.

"Make me...or I'll tell the white men what you are. And it will be the end of us both."

She was the woman I loved. I had to get her back to England, back to safety.

I looked down at my right hand.

My claws extended, slowly, over my finger-nails. I dragged one of them across my left wrist, making sure the gash was long and deep enough to remain open before my body healed itself. The blood came, and Virginia grabbed hold of my wrist and lifted it to her mouth. She drank until her mouth was full and the blood ran from either side of her lips—her eyes locked on mine. And when she'd drunk her fill, we kissed, the blood still running from her chin onto the front of her dress... between her breasts. We pulled each other's clothes off, each of us bleeding on the other. We made love—Virginia's body warmer than it would ever be again. Her eyes filled with the last tears they would ever shed. We made love until her eyes rolled back in her head and the sickness took her.

"My father...," she whispered. "My lover...my maker."

For three days and nights I looked after her, hold-ing her down when she writhed. Wiping the sweat from her brow and the sick from her face. I comforted her when she woke from her transformation, confused and overwhelmed by her new senses. I cleaned her and held her until she remembered me again. When she did, we made love as immortals, biting and clawing at each other, collapsing into each other. I drifted off to sleep in her arms. When I awoke, she was gone.

Virginia Dare, the first English child born in the New World, had disappeared into the American wild.

Henry looked across the table at Rockefeller. That old face. Gaunt and weathered but wise.

[Rockefeller] was smiling at me. He was clearly pleased with how the meeting had unfolded so far. It had all gone exactly as he'd envisioned. But then, everything did.

Henry felt sick. Off balance. The idea that Virginia was still alive after all this time...that she and Grander were one and the same...it didn't make any sense. And yet it made *perfect* sense.

I was too stunned to speak. Somehow, this rich old man across the table from me *knew*. Knew the people and places I had associated with hundreds of years before. He knew that I'd made Virginia immortal. But how? How the hell could he have known? And how the hell could any of it be true?

"Mr. Rockefeller—"
"You're dying to know how I came to possess this information."
You're goddamned right I am.
" 'Wealth' and 'information,' Mr. Sturges. Two of the most important words in the English language. And it just so happens that they mean exactly the same thing. One is interchangeable with the other, in any context. I have more *wealth* than any man on this earth. Therefore, by definition, I have more *information* than any man, too."

I was done being polite. I couldn't have him spouting off vague, bullshit axioms when he'd just dropped a bomb in my lap.

"Mr. Rockefeller, I have to insist that you—"
"I became aware of a letter about, oh, a year ago. A recommendation for the Medal of Honor. This letter was brought to my attention by certain men who work in my employ. Men whose job it is to keep a sharp eye out for signs of the strange and unusual. A rather vague description of duties, I know. But they're quite effective, these men. They alert me when there's an item in the newspapers that requires following up. Or

when, say, a letter lands on the desk of the secretary of war, telling tales of soldiers throwing hundred-pound shells great distances, inhaling mustard gas with no ill effects, taking bullets without yielding an inch of ground. This account reminded me of similar ones, in letters written by soldiers during the Civil War, describing the 'impossible feats' of a number of Confederate soldiers on the battlefield. Letters that I have collected over the years.

"I wanted to meet this extraordinary soldier," Rockefeller continued. "I wanted to see what the hero of Belleau Wood looked like firsthand and offer him further opportunities to serve his country."

"That's lovely," said Henry, "but I'm afraid you have the wrong soldier. I wasn't present at the Battle of Belleau Wood. And no one's ever recommended me for the Medal of Honor. Not that I know of, anyway."

"Oh, I know, I know. But you *were* a witness to the Civil War, were you not? I understand you were a trusted adviser to none other than Abraham Lincoln himself."

Again, I was surprised that Rockefeller knew of my friendship with Abe. But not shocked. Nothing could have shocked me after seeing Virginia's name. At least, that's what I thought.

"I had the privilege of being his friend."

"I voted for him in 1860, you know," said

Rockefeller. "And again in sixty-four. I thought him an eloquent man. He had his deficits, of course, but he had tremendous perseverance. I do not think any quality so essential to success as perseverance, don't you agree?"

Henry didn't answer.

"Perseverance, Mr. Sturges, in sufficient quantities, can overcome most everything. Even *nature*. Such a shame that he was cut down in his prime. To think of what he might have accomplished, if only he'd had more time."

"We are time's subjects," said Henry, "and time bids be gone."[10]

"Are we, Mr. Sturges? Are we *all* time's subjects?"

Again, Henry chose not to answer.

"Tell me, how did you receive the news of Mr. Lincoln's death?"

"I felt the loss deeply, as many did. It was too much to bear the thought of losing such a great man, such a cherished friend."

"Is that why you made him a vampire?"

My thoughts spiraled out of control, like a plane with one of its wings shot off. A dread began to fill my body. Cold water in an empty vessel, starting in my toes and flooding every compartment of me from the inside.

---

10. *Henry IV, Part 2*, act 1, scene 3.

I'd kept that secret locked deep in the vault of my mind for more than fifty years. I hadn't shared it with a single soul, and here—somehow—Rockefeller knew. And if Rockefeller knew, then others knew. And if others knew, knew that I'd broken my oath, broken a sacred code—*a vampire will make no other vampire*—then I was in imminent, mortal danger. What if [Rockefeller] hadn't called me here for a discussion? What if he'd called me here for some kind of—

"Relax. Your secret is quite safe, I assure you. I've made my fortune identifying valuable commodities," said Rockefeller. "Mr. Grander—or rather I should say, Ms. *Dare*—is a very serious problem. And it seems, given your history and abilities, that you are uniquely suited to deal with this problem, Mr. Sturges. That makes you a very valuable commodity indeed."

"Who told you that I made Lincoln a vampire?"

"I would very much like you to meet this hero of Belleau Wood. I believe the two of you could accomplish great things together. He's just in there," said Rockefeller, leaning his head toward the Shinto temple.

I hadn't sensed another presence with us. I'd been so distracted, first by meeting Rockefeller, then by the shock of what he'd told me, that I'd

just plain missed it. But there *was* someone...
someone just inside. I could smell him.

"Go on, Mr. Sturges. I'm sure he'll explain everything to your satisfaction."

On average, a vampire's heart beats once, maybe
twice a minute at rest. But mine raced now. I
couldn't bring myself to turn around, in part
because I was afraid—legitimately afraid that
this could be the end of me.

Henry pushed his chair away from the table, the
iron legs scraping over the concrete of the terrace. He
rose and walked slowly, slowly toward the front of
the temple. He felt as if he'd been drugged. His feet
seemed a mile away from his head. It was too much.
Too much revelation in too short a time.

I've made two vampires in my five centuries. In
both cases, it was because I loved them. Because
I couldn't bear the thought of living in a world
without them. And in both cases, I ended up
mourning them anyway.

I suppose there's no way to avoid losing the
things you love. Even if you live forever.

"Imagine my surprise," said Rockefeller, watching
Henry walk, "when my men tracked down this elusive

hero and brought him to me. Imagine my amazement upon hearing his sensational tale."

I walked into the relative dark of the temple. There was a man standing inside. A tall, slender man in a dress-green army uniform.

"There was only one man I wanted to meet," Rockefeller continued, "after meeting the hero of Belleau Wood. The man who had made it all possible."

His face was clean-shaven, except for a thin mustache that hugged his top lip. His hair was cropped short and neatly combed in military fashion. He wore thin, gold-rimmed spectacles with round lenses. It was a younger version of him—smooth faced, untouched by worry and wear. But it was *him*. Unmistakable. Alive.

"Hello, Henry," said Abe.

TEN

★ ★ ★

Burning

What is to give light must endure burning.
—*Viktor Frankl*

Abe didn't remember much about May 8th, 1865, but he remembered the burning. It felt as if his skin was being ripped from his body, one layer at a time. As if the air itself was on fire.

Decades later, in 1921, he would attend a lecture about the nature of time and space at Columbia University in New York. The lecturer, a German physicist who would win the Nobel Prize a year later, had opened with a fact that Abe found particularly fascinating, saying, with his thick accent:

"Every second that you and I sit here, the sun burns 680 million tons of hydrogen. Takes it and fuses it into helium. Every second of your life. Do you know how much 680 million tons is? It is more than a *trillion pounds*. A trillion pounds of fuel, every second, for billions and billions of years! Isn't it wonderful? And because it is so massive, this star, so heavy—gravity holds it all together! So you see, its power, the very thing that makes it want to tear itself apart, is the very thing that holds it together. And this, this is how the star spends its eternity. An eternity of this. Always the fight, the push and pull, between destruction and existence. Ah...but in the end, destruction always wins."

The burning had started the second he'd broken though the window. Before he'd even hit the ground. It had felt like he'd jumped into a skillet, his skin sizzling on contact. He'd thrown himself through the window, intent on returning to his grave. But the pain—a pain that couldn't be conjured in the devil's imagination—the pain had changed his mind. This was no way to die.

He ran toward the trees west of Tenth Street—desperate for the relief of their shade. He ran faster than any man has a right to run. *But you're not a man, Abraham.* Fast enough to draw the gaping stares of a group of children playing in the front yard of a neighbor's house. Running inside to tell their parents that a screaming man had just flown down Jackson Street. But Abe saw none of this. He was virtually blind. There was only the contrast of green leaves against the fiery sky, calling him to their comfort. Drawing him toward the woods, where the full May canopies would choke off the blinding, burning sun.

But even the shade burned. No, it wasn't the burning of the open, but it was still an agony unlike any he'd experienced in life. His arms, legs, face—every inch of him felt like the exposed root of a rotten tooth, constant, shocking agony as the dentist's pliers grabbed hold and yanked on the inflamed nerve. His skin slewing off, the pain doubling him over. *In the end, destruction always wins.*

Abe dragged himself along the ground. *Henry will be coming after me any minute now. He'll tell me how to make the burning stop.* His skin blistering and blackening. His eyes stinging. A trillion pounds of fuel making him suffer every second. Time seemed to melt along with his flesh, and where there was the floor of the forest there was now the floor of a horse stable; Abe dragged himself into the mercy of its innards, into one of its dark stalls, burying himself under hay and mud and manure, praying that it would keep the sun off him. That it would stop the burning.

It hadn't been easy. Not at first. Abe and Henry's reunion had come with all the drama of a rock band getting back together decades after an ugly breakup. But time heals all wounds, congealing around psychic injuries like a clotted mass of platelets and white blood cells. Eventually the wound scabs over. If you don't pick at it for sixty years, it becomes a scar.

> [Abe] was...chilly, at first. Standoffish. Frankly, I would have preferred anger. Anger I could deal

with. Passion and fury were emotions I understood. I'm not big on melodrama—which is frustrating, given that it's almost exclusively how my kind are portrayed in fiction. Abe wasn't melodramatic; he was just quiet. I almost wished he would lash out, strike me. Nothing cleanses the conscience quite so well as being wronged by the person you've wronged.

The turning point in our relationship came two weeks after our reunion, when I was finally able to make him a gift of something I'd been holding on to for decades.

Abe stood transfixed at first, staring at the gift, then at Henry, then back to the gift again. He reached over and hefted his ax for the first time in sixty years.

He held it in his left hand first, then tossed it into his right, a slow grin spreading across his face. He ran his fingers along the worn handle, over nicks and notches that had been there since his father first gave it to him. This ax wasn't just his weapon. It was his only link—besides me, I suppose—to a long-vanished past.

Like Henry's old vampire bodyguard, William Duell, Abe had accelerated his body's resistance to sunlight (though unlike Duell, he hadn't done it gradually, or by choice), allowing him unusual freedom of movement for a vampire still in his first century.

They resumed hunting together, just as they had a century earlier, when Abe was a young man and Henry his mentor.

> But that dynamic was gone. We were equals now. Partners, going on "errands" at the behest of our government.
>
> If you needed to know what vampires were up to in Europe or Asia or South America, [Abe and I] were your best option. Our orders came from the War Department, sometimes directly from the White House. And they kept us busy. Between 1922 and 1929, we were dispatched to six continents. But all that changed after the crash.

In October of 1929, the stock market suffered a series of unprecedented losses, kicking off the Great Depression. It marked an end to the "sky's the limit" economic optimism of the previous decade and left millions of Americans in financial ruin, rich and poor alike. Henry lost more than half his net worth in a single day (though he was still rich by any standard). Suddenly the government had its hands full trying to keep a sputtering economy from falling completely over the cliff's edge. Keeping tabs on foreign vampires was no longer a priority.

After the crash, we mostly worked on American soil with [director of the FBI, J. Edgar] Hoover— investigating the Osage Indian murders,[1] keeping the [Ku Klux] Klan in check, helping out with the Lindbergh kidnapping in '32.[2] [Hoover] didn't like us much. He thought vampires were "disgusting, amoral creatures." His exact words, and he said them to our faces. Imagine that, the director of the FBI, looking a former president in the eye and calling him "disgusting." Tell you the truth, I think he was just embarrassed by how effective we were compared to his golden boys.

---

1. Between 1921 and 1925, upward of sixty Osage Indians were murdered in Oklahoma. The murders went unsolved for years. Later, it came to light that the Osage had been murdered by neighboring white men who wanted to reclaim oil-rich land that had been granted to the Indians under the terms of a 1907 deal.

2. World-famous aviator Charles Lindbergh's twenty-month-old son was taken from his crib on March 1st, 1932. A letter was left at the scene demanding $50,000 in ransom. The story became an instant worldwide sensation, prompting offers of help from everyone from Wall Street titans to mobsters like Al Capone. On hearing of the kidnapping, President Herbert Hoover vowed to "move heaven and earth" to find the child. Abe and Henry were dispatched to New Jersey to investigate any possible vampire involvement, as Lindbergh was something of an American symbol. They failed to find any vampire connection, but an idea of Abe's (to pay the ransom in gold certificates rather than cash) eventually led to the arrest and execution of Richard Hauptmann, a German immigrant and resident of the Bronx.

Perhaps their most notorious brush with American crime came in 1930, when Abe and Henry were sent to aid a young treasury agent named Eliot Ness.

Ness was surrounded by corruption. Everyone he trusted had turned out to be an incompetent or a fraud—or worse. He needed dependable men willing to go up against Al Capone and his private army, and those men were almost nonexistent in Chicago. Ness had written letter after letter to the Justice Department in Washington, explaining the scope of the problems he faced and begging for reinforcements. He didn't need more cops; he needed soldiers. This was, after all, a war for the soul of a city, and the good guys were losing.

In 1930, his prayers were suddenly and mysteriously answered when two men arrived from D.C. to aid in his crusade. He didn't quite know what to make of the pair at first. One was awkwardly tall and melancholy. The other was quiet, intense to the point that Ness thought his dark eyes might pop right out of his skull.

Abe and Henry had been crisscrossing the United States, taking on one public enemy after another, all the while searching for the only enemy who really mattered: Virginia Dare. The revelation that "A. Grander VIII" was actually Dare hadn't made her any less elusive. After a decade of pursuit, Abe and Henry weren't any closer to tracking her down.

We couldn't exactly put out an all-points bulletin for a twentysomething redheaded woman. Not without putting innocent people in danger or arresting half the women in Western Europe. Or worse—without letting Virginia know that we were onto her. Nor could we rely on the Union for help.

The Union's steady decline had continued in the early twentieth century. During the Civil War, it had boasted nearly five hundred members in America alone. Now the best estimates put the number at barely one hundred members worldwide—an 80 percent drop in just seventy years.

There were a number of reasons, I think. It was becoming harder to kill without recourse, for one. There were fewer nameless immigrants and transients. People had begun to carry identification cards. Police were using fingerprints to match murderers to victims. And where the wealthy had long enjoyed a sort of unspoken immunity from prosecution, the rise of the working class meant that no man was above the law or above suspicion. In other words, it was getting harder to be a vampire. The world was changing faster than ever before, and the relics were struggling to keep up.

When Abe and Henry arrived to reinforce Eliot Ness, Prohibition was dragging into its tenth year.

Chicago was a city under siege, on the verge of breaking.

> I didn't care for [Ness] at first. His shoes were too clean, and he had no discernible sense of humor. People as brittle as Ness are what drive other men to drink in the first place. But he was relentless, determined. He was a Boy Scout, sure. But he was a man with a clear sense of justice and purpose. I remember asking him, not long after we got to Chicago, exactly what it was he wanted us to do. Kill Capone?

"No," said Ness. "If we kill him, another man'll just pop up in his place. We're in the *justice* business, men—not the execution business. If we resort to killing in cold blood, well...then we're no better than the men we're fighting."

Abe and Henry shared a look. *Whatever you say, pal.*

"So if you don't want to kill them," asked Henry, "what do you want to do?"

Ness thought a moment.

"I want to *scare* them," he said."

Ellington's "Sweet Jazz o' Mine" was playing as they walked in, brought to life by black musicians on a stage barely big enough for an upright piano and drum kit. A trumpet player rounded out the trio, the crisp notes of his horn splitting the smoke-filled air and rising above the din of drunken conversation.

Abe was wearing a long coat, his ax concealed beneath it, and a black fedora, the brim pulled low above his eyes. Henry also wore a hat, an expensive black suit, and a wide, short tie—the style of the day. Ness, as always, looked every bit the Boy Scout, with his cheap gray suit and naked head of close-cropped hair.

> The room was packed to the gills with gangsters and their girlfriends. Music blaring. There were no uniformed cops with us, no other agents. Ness had insisted on keeping it quiet. He didn't want any of Capone's men getting tipped off.

Ness stepped onto the small, crowded stage and stood beside the bewildered musicians. Abe and Henry stood on either side of him.

Ness yelled something to the speakeasy crowd.

> No one heard him over the band. I turned toward the musicians and held up a hand: *stop*. They did. Heads started to turn toward the stage, everybody wondering what happened to the music. In a low voice, I told [the musicians] it might be a good time to go have a smoke.

"This is a raid!" yelled Ness to the bewildered crowd. "You're all under arr—"

> Bullets started flying. I knew immediately that they came from a [Thompson submachine gun] because there were a lot of them, and none of them hit us. Somewhere a woman started screaming— a deep-throated and masculine affair that seemed entirely incongruous with her painted face and sequined party dress. The screaming stopped abruptly when the top of her skull was torn off by the tommy gun.

Abe pulled his ax from his coat and charged at the gunman, swinging his blade and cutting clean though the man's rib cage and into his heart. Ness took cover behind the upright piano and started firing with his service revolver.

Henry dove behind the bar as a second machine gun opened up, then a third. He unsheathed his claws and crept beneath gin-soaked tables until he came to the nearest of the men shooting at him. With a brutal swipe, he relieved the man of both his kneecaps. And when the man bent over to investigate the sudden agony below his thighs, Henry relieved him of his face.

He grabbed the tommy gun from its previous owner, slapped in a new drum, and started firing.

It was exhilarating, I admit it. This wasn't the old Springfield I'd used in [World War I]; this was a big, fat, flesh-ripping, kill-'em-all-and-let-God-sort-'em-out death sprayer. Even better than Tesla's ray gun. I swung the barrel from side to side like I'd seen the screen actors do. Fifty rounds gone in a blink, and without another magazine I chucked the gun aside. I surveyed the room, expecting to see the bullet-riddled corpses of bad guys sprawled over tables and hanging from chandeliers.

I hadn't hit a single person. Not even a bartender. I dove for cover again.

Ness stood up in Henry's wake and began to fire. Abe leapt over the tables, whirling his ax and leaving a trail of blood and body parts behind him.

With his size, when Abe had his claws and fangs out, he looked like a lanky demon. Gangsters— thieves and professional murderers—pissed themselves as he approached.

A bodyguard with a tommy gun aimed his weapon at Henry and fired, screaming. Henry slid across the wooden floor, narrowly dodging bullets, and buried his claws in the man's groin, severing the great saphenous vein, the longest in the human body. Blood burst forth like water from a ruptured main. He bled out in seconds.

As Henry drained Capone's men of their blood, Abe drained the barrels that lined the walls of their contents. He split them open with his ax, Canadian whiskey pouring out in a brown froth.

In all, eight Capone associates died that day, and many more escaped to spread the word. These agents, whoever they were, had moved so quickly— so unnaturally—that the surviving gangsters thought they were fighting ghosts. As one gangster told Capone, "I'd take a swing at the guy's face, only to see him halfway across the room by the time my fist came around. I couldn't get a hand on him, and none of the other fellas could put any lead on 'em, either."

The word was out. Eliot Ness had a private army of his own. And they weren't just fast . . .

They were untouchable.

In 1937, after five years of painfully slow recovery, America was hit with a severe recession, erasing most of the gains in employment and stocks and plunging America back into the depths of economic ruin. And it wasn't just money (or the lack thereof) making America miserable. Everywhere you turned in 1937, it seemed that something bad was happening: dustbowl conditions in the heartland. The mysterious disappearance of Amelia Earhart, aged thirty-nine, and the death of beloved composer George Gershwin, aged thirty-eight. For the first time in the nation's history, natural-born

American citizens were leaving and returning to the countries of their ancestors. In New York, Henry's old friend Tesla—then eighty years old—was hit by a cab while crossing the street and nearly killed. He would never fully recover from his injuries.[3]

> It was almost supernatural how bad things were. As if there was a curse on America. It might sound crazy, but that's how it felt at the time. The country couldn't catch a break.

But as bad as things were at home, they were even worse overseas. Spain was in the midst of a bloody civil war. The Gestapo was arresting political enemies in Germany. Mussolini had Italy in his fascist grasp. England had signed a treaty with Germany allowing an expansion of the German navy (a decision it would deeply regret). War had broken out between China and Japan, with Japanese soldiers slaughtering three hundred thousand Chinese soldiers, women, and children in a six-week period that would be known as the Rape of Nanking. Whether in America or abroad, it seemed a shroud of darkness had encircled the earth.

If it had been left to Abe, they would have meted out bloody justice with the same year-round, rain-or-shine

---

3. Tesla would die alone in his room at the New Yorker Hotel in 1943.

regularity of the postal service, but at Henry's insistence they occasionally took a break.

> I told him that we had to see more of the country, see the people, to help us remember why it was worth saving. He'd mumble something about not needing a reminder, but he'd usually give in. Murder—even righteous murder—is exhausting work.

It was on one of these brief interludes that they found themselves on the way to South Dakota, to see firsthand the nearly finished head of Abraham Lincoln on Mount Rushmore.

> Personally I thought it was hilarious, but Abe was dead set against it. Just as he hadn't wanted to go to the dedication of the memorial in '22, or the rededication of the tomb in '31, he wasn't interested in seeing himself in stone. It struck him as vain and a little perverse to—as he called it—"attend your own funerals."
>
> He could be a bit of a downer, truth be told. He still had that melancholy streak. And on top of that, he'd become paranoid about being recognized, especially after they'd slapped his face on the five [dollar bill] in 1914. I told him, "Calm down. First of all, even if someone thought you looked exactly like Abraham Lincoln, why on earth would they think you were *the* Abraham

Lincoln? Second of all, you look about twenty years younger than the man in those portraits. Different hair, no beard, new glasses..."

During their stopover in Minneapolis, Abe happened to glance at an item buried deep in the pages of the *Minneapolis Star*.

A teenage boy had been lynched in a small town a couple of hours outside the city. A black boy who'd forced himself on a sixteen-year-old white girl down the road. Of course, no suspects were named. No witnesses had come forward. It all happened in the dark, you see. Such a shame. But of course, the boy shouldn't have done what he did. Neighbors described him as "simple," or "slow." A "gentle soul" who'd never done anything like this before. "What a shame, what a shame, but then it just goes to show you they can't be trusted," and so on.

Abe and Henry decided to extend their stay. They made their way to the town[4] in question, purporting to be derrick workers on their way south after working a season in Canada. Just a couple of able-bodied white men looking for an honest wage.

---

4. Henry prefers to keep the name of the town off the record, citing the potential of civil and criminal consequences.

We'd become pretty adept at investigating these sorts of things. There were two general rules: one, ask as few questions as possible. These were tight-knit communities. They were inclined to be distrustful of outsiders, and if they got a whiff of suspicion, that was it. You were done. Two, you had to be willing to spend the time. If you waited around long enough and people got the sense that you were "all right," someone usually slipped up sooner or later.

While lynching was more prevalent in the Jim Crow South, it was present all over America, even as late as 1937, and even as far north as Minnesota.

There are dozens of pictures—you've probably seen some of them; everyone *should* see them: black bodies hanging from trees, from telegraph poles, bridges. Broken necks. Blood running from their noses. And in almost every one of these pictures, you'll see a group of white faces staring back at the camera defiantly. Faces smiling, pointing, even *laughing* at the dangling bodies. And you realize, *This is their keepsake of the moment.* This is their community, coming together to right a wrong—no judge, no jury, no consequences. Just some townsfolk and a rope. They don't see anything wrong with it. They're *proud* of it. The majority of their victims were young black men, some of them tortured before they were hanged. Some with fingers, limbs, genitals, missing. Almost all were savagely beaten before their deaths. In one picture, no less than ten young black men—some of them just *boys*— are hanging from the same tree. What their alleged crimes were, I had no idea. It didn't matter to their murderers, and it didn't matter to me.

Abe and Henry found lodging at a boardinghouse and spent the next two weeks minding their own business. They found work—hauling scrap away from a demolished mill (they didn't need the money, but it was important that they keep up appearances—people were undoubtedly watching). They went to church on Sunday and pushed food around their plates at the local dinette. They kept to themselves.

It's amazing what people will tell you when you shut up and let them talk. We hadn't been there two weeks when one of the waitresses at the dinette asked us if we'd heard about "the incident." It was still big news in town, in the sense that nobody wanted to be caught dead talking about it but it was all anyone wanted to talk about. She told us the name of the so-called white "victim," which they hadn't published in the newspaper. She told us the names of a few of the men who "done justice to the boy." I mean, it was incredible. She didn't know us from the next guys, and here she is giving up half the people in town, thinking we're just going to nod and forget about it.

"Boy should'a known not to mess around like that," she said. "He lived here his whole life. He knows what kind'a men we got around here. What kind'a *groups*."

Abe and I pieced it together pretty quickly: a teenage white girl stumbles in the front door after curfew with liquor on her breath and dried semen down the front of her dress. Her mother cries. Her daddy pulls off his belt and threatens to beat her senseless, so the girl does the only thing she can. She cries rape and tells her daddy that it was the black boy who lives down the road, only she doesn't use the word "black." He'd forced her to get drunk, she tells him. And then he forced himself on her, honest, Daddy. May God strike her down, Daddy. And so what's Daddy do? He *has* to believe her. He has to, or his little girl—his little *angel*—is nothing but a whore. He calls the sheriff, whom he's known since the two of them were kids. "Come on out to the house," he says. "Bring some of the boys with you, and leave your badge at home."

Meanwhile the black boy's asleep in his bed, unaware that any of this is going on. Unaware that a dozen angry Klansmen are on their way over. They barge in, tie his hands behind his back, and drag him off while his mother and sisters scream. They throw him in a car, caravan out into the woods. They beat him, make him a noose, and string him up, yelling every epithet you can imagine. Cheering as he thrashes like a fish on a hook. Cheering when the front of his trousers darkens as he pisses himself. And when he finally dies, they cut him down, douse him with kerosene, and burn him down to bone and ash, just to make sure there's nothing left of him for his mother to bury.

The boy never knew *why*, you see. Why he was dragged from his bed. Why those men were so cross with him. He'd gone to his death confused, and that, more than anything, was what got under my skin. Every time an innocent is murdered, it's a tragedy. But when it's a child or someone of feeble mind, as this boy was—someone who *doesn't understand*—my fists ball up and my teeth clench at the thought of that fear. That confusion. That look a dog gives its owner after it's been kicked. *What did I do? I don't understand.*

The firelight drew Abe and Henry in like moths. It cut through the night woods like a lighthouse through fog, guiding them home. They'd been small fires at first—fifteen or twenty flickering dots in the dark. Stars that had fallen to the ground, twinkling between the gaps in the trees. A chorus of voices had accompanied these little stars as they danced, chanting in unison, drawing the two vampires closer. As they crept nearer, the small fires had joined together, giving life to one towering flame that made the silhouette of every branch, and the white robes of every man they were about to kill, visible.

They were on the edge of the clearing now, close enough to see those faces that weren't obscured by hoods. There were forty of them, give or take. Men and boys, each of them holding a torch, their sheets rendered ghostlike in the glow of the flames. And the good ol' cross. That Old Rugged Cross, *the emblem of suffering and shame.*[5]

They stood in a circle around the cross, pointing their flaming torches at it, lifting and lowering them in unison. All of them wore white, save one. A portly one in a red sheet, his face uncovered, a red hood rising from his head like a dunce cap. He wore glasses, using the light of the torch in his right hand to read from a small book in his left.

"For God...," said the man in red.

"For God!" repeated the others.

"For country..."

"For country!"

"For race..."

---

5. From a popular hymn of the time, "That Old Rugged Cross," by George Bennard (1873–1958).

Klansmen burn a cross during a rally similar
to the one Abe and Henry attacked in 1937.
Though lynching was on the decline by the
1930s, there were still incidents in America as
late as 1968.

"For race!"
"For Klan..."
"For Klan!"
With that, the other men threw their torches at the
base of the cross, and up the flames went, climbing
the kerosene-soaked wood with a *whoosh* of air.

[The cross] was forty feet high, with the flames
jumping another twenty feet above its top. The
fire would've been visible for miles. Clearly,

they weren't worried about attracting attention or drawing the suspicion of the law. Half of them *were* the law.

Abe and Henry waited for the moment to strike. Once they revealed themselves, the rest had to be quick and vicious. It was dangerous, taking on so many men at once, even for a pair of vampires.

"In Jesus Christ's name!" said the man in red.

"In Jesus Christ's name," repeated the others, beginning a chant: "In Jesus Christ's name! In Jesus Christ's name!"

As they chanted, one of the Klansmen, who happened to be looking toward the woods beyond the circle of his white brethren, saw a shape come streaking out of the tree line. *Or was it two shapes?* It was hard to see much in the darkness that lay beyond the flames. He saw the shapes—*it's two shapes, I'm sure of it*—racing toward the other side of the circle with inhuman speed, coming into focus as they neared the light of the cross. *Are they animals? But why would animals come toward*—

One of his brother Klansmen—*from the size of him, I think it's Big Ray, but I can't tell with that damned hood on*—suddenly arched his back and dropped his torch. He fell to his knees; his hands came up to his throat.

The chanting stopped. All eyes on their kneeling brother.

"Ray?" said the man in red. "That you under there?"

Ray didn't answer. He couldn't, on account of his throat having been cut from ear to ear. None of the other Klansmen could see the color drain completely from Ray's face, tuning his skin the same pale shade as the hood that covered it, or see his eyes bulge as he strained for breath. But they saw his blood. Spreading from his collar out to his chest as the fibers of his white sheet soaked it up like the roots of a thirsty tree. Gravity making the blood empty out of his brain, his heart pumping the rest upward, out of the gaping wound, pouring out of him by the glassful, darkening his chest. Big Ray fell onto his stomach, his hands at his sides. Prostrating himself before the burning cross, his soul fresh on its way to what he prayed would be a segregated heaven.

Two men fell from the sky. They'd jumped clear over the Klansmen's heads, landing inside the circle with animal grace. They were wearing masks, these men. At least they *looked* like masks. Their eyes were black from lid to lid—windows into the surrounding dark. Their mouths were open to jaw-breaking widths, with fangs that looked like glass shards in the firelight. The tall one snatched a torch from the nearest Klansman's grip, drew his arm back, and drove the burning end clean through the man's chest and out his back. It had gone through so fast that it was still burning when it broke through his spine, making the back of his robe pop out like the center of a circus tent and setting him alight.

The Klansmen ran for their lives. The circle broke apart, white sheets fluttering in every direction. Henry made a beeline for the one in red.

It was important to make an example of the leader. (I assumed he was the leader—he was the only one wearing red, and he didn't exactly have the worker-bee physique.) I ran him down, which took all of a few steps, and tackled him. Pinned him. I rolled him onto his back and made sure he got a good look at my face. The eyes, the teeth. In most cases, I take victims unaware. It's over before they know it. Quick and relatively pain-less, even for the wicked ones. But when someone is *especially* evil, when they've taken pleasure in striking fear into others before death, [then] I don't mind them dying afraid.

Henry lifted the man in red up by his throat and threw him into the air—no small feat, considering he weighed in at better than three hundred pounds. Up he went, into the burning cross, his crimson robes waving like the red flags Henry had seen used to signal imminent danger during the Great War. *You're in imminent danger, all right.* The back of the man in red's skull cracked as it struck the cross, knocking him unconscious. He fell back to earth, his robes consumed by the flames.

He was [unconscious] for only a second or two. His eyes opened, and after a moment in the fog—you know, *Where the hell am I? What's that smell?*—I saw it register on his face. The pain of his broken bones and burning flesh. The gravity of his situation. He panicked, of course. Got up on his hands and knees and crawled away from the burning cross. But it didn't matter. His robes were burning like the fabric on those torches. All that fatty flesh was starting to sizzle beneath them. I considered feeding on him, showing him a little mercy. But then I thought of that boy, dragged from his bed and tortured, hanged. I decided to watch him burn.

One thing I distinctly remember—his hat was still on top of his head as he crawled. Even after I'd thrown him up in the air, even after he'd landed in a heap, that pointy red hat was still stuck on there. And so help me, the very tip of its pointy top was the only part of it that was on fire. I watched the poor fat slug drag himself along the ground, screaming, and I was suddenly hit with the image of a red candle. A big Disney cartoon of a red candle, screaming in pain. Its wick burning, making the red wax (in this case his skin) melt. I started to laugh. I couldn't help myself. Even with him squealing like a stuck pig, "Oh, Jesus, help me," and all that.

Henry began to sing as the man in red cried out for his savior:

"Happy birthday to you, happy birthday to you…"

Henry waved his arms back and forth as if conducting a symphony.

> I should've been off helping Abe run more [Klansmen] down, but I was transfixed. What's that quote? The one from the Hitchcock film?[6] "We all go a little mad sometimes." I suppose I did. Having a fit of laughter and song at the sight of a suffering man. What else can you call it but madness? And the truth is, to this day, I can't see a red candle without breaking out in a smile.

Abe, meanwhile, chased down another of the fleeing Klansmen and caught hold of his sheet, yanking it backward—and bringing the man inside to an abrupt halt. He tore the hood from the man's head and let him look upon his eyes, his pale, wild face and fangs. Abe knew the Klansman was terrified from the foul smell that wafted up from the seat of his pants—an all-too-common occurrence that never failed to turn Abe's stomach and put him off feeding. His appetite gone, Abe had to settle for grabbing the sides of the Klansman's head and turning it 180 degrees, so that his chin rested atop his spine.

---

6. *Psycho* (1960).

Most of the other Klansmen took off into the woods, ditching their robes in hopes that they would be harder to see. Some scooped up their children in their arms as they fled. A few ran to the cars and trucks parked nearby, fishing inside for pistols and rifles, intent on standing their ground. These defiant few took aim as the two figures approached from the middle of the clearing, silhouetted against the burning cross. They leveled their guns and shot. They shot straight and true. They saw the figures recoil as they were struck by the bullets. But they kept coming.

> Typically, we killed a few of them and let the rest run off to tell their friends. We always let them see our faces—that was key. Otherwise, they might run off thinking it was a group of local blacks that'd attacked them. There might be retributions. You might ask—where were the black vampires in all of this? It's a fair question. We never intended, as two white vampires, to act like the saviors of an oppressed people. But the truth is, I didn't know any [black vampires] in those days. Even if I had, it would have been a bad idea for them to join our raids, for the reasons I just mentioned.

The gunshots died, along with the remaining men. Abe and Henry stood in the silence of the clearing, listening to the snapping twigs and branches of men fleeing in the dark woods and watching taillights disappearing down country roads in clouds of dust.

At first light, the local sheriff, the mayor, and a handful of deputies (most of whom had been at the rally beneath sheets) stood in the clearing. The charred cross still stood, though its flames were long dead and the ashes damp with morning dew. The men held handkerchiefs over their noses and mouths.

There were three of them. Three white men, stripped naked, their bodies flayed open and cleaned out like gutted fish. Each with a rope around his neck, each hanging from a high, sturdy tree branch at the perimeter of the clearing—their entrails dangling from their bellies, all the way down to the dew-covered ground, like umbilical cords attaching their corpses to mother earth. And each of the three was completely bereft of skin, their red flesh and muscle exposed. Skinned like grapes, save for a thin strip of pale white left on each of their chests in the shape of the letter "K." In the center of the clearing lay the fat, charred body of their leader. His arms outstretched, his hands nailed to the beam of the burned cross in a Christ pose.

The number of cross burnings dropped dramatically throughout the South in the 1930s.

Abraham Lincoln entered the White House wearing his dress-green Class A army uniform, which bore the gold leaf insignia of a major. The military identification

card he presented at the security desk bore a different
name than the one he'd been born with. The signature
on his card was checked against the one he entered in
the visitors log, and he was ordered to surrender any
weapons at the desk. He wasn't carrying any. Nor was
Henry, who, although also an officer in the army, was
wearing civilian attire.

The two vampires had been summoned back to
Washington in April of 1937. They'd never reached
South Dakota, which was just fine with Abe, who'd
dreaded seeing his old, awkward self carved into the
side of a mountain. The memorial on the mall was
bad enough, and Abe avoided it like the plague whenever he was in town. But no structure in Washington
gave him greater fits of anxiety than the White House.

> It was hard for him, going back. It was a house
> filled with ghosts. The ghosts of his cabinet, his
> wife, his children. They were all dead. Except in
> the White House. There, their voices, their faces
> were all very much alive to him.

The West Wing and its Oval Office had become
the epicenter of the presidency by then, but Abe and
Henry had been ushered to the residence on their
arrival, into one of its bedrooms—a more discreet
place for FDR to meet with his two vampires. They
sat, waiting for the president to wrap up other meetings. It was an uncommonly warm spring day, and the

windows had been opened to let in the fresh, fragrant air. The curtains softening the sunlight, gently waving in the breeze. Abe and Henry sat opposite the room's dominant feature—a rosewood bed, elegantly carved in Victorian style, with an arching, oversize headboard.

> I noticed Abe looking at the bed. Fixated on it. Whether by coincidence or design, we'd been asked to wait in what was then called the Lincoln Bedroom.[7] Abe had been brought face-to-face with the bed his son Willie had died in seventy-five years earlier.

"You think you're the only one who's sacrificed for this office?" said a voice.

Franklin Roosevelt stood in the doorway, his weight resting on a cane. Under his trouser legs, metal braces had been fastened to his legs with leather straps, to help keep him upright. Abe and Henry stood out of respect as Roosevelt hobbled in with tremendous effort. Though paralyzed from the waist down after suffering a bout of polio in his late thirties, he still insisted on walking whenever possible, using a method of shifting his weight that he'd taught himself.

---

7. On the northwest corner of the second floor, this room was known as the Lincoln Bedroom from 1929 to 1948, when it was remodeled and renamed the President's Dining Room. The present-day Lincoln Bedroom (and its iconic rosewood bed) occupies the southeast corner of the second floor.

Every president I've ever known has had the weight of the world on his shoulders, but none looked more worn down or ill suited to carry the burden than FDR. Ironic, since he was one of the more resolute and robust presidents we've had.

"It takes everything from us, this goddamned job," said Roosevelt, sitting on a chair opposite Abe and Henry. "Look at me. Barely five years on and I look like death warmed over—no offense."

"None taken," said Henry.

"You've sacrificed, I've sacrificed," said Roosevelt. "Does any man achieve anything worth a damn without sacrifice? Hell, I'm held together by leather straps and nervous doctors."

"I died," said Abe.

"Ha!" cried Roosevelt. "Watching a *play*. Don't act like you charged headlong into battle dodging cannon fire and waving the flag!"

I'm not sure where [Abe and FDR's] relationship went sour, exactly. They'd been cordial at first. Roosevelt had been elected in '32. According to custom, he'd started receiving intelligence briefings before his inauguration, including a meeting with Abe and me. He'd been shocked to learn that Abraham Lincoln, one of his predecessors, was not only alive but a vampire, and on the War

Department's payroll, no less. I'd witnessed that same moment of presidential awe twice before, when Abe had been introduced to Coolidge in '22 and Hoover in '28. Both had revered Abe and frequently turned to him for advice on a number of matters during their own presidencies. And why not? He was still as wise a politician as ever, vampire or not.

But FDR had never sought Abraham Lincoln's advice. On the contrary, they'd bumped heads almost from the start. While Lincoln admired Roosevelt's political savvy and largely supported his policies, he just didn't care for the man.

To [Abe], FDR was an elitist. A man who'd been born with a silver spoon in his mouth and a bug up his ass. He'd grown up American royalty, educated at Groton, Harvard, and Columbia. He'd worked on Wall Street, where he'd earned himself a reputation as a serial philanderer. He also saw Roosevelt's "noninterventionist" stance in Europe as a cop-out. More than that, he saw it as downright un-American. "If only his cousin[8] were still in the White House," he'd say.

---

8. Theodore Roosevelt and Franklin Delano Roosevelt were fifth cousins. Not only were the two men only loosely acquainted with each other, but FDR, a lifelong Democrat, actually campaigned *against* his Republican cousin in the election of 1908.

Personally, I thought Abe a little too hard on FDR. Abe's *own* son had been raised in the lap of luxury and attended Harvard, hadn't he? Never mind the fact that Roosevelt could have chosen a life of idle leisure but entered public service instead. He'd spent most of his life sick, and he'd been crippled by disease, yet he hadn't retreated from service. That counted for something, in my book, but Abe couldn't have cared less. Maybe he was jealous of Roosevelt. Maybe he was insulted that Roosevelt hadn't revered him as much as the others had. Maybe they were just oil and water. You never know with exceptional people.

"The world is in peril," Roosevelt continued. "We stand at the brink of a war unlike any history has ever seen. If we act quickly, we may be able to save untold millions of lives."

Throughout his first term, Roosevelt had taken a noninterventionist approach to foreign policy, choosing to fight the Axis powers with embargos rather than guns. America had no business meddling in other nations' affairs until its own financial house was in order, he thought. But now, with the Chinese and Japanese at war in Asia, and Hitler poised to launch attacks on his European neighbors, "the ostrich was running out of sand to stick its head in," as he told his advisers.

FDR had seen the newsreels, as we all had. Crowds a million strong, all hailing their chancellor. There was something undeniably enchanting about Hitler. He had an almost...supernatural draw. Something about his obsession with "the purity of blood" and "superiority of race." His vision of a world dominated by a chosen few. It all sounded eerily familiar.

"He's gearing up for war," said Roosevelt. "The only question is with whom, and when he's going to strike."

"So what is it," asked Henry. "You'd like us to gather some intelligence on what Hitler's up to? See if he's working with any of our kind?"

"No," said Roosevelt. "I want you to kill the son of a bitch."

To many Germans, the feeling of being driven out, of being humiliated, went all the way back to 1 AD, when Rome invaded Germania and drove its tribes back to the Rhine and the Danube. The bitterness of that defeat was passed down, generation to generation, evolving into the nationalism that exploded when Napoléon invaded German territory in the late eighteenth century. That nationalism gave rise to the concept of *Lebensraum* (living room)—the idea that Germans, being culturally and genetically superior to their neighbors, had the right to claim new territory and expand. Those expansion plans failed during World War I, and defeat led to its borders being squeezed even tighter. By the early 1930s, there was barely enough farmland to feed the country's booming population. And there was a widely held belief among Germans that they *would have* won the war, but for the "Jews and Marxists," who'd undermined them on the home front.

> That feeling—that Germany had been betrayed and that the German people had been shit on for centuries—is what opened the door for Hitler.

Adolf Hitler arrived in Vienna in the spring of 1910, a typical twentysomething. Rootless. Passionate. Unsure of what he wanted to do with his life. His parents were dead, and he got by with the help of a meager orphan's stipend that came monthly from the state. That, and whatever money he could make with his watercolor paintings of buildings and landscapes (most of them sold to Jewish art dealers). Vienna was a bohemian city in those days. A mecca for the arts. It also happened to be a hotbed of anti-Semitism. The papers carried almost daily treatises on the looming threat of an "invasion of Jews" from the East.

Unable to afford his own apartment, Hitler lived, along with some five hundred other residents, in a men's dormitory, where he rented a room by the week. It was a sparse, almost prison-like building, but it was an improvement over the homeless shelter he'd been staying in before that. He took his meals in its mess hall, where, amid the clatter of silverware and the clinking of plates and coffee cups, Hitler first heard others speak out against the Jews. There's no evidence that he shared those views at the time. In fact, even in his carefully worded piece of autobiographical propaganda, *Mein Kampf,*[9] Hitler admitted that he found the views of the anti-Semites "radical" during his days in Vienna. As late as 1913, Hitler counted Jews among his friends. Even at the height of his power in Nazi Germany, he remained grateful to the Jewish family doctor who had stayed by his mother's side, caring for her to the end.

Yet by 1920, just seven years after leaving the men's dormitory in Vienna, Hitler was giving fiery speeches in Munich, rallying thousands around anti-Semitic principles. It seemed as if he'd become completely consumed with hatred for the Jewish people. For decades, questions have persisted regarding the timeline of his radicalization. When did this shy, quiet drifter adopt his virulent views? How did he transition from a quiet bohemian artist to an impassioned, captivating speaker, with an almost mystical hold over an entire nation, in just a few short years?[10]

---

9. Written while Hitler was imprisoned for an attempted coup in 1923.
10. There have been countless books and research papers into the Nazis' obsession with all things occult. Pope Pius XII even tried to perform a long-distance exorcism on Hitler from Rome, believing he was possessed by the devil.

Abe and Henry arrived in Berlin on Thursday, April 22nd, 1937, after crossing on the French ocean liner SS *Normandie*—then the fastest, most luxurious passenger ship afloat. Abe traveled under the name Joshua F. Speed, a nod to his old friend from Springfield. Upon checking into their hotel, they opened their steamer trunks and began dismantling the various radios, cameras, and typewriters inside—all of which had been modified to include the necessary parts to build a compact, powerful bomb.

If the experience of killing Rasputin had taught Henry anything, it was this: the simpler the plan, the better. There would be no electrical death rays this time. No overly complex plots or reliance on untested coconspirators. This time, they would get as close as they could and, in FDR's words, "kill the son of a bitch." Getting close to Hitler was going to be a challenge, even for two men as fast and powerful as Abe and Henry. The Reich chancellor was surrounded by heavily armed, highly trained guards, at least some of whom, it was suspected, were vampires.

> It was tempting to just say, "Fine, we'll just wait for a rally or a parade. We'll wait for him to get close enough and then rush him with our claws and fangs flying." But even if we got to him—no doubt through a hail of machine-gun fire—we'd still have to escape, with every Nazi within a country mile on our tail, emptying clips into our

backs. Vampires are resilient, but we're not bulletproof. Shoot us often enough, and we die.

It had to be a plan that could be carried out
by Abe and me alone, and one that would leave
no trace of American involvement. We knew
there were Germans who wanted Hitler dead,
but FDR was adamant that we recruit no one.
He couldn't have the front pages of the world's
newspapers carrying headlines of a failed American plot. Not only would it embolden Hitler,
but it would almost certainly draw America into
the war, which is exactly what he was trying to
avoid.

Abe and Henry had considered every option,
assisted by a small, handpicked group of analysts and
officers from the War Department, who were told
only that they were assisting two American operatives
in planning the assassination of a high-level target.
Abe and Henry never met with them in person—so
critical was the protection of their identities and the
ability of the United States to deny involvement.

Nothing was off-limits for discussion: Slipping
into Hitler's residence under cover of darkness
and killing him in bed. Perching ourselves on a
roof opposite the Reichstag and taking him with a
sniper rifle. Posing as members of a foreign delegation and getting a face-to-face meeting with

him. But these came with too many variables and little or no chance of escape.

In the end, it was decided that a bomb would be the most effective and least traceable means. It was given the name Operation Sunshine—a play on one of the passages from *Mein Kampf*:

```
If you want to shine like the sun,
first you have to burn like it.
```

Rather than sticks of dynamite, they were given the then state-of-the-art compound known as RDX, or Research Department explosive—a white, crystalline powder, the primary ingredient in future moldable explosives like C-4.

We had eight ounces of this stuff, hidden in four separate film canisters—enough to turn a man into a cloud of blood and brain from twenty feet away. We'd been given instructions on how to handle it and had been assured and reassured that it was perfectly stable, that there was no way it would explode unless we wanted it to. Naturally, it scared the shit out of us.

Abe and Henry completed the bomb on the twenty-fifth, five days before Hitler was scheduled to speak at a rally at Berlin's Sportpalast (Sports Palace). That left the issue of getting into the venue undetected, and planting the bomb close enough to do its work.

They took in the warm spring evening, strolling past busy biergartens, where Nazi officers drank toasts to their führer and bounced pretty girls in their laps. Abe and Henry soaked up the old city. Henry was relieved to be a safe distance from their potentially explosive hotel room, though he couldn't escape a certain level of background anxiety. Henry didn't care for Berlin. He hadn't felt quite like himself since their arrival.

> I'd been dogged by an indefinable sense of dread since we'd arrived. I felt foggy and forgetful. I had trouble sleeping. I chalked it up to the anxiety of our mission and being surrounded by so much hatred.

Still, for vampires who fed only on wicked blood, Nazi Germany was an all-you-can-eat buffet. And Abe and Henry were hungry.

> There were SS officers everywhere you turned, some on duty, some drunkenly walking in the streets, singing and pissing in dark alleys. It was just a matter of finding two with the right jacket sizes.

As the Olympic Stadium Bell Tower[11] chimed two a.m., Abe and Henry followed a pair of officers—one of average height and build, the other uncommonly tall. They took care to keep from being noticed, both vampires having become adept at following prey on their own, but neither accustomed to killing in pairs. The Nazis walked arm in arm, both exceedingly drunk, but the taller of the two a shade drunker, and therefore leaning on his shorter friend for balance.

They were laughing and stumbling along. The taller one was wearing a woman's scarf around his neck—violet, I remember—clutching one end of it in his hand, using it as a prop in a story he was telling the other. Something about a woman named Liesl, whom he'd fallen hideously in love with, despite having met her at a beer garden two hours earlier. Whether this was Liesl's scarf or not, I have no idea.

The two officers stepped into an alley between two brick apartment buildings—all but one of the

---

11. Built for the 1936 Summer Games, which are most remembered for the four gold medals won by African American athlete Jesse Owens. Hitler was said to be furious that a black American stole the spotlight away from his so-called superior German Olympians. Owens returned to the United States a hero, though FDR never invited him to the White House or so much as sent him a telegram. The year 1936 was an election year, and the president was worried about seeming *too friendly* with the black track star. Owens would later work as a gas station attendant and declare bankruptcy.

windows above dark, the tenants long asleep. Abe and Henry waited on the sidewalk while the Germans relieved themselves against the trash cans that lined the walls.

It was important that their bladders be empty. We didn't want to go through the trouble of laundering their uniforms, you see. When we heard them finish, we stepped into the alley, our arms around each other, putting on a pretty good show of being shitfaced ourselves.

"Tut mir leid," said the shorter of the officers, a blissful grin on his face. "Das bad ist leider besetzt." *Sorry, the bathroom is occupied.*

The four men shared a laugh as the Nazis zipped up their trousers. Abe reached into his coat pocket and pulled out a silver cigarette holder.

"Haben sie feuer?" asked Abe. *Do you have a light?*

Both of the Nazis reached into their jacket pockets. It's doubtful they ever saw the fists coming, moving with dive-bomber speed and striking their skulls with savage force. They were cows in a slaughterhouse, rendered instantly and forever unconscious, with not the slightest hint of suffering or the faintest hope of reprieve. Abe and Henry caught the officers before they could fall all the way to the pavement (where their uniforms might come into contact with dirt or grime or recently expelled bodily fluids). They drained the men of their blood through careful bites on the wrists and neck, taking care not to spill a drop. When they were finished feeding, they stripped the men of their uniforms and dragged the bodies to the far end of the alley, below the darkened windows of dreaming apartment dwellers.

> I found a cigarette lighter in the smaller officer's jacket pocket. Usually I dispensed with personal items, but this was an intriguing piece—a silver Zippo lighter, emblazed with a gold swastika. Given that we were there to kill Adolf Hitler, I thought it might make for an interesting souvenir. Besides, you never knew when someone might need a light.
>
> I did, however, leave the purple scarf.

On Friday, April 30th, Abe and Henry, resplendent in their unsullied uniforms, joined thousands of soldiers and citizens in the Sportpalast. A stage had been constructed at one end of the arena, adorned with hanging garland and framed by a pair of floor-to-ceiling red swastika flags. Center stage, directly behind the podium, a giant golden eagle—the *Reichsadler*—sat with its wings outstretched, its head forever turned to the right. The symbol of Nazi Germany.

> Here we were, at the biggest Klan rally of them all. Tasked with killing the grandest of the grand

wizards. This was no remote wooded clearing, mind you. This was a public place, with thousands of screaming Germans, each of them willing to lay down his life to protect the führer. I'd seen astonishing public speakers before. Frederick Douglass was mesmerizing, and of course Abe could move people to tears—and to war—with his words. But this crowd was different. They were whipped into cabalistic frenzy, wild-eyed fury. Red-faced, they screamed, flecks of spit flying from their mouths. These men had surrendered all pretense of humanity.

By the time the opening acts had finished their speeches, the standing-room-only crowd was vibrating like excited molecules in boiling water. A party official rose to introduce the man everyone was waiting for. Standing behind the gleaming-white podium, he lifted his hands in an attempt to silence the crowd, which by then had risen to a chant of "Heil! Heil! Heil!" in deafening unison. Stomping their feet on the wooden rafters, making the whole building shake.

"Tonight," the official yelled into the microphones. But the crowd was relentless.

"Heil! Heil!"

Abe and Henry checked their watches. Hitler's speech was scheduled to begin at ten o'clock. It was already five minutes past.

Hitler speaks to the crowd at Berlin's Sportpalast, unaware that a powerful bomb is only a few inches below him. Note the glass of water on the podium, replenished after being spilled earlier.

"Tonight," the official continued, his voice booming from the public address system and echoing through the room, "let not only the German people but the entire world hear us chant!"

"Heil! Heil!"

"Tonight, let us speak with one voice!"

A large glass of water had been placed atop the podium for Hitler, who was known to scream himself hoarse during speeches. The party official (perhaps imitating his beloved führer) built to his own screaming crescendo: "The voice of a man who speaks for *all* of Germany!" He jerked his hands outward in a chopping motion on the word "Deutschland," emphasizing the first syllable and knocking the water glass over—spilling its contents across the top of the podium and over a typed copy of Hitler's speech. The crowd might not have noticed, had the official not jumped back, fearful of getting his khaki-colored uniform wet. He recovered and set about rescuing the typed pages.

> The crowd went silent for a fraction of a second, then broke into laughter, more at his cowardice than at his clumsiness. The laughter turned to boos and jeers. Distant shouts of "Asshole!" "Give us the führer!" and "Get off the stage!" But not from Abe and me. Our jaws were hanging off their hinges. We were horrified.

Horrified, because inside that podium, where rivulets of water were now beginning to seep through the cracks, was the bomb they'd so meticulously constructed and carefully planted—getting to the Sportpalast at dawn with the riggers and electricians, hauling bundles of wire and stringing garland wherever they were instructed to. And while the sound system was being tested, planting the bomb and setting its timer for ten minutes after ten that night. When the timer went off, an electrical charge would ignite the white crystalline RDX powder inside the bomb, turning the wooden podium into a trillion supersonic splinters and liquefying anyone standing by it. That is, as long as the powder didn't get wet.

> Hitler stepped to the podium and began to speak. We waited, fists clenched, unable to breathe. Ten past ten came and went. Ten fifteen...ten twenty...ten thirty...

After forty minutes of screaming and gesturing, Hitler ended his speech to thunderous applause, shouts, and stomps. He stood at the podium, a deity before the pious. Abe and Henry had failed.

"Let's go," said Abe.

"And do what?" asked Henry.

But Abe was already on his way. Henry followed him to the rear of the balcony, down the stairs to the main level. He followed as Abe ran down a wide, mostly empty corridor, the bulk of the crowd still chanting and stomping in the arena—hurrying through doors marked *Verboten!* and twisting through the dark, staff-only innards through which they'd lugged bundles of cable and garland hours earlier. Hurrying to intercept Hitler before his entourage led him out of the arena.

"Abe!" yelled Henry, running after him. "We can't! We have to let him go!"

Abe kept running.

Here I was, following a vampire through the recesses of a packed theater. A vampire who was determined to assassinate a world leader. And I had a thought. A ridiculous thought:

Abraham Lincoln had become John Wilkes Booth.

The dark recesses led them back to the light of the arena. They emerged just in time to see the führer himself step off the stage, trailed by advisers and surrounded by SS guards—the latter wearing helmets and compact machine guns, a curtain of protection through which nothing had much hope of penetrating. They led Hitler toward the exit, beside which the two vampires now stood, looking no different from any of the other thousands of Nazis in attendance.

"Abe!" said Henry again, tugging at the sleeve of his jacket. But Abe didn't acknowledge. He stood, tense and tall, staring at Hitler as the guards led him toward the exit.

I was afraid. I don't mind admitting it. But I didn't *show* it. To show fear would've tipped the guards off that something was wrong. I stood there, willing calmness onto my face and shouting out the side of my mouth.

"Goddammit, Abe, our orders!"

If Abe decided to pounce, we were both as good as dead. We might get to Hitler, and we might take a few of them with us, but we would never leave the arena alive. Not with that many machine guns tearing us to pieces. Not with thousands of Nazis chasing us down and exacting their vengeance. These would be our last moments. Abe knew it as well as I did.

Hitler grew close, gliding along in the middle of that machine-gun ring. Chants of "Heil!" blustering behind him, the wind in his invisible sails. Flashbulbs popping with strobe-light frequency as he neared the two officers standing to the side of his exit—one smiling awkwardly; the other, an uncommonly tall fellow, staring at him intensely.

We were face-to-face with him for a moment. I mean, this close [reaches out an arm's length]. Just a fleeting moment. He and I were the same height, same build—though his face was older and more severe. He had striking blue eyes. Most people don't know that. Intense, sunken eyes, which reminded me of Rasputin's. That hair, with its obsessively perfect part. And the mustache. I was close enough to see the pores of his skin. To feel the heat coming off him. It was just an

instant, but it was long enough for me to know—
he was no vampire.

There was no mystic spell being cast on the
innocent people of Germany. No supernatural
darkness taking them unaware. He was just a
man, and the shouting masses were willing participants in his madness.

Hitler considered Abe and Henry in that slow-
motion second, time itself seeming to grow weak, as if
the Great Clock of the Universe was in need of winding. The flashbulbs popped with less frequency, their
light seeming to grow fainter, the shouts of "Heil!"
more distant as all else fell away but the choice.

Only a few feet away from them...

"The hell with it," muttered Abe.

His claws shot out over the tops of his fingernails.
His fangs broke through his gums as if fired from tiny
mortars. All of this in a single beat of a fly's wings. He
lunged at Hitler, so fast that the guards didn't have
time to close ranks or level their guns. He dove over
the top of the ring of men, extending his long arms
out in front of him, swinging his claws with absurd
strength, just as he once swung an ax, dragging the
bony blades across Hitler's throat. There was no blood.
No wound. Just a startled look in Hitler's sunken
eyes. He brought his hands up to his throat, up to the
boiling pain that was just now coming across the Tele-
type machines in his brain, warning him, *This just in:*

something—we're not sure what it is yet—but something is terribly wrong.

All of this in barely the pop of a single flashbulb.

Henry lunged at the nearest guard and ripped the machine gun from his hands. The chants still there, muffled and distant:

"Heil! Heil!"

Henry fired into the ring of men before most could even find their triggers, cutting down the four SS guards closest to him, shocking the crowd into silence. The guards didn't flail their arms or fly backward firing their guns the way men do in the movies. They simply fell where they stood, limply, unceremoniously erased. The remaining guards opened fire, dividing their muzzles between Abe—who had landed on the ground at Hitler's feet—and Henry. The bullets tore into the vampires' arms and legs. Splintered their ribs and spines. All of this in a single chant of "Heil!"

Hitler clutched at his throat as beads of red began to appear, clinging to a perfectly straight, invisible line. Rubies on a necklace with no chain. More droplets began to appear along the length of the paper-cut-thin wound, held shut only by the surface tension of his skin. The dam broke with sudden fury, and the blood poured forth in waves, over the top of Hitler's hands, through the spaces between his fingers. He began to sputter and cough. He went ghostly white. His knees buckled. He fell, his blood mixing with that of his fallen guards. Mixing with the blood that trickled from the bullet-addled body of the tall vampire.

Henry fell, flailing his arms, firing his gun *exactly* the way men do in the movies. He writhed on the concrete, bullets lodged in every extremity. His gun barrel still smoking.

All of this in less than three seconds, from the first leap to the last shot.

And all of this, solely in Henry's imagination.

> The truth was, we just stood there and watched [Hitler] pass...watched his entourage lead him away as the crowd continued to chant. As much as Abe wanted to—as much as we *both* ached to—and as close as we were, we had our orders. No one could know who we were. No one could know that America had sent us. There was the country to consider.

The country...always the country...

> In the years to come, I would think about that night over and over, turn it in my mind a thousand different ways, wondering how many millions of lives might have been saved had we succeeded in blowing him into a million pieces. Or if Abe really *had* said, "The hell with it." How much suffering would have been spared, and how different today's world would look...if not for a fucking glass of water.

Abe and Henry boarded a train out of Berlin that night, going to great lengths to make sure they weren't followed.

But they were.

Back in their civilian clothes, fake passports in hand, Abe and Henry left Frankfurt by Zeppelin on the evening of May 3rd. They'd spent two days zigzagging through Germany by rail, as news of A FAILED PLOT ON THE FÜHRER'S LIFE! filled the front pages.

> They'd discovered the bomb while taking the stage apart that night and started looking for the saboteurs right away. Everyone who'd had access to the stage was rounded up and questioned, except, of course, for the freakishly tall officer and his smaller friend, who couldn't be found anywhere, and whom—come to think of it—no one had ever seen before. Within an hour of their finding the bomb, there were leaflets with our descriptions being passed out at beer halls and train stations and orders being radioed around the city to be on the lookout. You have to give it to the Germans... they're nothing if not efficient.

Abe and Henry had cabled a prearranged coded message back to Washington on the morning of their departure:

```
BER 1102A 3MAY 1937

SEC H WOODRING 1650 Pennsylvania Ave
N.W., Washington, D.C.

FORECAST CALLS FOR RAIN. DRESS
APPROPRIATELY.
```

It was a three-day crossing to New Jersey by air, and though still stinging from their failure, Abe and Henry were relieved to be headed home.

Henry had crossed the Atlantic countless times by then and had marveled at the speed and luxury of modern ocean liners.

Now man had built ocean liners of the sky. Defying

The dining room aboard Abe and Henry's Zeppelin. Henry passed much of the three-day voyage looking out the windows on the left, while Abe preferred to stay in his stateroom—a decision that nearly cost him his life.

Newton's laws in high style. Unlike twenty-first-century air travel, with cattle crammed into pressurized tubes, the fortunate few staring out of tiny windows at a strange collection of colors and patterns some five miles below, travel by airship was intimate. Slow and low. Gliding over the earth no faster than a car, a mere five hundred feet above the ground. Passing ships bobbing in the waves of the Atlantic. Over cities, low enough to make out people waving from their backyards.

This particular airship had two decks, the upper for staterooms, the lower for recreation and dining. There was a lounge on one side of the lower deck and a dining room on the other, both with large picture windows where passengers could idle and take in the view. There was also a small smoking lounge—the only place passengers and crew were permitted to light up, on account of their being seven million cubic feet of highly flammable hydrogen over their heads. There was even a crewmember whose sole responsibility was to make sure no one left the smoking lounge with a lit cigarette or pipe.

> Abe passed the time in his stateroom, reading. I preferred the lounge, soaking in this flying won-der of the modern world, the constant drone of the propellers the only noise, save an occasional rattle of china.

As it happened, this particular crossing was only half-booked. There were thirty-six passengers aboard of a possible seventy, and more than sixty crew. Unusually strong headwinds slowed the voyage, and by the time the American coastline appeared three days later, they were hours behind schedule.

> We passed over Boston, low enough to make out the clock on the steeple of the Old North Church. It was the first time I'd seen America from the air, and I was struck by how grand, how built up and packed in it all was. My first memories of Boston were of the ultramoral Puritan settlement I'd sought refuge in some three hundred years earlier, in the spring of 1660, when the colonial authorities hanged a woman named Mary Dyer for the crime of forsaking Puritanism. Not to become a Satanist, mind you, or even an atheist—but to become a Quaker and daring to suggest that men and women deserved equal standing in the eyes of God. Imagine what they'd have done if they'd known there was a vampire twenty feet from her gallows.

Further delaying the already late airship, there were thunderstorms over the landing site in New Jersey, forcing the captain, a forty-six-year-old veteran aviator named Max Pruss, to circle Manhattan and wait for the weather to clear. There was a minor stampede as New Yorkers scrambled out of their office towers to catch a sight of the glorious ship sailing overhead, seemingly just out of reach—lower even than the

Empire State Building's antenna. A biplane appeared and circled the Zeppelin, its newsreel cameraman taking footage of the spectacle.

> I was in my stateroom, collecting my things in anticipation of landing. I could hear the engines idle, the hiss of gas being valved to reduce the ship's buoyancy. I could feel the ship beginning to slow, and heard drops of rain begin to patter on the hull around me. Distant thunderclaps. I locked my trunk, grabbed my coat and hat, and decided to check in on Abe.

Abraham Lincoln, while brilliant and virtuous in many ways, had never been a punctual man. He was prone to getting lost in his own head, time slipping past him like a thief past a snoozing night watchman. Henry, to Abe's constant annoyance, had taken on the role of valet over the years, eyes on his pocket watch, nudging Abe along whenever there were trains to catch or appointments to keep.

> I knocked on his cabin door. No answer. I knocked again and called his name.

Henry turned the handle, expecting to find Abe asleep on the other side, a book on his chest. But when he opened the door, he nearly gasped. He dropped his coat and hat without thinking and extended his claws.

[The room] had been torn to pieces. There were craters and claw marks in the walls, tears in the mattress, feathers spilling out every which way. Flecks of blood, too. But the thing that drew my eye was a hole in the cabin ceiling. A big, gaping hole that had been punched in from *above*. Someone had forced their way in through a crawlspace. I stepped inside and closed the door behind me.

Henry stared up into the darkness of the gaping hole, which let cold air and engine noise in from the vast superstructure above. *Abe is up there,* he thought. *Dead or alive, he's up there, along with whoever made this hole.* Henry reached up and grabbed the sides of the hole, pulling himself into the darkness.

Getting the drop on Abraham Lincoln wasn't easy. Beating him up and dragging him away was nearly impossible. Whoever I was looking for was powerful and likely to do the same to me.

Contrary to the imaginations of most of those skyward-gazing New Yorkers, the "bubble" portion of the Zeppelin was not, in fact, one giant balloon. It was a rigid structure, and only part of it actually held the gas that kept the airship afloat. The rest was open space, connected by a series of catwalks and ladders that ran the length of the Zeppelin, giving the crew access to the gas cells, the engines, and the water tanks where ballast was stored to control pitch and buoyancy.

There were sixteen massive bags, or "cells" hidden inside the airship's silver shroud. Like the watertight compartments on a seagoing ship, they were designed so that the Zeppelin could stay afloat if any one—or even several—of them were punctured. All of this was contained within an aluminum alloy skeleton, covered by thin silver fabric to keep the elements out. Being inside the bubble felt more like being in a vast, dark factory than in an oversize balloon. There were no lights inside the structure (they were too dangerous so close to the gas cells), but just enough daylight seeped through the silver skin to ward off total darkness.

Henry made his way aft along a catwalk, his vampire eyes making day out of the dark. His nose following the familiar scent of his friend. And all the while, ready for the monster to spring from hiding.

> When you walk through a Halloween maze or watch a horror film, it's not the scare that gets you; it's the *anticipation* of the scare. I knew that I was walking into a trap, and I was eager to spring it. Eager to cut through that terrible anticipation and get to the screaming.

There was Abe. Alive, his hands bound behind him, his body tied to a vertical support beam with steel cable, likely ripped from one of the airship's control mechanisms. Henry didn't know it yet, but two fingers on Abe's hand were missing—cut off during the struggle in his cabin. He'd been tied up at the very rear of the hull, where the exterior's football shape narrowed to a point. On the other side of the fabric skin, four giant fins protruded from the airship's tail.

"Abe..."

"Don't," Abe whispered, half conscious. "It's a—"

"A trap. You don't say."

All the same, Henry began to yank at the cables, trying to loosen their grip on Abe's body.

"It was *her*."

> I sensed her presence moments before I heard her.
> It had been centuries, but her voice was unchanged.

"Hello, Henry."

Henry let go of the cables, leaving Abe still partially tied up, and turned.

> She was exactly as she looked when I'd last seen her in James Fort, hundreds of years earlier. Still striking. Still young, outwardly, with the same wavy red hair and blue, blue eyes, the color of shallow waters. She wore black pants and a black leather waistcoat with a dozen or more heavy brass buckles and held a small sword—barely longer than a knife—in each hand. I felt everything: surprise, hatred, fear, love. When you've

loved someone the way I'd loved her, you never stop. Not completely.

Henry couldn't find the words. Couldn't get his mind to pop into any particular gear. He was stuck, looking at her. She was flanked by two broad-shouldered brutes, their fangs glistening, claws scratching the metal hull of the ship in anticipation of conflict.

I'd known she was still alive, ever since Rocke- feller had revealed the hidden name behind the mysterious "Grander." But knowing something and seeing the proof standing in front of you are two very different things. The difference between believing in ghosts and waking up with one hov- ering at the foot of your bed. One is theoretical; the other is emotional.

"Virginia...," Henry whispered.

I was, a long time ago, said a voice in Henry's mind. *Her* voice. Henry was suddenly and completely aware that she'd been there, inside his head, since they'd arrived in Berlin. That indefinable dread he'd felt, that fogginess and forgetfulness...it had been *her,* all along. Henry felt like a gazelle at a watering hole, lapping up the cool droplets with his tongue, only to have his face snapped up in the jaws of the crocodile that had been waiting just under the surface the whole time. Waiting for the moment to reveal itself...until it was already too late. *I was there before you even saw the watering hole. I was there when you drank. I was always there.*

"You shouldn't have come to Germany," she said.

Abe pulled on the steel cables that affixed his wrists to the beam, trying to free himself. The cables cut into his skin, down to the bone—but they didn't give.

There were a million things I wanted to say. A million questions. Here we were, reunited after what, three centuries? More? Face-to-face for the first time since I'd made her. My mind was frozen, its processors overloaded, and she took full advantage of it.

Virginia came, fiery and perfect, swords spinning. Up came her leather boot, the heel connecting with Henry's chin faster than he could get his hands up to block it. Before his neck had time to snap back into position, Virginia plunged one of her blades into his chest, missing his heart by less than an inch. Henry instinctively grabbed the blade and held on as Virginia withdrew it—cutting deep gashes in both of his palms. She kicked him again, cracking his ribs and sending him stumbling backward on the catwalk.

She took a step back and let her brutes surge forward, a beneficent lioness, letting her cubs have their way with the scraps. The first leapt through the air, his jaws opening impossibly wide. Henry dropped onto his back and kicked upward with both of his legs, sending the vampire sailing off the catwalk. He fell fifteen feet to the canvas below, the force ripping a hole in the fabric directly above one of the airship's four propellers. He fell through, the spinning blades severing his legs as he fell five hundred feet to the New Jersey countryside.

The second brute was more cautious, slashing half-heartedly at Henry's throat as if afraid to commit himself. When Henry dodged, the vampire tried to kick his legs out from under him. Henry jumped forward instead, plunging all ten of his claws into the vampire's throat. When he withdrew them, blood spurted from ten perfectly round wounds. The brute struggled to keep himself from bleeding out, but he was leaking like a sieve. Henry grabbed his head and twisted it violently. With a snap he broke the vampire's neck and let him fall to the ground, his face now gawking at his own back.

Henry looked up at Virginia, who'd been watching with a wry smile. She was upon him in an instant, swords flashing through the air. Henry's only chance was to get in so close that her blades couldn't find momentum. He threw himself at her, embracing her as he had centuries before and trying to bite her face. Virginia slipped from his grasp and slashed at him again and again. Sparks flew as errant strikes connected with the metal frame of the airship.

She was the best fighter I'd ever faced. Ten times more powerful than Rasputin, despite being half

his size. She was, to put it mildly, kicking my
ass—cutting me to ribbons.

Virginia spun and kicked Henry a second time
in the face, her red ringlets twirling outward like the
streamers on a Maypole. He fell backward onto the
metal catwalk, hitting the back of his head hard enough
to rattle his brain in his skull, flicking his consciousness on and off, like a toddler who's got ahold of a light
switch. He could hear the four Daimler-Benz engines
pick up again, this time in reverse, bringing all 803 feet
of Zeppelin to a near halt, as Virginia raised one of her
swords and plunged it into Henry's middle. She twisted
the blade and withdrew it. It made a sucking sound as
it left Henry's body. Blood trickled out around the red
entrails that peeked through the wound.

Virginia turned her attention back to Abe, who'd
cried out at seeing his friend disemboweled. He began
to struggle against his bonds with renewed urgency.
She was intent on finishing the old vampire hunter,
now that his role as bait was fulfilled. The engines
idled again, the airship slowing almost to a stop as the
mooring lines were dropped beneath them. Virginia
drew back her blade to cut off Abe's head.

But something stopped her.

A sound.

The unmistakable sound of a Zippo lighter opening.

A silver Zippo, adorned with a gold swastika—
a souvenir of a failed mission. Virginia turned and

looked into Henry's eyes, and for a moment, that's all there was. Just the two of them...back in the days of understanding. In love forever. Somewhere in this moment, Henry struck the lighter's flint and let it fly.

It flew as if in a dream, all slow motion and angels singing, gracefully arcing toward the nearest hydrogen cell. Its flame licked the side of the giant bag, the atoms of its fabric excited by the heat, their electrons moving to higher orbitals...the fire spreading on a quantum level, its time disassociated from that of the real world.

The explosion sent a quake through the entire airship and swallowed Virginia Dare up in a temporary sun. Abe and Henry felt their eardrums rupture from the shock wave of the explosion, felt the searing heat that singed their hair and baked their clothing onto their skin. They tried to keep their footing as the bow lurched upward, tilting the blimp at a forty-five-degree angle, breaking the back of the ship's rigid skeleton and sending her freefalling the last hundred feet to earth. The tail crashed into the ground, sending a shock wave of hydrogen all the way to the bow, where the resulting wall of flames ignited what was left of the frame and shattered the control car, killing eighteen of the crew in an instant. Smoke and fire filled the passenger and crew areas in a matter of seconds.

All was light and heat. My clothes burned away, and I could feel us falling—the tail, falling to the ground. As the fabric over the hull burned away, I caught the briefest glimpse of the ground crew below. Their faces lit by the flames—the superstructure falling toward them, and us with it.

The beam that Abe had been tied to split in the crash, freeing him. His skin was burning, just as it had all those years before in Springfield. But this was a different fire. This fire was a liquid that clung to the surface. Melted his clothing and flesh, joining the two together.

The ship lurched again as the other cells began to explode—silver and china flying from the shelves of the galley. Stacks of luggage falling over along with their well-appointed owners. All the while the newsreel cameras turned, the radio announcers broadcasting live—"oh, the humanity!"—a close-up catching the word "Hindenburg" burning away along with the rest of the hull's fabric covering.

Suddenly I was on the ground. My clothes had burned away, along with some of my hair. All of creation smelled like diesel fuel. The hydrogen burned away in a few seconds, but the diesel—the stuff they used to run the generators and propellers—the diesel covered everything and kept burning. I saw the silhouette of a woman against the flames. The glowing, red-hot tips of her singed hair, ten thousand fiber-optic strands, billowing in the hot air.

The canvas covering of the *Hindenburg* burns away seconds after the initial explosion. It was reported that thirty-six people perished in the disaster, but that figure didn't account for Virginia Dare or her two associates.

Virginia was drenched in fuel, battered, disfigured, but still somehow alive. The flames licked at her ankles, caught the taste of the fuel on her skin, and engulfed her in seconds. Even then, with her skin blackening and rivulets of blood running down her face, she crawled forward.

It was only when the *Hindenburg*'s metal skeleton collapsed atop her naked body like a great molten mountain that she was finally extinguished.

ELEVEN

'53

Every man's a would be sportsman, in the
  dreams of his intent,
A potential out-of-doors man when his
  thoughts are pleasure bent.
But he mostly puts the idea off, for the
  things that must be done,
And doesn't get his outing till his outing
  days are done.
So in hurry, scurry, worry, work, his living
  days are spent,
And he does his final camping in a low
  green tent.

—*Reuben Anderson*

Of all the battles he'd fought in, all the years he'd
spent and horrors he'd witnessed in Europe,
Henry only ever dreamed about the beach. An excerpt
from a letter he wrote to Abe on June 6th, 1953:

The ramp comes down, too far from shore, much farther than we'd drilled for. I see the muzzle flashes from the bunkers. A half second later, the bullets start whizzing past us. I jump in, taste the salt water as it goes up my nose, my feet trying to find the bottom as the tide bats me around, but finding nothing. So I swim. I have an advantage. I'm stronger, not weighed down by all that gear, so I make it. Crawl to shore, crouch behind a hedgehog,[1] get my bearings. I look back toward the LV and see half the boys from my boat floating facedown in the ocean, bobbing with the waves. I see the color of the water changing, cursed by the same plague that touched the Nile. The salt of American blood mixing with the salt of the English Channel.

I look up the beach—boys of eighteen, twenty, faceup, facedown, torn to ribbons. Crying out for their mothers, medics hovering uselessly over them, telling them lies. Priests doing the same. There's so much blood in the water, on the beach, that I can't help the thought of feeding on it. I feel guilty for even having the thought, but it's there. I remember the mission, steady myself, and run, making no effort to disguise my vampire speed; zigzagging to throw

---

1. "Hedgehogs," or "Czech hedgehogs," were angled iron obstacles used as antitank defenses.

American forces land on Omaha Beach, June 6th, 1944. Henry was among those to storm the beach during the first wave of the attack. Though he survived, the images of D-Day would haunt his dreams for years to come.

> off the German gunners as I dart between
> obstacles, taking cover behind one of the
> few DD Shermans[2] to make it. [An artillery]
> shell goes off ten yards behind me, filling my

---

2. A Sherman tank modified with a DD, or "dual drive," system (tank treads for land use and a rear-mounted propeller for water use) and a floatation curtain, transforming it into an amphibious assault vehicle. Twenty-nine tanks were launched at Omaha Beach, two miles off the coast. Only two made it ashore, leaving the landing forces exposed and vulnerable to German machine-gun fire.

back with shrapnel, knocking me off my feet.
I'm facedown, dazed, in pain, but when I look
up and get my bearings, I'm at the entrance of
one of the concrete bunkers, having skipped
distance and time the way you can only do in a
dream.

I pull the pin on a grenade, count off in my
head, one one thousand, two one thousand...I
throw it into the bunker a split second before it
goes off. The blast sends a plume of smoke out
the door. The machine-gun fire stops. I wait a
moment for the smoke to clear, to see if any of
them come running out. None do, so I charge
in. There are three Germans inside, one clearly
dead from the blast, the other two stunned and
wounded. I grab one of them, the gunner, around
the neck, push my thumbs into his throat, and
make a hole in his Adam's apple. I pry his neck
open from the middle and leave him to bleed
out. I take the other's head in my hands, press
my palms flat against his temples, and squeeze.
He grabs my wrists, tries to pry my hands
away, but it's useless. I'm too strong. He looks
right at me, blood starting to trickle from his
nostrils...his tear ducts. Crying tears of blood,
like a miraculous statue of the Virgin Mary. He
screams, agony, but it lasts only a second, before
his head caves like an eggshell and his brains

spill out his ears, around my fingers. The blood cascades over my wrists.

There's another break in time. The operation is over; the beach is full of GIs, cleaning up the mess, carrying away the dead. One of my men tells me there's a wounded officer asking for me. Moments later I part a small crowd on the beach...and see that it's you, Abe. Everything below your chest has been blown away; blood foams at the corners of your mouth. I kneel, take your head in my hands. You look at me, glassy-eyed but lucid, and you whisper, "You did this, Henry...you did this."

And that's when I wake up.

Nat King Cole crackled over the AM, mixing with the wind and engine noise:

If you ever plan to motor west, travel my way, take the highway, that's the best.

Henry had gotten hip to that timely tip. He was driving on Route 66, headed toward a sun that just then took its deep-orange bows for the evening and dipped below the edge of the world, off to begin its next performance. He drove due west, doing a hundred miles per hour on the straightaways of the Texas plains. Los Angeles was only one night and one road away, and he meant to power through till dawn, blowing past one-pump gas stations and one-horse towns like he'd been shot out of a pistol, riding on the back of a red bullet—the bullet, in this case, being his Porsche 356 convertible.

I'd never been what you'd call a "car person," but *that car*...

It had shown up on his doorstep one morning, on the back of a truck, with a letter taped to its steering wheel:

From: General Dwight D. Eisenhower (ret.)
President, Columbia University
To: Henry Sturges

Dear Henry,

This was recently given to me by
Mr. Ferdinand Porsche, who I became
acquainted with while serving as military
governor of American-occupied Germany.
I'm told it's one of only six of its kind, and
that it has an engine to rival that of any
race car.

It's far too flashy a vehicle for an old
soldier and college president, but it

made me think of you. A rare breed,
faster and more powerful than most,
but possessing an unexpected elegance. I
hope you'll accept it with my compliments,
as small thanks for your many acts
of bravery and valor, on behalf of the
United States of America, her allies, and
all the free peoples of the world during
the war.

Your friend,

Dwight D Eisenhower

War was over, and once again everyone seemed to be in a big hurry to forget it. Optimism was the new patriotism. The whine of air-raid sirens had given way to the beat of Cole Porter. *Buy War Bonds!* had become *See the USA in Your Chevrolet!* Henry was all too happy to oblige (albeit in a Porsche).

The whole country seemed showroom new in 1953. The red paint of Henry's car. The mirrored lenses of his Ray-Ban aviators, which reflected the last of the dying sun. His crisp white T-shirt. His bright-blue jeans and close-cropped, slicked-down haircut. Like the car, Henry looked like he'd been built for speed. Cutting through the air as the chill of a desert night began to set in, his tires stirring up the last of the heat devils that danced above the black tarmac.

I think that after those years of hell, I just wanted to be as far away from Europe and its ghosts as possible.

Abe and Henry had spent years on the battlefields of World War II, but they hadn't been side by side.

We went our separate ways for a while after [the *Hindenburg*]. I'd been asked to go to London and liaise with SIS Section D,[3] relay the Brits' findings back to the White House, and so on. Strictly speaking, I was there in an "advisory" capacity, but FDR had let it be known that I was also an asset they could use in the field, and they did. It was one of the ways America was helping the Allies fight the Nazis, without going all in, see. But Abe...Abe was frustrated with Roosevelt's reluctance to get into the war. He thought it was cowardice, frankly. He was ordered to Russia to liaise with their intelligence people, same as me. But after a week or so of doing that, he walked out of the American embassy and loaned himself out to the Russian army as an infantryman, despite his [permanently disfigured left] hand. He didn't want to observe and report; he wanted to *fight*.

---

3. Designated the "Special Operations Executive" in 1940, but often referred to as "the Baker Street Irregulars," a name borrowed, ironically, from Arthur Conan Doyle's *Sherlock Holmes* stories.

That's Abe. He always needs to do what he feels is right...consequences be damned; opinions be damned.

Abe fought with the Russians in Poland in 1939, in the Baltics in 1940, and on the front lines at Minsk and the Dnieper River as Germany invaded Russia in 1941. In October of that year, he wrote a letter to FDR—his first communication with the president (or any representative in the U.S. government) in nearly four years.

Lincoln scholars call it the "senses" letter,[4] due to Abe's use of the verbs "See!" "Hear!" "Smell!" in an attempt to engage Roosevelt on a visceral, emotional level—imploring him to commit American forces to Europe and stem the advance of the Nazis and their slaughter of innocents. It's one of the longest letters Abe ever sent, and one of the most emotional, written in the immediate aftermath of the massacres at Babi Yar—a ravine in present-day Ukraine where the Nazis executed nearly thirty-four thousand Jewish men, women, and children over a two-day period during their campaign in Russia.

---

4. The letter is currently housed in the collection in the Franklin D. Roosevelt Library and Museum in Hyde Park, New York—just a stone's throw from Henry's estate in Rhinebeck. The letter is addressed from "A. Lansing," an alias Lincoln was using for correspondence at the time.

A. Lansing
Moscow
October 16th, 1941

F.D. Roosevelt
The White House
Washington, D.C.

Mr. President,

I have this day returned from Kiev,
where I learned of a horrendous
massacre of innocent civilians
outside that city. This massacre took
place on September 29th and 30th. It
was perpetrated by the Germans, with
the assistance of the local Ukrainian
police.
  There are photographs, which I
have seen with my own eyes, of the
victims before, during, and after
their executions. Mothers, young and
old, forced to strip naked before
being shot unceremoniously in the
head, their bodies dumped in mass
graves. Can you see them? Stripped of
their dignity before being stripped
of their lives? Can you see that in
the hands of many of these women are
babes of two years...a year...four
months old? Their bodies likewise
stripped naked in the cold?

These women, their children in their arms, are confused. Confused as to why the trains haven't come to whisk them off to safer, distant cities, as they were promised. They stand in line, these women. They stand in line, waiting, waiting...waiting their turn. Can you feel the chill of the autumn air as it hits their shivering, naked flesh? As they press their infants to their chests, trying to give what little warmth they have to their crying young? Can you hear them cry out for their men, who have been taken elsewhere, out of sight, never to return?

These women, these mothers reach the front of the line. They're told to spread out, at the edge of the trench. Told to face the other direction, still clutching their young to their breasts. Still holding the hands of those children who are old enough to walk on their own. Still clinging to the hope that somehow, this will end well. That it's all been some misunderstanding, even as they look down at the freshly bleeding bodies in the trench below. As they look away, pistols are held an inch from the back of their heads. There is no fuss or ceremony in this;

it's all done quickly, efficiently, for
there are many left to kill. With no
more effort than it takes to turn off
a wall switch, a trigger is pulled,
gunpowder ignites, and a bullet rips
through their brains. It ends them,
as they stand their holding their
babies in their arms. Their babies,
who fall with their mothers as they
collapse, already dead, into the open
trench. They fall, like marionettes
whose strings have been suddenly and
forever cut, onto the bleeding bodies
that fell in the group before them.
Can you smell the gunpowder in the
air? Can you hear the children cry
out in the arms of their mothers?
Do you see the face of the three-
year-old who cries out beneath his
mother's lifeless body, his mother,
just seconds before, the steadiest
and most loving thing in his life,
now gone? Do you see the round, fair-
haired head of the infant, as the
barrel of a German pistol is held an
inch away from it?

See it. See the infant's head as
the trigger is pulled and the pistol
recoils. See the force of the bullet
move the head violently as it dashes
the skull apart. As it tears through
the brain, extinguishing one of

An unidentified woman clings to her child moments before both are shot to death at Babi Yar, outside Kiev. Abe wrote an impassioned letter to FDR after seeing this and other pictures of the massacre, which claimed upward of 34,000 Jews over a two-day period in 1941.

God's good lights. Extinguishing,
in a callous, effortless instant, an
untold future. A full and fruitful
life of eighty...ninety...a hundred
years of laughter and tears and
joy and sorrow and love and loss
and learning and travel and wisdom
and contribution and complexity.
A hundred generations of promise,
snatched away by a five-cent bullet.
    See it. See the spark go out of the
tiny child's eyes as the bullet exits

his forehead. See the blood shoot
from his head in long arcs—pump,
pump—as his tiny heart continues to
beat a moment longer. See it. Now
multiply it by ten thousand. One
hundred thousand. Multiply it by the
millions, until the sheer volume of
it washes over you and blankets you
with the warmth of its impossibility.

I once believed that the best way
to destroy my enemy was to make him
my friend. But that belief seems
naive in the face of such evil.
The world is facing a darkness the
likes of which it hasn't seen since
the Angel of Death descended on the
homes of Pharaoh's slaves. An enemy
motivated not by greed or need,
but by hatred. By a deep, almost
religious conviction in its cause,
bred in its bones since an ancient
age. This enemy will never relent.
It will never surrender. It must be
erased, its every cell cut like a
tumor from the flesh of the earth.

America must enter this war.
She must enter it immediately and
unreservedly, and she must employ her
every asset. She must come to the
shores of Europe before Europe lands
on hers. Before women and children
are stripped bare and shot like

animals on the streets of New York,
Springfield, and Los Angeles.

I have led America, as you lead it
now. I have steered the Great Ship
through turbulent waters, as you are
faced with doing. I know what it is to
send boys to their deaths in the name
of a cause, and I know what it is to
write letters to the mothers of the
lost. But as great as their sacrifice
will be, it will pale in comparison
to the horrors of a world in which
this darkness is left unchecked.

You and I have had our differences
of opinion about this war, and a
great many things. But surely no man
of character, no nation of honor, can
look away as these atrocities befall
innocent people.

Think not that I am come to send
peace on earth: I came not to send
peace, but a sword.[5]

Yours,

A

FDR never responded to the letter. He didn't have
to. Six weeks after Abe sent it, the Japanese bombed
Pearl Harbor, leaving America no choice but to enter
the war.

---

5. Matthew 10:34.

Henry drove west on Sunset Boulevard, his car a tiny novelty compared to the bulky Buicks and Chryslers, all of them in muted colors and built like tanks. He shared the road with electric streetcars, packed with smartly dressed men and women on their way to work, the marquees of movie palaces promoting films like *Roman Holiday* and *Gentleman Prefer Blondes*. The dilapidated *Hollywoodland* sign in the hills above.

> I needed something new to wash away the memories of those rain-soaked, ancient European cities. The rubble, the death, the strife...the insides of ships and rucksack straps making you feel claustrophobic and heavy and hopeless around the clock. Multiply that by four, five, six years...and you start to get a picture of how crazy, how restless I was when I came back.

He wasn't the only veteran who wanted to start fresh. Abraham Lincoln had also returned home eager to forget the concussive blasts of artillery shells and the hasty field burials of too many friends.

> I saw him briefly in '45, in the American Sector [of occupied Berlin]. He'd come in with the Russians in April or May; I'd come in with the Eighty-Second [Airborne] in June. We only had

an afternoon to catch up, and like most soldiers, we weren't interested in sharing war stories, so we filled the time with small talk. (Come to think of it, that was the last time I saw him in person, until '63.) Abe told me he'd read a book—it was a popular book at the time, I forget what it was called[6]—but it had to do with getting back to the land and all that. Anyway, he'd read this book and gotten it in his head that he should become a farmer. And that's exactly what he did. As soon as he got back to the States, he bought himself a little farm near Springfield and started raising cattle. Some of them he sold to slaughterhouses; some he kept for himself and fed off in increments. He'd had his fill of killing men, and now that he was back in the U.S., he wanted no part of it—even if it meant feeling a little run down.[7]

In all his centuries in America, Henry had never made it as far west as California. Now, as the world took a breath between a hot war and a cold one, he made a pilgrimage to America's second shore, some four hundred years after landing on its first one.

---

6. *The Egg and I*, by Betty MacDonald (1945).

7. While a vampire can survive on animal blood, many liken it to putting cheap gas in a sports car. The vampire typically experiences mild exhaustion, consistent with how a human feels when fighting a cold. For this reason, animal blood is usually used as a last resort or by those, like Lincoln, who choose not to feed on humans for moral reasons.

Everything alive and modern. All neon and glamour. I remember how strange it was, seeing palm trees on American soil. How different the light seemed; how different the air smelled. There was a still a Western feel to [Los Angeles] in those days. Orange groves and farmland still mingled with concrete at the edges of Hollywood. And as many people as there were, it never felt the least bit crowded. There was plenty of room, plenty of air, everything flat and vast, like the world's biggest small town.

Howard Hughes was many things—genius, pilot, engineer. He was a film director and producer and the sole owner of RKO Pictures. He was a famous womanizer, having worked his way through a long line of Hollywood starlets, from Katharine Hepburn to Ava Gardner. He was prone to wild mood swings and a notorious obsessive compulsive.

He was also, much to his dismay, a vampire.

Hughes had been killed in a plane crash on July 7th, 1946, while testing his company's experimental XF-11—designed as an army reconnaissance aircraft. An engine failure had sent him careening into a Beverly Hills neighborhood, destroying several houses but miraculously sparing the people inside them. Hughes's badly burned and broken body had been pulled from the wreckage and taken to a hospital, where surgeons had been unable to save him. With a cold war looming, the army had decided that a man of Hughes's engineering genius was too valuable an asset to lose, so they'd made arrangements to have his death reversed.[8]

When Hughes woke from his transformation and realized what had happened, he fell into a deep depression. Not long after being resurrected, he'd famously spent four months in a dark screening room, watching movies around the clock, refusing to bathe or shave, and writing extensive memos on legal pads, instructing his employees to avoid looking at him or speaking to him. Once the initial shock wore off, however, his vampirism became just another problem for the genius to solve.

A lifelong germophobe, Hughes abhorred the idea of biting into another being's flesh and sucking out its "dirty, unfiltered blood." To this end, he employed an ever-changing stable of some fifty donors (they were told they were part of a clinical research trial). Each of the donors was given an extensive background check, screened for diseases, and forbidden from smoking, drinking, or taking drugs for the term

8. Henry was approached by Secretary of War Robert Patterson on July 8th, 1946, and asked to fly to California to revive Hughes. He refused, telling the secretary he could not in good conscience make another vampire. Patterson was so furious that he tried to have Henry dishonorably discharged (only the intervention of Army Chief of Staff Eisenhower prevented him from doing so). All the same, Henry and Patterson never spoke again, and Harry Truman never asked Henry to the White House (it's unclear if this was related to the Hughes affair). There is no record of who Patterson ultimately got to do the job.

of their employment. Even so, Hughes demanded that all the collected blood be run through a dialysis machine[9] before he used it. Hughes even designed a machine that injected the blood directly into his fangs at high pressure, filling his body in a third of the time of a conventional feeding.

Henry's Porsche pulled up to the guard gate of RKO's backlot in Culver City. Affectionately known as Forty Acres, the lot had been in use since the silent era, home to productions like *King Kong* and *Gone with the Wind*. And in 1953, it was the sole property of the reclusive Howard Hughes.

> I'd arrived early, so I parked and walked around a bit, this being my first time on a movie back-lot. Here, ancient Greece. There, a bombed-out European square. Tarzan's jungle next to a plantation from the antebellum South. It was a journey through time, ancient places, previously existing only in the imaginations of readers, rendered real with exquisite detail. I wandered down a street where they were building a full replica

---

9. Though not yet widely available, experimental dialysis machines were in use at several hospitals in the United States. In 1949, Hughes purchased one from Mount Sinai Hospital in Los Angeles and had it moved to his home in Hancock Park.

of a small 1860s town—dirt streets, horse-drawn carts, everything exactly as it would have been. I stood in the middle of this imaginary town, nearly a century removed from the real thing, and was awash in the strange feeling of having been transported back in time.

Henry was ushered into Hughes's office at precisely twelve o'clock noon. Not a second before or after. It was a perfect, sparse square of a room, everything pristine and white, from the walls to the carpet to the furniture. So white that the tiniest speck of dust would stand out like tar on a wedding dress and be mercilessly annihilated by the attentive and retentive staff. The only nonwhite features in the room were the large windows that dominated two walls of the corner office. Their panes had been painted black, barring even a single photon of sunlight from slipping through. A pair of frosted spherical overhead light fixtures provided dim, even illumination.

The frail, lanky figure of Hughes stood up behind his white lacquer desk. He had a thin mustache, his graying black hair parted in the middle and draped over both sides of his face. He wore black trousers that looked two sizes too big and a crisp white shirt, completely unbuttoned, revealing his pale, almost skeletal chest beneath. Henry was shocked at Hughes's appearance but gave no outward sign of it.

Vampirism hadn't made him more youthful. In fact, Hughes looked worse than ever. Maybe it was a side effect of having the blood filtered before drinking it. Maybe he was protecting himself from germs but also stripping the blood of some mysterious yet essential property.

"Mr. Hughes," said Henry, reaching out his hand. Hughes didn't take it.

"You'll forgive me," said Hughes, looking at Henry's outstretched hand like there was a gun in it. "Filthy things, hands. Disgusting repositories of germs. Did you know that the average hand has *hundreds of thousands* of fecal particles on it?"

"I can't say that I did."

"When I see a pair of shaking hands, all I see is two people politely smearing their shit together. It's an abhorrent practice, abhorrent, abhorrent, ab—"

Hughes swallowed hard, choking back the word. He gestured for Henry to take a seat on one of two firm white sofas that faced each other in the center of the room. Henry obliged, while Hughes pulled four tissues from a dispenser on an end table, unfolded them, and placed them gently on the cushion, ensuring that no part of his trousers made contact with the couch, before he sat.

I'd heard the stories, and I'd been prepared for the idiosyncrasies. Still, he must've caught me

looking at the tissues, because he felt compelled
to say—

"Disease is everywhere, Mr. Sturges."

"Disease can't harm you anymore, Mr. Hughes."

"Just because I no longer feel the effects of a disease
doesn't mean it's not there . . . growing under the surface
of my fingernails. Festering in the pores of my skin.
Festering, Mr. Sturges, festering, festering, festering—"

Hughes kept repeating the word, squinting his eyes
and screwing up his face, caught in a feedback loop
from which he was powerless to free himself:

"Festering, festering, festering . . ."

I'm sitting across from a madman.

"With all due respect, Mr. Hughes," said Henry,
cutting him off, "did you invite me to come all this
way to talk about disease?"

Hughes paused, his eyes opening again. He swallowed, then continued as if nothing strange had
happened:

"As a matter of fact, Mr. Sturges, I did."

Hughes gave a nod to one of his assistants. The
lights dimmed, and a projection screen lowered
out of the ceiling behind Hughes's desk. A beam
flickered out of a small glass square embedded in
the wall, filling the screen with black-and-white
footage. First, a title card—I don't recall exactly
what it said, but it was something along the lines

of THE FOOTAGE YOU'RE ABOUT TO SEE HAS BEEN CLAS-
SIFIED TOP SECRET. Then, images of a laboratory.
Medical researchers, microscopes, and test tubes.
Men in white lab coats, some of them smoking
pipes, discussing things, looking at charts. Real
doctors and researchers, awkwardly re-creating
their daily routines for the cameras.

"A thousand years from now," said Hughes, "humanity will look back on 1953 as the year the future was
born. For this year, there have been not one, but two
landmark announcements in the field of medicine."

The footage changed to a pair of young scientists
giving a demonstration with a large metal model
that reminded me of an overgrown Erector Set.

"James Watson and Francis Crick," said Hughes,
"who recently published a groundbreaking paper in
which they described, for the first time, the double-
helix structure of DNA."
The footage changed to a smiling man wearing
a lab coat and horn-rimmed glasses, holding up two
large glass bottles of dark liquid. Without missing a
beat, Hughes continued:
"Dr. Jonas Salk, who this very year announced
his successful vaccine for polio, eradicating a disease
that has plagued mankind since Moses led his people
through the desert."

Every word was perfectly timed to match the film. I imagined [Hughes] sitting there, alone in the dark, obsessively watching the reel hundreds of times, practicing his narration before I arrived. Why not just record it in advance? I'm sure he had his own bizarre reasons.

The scene changed again, this time to an overhead shot of a man lying on a table, wearing a surgical gown and scrub cap.

Title Card: PHYSICAL EXAMINATION

[The man was] a vampire—one I didn't recognize. His fangs were being examined by a team of masked human doctors. They took measurements, tested his reflexes, drew his blood. I was intrigued. I'd never seen a real vampire captured on film. Not with its fangs out, anyway. And certainly not interacting with humans in such a clinical, cooperative manner. Being poked and prodded for all to see, captured on film for all time.

Title Card: ASSESSMENT OF ABILITIES

[The vampire subject] ran across the screen in slow motion, from left to right, the wall behind him painted with black-and-white distance markers—the same you would see in a car crash test. Next came a close-up of his claws extending, then a wider shot—again, all of this was in slow motion—of him taking a swipe at a pig carcass that had been hung from the ceiling. His claws opened four deep gashes in the pig's skin and sent slow-motion ripples through its body. Next came the eyes. A close-up of the whites clouding over black as he took his vampire form. Then a split screen. On the left, nothing but darkness, with a tiny flickering dot of light in the center. The words "HUMAN SUBJECT—20/20" superimposed at the bottom. On the right, a brightly lit office—probably one of the researchers'—with a desk, chairs, and piles of papers all clearly visible. A man in a white lab coat standing in the center, with a lit candle in his hand, its flame in exactly the same position as the flickering dot of light on the left. The words "VAMPIRE SUBJECT—20/5" superimposed.

Title Card: FEEDING MECHANISM

The vampire stood against a black background, staring into the camera, a mannequin beside him. On cue, he extended his fangs and bit into the mannequin's neck. In a close-up, the fangs were shown entering the rubber skin in slow motion. As weird as it was, sitting there, watching this with Hughes, it was also fascinating. As many necks as I'd sunk my fangs into, I'd never seen the mechanics of the process revealed as clearly as they were here—slowed down to a fraction of real time. The fangs punching through tiny holes in the gums, the hollow tips tearing into the flesh.

Title Card: METABOLISM

This dissolved into an animation of blood being drawn out of the neck and into the hollow fangs. The animation zoomed out, becoming a cross section of the vampire's entire body. It showed the blood running though a pair of veins from the fangs into the aorta, where the heart slowly pumped it through the rest of the vascular system. A hand-drawn clock appeared in the upper right-hand corner, the hour hand spinning wildly to show the passage of time, as the blood was slowly absorbed into the tissue over a period of days, nourishing it like water in a flowerpot.

A final title card appeared on-screen: PRODUCED BY RKO PICTURES FOR THE HOWARD HUGHES MEDICAL INSTITUTE. COPYRIGHT MCMLIII.

The light of the projector went dark. The screen retracted into the ceiling, and the room slowly brightened.

"You're looking for a cure," said Henry.

Hughes smiled. It was all the confirmation Henry needed.

It was a question that had occupied me, occupied virtually every other vampire since the beginning of history: *Is there a way out? A way back? Is death the only cure for our curse? Is "curse" even the right word?* I'd heard of vampires traveling to Asia and Africa in search of shamans and witch doctors. Concocting herbal remedies or sitting in steam baths, trying to sweat the impurities out. I'd seen vampires sitting in churches with their rosary beads in hand, humbling themselves before God in a vain effort to gain His forgiveness. I'd seen all of the fad "cures," and I'd be lying if I said I hadn't tried a few of them myself.

"Others have tried," said Henry.

"Yes," said Hughes. "But they lived in simpler times. They thought of vampirism in religious terms, and they shunned the affected. Feared them, just as lepers and hunchbacks were shunned and feared. But never, in the thousands of years that vampires have roamed this earth, has anyone bothered to *study* them."

He was wrong, actually. Plenty of people had studied vampires over the centuries—most of them vampires themselves. Hell, Tesla took

X-rays of my fangs fifty years before I ever met Howard Hughes.

"It's a dream," said Henry. "One that vampires have been dreaming for a thousand—"

"*No one dreams as big as Howard Hughes!*" he yelled.

Silence. The rage had come from nowhere, like a bolt of lightning on a cloudless night.

"Mr. Hughes, I didn't mean to—"

"After the shock of my transformation wore off," said Hughes, all traces of his anger gone, "I thought— what if this isn't some old black magic? What if it isn't a 'curse'? After all, a man gets cancer, we cut it out. He gets polio, which changes the shape of his body, alters the makeup of his muscles and density of his bones. And what do we do? Do we call him a demon? In the Dark Ages, maybe. But nowadays we look for a *cure*."

"Vampirism is different. The changes are more radic—"

"*Is* it? It's passed from host to host, through the blood. It alters the makeup of our bodies, changes our muscles and our bones, affects our hearing and sight. But we're so conditioned to think of sickness making our bodies worse, we almost can't conceive of one that would make us *better*. It's a disease...and for every disease, there's a cure."

"Let's suppose you're right. That it's no different than cancer. Finding a cure will be every bit as hard—if not impossible."

Hughes smiled again and gave another nod to one of his hovering assistants, who carried an easel to the end of Henry's sofa and set on it a full-color rendering of a large building surrounded by palm trees.

"The Howard Hughes Medical Institute,"[10] said Hughes. "Already under construction in Miami. When it's complete, it will house the finest scientific minds in the world, all of them looking for the secrets to life itself. I'm raising a $100 million endowment, $50 million of which comes from my own pocket."

Henry looked at the rendering—its vibrant colors and sun-soaked palm trees a stark contrast to the darkened, grayscale lunatic sitting across from him.

"Mr. Hughes," he said at last, "I admire your passion. But it seems like an awful lot of money to spend on a relatively small problem. I'd venture there are fewer than a hundred vampires in the United States."

"Ninety-three, including you and me."

The way Hughes said it left no room for doubt. I imagined a small army of well-paid emissaries conducting an exhaustive vampire census with

---

10. Founded in 1953, the Howard Hughes Medical Institute is still in operation today, spending more than $800 million annually in biomedical research, though it is unclear how much of that money remains dedicated to the study of vampires.

the obsessive attention to detail their boss would
have demanded.

"Point is," Henry continued, "the breed is dying
out, all by itself. Besides, I'd think a man like you
would jump at the chance to live forever. Think of the
things you could accomplish."

"Oh, I intend to live forever. But I'd like the option
of doing it as a *man* and not a monster. Think about
it—freedom from aging, freedom from death. Perfect
eyesight and hearing. Perfect health. Now imagine
being able to grant those gifts to *everyone*, in the form
of a pill. Eternity in a bottle, Mr. Sturges. A world
without hospitals or graveyards."

Hughes spoke as if it was some kind of utopia.
But there was something about his vision that
unnerved me.

"You're talking about creating a race of superhu-
mans," said Henry.

"I'm talking about a revolution in what it means to
be human. What it means to be *alive*. I'm talking about
erasing the boundaries between vampire and man—
taking the best qualities of each and cutting the rest
out like a cancer. For vampires, an end to darkness and
murder. For humans, an end to fear and suffering."

"And a beginning to overpopulation, religious tur-
moil, unwinnable wars..."

"We already live in that world."

Crazy or not, he has a point...

"The government might have something to say about it," said Henry. "A private citizen, tinkering with the building blocks of human life—"

"The government?" Hughes laughed. "The government is my biggest investor![11] 'Imagine,' I told them, 'whole battalions of American super-soldiers—faster, stronger, quick healing, able to see in near total darkness, and with a limitless shelf life. And all without the unfortunate side effects of sun sickness and drinking blood.' You should've seen them. They practically fell over each other trying to write me the check! Forget hydrogen bombs, Mr. Sturges—this is the *real* arms race."

"Why me?" asked Henry.

"Because...you are, to my knowledge, the oldest vampire in the United States. If I can convince you to join our board of directors and sign up for treatment when the time comes, then I can convince others.

---

11. Project MKULTRA was launched in 1953, the same year as the Howard Hughes Medical Institute, approved by CIA director Allen Welsh Dulles, and headed by Dr. Sidney Gottlieb—known in the agency as "the dirty trickster" for his use of LSD and other psychotropic drugs on unwilling participants, and for his plots to "chemically assassinate" America's enemies, like Fidel Castro. While long rumored to be a covert program researching drug-based mind control and telepathy, the real goals of the program were the study of vampire biology.

That...and I need your money. Seats on the board start at a million dollars."

> The whole thing made me nervous. The hubris of meddling with nature. The danger of getting it wrong.
>
> Still...it's hard to describe how intrigued I was. If there was even a grain of truth to what Hughes was saying—if I could be done with killing, done with dark glasses and cold hand-shakes...if I could fall in love with a woman without having to watch her wither and die, if we could have a child...if I could sit down in a res-taurant and have a fucking *steak*...
>
> If there was even one atom of possibility...

In March of 1976, a refrigerated case arrived at the penthouse of the Fairmont Princess Hotel in Aca-pulco, Mexico, accompanied by armed couriers. In it were twenty vials of clear liquid labeled *Compound 16*. These inauspicious vials were the result of two decades of intense work by the world's leading scien-tists operating at the razor-edge of molecular biology. Compounds 1 through 15 had never made it past the Petri dish. But Compound 16's initial test results had been encouraging, if inconclusive.

"Encouraging" was enough for Howard Hughes.

He'd long since sold RKO and retreated from the world, buying up hotels in Las Vegas, London, the Bahamas, and now Mexico—living in their penthouses, shunning visitors, and obsessively pursuing his dream of a cure from afar, via a dedicated phone and fax line that could connect him to someone at the institute at any hour, any day of the year.

Against the advice of everyone on his payroll, Hughes began self-administering a course of Compound 16 injections on March 30, 1976.

Usually, it would have taken years of clinical trials on animals before a human—or in this case, a vampire—would've been subjected to the risk. But this was Howard Hughes. Even after the adverse side effects started to kick in, he stuck with the treatment, stubbornly—as if he could pull his body out of a nosedive, like a plane that had lost an engine.

Within days, he began aging rapidly. His hair and his fingernails grew almost an inch a day. His muscles began to atrophy and he started dropping weight. He tried to eat regular food, believing that he could fight off the weight loss by force-feeding. But his fragile stomach, out of use for thirty years, rejected everything he put in it. All his subordinates could do was watch as he wasted away. [Hughes] was so desperate to be done with blacked-out windows and dialysis machines that he ignored the pain.

On April 5th, 1976, Howard Hughes died on a private jet en route to a Texas hospital. X-rays of his corpse revealed broken needles embedded in his arms.[12]

Toward the end of his life, he'd taken to having his every waking moment recorded on audiotape, protection against the schemers and backstabbers he perceived to be lurking all around him, waiting for him to slip up so they could sue him for his billions. The recorder built into the cabin of his jet captured his mumbled last words for posterity:

"No one dreams bigger than Howard Hughes…"

[Hughes had] been too desperate, too impatient. But he was right about one thing—'53 was the year everything changed. It *was*, looking back, the year that gave birth to the future…just not the one that Hughes had imagined.

It was the year Stalin died and Khrushchev began ratcheting up the Cold War; the year America propped up the shah in Iran and began making a mess of things

---

12. The official autopsy listed kidney failure as the cause of death. X-rays revealed five broken hypodermic needles in the flesh of his arm. Doctors assumed these were to administer codeine into his muscles.

in the Middle East. And it was the year Hughes and Henry started looking for the cure.

> All of it would come back to haunt us, one way or another... and all of it can be traced back to 1953. But of all the things that happened that year, the one that would haunt me the most was something I took no notice of at the time. The swearing in of a young senator...

His name was Jack Kennedy.

TWELVE

★ ★ ★

Two Presidents

Has anybody here seen my old friend Abraham?
Can you tell me where he's gone?
He freed a lot of people,
But it seems the good, they die young.
I just looked around, and he was gone.

— *Dion, "Abraham, Martin and John"*

October had always been special to the marine. He'd been born on the eighteenth day of that month, 1939—two months after his father died of a heart attack and twenty-two years after Russia's October Revolution had given rise to the Soviet Union. These two seemingly unrelated events—the birth of a fatherless boy in New Orleans and the birth of a communist superpower in Russia—would, in fact, conspire to shock the world and forever change America's destiny.

The marine had been what they called a "troubled" child. Lashing out at his mother, schoolmates, and teachers. He was scrawny. Fragile. But for as long as he could remember, there'd been a giant living inside him. A giant with red, leathery skin. Muscles and veins bulging just under the surface. It had wild red hair, the clear, comb-like teeth of a deep-sea fish, and solid red eyes—the same kind of eyes the marine had seen on the white mice they fed to snakes at the pet store. The giant called itself "Redhead," and it lived deep, deep in a cave, in a secret part of the marine's mind. The marine liked to imagine Redhead luring people into his cave—parents, teachers, schoolchildren—the same people who teased him or made him do things he didn't want to do. He liked to picture Redhead luring them in, then gnashing them apart with its terrible fish teeth—a teacher screaming as her body was torn in half, spilling her foul, shit-stuffed guts onto the cave floor. A schoolboy crying as his arms were pulled out of their sockets, skin and sinew hanging at his sides like red tassels off bicycle handlebars.

In this cave, along with the strewn bones of the marine's enemies, sat a rotary telephone (it looked positively tiny in Redhead's hand—tiny enough to make the marine giggle at the sight of it). When Redhead had something important to tell him, the phone would ring in the marine's ear, and he would answer. Sometimes, he and Redhead would stay up half the night, telling secrets to each other.

Otherwise, the marine had few friends. He avoided interaction, preferring to bury his face in paperback novels—spy adventures, Westerns, and detective pulp.

Stories about big men with big guns. When he was a little older, he discovered books about altogether *different* types of men. Men like Karl Marx and Henri de Saint-Simon. The marine became fascinated by the idea of a system in which *everyone* was important. In which no man could look down his nose at another man. An idyllic world in which a slight, fatherless boy was just as important as a president. He wrote letters to the Young People's Socialist League and the Socialist Party of America requesting more information but told no one of his interests. He knew these were dangerous pursuits for an American boy.

In seventh grade, the marine was sent to a juvenile psychiatric ward after striking his mother during an argument. There, on a cot, in the silence of his white-walled room, he'd fantasized about what it would be like to be one of the characters in those paperback adventures. A lone gunman in the Old West. A private eye. A big man with the power to mete out life and death as he pleased. Redhead told him not to share these thoughts with the court-appointed psychiatrists (who wrote nasty words about him in their notebooks and tried to trick him into saying the wrong things).

In October of 1956, he'd dropped out of high school, left his mother in Texas, and joined the marines. There, at last, he found the structure and family he'd craved his whole life and found something he truly excelled at: shooting a rifle. He loved his rifle, as all marines did. And like all marines, he knew the Rifleman's Creed by heart:

```
This is my rifle. There are many like
it, but this one is mine.
   My rifle is my best friend. It is my
life. I must master it as I must mas-
ter my life.
   Without me, my rifle is useless. With-
out my rifle, I am useless. I must fire
my rifle true. I must shoot straighter
than my enemy who is trying to kill me.
I must shoot him before he shoots me.
```

High scores on the gun range earned him the designation "sharpshooter," and his aptitude tests earned him a security clearance. It seemed that here, within the yelling and rules and straight lines of the Marine Corps, he'd finally become the man he was always destined to be. A big man who could dispense death at will.

But Redhead didn't like the marines. It didn't like the yelling or the rules or the straight lines. It didn't like being told what to do or when to rise or when it could and couldn't dispense death. Redhead's phone calls grew more frequent. Its whispers turned to shouts. The marine began to lose focus. He accidentally shot himself with his service pistol. He was sent to the brig after threatening an officer. But his biggest mistake—the one that made his life a living hell—was talking

about the *ideas*. Ideas like socialism, communism…
visions of a world in which *all men* were created equal.

Now, instead of psychiatrists writing nasty words
about him in their notebooks, it was other marines
giving him nasty looks in the mess. Shunning him
in the barracks, calling him a "traitor" or giving him
nicknames, like "Ivan" and "Red."

Red…

Late at night, in the secret sharing time, Redhead
would pester him with questions: *Why should we have
to salute the officers who do nothing but belittle us? Why
should we risk our life for a country that doesn't appreciate us? What's America ever done for us, anyway?*

Redhead told him to remember the mice. The helpless red-eyed mice they used to feed to snakes in the
pet store. The marine had always liked watching them
die. He found it fascinating, the way they scurried
around the terrarium, searching frantically for a way
out. They way they gasped for breath as the snakes
coiled around their bodies, crushing them. Redhead
made him watch the mice die over and over in his
mind, all the while asking the same question:

Are you the mouse, or are you the snake?

In October of 1959, just shy of his twentieth birthday, the marine did something unthinkable for a U.S.
serviceman: he packed up his meager belongings,
withdrew his $1,500 life savings, and defected to the
Soviet Union.

Upon his arrival in Moscow, Soviet officials were

instantly suspicious. They found it incomprehensible that a U.S. Marine would want to defect. He was accused of being a spy. He was followed by the KGB. After a week of pleading his case to a parade of bureaucrats and having every door slammed in his face, the marine's visa was revoked and he was ordered to leave the country.

Desperate, the marine went back to his hotel, slipped into a hot bath, and took the blade out of his razor. He wasn't going back. He *couldn't*. The phone started ringing in his ear (Redhead, no doubt, calling to talk some sense into him). But the marine didn't answer. This was *his* decision. If he couldn't live in the Soviet Union, at least he could die there. He pressed the corner of the blade down on his left wrist until it broke through, then dragged the blade up his forearm, opening a large vein and spilling his blood. He did the same to his right wrist, then set the blade gently on the edge of the tub and relaxed into the warmth of the water. As the red clouds spiraled outward from his wrists, he closed his eyes, sad that it had to end like this but proud of himself for having the courage to see it though. But rather than peacefully drifting away to sleep, the marine was suddenly overcome by the feeling of a powerful presence in the room with him. Something with him in the dark. He opened his eyes one last time and saw a woman—an *angel*—standing over the tub, smiling down at him. A beautiful woman with wavy red hair.

Redhead...

She was the last thing he remembered before the darkness crept in from the corners of his eyes and took him. And she was the first thing he saw when he woke—sitting beside his hospital bed, keeping him company as the Soviet doctors bandaged his wrists and pumped him full of fluids. She spoke to him in perfect English, her demeanor warm and caring. She asked about his life. What he thought of the United States. Why he'd defected. Why he'd tried to kill himself. The marine answered her questions honestly. He felt a strange, instant connection with her. As if she understood exactly how he felt.

When her questions had been answered, the woman told the marine that there *was* indeed a place for him in the Soviet Union. An important place. He was overjoyed. That night, as he lay alone in the hospital bed, he picked up the phone and dialed Redhead. He wanted to tell his oldest friend about the woman and what she'd said. But Redhead didn't answer. It didn't want to talk about the woman.

It was *afraid* of her.

For the next two years, the marine lived the ideal Soviet life. He was given a furnished apartment in Minsk and a monthly stipend. He was assigned a Russian language tutor. He met a young Russian girl, married her, and got her pregnant. All of these things pleased the marine. But none pleased him so much as his time at the Factory.

Every morning, six days a week, a car driven by two nameless, silent men picked him up in front of his building and took him to what looked like an ordinary factory—a vast brick building with three smokestacks protruding from its top, seeping white smoke into the atmosphere. But inside, beyond the guard posts and layers of barbed-wire fence, was a space that looked more like an amusement park than a factory floor. There was an obstacle course. A gun range. A mockup of a multistory house, and a row of office windows overlooking it all, like the press boxes in a stadium.

Here, in the Factory, the marine was slowly disassembled and rebuilt. Already a sharpshooter, he was drilled until he could hit a moving target at five hundred yards. He was taught evasion tactics. Hand-to-hand combat. The rapid assembly and disassembly of different weapons. He was trained in the basics of bomb building, surveillance, and counter-surveillance. Every so often, he would glance up at the office windows and see a familiar shock of red hair behind the glare of the glass.

Two years later, when he emerged from the Factory, he wasn't the marine anymore. He was the *Asset*. He liked the name. It suggested value.

In 1962, the Asset walked into the American embassy in Moscow and announced that he wanted to return to the United States. His defection had been a mistake, he told them. He was ready to go home and spread the word of the evils of communism, so long as his bride and infant daughter could join him. The Americans, always eager to slander the Soviets with their propaganda, could hardly stamp his passport fast enough. They even paid for his ticket.

The Asset and his family settled in Texas, where he used the skills he'd been taught to blend in. He joined the Anti-Communist League (it was all he could do to keep his mouth shut in the meetings, as the bloated Americans called for witch hunts and demanded loyalty oaths and whipped themselves into an outright paranoid frenzy over the likelihood of "red spies" in their midst). They weren't back in the States long before October came around again. The month of his birth and every important change in his life since. It was the month he'd joined the marines and the month he'd arrived in the Soviet Union. Once again, October delivered on its promise of renewal.

That month, the Asset got a job working in the Texas School Book Depository building in Dallas.

Henry prepared to kick the door in.

The evidence had led them here, to a third-floor walk-up in Hell's Kitchen—a neighborhood synonymous with crime, home to dope peddlers, streetwalkers, and gangsters who callously blew each other's brains out in front of family restaurants. A neighborhood where children played in trash-strewn alleys and traveled in packs.

It was here, in New York's roughest neighborhood, that Virginia Dare's trail had gone cold. Here, in a tenement building on Eleventh Avenue—once called "Death Avenue" for the number of pedestrians trampled under its horse-drawn carriages. They had been investigating for two months, interviewing those few vampires who remained on American soil, following a trail of fake names and false leads, and cobbling together a picture of a conspiracy both vague and vast. They'd worked tirelessly for weeks on end, yet what they'd learned barely filled a single page of a reporter's notebook:

1. The woman Henry had known as "Virginia Dare" was still alive and had been in the Soviet Union since at least 1950, splitting her time between Moscow and Minsk.

2. There was a facility in Minsk, commonly called "Zavod" (the Factory), where the KGB trained assets for service in foreign countries.

3. An unknown number of Soviet sleeper agents were currently in the United States.

4. Increased chatter on coded Soviet spy networks indicated that "something big" was coming.

5. Someone matching Virginia Dare's description had recently been photographed leaving a meeting of the Young Communist League in Philadelphia.

Dare was adept at covering her tracks, and for two months, Abe and Henry had chased one dead end after another, always a step behind. But recently, she'd made a critical mistake: she'd underestimated the paranoia of J. Edgar Hoover.

Hoover had tapped the phone of practically every Russian, Cuban, Vietnamese, Chinese, and Korean expatriate in the United States.[1] Three days before Abe and Henry found themselves in that Hell's Kitchen apartment building, a low-level analyst had been poring over a backlog of phone transcripts, when he'd stumbled on a brief exchange—translated from the original Spanish—between a Cuban exile named Ernesto Mosqueda Ramos, suspected leader of a pro–Fidel Castro group, and an unidentified female:

> **EMR**: Hello?
> **UF**: It's time, Ernesto.
> [:04 seconds of silence]
> **EMR**: What's our target?
> **UF**: I'll be there on Friday morning to discuss it in person. Eleven o'clock. Bring the others.

Ramos then immediately made a call to one of his top lieutenants, beginning with:

> **EMR**: I just talked to the red-haired woman. She said it's time.

---

1. Between 1953 and 1963, Swiss manufacturer Nagra sold more reel-to-reel tape recorders to the FBI than it did in all of Switzerland.

It wasn't much, but it was enough to send Abe and Henry racing to New York, and enough for the Secret Service to start round-the-clock surveillance on Ramos's apartment. On Friday morning, with cameras clicking from adjacent rooftops, they'd watched two men—both members of Ramos's pro-Castro group, and both Latinos—arrive together at his apartment. Ten minutes later, a white woman with wavy red hair had approached from the south, wearing sunglasses and a long coat. She, too, disappeared into Ramos's building.

Minutes later, Abe and Henry had their bodies pressed against the wall on either side of the apartment door, preparing themselves for a fight to the death with Virginia Dare. Henry in a light brown jacket, a white T-shirt, and jeans; Abe in a long black coat and gray trousers. Neither man would change his clothes for the next seventy-two hours. Three Secret Service agents joined them, guns drawn. Five New York City policemen waited on the sidewalk outside, just in case anyone tried to climb down the fire escape.

Henry nodded to Abe. He kicked in the door.

Abe was sitting with his back to the door as Henry entered, writing in his journal by a window that looked out onto the South Lawn. The old friends hadn't laid eyes on each other for more than a decade, and when

Abe stood up and turned around, Henry burst into laughter.

> [Abe] was sporting a huge, bushy beard and hair down to his shoulders.[2] He'd taken to wearing a floppy-brimmed hat and little circular sunglasses with gold wire rims. I would've called him a "hippie," but this was a good five years before anybody knew what a "hippie" was.

Abraham Lincoln had spent the 1950s raising cattle on his Illinois ranch. He hadn't left the Springfield area in more than a decade, and he hardly ever left his property—preferring to spend his downtime reading, listening to the news on the radio, playing records (classical and jazz, mostly), and painting—a hobby that had grown into a passion.

But hermit or not, Abe couldn't ignore the president's invitation to the White House to commemorate the one hundredth anniversary of the signing of the Emancipation Proclamation. On August 3rd, 1963, he and Henry joined a quarter million people on the National Mall, a black umbrella over their heads to ward off the midday sun as they listened to a thirty-four-year-old preacher deliver the keynote address on the steps of the Lincoln Memorial:

---

2. A vampire's hair continues to grow throughout its life, though due to metabolic differences, it grows at roughly half the rate of a human's.

"Five score years ago, a great American, in whose symbolic shadow we stand today, signed the Emancipation Proclamation. This momentous decree came as a great beacon light of hope to millions of Negro slaves who had been seared in the flames of withering injustice. It came as a joyous daybreak to end the long night of their captivity. But one hundred years later, the Negro still is not free."

Abe and Henry found themselves in the Oval Office that night, its windows dark, the corridors of the White House quiet around them. There'd been a reception for the leaders of the March on Washington earlier, including the young Dr. King, fresh from giving the speech of the century. But the festivities were over. The crowds had gone home, and now three men, two of them presidents, sat alone by the glow of two silver lanterns, a gift from the White House Correspondents' Association, replicas of the lanterns that had signaled the British invasion on the night of Paul Revere's ride—a night that Henry remembered well.

To his admirers, John F. Kennedy was a reinvigorating, transformative figure—a brilliant scholar and war hero. To his detractors, he was the product of old money and old political machinery—an arrogant playboy who never would've attained the presidency had he not won the birth lottery.

He *was* brilliant, and he *was* arrogant. You don't have much business being president if you're not both, to some degree. But if you judge a man by what he makes of his advantages, Kennedy surely made more than most. Like FDR, he could've chosen a life of leisure or business—but he chose combat. Boldness. Justice. And ultimately, he gave his life for his choices. Kennedy said something about his friend [the poet Robert] Frost once—something about how poets and politicians could both be judged by how they rose to the challenges of their lives.[3] That, to me, summed up the spirit of Jack Kennedy. Not only did he rise to the challenges, he went looking for them.

Abe had always liked Kennedy. And like Abe, the young president had always had a fascination with death—namely, his own.

He and Kennedy had corresponded several times since the election. As president elect, Kennedy had sought Abe's comments on a rough draft of his inaugural address.[4] He'd been the first

---

3. The exact quote is: "I think politicians and poets share at least one thing, and that is their greatness depends upon the courage with which they face the challenges of life."

4. Kennedy and his speechwriter, Ted Sorensen, had studied the Gettysburg Address in crafting the main ideas of the speech. The draft they sent Lincoln for notes contained the line "And so my fellow citizens, the question is not what America can do for us, but what we can do for America." Lincoln crossed it out and wrote a now immortal line in its place: "And so, my fellow Americans, ask not what your country can do

president elect to do that, by the way—which is amazing, when you consider that Abe wrote the two greatest inaugural addresses of all time.

[Kennedy] didn't bother Abe with the questions most presidents did. You know, "Do you have any advice on current affairs?" "What was it like during the Civil War?" And so on. All Kennedy ever wanted to know about was Ford's Theater. Namely, what Abe remembered and didn't remember. And now that he finally had him in the Oval Office, that's all he wanted to talk about. At the time it was nothing. Just conversation. Looking back, though, watching those two men talk about what it was like having a bullet shot through the back of your head . . .

There are few things in my long life that truly haunt me. That night is one of them.

"Did you see anything?" asked Kennedy. "Afterward, I mean?"

"You mean, did I see any sort of bright light," said Abe, "or flights of angels coming to carry me to my rest?"

"Yes."

"No," said Abe. "I didn't see anything."

Kennedy's face visibly fell. For all of his playboy

---

for you, ask what you can do for your country." He then added a second line, expanding on the idea: "My fellow citizens of the world, ask not what America will do for you, but what together we can do for the freedom of man."

confidence and marital shortcomings, he was a deeply religious man. He'd been hoping for some confirmation from Abe, some tiny hint that his lifelong devotion to the cross hadn't been in vain.

Sensing his disappointment, Abe smiled warmly at the young president and said, "I didn't see anything... I saw *everything*."

Now it was Kennedy who smiled at Abe.

"But with all due respect, Mr. President—"

"Jack."

"With all due respect, Jack...you haven't called us here to discuss the mysteries of existence."

Kennedy looked at Abe a moment, studying his eyes. For all the changes—the smooth skin, the long hair, the bushy beard—they were still the wizened eyes of Abraham Lincoln. *Incredible.* Kennedy reached into his jacket pocket and lit a cigarette. He took a puff, shook out the match, and threw it onto the glass table between them. Like all great politicians, Kennedy was a malleable man. He had made room in his belief system to accommodate vampires. If they existed, then God must have created them, and if God created them, then Kennedy could accept them.[5]

---

5. Colossians 1:16, 17: "For by him were all things created, that are in heaven, and that are in earth, visible and invisible, whether they be thrones, or dominions, or principalities, or powers: all things were created by him, and for him: And he is before all things, and by him all things consist."

"I need you," he said.

They were the three words I least wanted to hear. I'd been happily jetting back and forth between [upstate New York], where I was building a permanent home, and Florida, where the [Howard Hughes Medical] institute was headquartered. I was making a fortune in the market, and we were making real progress on a cure. The last thing I wanted was to drop everything and become the president's errand boy again.

The Soviets were up to something, Kennedy told them. He wasn't sure exactly what it was, but their people on the ground were sure they were gearing up for some kind of strike against the United States— retaliation for the embarrassment of the Cuban missile crisis. The president's advisers had warned him about traveling overseas, and his personal Secret Service detail had been increased.

"You two," Kennedy continued, "well…you're the last of a dying breed. There are only a handful of vampires left, and of that handful, virtually none with any sense of allegiance to the United States."

"Forgive me," said Henry, "but why us? Can't the CIA handle this?"

Kennedy pressed a button on the end table beside his chair. Abe and Henry looked up as a man walked into the Oval Office—a smartly dressed man of sixty or so, with neatly kept gray hair, wearing glasses on his pleasant face. Abe and Henry had never met this man, but they recognized him as John McCone, director of the CIA. His face had been a fixture in the papers during the Cuban missile crisis the previous year. It was, in fact, McCone's deep mistrust of the Soviets that had led to the discovery of Russia's nuclear designs on Cuba, and, along with the president's steady hand, he had pulled the world back from the brink of a nuclear holocaust.

> [McCone] introduced himself and sat on the sofa opposite Abe and me. He laid a manila folder on the table and slid it over to us.

Henry opened it. There were several eight-by-ten black-and-white photos inside. Long-lens pictures of a woman walking out of a building. Sunglasses and long wavy hair. They were grainy and slightly out of focus, but it was Virginia Dare. Unmistakable.

"I understand she's an acquaintance of yours," said Kennedy.

"Was," said Henry. "She's been dead for twenty-five years."

"Are you sure?" asked Kennedy.

"I watched her burn to death in '37," said Henry. "We both did."

McCone reached forward and tapped the top of one of the photographs with his index finger.

"These were taken less than a week ago," he said.

It never occurred to me that she might've survived. She'd been so engulfed, so blackened and disfigured, drenched in diesel fuel. That image of her dragging herself along, being crushed beneath the hot metal skeleton of the *Hindenburg* . . . that image had been seared into my memory.

No, it can't be her, thought Henry. *Impossible. Impossible! No one could've survived that inferno, not even her.*

But Virginia had always been a survivor. She'd survived the wilds of the New World. Survived a crossing to Europe. Survived with nothing but her wits and her hatred, whittling her fears away until all that remained was a sharp point. And it was Henry Sturges who'd set her on this path.

"Whatever they're up to," Kennedy said, "*she's* the tip of the spear."

McCone spoke up and told us what they knew: the Factory in Minsk. The sleeper agents, all of them seemingly recruited by the same woman. A woman who went by many names and was almost never seen in public.

"It's my fault," said Henry when McCone was done. "All of it."

Kennedy looked surprised. "What do you mean?"

I hesitated. It wasn't that I was afraid to admit it to the president. I was afraid of admitting it to *myself.* I got a taste of how the parent of a school shooter must feel—going down a list of things I could've done differently. Points at which I could've intervened. Was I the one who'd pulled the trigger? No. *But I'd created the finger that did.* It was my choice that set her down the path. My blood that ran in her veins.

"I created her," said Henry. "I made her what she is...a long time ago."

Kennedy turned this over in his mind for a while, silently.

"Well then," he said at last, "you'll just have to destroy her."

Henry was first through the door. Abe was next, his beard obscuring his famous face, his long hair tied back with a rubber band; like Henry, he was wearing sunglasses. The Secret Service agents were behind them, pistols in hand, their bodies tense and trained, taking corners at precise angles and announcing themselves in shouts as they made their way into the cramped apartment, its walls covered in revolutionary sentiments and peeling paint, its curtains drawn. A short entry hall led into the living area, where Ramos and his two accomplices were meeting with the red-haired woman. They'd taken only a few steps inside before the shooting began.

I heard the first bullet whiz by my left ear. I'd guess it missed me by less than an inch. I spun in the direction of the shot and saw one of Ramos's men aiming his revolver at me. The other was trying to pull a gun from his waistband, but the hammer had snagged on his shirt. Ramos had grabbed the red-haired woman, pulling her into an adjacent room. As the second shot went off, Abe pushed me out of its path. It hit the wall directly behind where my head had been a fraction of a second earlier, blowing a crater in the plaster. Before I could get my wits about me, there was a *Pop! Pop! Pop!* as the Secret Service men emptied their revolvers into the two accomplices. The agents around us had no idea we were vampires, and we were strictly prohibited from revealing ourselves. The red-haired woman started to scream in the next room. I remember thinking it strange that a woman like Virginia would scream.

Abe and Henry ran past the dead accomplices and into a bedroom, where Ramos was trying to pry open a window so he and the red-haired woman could climb down the fire escape. *Why is she running away?* Henry thought. *Why doesn't she turn around and tear us apart?*

The heat of the radiator beneath the window had made its frame expand. Ramos couldn't get it to budge. Cornered, he turned and fired a .38 revolver, hitting Henry in the chest—a minor annoyance that Henry responded to by swatting the gun from Ramos's hand and pushing his head through the window, breaking the glass, splintering the wooden frame, and opening deep gashes on Ramos's face and neck. Abe, meanwhile, had put a hand on the woman's throat and pushed her up against the wall.

> She was hysterical, hyperventilating. Abe grabbed her hair and pulled. Off came the wavy red wig. Under it, nothing but straight blond hair and a terrified human girl.

Minutes later, the apartment was filled with police, dusting surfaces for fingerprints, measuring bullet holes, and taking pictures of the two corpses in the living room—one with a hand still clinging to the stuck pistol in his waistband. Ramos sat handcuffed in the bedroom, surrounded by police and Secret Service men as a medic patched up his wounds. Abe and Henry sat alone with the blonde as she smoked a cigarette in the small kitchen.

"When?" asked Henry.

"A few days ago," said the girl. "I'd seen her around a little, talking to some of the other girls. I figured she was working, but I never saw her get in any cars or go off with anybody. She was just there, and then she wasn't."

"And what did she say, exactly?"

"She told me she'd give me a hundred bucks if I showed up here at exactly eleven o'clock, wearing the wig and the sunglasses. I figured it was work, you know? Covering for her with one of her regulars. She gave me fifty up front and told me I'd get the rest after."

The girl's expression darkened suddenly.

"Wait...," she said, "does this mean I don't get the other fifty?"

"The woman," said Abe. "Did she say anything else? Anything about where she might be staying or traveling?"

The girl thought for a moment.

"Yeah, actually. There *was* something else. She told me to say hello to somebody. 'Denny' or something. 'Harry' maybe. Shit, what was the name..."

"Henry?"

"Yeah! Henry! She told me, 'Say hello to Henry.' You guys know him?"

Abe and Henry shared a look. They thanked the girl for her time, excused themselves, and headed through the living room, toward the bedroom where Ramos was being kept. Maybe he would have the information they needed. But probably not. Virginia knew she was being followed, and she knew exactly who was doing the following. Once again, she was five steps ahead.

Abe and Henry were careful not to disturb the evidence as they stepped around the two corpses on the living room floor—no easy feat, since the vampires were half-blind from the constant popping of the police photographer's flashbulbs. Henry reached for his sunglasses and put them on. His vision restored, he was able to make out the date on the blood-spattered calendar hanging on the living room wall:

November 22nd, 1963.

It had rained all morning in Dallas, but at ten a.m. the skies had begun to clear, and by noon it had become an unseasonably warm and sunny autumn day. One hundred and fifty thousand people had skipped school or taken off from work to line the streets of downtown, hoping to catch a glimpse of the president of the United States. Cameras clicked Kodachrome stills and small children sat on their parents' shoulders, some waving American flags, all cheering as the midnight-blue 1961 Lincoln Continental drove past at an average speed of eleven miles per hour, flanked by motorcycle escorts and followed closely by a Cadillac convertible, four Secret Service agents standing on its

The president rides through downtown Dallas, just minutes before being shot. Abe and Henry were still fifteen hundred miles away in New York's Hell Kitchen, having been lured by a decoy working for Virginia Dare.

running boards, ready to jump off and deal with any threat from the crowds with their service revolvers or with the AR-15 rifle they carried in the car.

But there'd been no cause for alarm. The motorcade had been winding its way along for more than forty minutes, the president and first lady waving all the while, occasionally stopping to shake hands or take pictures. Despite worries about a liberal northern president traveling in the Deep South, the people of Dallas had been welcoming and enthusiastic. The crowds began to thin out as the president's limousine reached the end of the parade route and made a tight left turn onto Elm Street—where it would proceed for one final block of waving and smiling before turning onto the freeway and proceeding to a luncheon, five minutes away.

This is my rifle…

The Asset aimed out the sixth-floor window. This particular rifle was a 6.5 mm Italian model with a 4X scope, built in 1940. It was the exact rifle he'd trained with during his two years at the Factory, delivered to him by the KGB though a fake mail-order service. He'd taken it out for target practice and had been pleased to find he could still shoot the wings off a honeybee at two hundred yards. He and his rifle were one.

There are many like it, but this one is mine…

The Asset took aim. The president was fifty yards out, moving away from him at ten, maybe eleven miles per hour. At this distance, he couldn't miss. He looked through the scope, exhaling as he'd been taught. Slowing his breathing, his heartbeat. Relaxing his finger against the trigger.

My rifle is my best friend. It is my life. I must master it as I must master my life.

He was indeed the master of his life. In this moment, he was all powerful, just as he'd always known he would be, even as a boy on his cot in that white-walled room, as those devious psychiatrists tried to trick him. Even as his fellow marines shunned him.

Without me, my rifle is useless. Without my rifle, I am useless.

Through the scope, the Asset watched Kennedy wave to the relatively few people gathered on both sides of the street. The Asset tracked him, aiming for the back of his head. *One shot, one kill.* Kennedy was still inside seventy yards. The Asset's accuracy inside that distance was better than 97 percent. It was as good as done. Still, he could feel his heart beating in the tips of his fingers.

Are you the mouse, or are you the snake?

The Asset fired.

He missed.

The bullet sailed wide left, striking the concrete curb on Main Street. A fragment of the bullet broke off and hit a spectator named James Tague on the right cheek, drawing blood. Heads turned toward the sound of the rifle shot. Had it been a firecracker? An exhaust backfire? Kennedy—a combat veteran— was one of those who turned.

"Impossible...," the Asset whispered to himself. "Imposs—"

Shut up! There's still time...

The Asset exhaled.

I must fire my rifle true. I must shoot straighter than my enemy who is trying to kill me...

Eighty yards. He aimed at the president's back, a bigger target, hoping to blow his heart to pieces or, at the very least, sever his spinal cord.

I must shoot him before he shoots me...

He chambered another round with astonishing

speed. Took aim. Squeezed off a second shot. Kennedy flinched in the scope, then awkwardly raised his elbows and clutched at his throat. The bullet had entered the president's upper back, nicked his spine and right lung, then exited out the center of his throat, tearing his tie knot, before continuing forward into Governor Connally's back just below his right armpit, shattering his ribs and exiting out his chest.

It was a clean hit, but it wasn't a kill shot. The Asset had to be sure. He pulled back on the bolt and chambered another round. He exhaled again and aimed at Kennedy's head, now slumped to the left as the first lady put her hands on his shoulder, bracing him, asking him what was wrong. *Ninety yards.* He pulled the trigger with a feather touch.

Kennedy's head exploded.

Redhead...

The bullet had entered the back of Kennedy's skull dead center and broke into fragments, each of those tearing through his brain, the shock wave creating incredible pressure in his skull, forcing blood and cranial fluid outward as if a bomb had been set off in the center. The front of the president's head bulged out, then broke—pieces of skull, brain, and blood flying out of the massive hole in his head. All of this in roughly one-eighteenth of a second. The time it took Abraham Zapruder to record one frame of his famous motion picture.

Blood, skull fragments, and pieces of brain were

ejected all over the interior of the Continental—both the inside and outside of the windshield. They landed on the Secret Service driver's suit jacket, on the car's front hood...even on the faces of two of the Dallas motorcycle policemen who were following a car's length behind. One of those policemen—hit in the face with what he described as a "fine mist"—would never forget the salty taste of President Kennedy's brains on his tongue.

The Asset sucked in a breath, as if breaking the surface of a lake after nearly drowning. His whole body tingled. It was almost orgasmic, watching the leader of the free world's head break apart and spill its contents. He watched through the scope as Mrs. Kennedy tried to climb out of the line of fire, only to be stopped by her personal Secret Service agent, Clint Hill, who'd come running from behind.

As the limousine sped away, the first lady screamed, "I have his brains in my hand!" and then leaned over to her husband and asked, "Jack? Jack, can you hear me?" over and over again. Jack could not. Jack was dead. He'd been dead before his head recoiled. For all the fuss about last rites and the tearful official pronouncement that would come less than an hour later at Parkland Hospital, he was, for all intents and purposes, gone before his limousine reached the end of Main Street.

The Asset was pleased, but this was no time to sit and admire his work. There was a procedure. A strict schedule to adhere to. He hid the rifle and walked, calmly, toward the stairs.

Better late than never, thought Virginia.

The assassination had originally been assigned to a *different* group of assets, twenty days earlier, in Chicago. As Kennedy's motorcade drove from O'Hare Airport into the city, three men, each with a high-powered rifle, were to have been stationed at the Jackson exit off the Northwest Expressway, where the limousine would be forced to slow and take a precarious turn. All three would've fired at once, trapping the president in a turkey shoot, while a fourth gunman waited on an overpass a few hundred yards down the street to finish the job in case the others didn't.

At the exact moment Kennedy was gunned down in Chicago, her other assets would have struck halfway around the world, assassinating the president of South Vietnam. With the dual strikes against the American and Vietnamese heads of state, the American appetite for intervention in Southeast Asia would have evaporated, clearing the way for the dominos—Laos, Cambodia, Thailand, Malaysia, Indonesia, India—to fall and establishing the Soviet Union as the world's sole superpower and communism as its dominant ideology. America's time in the sun would finally be over.

But her assets in Vietnam had carried out their mission three hours earlier than scheduled, giving

time for news of the assassination to reach Washington. Fearing a plot, the Secret Service had scrapped
the president's trip to Chicago at the last minute, leaving Virginia scrambling to get everything in place in
time for the next window.

Unfortunately, that window was Dallas, where by
far the weakest of her assets was stationed. He was a
troubled man, this asset, with delusions of grandeur
and a personality disorder bordering on schizophrenia.
But he was zealous and easily manipulated, and he was
a crack shot with a rifle. To Virginia's immense relief,
he'd done brilliantly. Now only one thing remained.
The most important step in any assassination:

Kill the assassin.

Guiteau[6] had hanged for shooting Garfield. Czolgosz had sizzled and smoked in the electric chair for
killing McKinley. The asset who'd poisoned Taylor[7]
was never caught, so Virginia had dispatched him
herself.

But this idiot…this idiot had gotten himself
arrested.

Virginia had given him specific instructions: he

---

6. Charles J. Guiteau (1841–1882) shot President James Garfield on
July 2, 1881. Garfield died eleven weeks later, after just 199 days in
office.

7. President Zachary Taylor (1784–1850), who had committed himself to preserving the Union a full ten years before Abraham Lincoln
took office, fell ill suddenly on July 4, 1850. He died five days later.
Assassination theories have hung over his death ever since.

was to take the bus to the Texas Theatre on Jefferson Boulevard, where a KGB agent would contact him and accompany him out of the city. He would be driven across the border, to Mexico, and from there flown to Havana, where his wife and daughters would be waiting for him. They would all be flown to Finland, then cross the border into the Soviet Union, where the Asset would receive a hero's welcome, a high-level job, and a lifetime pension. (It was all a lie, of course—in truth, they would drive him and his family into the middle of nowhere, kill them, burn them, and bury their charred bones in an unsuspecting farmer's field.) In any case, all he had to do was sit in an air-conditioned movie house and wait.

Instead, he'd panicked and shot a Dallas police officer[8] who'd stopped to question him as he fled the scene of the assassination. At least a dozen witnesses saw the shooting, after which the Asset—instead of improvising an escape—continued into the Texas Theatre as planned.

He was a crack shot, but he was no scholar.

No matter. Virginia always had a contingency plan in place. She called another asset—one who'd been in semiretirement for some time. He was a Dallas local, a nightclub owner and mob associate whom Virginia

---

8. J. D. Tippit (1924–1963) was a married father of three young children, and an army veteran of World War II. In addition to serving on the Dallas police force, he also worked at a local barbecue restaurant at the time of his murder.

had recruited and trained in Havana years earlier. His name was Jack Rubenstein, but he went by Jack Ruby.

Abe and Henry were thirty-six thousand feet above the earth, aboard Henry's Lockheed Jetstar,[9] its four engines pushing it toward Dallas at five hundred miles per hour. The pilots relayed news from the ground: at twelve thirty p.m., the president had been shot in the back of the head by an assassin's bullet (the similarities to Abe's assassination were striking, though Abe and Henry felt no need to discuss them). At 1 p.m., doctors at Parkland Hospital had pronounced him dead. At 1:15 p.m., a Dallas patrolman had been shot by an unknown assailant, who fled to the Texas Theatre, where he was taken into custody at 1:50 p.m. It would be another twelve hours before that suspect was officially charged with the president's murder, but there was a feeling among the Dallas detectives that they had their man—the coincidence of the two shootings so close together, and by a man with similar descriptions, was just too great.

There was nothing they could do for Jack Kennedy. One of the president's closest aides, Kenneth

---

9. The Lockheed Jetstar, which entered service in 1957, is regarded as the first private or executive jet aircraft. Henry purchased his 1962 model for just under $1 million—the equivalent of roughly $8 million in 2015 dollars.

O'Donnell, had spoken to Henry from Air Force One as it had carried Kennedy's body back to Washington.

> He asked me if there was any way to restore the president. I'd brought Lincoln back, he said, why not Kennedy? But it was impossible. Half of Kennedy's brain was missing, parts of it still embedded in motorcycle tires and dashboard vents. Even if I *could* bring him back, what would've emerged from the fog would've been nothing like the president and, in all likelihood, severely impaired.

All they could do was get to Dallas as quickly as possible. Get in front of the shooter. Interview him. Intimidate him. There was still a chance he could lead them to Dare. And if he did, there was a chance they could catch her before she vanished into thin air again, if she hadn't already.

Darkness had fallen by the time Abe and Henry landed at Love Field, where the president himself had landed earlier that very day. They sped to the Dallas police headquarters on Harwood Street, where the suspect was being interrogated. But instead of walking into a police station, Abe and Henry found themselves in a madhouse.

> There were reporters everywhere, clogging the hallways, hot television lights and huge studio

cameras on wheeled pedestals. We decided to wait until the commotion died down.

Hours passed. At 11:31 p.m., the Dallas police trotted their suspect out in front of a crowded room of reporters, for what would become known as "the midnight press conference." Abe and Henry stood near the back of the room as the suspect was allowed to answer just a few questions. Jack Ruby was also in attendance, a loaded Colt Cobra .38 revolver in his jacket pocket.

It was five in the morning by the time we were finally able to sit down with [the suspect]. A detective brought him into a small interrogation room, where Abe and I had been kept waiting for more than three hours. He was exhausted. He'd been beaten at least once. He hadn't been allowed to talk to an attorney or make a phone call. And now here he was, delirious and hand-cuffed, led into yet another endless room to be asked the same three questions. So imagine his surprise when he sat down and I asked him—

"Where's the red-haired woman? The one who trained you in Minsk?"
The suspect looked up, his eyes suddenly alive with mischief. He stared at Abe and Henry for a moment.
"Who are you?" he asked.

"Answer the question," said Abe.

"We know she recruited you," said Henry, "some-time after you defected. We know she was there when you were trained at the Factory in Minsk. And we know that she's been in contact with you as recently as yesterday."

> This last part was a bluff—we didn't know *when* he'd been in contact with Virginia, but it was reasonable to think he had.

"I don't know what you're talking about," said the suspect through a smile.

"She's going to kill you," said Abe. "You, your wife...your daughters."

The twinkle left the suspect's eyes.

"Cooperate with us," Abe continued, "and we can protect them. We can protect *you*."

The suspect looked at them for a few moments, then smiled and lowered his head so that his chin was touching his chest.

"Like I said," the suspect continued, "I've got no idea what you're talking about...I'm just a patsy."

> Those were the last words he spoke to us. Every-thing else was met with silence. He wouldn't talk to us or even look at us. It was clear we were getting nowhere. We'd been at it for twenty-four hours straight, from Hell's Kitchen to Dallas. We

were tired and frustrated. We decided to grab a few hours of sleep and try [interviewing him] again in the morning.

But the second interview never came. By the time Abe and Henry returned, at just after ten a.m., the

Jack Ruby lunges at fellow Dare asset Lee Harvey Oswald with a .38 Colt Cobra revolver in the basement of Dallas police headquarters. Abe and Henry were only a few feet behind and to the left of the photographer when this picture was taken, but they were unable to stop him.

decision had been made to move the suspect to a jail on the other side of Dallas, where the press would have less access. At 11:21 a.m., as Abe and Henry watched with a crowd of reporters, the suspect was escorted through the basement of police headquarters toward a waiting armored car. He made it a few feet before Jack Ruby stepped forward and shot him in the gut.

It was late. The morgue was empty—a vast, dimly lit space, tens of thousands of light-blue tiles making up its floor. There were corpses everywhere, some off in the dark corners of the room, stacked floor to ceiling like items on a store shelf, wrapped in plastic, or covered with white sheets. Other corpses lay on stainless-steel tables, their shiny surfaces slightly tilting toward a drain at one end, which collected blood and other fluids for disposal. Electric saws, designed to rip through bone with their circular blades, and other surgical instruments sat on wheeled tables beside them. Scales for weighing organs hung from the ceiling under light fixtures, most of their fluorescent bulbs dark, only a few flickering here and there, creating pockets of sterile light. One of the walls was covered with the shiny doors of sliding storage lockers—full-size for adults, smaller for infants and children.

Virginia walked across the cold tile, slender legs jutting from her skirt, each high-heeled step echoing off the hard surfaces. She would've preferred more functional clothing, but she'd had to charm her way into the building, and that had called for skin. Her vampire senses soaked it in: the smell of death and chemicals everywhere, formaldehyde and bleach, mixed with the faint smell of gas, which was used to fuel the cremation furnaces built into the far wall. The low hum of the refrigeration units, staving off decomposition by keeping everything at a constant forty degrees Fahrenheit.

Her Asset was somewhere in here, dead nearly twelve hours, if you believed the official story. There were rumors he'd survived Ruby's bullet to the stomach. Virginia had to see him with her own eyes. She had to be *sure*.

The morgue staff had gone home for the night, no doubt glued to their radios and televisions along with the rest of the country. She was alone with the dead of Dallas. The president himself would've been on one of these slabs, had the Secret Service not insisted (by pulling their guns and threatening to shoot Parkland Hospital staffers) that his body be taken back to Washington.

Virginia began with the stacked corpses, lifting each sheet or peeling away just enough plastic to get a look at the toe tags. Her Asset wasn't there. She continued to the bodies on the autopsy tables, studying the faces of the freshly dead—some of their chest cavities splayed open, some with the tops of their skulls cut off, brains exposed or altogether missing.

Her Asset wasn't there, either, which meant he'd been put in one of the storage lockers. Virginia walked along the metal wall. The front of each locker bore the name of the deceased, written in white grease pencil. Sure enough, on the last door of the bottom row, all the way in the corner of the morgue, she found the name she'd been looking for.

She smiled, reached for the metal latch, and pulled. The locker slid open, revealing a body covered in a white sheet. Virginia reached for the top of the sheet and began to pull it—

Someone's in here.

She wheeled around, startled by a presence in the room. She'd been so focused on finding the Asset, she'd missed the sound of careful footsteps on the tile floor; the soft shuffling of clothes.

A tall, slender man with a thick beard stood at the far end of the room, silhouetted by one of the flickering bulbs. It was Abraham Lincoln—still missing the fingers she'd taken from him on the *Hindenburg*. He was dressed in blue jeans, boots, and a white T-shirt, sunglasses hanging from the collar, his long dark hair resting on broad shoulders. He was holding an ax in his left hand.

But if Lincoln's here, that means—

The Asset's corpse sat up beside her; the white sheet fell away from its face.

Henry.

Dressed like his partner, only in a black T-shirt

instead of white. Virginia took a step back, her eyes flitting between Abe and Henry. She needed to be aware of both of them now. Every step, every twitch.

"It's over," said Henry, swinging his feet over the side of the locker. "There are men covering every exit. They know what you are, and they have the weapons to stop you."

"Do they?" asked Virginia.

"There's still a way out for you, Virginia," said Henry. "Help us. *Work* with us. Expose the other people behind this."

"You're offering *me* a way out? Henry...I don't think you understand—"

"Shut up!" he yelled. "No more games. Either you surrender yourself right now and help us...or you die."

> We looked at each other for a second or two. I think of those seconds sometimes. So much going on behind her eyes: hatred, pity, regret, love. And the truth, sinking in...The truth that one of us was never going to leave that room.

"Think," said Henry. "They know your face. Your associates. They know you orchestrated the death of a president. Even if you kill us, even if you fight your way out of here tonight, they'll never stop hunting you. They'll find you, and when they do they'll take their time killing you."

"And if they do," said Virginia, "there will be others to take my place. Others who won't rest until this country crumbles."

"Why?" asked Henry. "Where does this hatred come from? You would slaughter innocents in the name of what—fascism? Communism? Because one form of tyranny suits you better than another?"

"*Slaughtering innocents* is all men have been doing since they landed on these shores. Burning witches at the stake, driving people from their lands, persecuting and purifying and segregating. How many innocents have died in the name of 'democracy' and 'freedom'? You, Henry...how many innocents have *you* slaughtered in your time?"

Henry gave no answer.

"America's time is over," she said.

"And yet we remain."

Abe's voice had come softly from the darkness, echoing through the room.

"For all of our imperfections," he continued, "all of our sins and hypocrisies—and they are many, I grant you—through war and disagreement and tragedy... we remain."

He took a small step forward, twirling his ax. "We may yet destroy ourselves," he said. "I can't say I'd be all that surprised if we did. But I promise you...this country will never be destroyed from the outside. Not by any ideology or foreign power...and certainly not by *you*."

Virginia looked at both of them. She smiled.

"You wouldn't understand," she said. "You're Americans... You've *always* been Americans."

Virginia's fangs punched through her gums and her eyes went black. She broke her stare with Henry and lunged toward the collection of sharp instruments laid out beside the nearest autopsy table. Abe took off running across the tile floor, intent on stopping Virginia before she reached them, as Henry sprang from his seated position and gave chase from behind. All of these things in the same instant, almost imperceptible to human eyes.

Abe beat Virginia to the table by an arm's length, knocking the instruments out of her reach, spilling all manner of scissors and scalpels across the floor. He swung his ax at her neck, but she moved from its path and swung her clawed hand at him in return, tearing the front of his T-shirt and drawing blood. Henry was there a fraction of a second later, the three vampires colliding in a blur of gnashing teeth and swinging claws. They fought the length of the room—Virginia kicking and punching; Abe swinging his ax from the front, only to have it blocked; Henry with his claws out, thrusting them like daggers at Virginia's back but doing little more than landing scratches.

Even with the two of us [fighting her] together, we were barely holding our own. There's no overstating how talented she was. How fast, how strong. She seemed to anticipate our every move, have a counter for our every attack.

Abe brought the blade of his ax down on Virginia's head, only to have her grab the handle in midflight and use it as a brace, lifting herself off the floor and landing a kick to Henry's neck behind her—the sharp heel of her shoe punching a small hole in his throat. Henry brought his hands upward, just as Kennedy had done when the assassin's bullet tore through his vocal cords.

Without missing a beat, she flew at Abe like this [drags fingers across his face] with her claws and opened four deep gashes across his face, from here [his left temple] to here [his right cheek].

With both Abe and Henry stunned, Virginia grabbed the front of Henry's shirt, lifted him off the tile, and drove him into the wall of metal storage lockers. He slid to the floor, dazed. The lockers teetered, then collapsed on top of him. He tried to roll out of the way, but he couldn't muster the speed. His left arm was pinned beneath the cold metal.

She left me trapped there, still bleeding from my throat, my arm crushed beneath a ton of metal.

Virginia turned back to Abe. Now with only one opponent, she attacked with twice the fury, avoiding his ax by contorting her body out of its path, and countering with sharp-clawed punches and high-heeled kicks—one of which knocked the ax out of Abe's hand.

It slid across the floor, and Virginia went for it. She was faster, but Abe's body was longer—he dove after her and wrapped his arms around her legs, tackling her before she could get to it.

Abe held on to Virginia's legs as tightly as he could. With the same strength that had once made him a feared wrestler in Illinois, he stood up and swung her body off the floor and into the air—throwing her down onto one of the empty autopsy tables, hard enough to leave a dent in its stainless-steel top. He held her there on her back, his left hand pressing on her chest, and reached for a nearby electric bone saw.

> He got his hand on it and powered it up. The round blade started to whir, a terrible, high-pitched shrill sound. [Abe] brought it toward her neck, stretching the electric cord to the limit and getting within a foot of taking her head clean off.

But Virginia got her heels up and kicked Abe in the chest, knocking him backward and onto the ground.

His head cracked against the floor, shattering several of its soft-blue tiles. Virginia was up in an instant, grabbing the bone saw and starting it up. Abe tried to lift his head, but Virginia stepped on his throat, pinning his neck against the floor with her heel. Henry tried to pull his arm free to no avail. He was trapped.

> If it had been a movie, Virginia would've brought the blade [of the bone saw] down slowly, so that [Abe] could see it coming and have a few seconds to scream or beg for mercy. In reality, she just revved it once and jammed it into his skull.
>
> Imagine the piercing whine of a dentist's drill as it excavates a particularly stubborn tooth. *That's* what it sounded like as the saw bit into Abe's forehead. A flower of blood blossomed in the air above him, followed by the smell of burning hair. It was Abe's skull. I was smelling Abe's skull as the bone saw's carbide blade chipped greedily away at it.

Still on his back, Abe brought his long legs up and kicked Virginia off, sending her flying halfway across the morgue. The bone saw ground to a halt, its blade still embedded in his forehead. He wrenched it free and pawed at his face as a sudden sheet of blood obscured his vision. Virginia saw her chance and took it.

She went for the ax again . . . This time she got it.

Abe ran at her and dove, thinking that he could tackle her again before she started swinging. Better to grapple with her on the ground than face a blade out in the open. But Virginia was a step too quick, moving out of his path and swinging the ax downward as he flew past her.

The blade found purchase in Abe's lower back. Henry cried out.

> [Abe's] whole body tensed up, all at once. He hit the floor hard—didn't put his hands out in front of him to soften the landing, didn't try to roll over or get back on his feet. And I knew. I *knew*, in that instant, she'd paralyzed him.

Abe was facedown on the floor, helpless to move his limbs. Blood ran freely down his face. Virginia dislodged the ax and swung again, hard enough to split a tree stump. She broke Abe's spine clean in two and cut through his organs. Only the tile under his belly kept her from cutting any deeper. With the blade still buried inside him, Virginia pulled on the handle and put her heel against Abe's hip. With a grunt of effort, she ripped the two halves of his body apart. His legs and torso slid off in different directions, like two like poles of a magnet repelling each other. The wet sounds of blood and organs spilling onto the floor.

Henry gritted his teeth and yanked on his left arm.

With a sound that belonged in a butcher's shop, muscle, fat, and sinew tore. There was a stomach-churning jolt and the shoulder joint separated—then suddenly his arm was free.

> I was desperate to get to Abe and help him. But I couldn't do that until I finished *her*. I felt wild, savage.

With one arm hanging useless, but feeling no pain, Henry ran at Virginia, no plan other than charge. No weapon other than rage. Virginia drew the ax back and swung for his head. But Henry dropped to his knees, sliding across the floor, freshly wet with Abe's blood. As the blade passed over him, he dug his claws into Virginia's upper thigh and dragged them down toward her knee, tearing the ligaments apart and making her leg buckle. She fell to the floor beside him.

Henry hit her with a closed fist, breaking four of the knuckles on his right hand and shattering Virginia's jaw. She was stunned just long enough for Henry to hit her again—square in the face this time, breaking her nose and eye socket. Blood seeping from her tear ducts and nostrils.

Henry knelt on top of her and grabbed a scalpel off the floor—one of the instruments Abe had knocked off the table. He squeezed her throat with his left hand, his muscles shaking with effort, grunting, pushing the blade ever closer to her face as Virginia grabbed his wrist and pushed back, both of them fighting for every inch. She dragged her claws along his wrist, slicing away bands of flesh, but Henry hung on. Even as the bones of his wrist were exposed and his blood began to pour over his hand and onto Virginia's porcelain throat.

He pushed...the scalpel's blade pressed against Virginia's closed eyelid, droplets of blood beading around it. Harder...until the blade cut through the closed lid and into the cornea beneath it. Harder... through the cornea and pupil, into the lens, slicing through to the retina.

> She screamed. I kept pushing—burying the blade deeper into her eye, until half of the handle had disappeared into her face. I yanked [the scalpel] out, taking some of her eyeball with it, and plunged it into the other eye.

Virginia screamed, a sound more shrill and terrible than the whir of the bone saw. He'd blinded her. With the scalpel handle still sticking out of her eye, Henry let go, drew his arms up, and clapped his palms against the sides of her skull as hard as he could—hard enough to burst her eardrums. She brought her hands up to her ears as blood began to pour from them, and cried out again. *Blind and deaf.* Henry grabbed the handle of the scalpel and yanked it out, a useless, gelatinous mess where those pretty blue eyes had been moments before. He tried to pry her mouth open with his free hand, determined to cut out her tongue.

> Whatever parts of me that were human had been sent away. This was the vampire, acting of his own accord. Merciless and unbound.

Perhaps sensing his intent, Virginia clamped her jaw shut. Undeterred, Henry pressed the scalpel against her chin and dragged it down her throat, severing the digastric muscle. As she thrashed, trying to free herself, he pried the incision open with his fingers and pulled her tongue out through her throat. He severed it with the scalpel and threw it across the floor.

Henry got to his feet and tugged on the bottom of his T-shirt, straightening it—an unconscious habit. He watched Virginia drag herself across the floor, blind, deaf, and mute. Feeling her way around as blood seeped from the exposed muscle of her throat and the remnants of her severed tongue. He walked to her, grabbed her by her wavy red hair, and dragged her across the tile. The same beautiful hair of the infant he'd cradled in his arms, of the little girl he'd watched grow into a young woman, the young woman he'd fallen in love with. But all of those people were long dead. What had been left in their wake was something completely devoid of humanity. What Powhatan would have called a "bad devil."

And it was time to send the devil back to her maker.

Henry dragged her to the cremation furnace as she moaned through the blood pooling in her mouth. He gripped the bloody scalpel in his right hand and lifted Virginia up by her hair with his left, pressing the blade to her forehead.

He took her scalp.

She tried to scream, but all she could manage was a kind of wet, pathetic moan.

Henry opened the furnace's metal door, its stone innards barely bigger than a coffin. He threw the scalp inside, then lifted the rest of Virginia up and tried to force her in, feet first. She was weak, and she'd been robbed of two senses, but she was still aware enough to fight back. She grabbed the sides of the furnace with her fingertips and held on, scraping the walls with her claws as Henry forced her deeper inside. His patience depleted, his sympathy nonexistent, Henry swung the furnace's heavy metal door on its hinge and slammed it shut, crushing the tips of her fingers. He opened it again as she moaned loudly, a fresh wave of hot pain. She retracted her hands, and Henry shut and latched the furnace door for good.

He planted the palm of his one good hand on the red button beside the door and pressed down. There was a loud whoosh of gas, following by the *click-click-click* of an electric igniter. The flames came with jet-engine intensity, screaming from nozzles that ran the length of the furnace, top and bottom. The stone coffin was full of fire.

Henry wasn't sure if Virginia was moaning inside; he couldn't hear over the roaring flames. But he *could* hear her bony fingertips scraping against the other side of the iron door. Desperate to free herself from the agony. Blind, deaf, and burning alive. The blood running from her face, sizzling as it hit the stone floor of the furnace.

There would be no improbable escapes this time. No survival. She would burn.

But Abe...

The reality came flooding back all at once. Henry turned away from the flames and rushed to his friend's side. He'd been cut clean in half at the waist. His long legs were on the other side of the morgue floor. Henry knelt down and turned him over...his face ghostly white except for the vivid red wound on his forehead, his brown eyes tired, their lids half-closed.

"You'll be all right," said Henry. "We'll get you put back together. Your body will heal its—"

"Henry," said Abe through the sputters of blood in his throat.

Abe looked up at his old friend. The time had come to conduct the last of his earthly business. And it was so clear to him now, so clear what his last word on this earth must be. So clear why time had delivered him to this place, this moment. Abe found just enough breath to whisper to Henry the same word his mother had said to him as she lay dying in a cold Kentucky cabin, 150 years earlier:

"Live..."

And with that, Abraham Lincoln died.

"Abe?"

There was nothing behind his open eyes.

"Abe!"

But Abe was elsewhere, his mind cycling through its shutdown sequence. Firing off its last few electrons before it was hauled off to the Great Scrapyard in the Sky. The picture book flipped past, pausing on random (and not so random) pages: the room above Speed's store, summer in full, near-poverty bloom. His sons, all four of them, waiting for him on a train platform. Waiting to become one with his consciousness, their atoms rejoining his, completing their cycle. His mother, with whom this adventure had begun a century and a half before. All of them together again, closer than any physical embrace could bring them. All of them melting into one another's love and becoming one with the universe, where consciousness was merely a matter of mathematics and all possible outcomes coexisted in eternal harmony.

I'd watched many men die...human and vampire alike. I could tell the precise moment death touched them with the tip of a skeletal finger and they became nothing but an empty vessel.

I saw that moment come for my friend.

Henry lowered Abe's head to the tile floor. He cried awhile, alone.

Abe's ax lay on the tile floor nearby . . . the same one he'd had since his earliest vampire-hunting days, when he was barely more than a teenager. The one he'd carried with him to the White House as president and swung at Henry in anger during the Civil War. The ax that Henry had kept after Abe's assassination—a keepsake of their friendship.

Henry picked it up off the bloody tile and held it a moment, feeling the weight of its blade, of its history. He walked to the cremation furnace and opened the heavy door again, the flames still raging inside, hot air rushing past him into the cooler morgue, making the follicles on Henry's head dance. Virginia's body was blackened and still, skin giving way to charred muscle and sizzling yellow fat. Henry half expected her to lunge toward him, a half-melted monster, intent on grabbing him and pulling him into the flames with her. But nothing of the sort happened. She was dead.

Henry threw the ax in with her.

He watched its wooden handle start to blacken, then catch fire, burning away the worn grooves where Abe had placed his hands a million or more times; watched its reflective blade darken as carbon blackened its surface.

The two people he'd loved most in his long life had died in the same room, on the same day. And before the day was done, he would burn both of them to ash.

The men with guns came. The covering up began. The scrubbing of surfaces and destruction of evidence. Dawn was breaking over Dallas, bringing unwanted sunshine—that best of all disinfectants. They had to hurry. There were witnesses to discredit. Cameras to confiscate. Busy, busy, the cover-uppers.

Henry was ushered out of the Medical Examiner's Office building and into the early morning sun, toward a black government car—Abe's and Virginia's blood still on his torn clothes.

> Men with radios everywhere yelling, hurrying this way, that way. Chaos. A younger man ran up to me before I got in the car. Judging by his suit and buttoned-down demeanor, he was an FBI agent. Judging by his youth, he hadn't been one for very long.

"Mr. Sturges?" said the FBI man. "I'm to take you to the airfield. President Johnson would like you in Washington right away."

"I'm going home," said Henry, stepping into the black car.

"Sir, but the president—"

"You can tell the president to go fuck himself for all I care."

Henry closed the car door. He told the driver to go and sank into the seat. They left the FBI man and his shocked expression behind.

President Johnson, thought Henry.

There was no hope in the sound of it. No life. Henry stared out the window as the car drove him back to his plane. Everywhere, flags at half-staff. *They're mourning more than their president,* he thought. *They're mourning what America might have been. What she came so close to being.*

They all know, thought Henry. *They* know *it'll never be the same.*

As fate would have it, Jack Kennedy wasn't the only famous man to die on November 22nd, 1963. *The Chronicles of Narnia* author C.S. Lewis and *Brave New World* author Aldous Huxley also shed their mortal coils that day. The world had little noted their passing, the noise of their deaths drowned out by the American president's. But Henry had spotted their obituaries in the *Dallas Morning Herald*, and he'd been struck by the symbolism of it.

I thought it fitting that those two, especially, had gone to their eternal rest on the same day as Kennedy. Lewis, whose Christianity was at the center of his life and his work, like Kennedy's

Catholicism was at the center of *his*. And Huxley, with his vision of an authoritarian world—a world in which genes would be manipulated, and individualism and capitalism outlawed. A vision that now looked perilously poised to come true.

I felt exactly as I had in the wake of Abe's assassination a century earlier. I didn't see any light on the horizon. I didn't feel any sense of purpose. I began to think of what Virginia had said...that the Great Experiment had failed. That America really *was* done. I didn't know. But I knew one thing...

I was done fighting for her.

EPILOGUE

★ ★ ★

The Last American Vampire

In the end, it's not the years in your life that
count.
It's the life in your years.

—*Abraham Lincoln*

Henry didn't much care for knocks on his front
door, especially when he wasn't expecting any
visitors.

He'd built his country estate for the purpose of
keeping people away, and he'd surrounded it with
high walls and heavy gates to underscore that point.
In more recent years, an Orwellian array of cameras
had been added to the list of deterrents, giving Henry
a live view of every corner of his property, day or night.
He'd made a lot of enemies in his five centuries. Most
of them were dead, but you could never be too careful.

Henry had been sitting in the nook of his large,
brightly lit kitchen that evening, its pantries empty, its
stainless-steel refrigerators filled with bags of donated

blood (one of the perks of owning a private chain of hospitals), and catching up on his newspapers, their front pages plastered with the smiling face of a White House intern. A small television on the kitchen's marble countertop was tuned to CNN, the word "impeachment" on the lips of every anchor.

Henry had largely retreated from the world, but he still liked to have the information, and it was easier to come by than ever. Recently, a cardboard envelope had shown up in the mail. Inside was a shiny compact disc with the letters "AOL" emblazoned on the front. The next day, Henry canceled all but a few of his newspaper subscriptions. The world was at his fingertips now, anytime he wanted it.

I've always prided myself on my ability to adapt. To change my hair and clothing, alter my manner of speaking to stay current. I've gone out of my way to remain connected to popular culture, whether it's books or music or television or cinema. There are some vampires who pride themselves on being anachronistic. You see them strutting around, flaunting their outdated fashions and idioms, passing themselves off as "Goths," or "Steampunks." I've never understood that. To me, when you can't keep up with the world anymore, it's time to get off the merry-go-round and make room for another rider.

The curtain was falling on the twentieth century, and in true theatrical tradition, things were a bloody mess heading into the finale. The president was embroiled in scandal. Fanatics were running around proclaiming the end was at hand. Scientists were predicting a global computer meltdown at the stroke of midnight 1999. India had gone from Gandhi to nukes in the space of fifty years and had its finger on the button, ready to destroy neighboring Pakistan. Pakistan, in turn, stood ready to destroy India. Just about everybody wanted to destroy Israel.

To those living their first lifetimes, it all seemed like an escalation. As if the world *was* indeed growing more violent. As if we really *were* building toward some kind of catastrophe. To me, it was simply par for the course.

There are certain constants in the laws of human nature. Like the speed of light, they're fixed and universal. And the biggest one of them all, the one constant that thundered down the mountain long before Moses and his stone tablets, is this: each generation will hold the next in contempt and cherish the imaginary memory of "the way things used to be." It's as baked into our bones as the need to breathe and screw. For five hundred years, I've heard men lament the fact that the world was "going to hell."

It would be lovely if we could go our entire lives believing in Santa Claus or be awestruck at the sight of jingling car keys well into adulthood. But that's not the way it works. Some of us grow cynical. Some of us grow wise. But *all* of us grow old, if not in body, then certainly in spirit.

Henry had been born into a violent world. A world of plagues and panics and mass killings. And so it went, decade upon decade. Plagues and panics and mass killings. The methods changed, nothing more.

I was content to stay holed up in my little country manor like a lord of old. Writing letters, attending board meetings, taking the occasional jaunt into town, strolling past the shops on East Market Street, exchanging nods with familiar faces. Watching the seasons change and the living change with them. Watching them share in the experience of life together. Growing old together. Birthdays and graduations and weddings and funerals and birthdays and graduations and weddings and funerals and so on, and so on, and scooby dooby doo.

Always one for secretive associations, he joined as many as he could now, becoming a member of the Knights of Columbus, the Kiwanis, the Elks, the Masons. Realizing he'd never had any formal schooling, Henry enrolled in Dutchess Community College and got a bachelor's degree in English litera-ture. Suffice it to say he was the only member of his class who'd been friends with many of the authors on the reading list.

When there was somewhere to go (and there rarely was, other than the occasional board meeting), a black town car[1] would show up at Henry's doorstep and chauffeur him an hour north to Albany, delivering him right onto the tarmac, where his jet[2] was fueled and ready, its engines already spinning. No more than two minutes after climbing aboard, he was airborne, on his way to Europe by way of London, or Asia by way of Los Angeles or Seattle. Or anywhere he wanted to go. It was all a phone call away now.

His most frequent flights were to Maryland, where the Howard Hughes Medical Institute was now head-quartered, and where Compound 220 was being developed behind a veil of secrecy. It was the result of decades of trial and error, and unlike many of the com-pounds that came before (including the one that had killed the institute's founder, Howard Hughes), Com-pound 220 required only a single dose. One injection, and the body would revert back to its human self.

---

1. More recently, Henry has taken to using a helicopter to transport him when weather permits, cutting the travel time from an hour to fif-teen minutes.
2. Henry sold his JetStar in 1972. He's continually upgraded his pri-vate aircraft since the 1960s.

At least, that was the theory. It was still a long way off from animal testing, let alone any sort of real application. Still, I was hopeful that my vampire days were coming to an end.

But Henry was grateful for his claws and fangs that summer night, when the unexpected visitor came.

The staff had gone home. He could have afforded to keep a round-the-clock army of help on hand, but he liked having the house to himself at night. He didn't venture out to feed anymore—he didn't have to, thanks to the well-stocked refrigerators and the nondisclosure agreements signed by his staff. Still, killer or not, Henry couldn't shake four hundred years of sleeping habits.

The night was still a vampire's domain, even if that vampire chose to spend it watching CNN in his breakfast nook.

The knock came just after ten o'clock. He put his papers down and walked to a dark monitor on the counter, just beside the small television. He touched a button on the monitor, and its screen came to life with eight small black-and-white boxes, each a live feed from one of the cameras on his property.

There was a boy at the front door. He looked to be about thirteen or so. Probably just some kid from the neighborhood, asking if I'd seen his lost dog, or selling raffle tickets for his Boy Scout troop.

How he'd gotten onto the property was another matter. The maid forgot to close the gate on her way home from time to time.

Henry walked the long hall from the kitchen to the foyer, passing neatly hung photographs that had been laid out in chronological order, with the oldest closest to the kitchen, becoming more contemporary as he neared the front door.

It was intentional, meant to subtly urge me out of the past and into the present as I stepped into the world on any given day. It's one of those little things that only people with way too much time on their hands think to do.

The hallway began with old daguerreotypes and wet plates, some dating back to the 1840s, the blurred suggestions of landscapes and portraits growing sharper as the nineteenth century approached the twentieth.

Most people look at them, these [photographs of] men with their grand mustaches and decorative canes, of women with their oversize hats and bustles, with a sort of passing fascination. In books, on screens, in museums. They look at them as if they're looking at a fiction. Something elaborately staged to give their present day some context.

I look at them and remember *being* there. I remember the noises. The smell of the air. The unspoiled burnt orange of a new brick town house. I remember sunsets every bit as colorful and breathtaking as they are today. The feeling of warm, living flesh against my own. I remember the faded laughter of friends now centuries in their graves. The pitch of their voices, the color of their eyes, their hair. As alive as you and me. Briefly, brilliantly. Grabbing onto as much as time would let them.

Here was his old friend Twain, holding a lightbulb in Tesla's lab...Abe, Henry, and Eliot Ness, the original Untouchables, posing with a pile of confiscated whiskey barrels...Henry and a few of his brothers in the Eighty-Second Airborne, flashing victory signs in Salerno, Italy. Here was Henry standing on Venice Beach in 1953, laying eyes on the Pacific Ocean, nearly four hundred years after crossing the Atlantic...A picture of his brand-new Gulfstream II jet, the day he took delivery in 1976...An image of Halley's Comet in the night sky in 1986, when it had returned for the fifth time in Henry's memory. The ribbon-cutting ceremony for the Howard Hughes Medical Institute's new Maryland headquarters in 1991...

I hesitated before opening [the front door]. There was something off about it, something strange about what was on the other side. My instincts told me to fear it. This thing that looked like a thirteen-year-old boy.

It had been a long time since Henry had been in a fight. Physically, he was still the same specimen he'd been in 1963, but decades of rust had dulled his technique.

I opened the door. Our eyes met, and I knew, instantly, where the hesitation had come from.

There was a vampire on my doorstep.

"Hello, Henry," said the boy.

"Who are you?"

The boy smiled. "Alex," he said. "But you would have known me as Alexei Romanov."

It had been eighty years since the night Alexei had been dragged from his bed and riddled with machine-gun fire, along with his parents and sisters. Eighty years since he'd played dead, lying in the back of a truck, next to their bodies, not moving a muscle as he was thrown into a shallow grave beside their still-warm bodies, waiting for night to fall so that he could make his escape.

They sat in Henry's study, Norman Rockwell's large 1964 painting *Young Lincoln* hanging prominently on the wall. It was Henry's favorite image of his old friend, for it captured him in the heart of his youth, his ax in his right hand, a book in his left, looking down, reading as he strode tall and confident though an Illinois prairie. His emotional connection to the painting was bolstered by the fact that Rockwell had created it, unknowingly, less than a year after Abe's death.

To a casual observer, it looked like a man of twenty-five sitting with a boy of thirteen. But here were two old men—one in his nineties, the other well over four hundred—both refugees from the countries of their birth, forced to find their own way in a strange and hostile world.

"You aren't an easy man to find," said Alexei.

"I've gone to great lengths to remain unfound. How did you, if I may?"

"Well...I can't take all of the credit. I had to enlist some of my friends in the Union."

"The Union?"

I was surprised to hear the word. The Union—at least the one I'd known—hadn't been a viable organization for more than sixty years. The [headquarters in New York] had sat empty since the 1930s, all that marble and gold gathering dust in the dark. All those mirrors with nothing to reflect.

"I've been working with them," said Alexei. "Lending a hand when needed, just as you did."

"I didn't know there was a 'them' to work with."

Alexi studied him for a moment. A smile.

"My God," he said. "It's really you. It's just—forgive me, but it's just that I've heard so many stories."

"Oh? Is there anyone left to tell them?"

"A few old relics, holed up in their houses, waiting for time to swallow them up."

Alexei realized what he'd said, then added: "No offense."

"None taken," said Henry. "We relics have thick hides."

"They told me about your days with the old hunters. The early days, when we recruited humans to our cause. Trained them to fight as we do. They told me about you and Lincoln. They said he was one of the best vampire hunters there ever was."

"Not *one of* the best," said Henry.

"Forgive me," said Alexei. "Of course. They also told me that no vampire ever fought as valiantly or as often for the Union as Henry Sturges."

"Why have you come?" asked Henry. "Why'd you go through all of the trouble of tracking me down? Was it curiosity? The need to put a face to all these stories you've heard?"

I knew, of course. He was young and still clumsy at hiding his thoughts. I'd known what he wanted since the moment we'd sat, but I wanted to hear him say it.

"I thought," said Alexei, "perhaps, if you ever wanted to venture out into the world again; if you wanted to—"

"If I wanted to leave my lonely estate behind and don my cape again? Fight for truth, justice, and the American way?"

Henry couldn't help a smile. *Here's a vampire, all of ninety-three years old, trying to lead me back to the light, as if I myself haven't been in that chair a thousand times, full of purpose, sounding the rallying cry.* Henry was overcome with fondness.

"I'm flattered," he continued, "but I've done my bit for king and country. I'm content to be a relic, I'm afraid."

Alexei smiled.

"I envy you," he said. "The things you've seen... the battles you've won. You've made a difference."

"I envy *you*," said Henry. "You still want to."

Henry walked Alexei to the front door, the Hallway of Time bringing them closer to the present with each step. The sun would be rising soon, and the younger vampire was still sensitive to light, though less so with each passing year. He had a chauffeured town car waiting out front (he preferred to drive himself, he told Henry, but was always getting pulled over for looking underage).

[Alexei] handed me a card with his phone number
and e-mail address and told me to call or write
if I changed my mind. I knew I wouldn't. Hell,
I'd probably throw the card away as soon as he
left. But I thanked him and promised I'd consider
it. Better to be polite.

"There are more of us than you know," said Alexei.
"Not as many as in the old days...but enough to
make a difference."

Henry shook Alexei's hand and watched him drive
off...the taillights of his town car growing dim as
they twisted down his wooded drive.

To be young again, he thought.

When you approach your five hundredth year, the
bar for what's considered "memorable" is impossibly high. But that was a memorable morning.

Henry had been roused from sleep by the sound of
weeping. He'd found the maid in the kitchen, watching the small TV on the counter—the one that was
always tuned to CNN. She had her hands clutched
at her mouth, tears in her eyes, mumbling, "Ay, Dios
mío...," again and again. She'd never seen anything
so horrible in all her life.

Henry had. Many times.

I knew, within minutes of the first breaking news. I could see it clearly, even through all that dust and chaos.

A war was coming.

It wouldn't be a war between two armies, shooting it out on the battlefield. It would be fought face-to-face, in dark alleys and far-off hotel rooms. It would be savage and secretive and would violate every article of law or code of moral conduct ever devised by man.

Henry turned the television off. He didn't need to see any more.

I sent the staff home early and retreated to my study.

He walked up to the painting of Abe, swung it away from the wall on its hinges, and opened the small safe behind it. Inside were twelve little leather-bound books, their pages filled with tightly packed musings on the nature of life, confessions, fears, triumphs.

The secret journals of Abraham Lincoln.

I flipped through them that morning, knowing that America would never be the same, just as I'd felt in Dallas, forty years earlier.

He came to a passage toward the end of the eleventh book, written on Christmas Eve 1862, less than two weeks after a stunning Union defeat at Fredericksburg—the lowest point of the war, when Abraham Lincoln had every reason to believe that all was lost. It read:

```
And so I renew myself to the cause,
even if it proves a lost one. I pledge
my heart and mind to these things
because they are right, not because
they are prosperous, or even likely to
succeed. I echo the last sentiments of
Nathan Hale, uttered from the gallows
in 1776, "I only regret that I have
but one life to give for my country."
```

Henry closed the journal and smiled.

In the end, he thought, *you had two.*

He returned the journals to the safe. There, among their priceless yellowed pages and worn covers, another small object stood out—bright, unsullied by time. Henry picked it up and stared at it, a single word turning over in his mind from beyond the grave:

Live…

It was Alexei Romanov's card.

ACKNOWLEDGMENTS

You did it. You finished the book. Okay, maybe you just skipped to the end because you're one of *those* people. But either way, let's start by acknowledging you. *You*, Dear Reader. Let us sing songs of your glory from on high the mountain! Let tales of your greatness ring through the ages! Because let's face it—without you, these books would have no life, and I'd have no fun writing them. You are hereby...acknowledged. To my editor and man-friend, Ben Greenberg, whose last nerve I so frequently work, and whose strong, safe hugs I crave at all hours...I acknowledge you, sir. To Jamie Raab and Michael Pietsch, and my entire Grand Central family, who've been the most supportive and enthusiastic partners a middle-class white kid from the hardscrabble streets of Connecticut could hope for...here's some much-deserved acknowledgement. To Elizabeth Connor, for her brilliant design (and another killer cover); and Stephanie Isaacson Greenberg, who makes pretty pictures and even prettier babies...consider yourselves acknowledged. To

Claudia Ballard and my William Morris Endeavor family, who earn 10–15 percent of my paycheck but 100 percent of my love…I acknowledge you. To Erin, Josh, and Jake, and the rest of my *actual* family, who so frequently ask me, "Can't you slow down and enjoy yourself a little more, be a little less serious?" I acknowledge you. But my answer is still "No." And finally, to Stephen King—because it's my acknowledgements page, and why the hell not.